PENGUIN BOOKS

Singing to the Dead

Caro Ramsay was born in Glasgow and now lives in a village on the west coast of Scotland. This is her second DI Anderson and DS Costello novel, following the critically acclaimed *Absolution*. *Dark Water* is the third book in the series and the fourth, *The Blood of Crows*, is published in Penguin Books in September 2012

Praise for *Absolution*

'A cracker of a debut . . . Many shivers in store for readers, followed by a shattering climax' *The Times*

'Ramsay handles her characters with aplomb, the dialogue crackles and the search for the killer has surprising twists and turns. A most auspicious debut' *Observer*

'Undoubtedly one of the most impressive debut novels in the field in some time' Barry Forshaw, *Amazon*

'Among the year's best literary thrillers' *Washington Post*

'Edgy and fast-paced, this crime thriller is a cleverly understated page-turner . . . Deliciously dark, this well-written debut will leave you wanting more' *Woman*

'Glasgow comes alive in Caro Ramsay's dark, vivid and daring thriller' Val McDermid

'A cracking debut [4 stars]' *Mirror*

Singing to the Dead

CARO RAMSAY

PENGUIN BOOKS

PENGUIN BOOKS

Published by the Penguin Group
Penguin Books Ltd, 80 Strand, London WC2R ORL, England
Penguin Group (USA) Inc., 375 Hudson Street, New York, New York 10014, USA
Penguin Group (Canada), 90 Eglinton Avenue East, Suite 700, Toronto, Ontario, Canada M4P 2Y3
(a division of Pearson Penguin Canada Inc.)
Penguin Ireland, 25 St Stephen's Green, Dublin 2, Ireland (a division of Penguin Books Ltd)
Penguin Group (Australia), 250 Camberwell Road,
Camberwell, Victoria 3124, Australia (a division of Pearson Australia Group Pty Ltd)
Penguin Books India Pvt Ltd, 11 Community Centre, Panchsheel Park, New Delhi – 110 017, India
Penguin Group (NZ), 67 Apollo Drive, Rosedale, Auckland 0632, New Zealand
(a division of Pearson New Zealand Ltd)
Penguin Books (South Africa) (Pty) Ltd, Block D, Rosebank Office Park, 181 Jan Smuts Avenue,
Parktown North, Gauteng, Johannesburg 2193, South Africa

Penguin Books Ltd, Registered Offices: 80 Strand, London WC2R ORL, England

www.penguin.com

First published 2009
This edition published 2012
001

Set in Monotype Garamond
Typeset by Rowland Phototypesetting Ltd, Bury St Edmunds, Suffolk
Printed in England by Clays Ltd, St Ives plc

ISBN: 978-1-405-90935-8

www.greenpenguin.co.uk

ALWAYS LEARNING　　　　**PEARSON**

To Mum and Dad

Author's Note

Singing to the Dead is a work of fiction. Names, characters, places and incidents either are the product of the author's imagination or are used entirely fictitiously.

Acknowledgements

I would like to thank Jane and all the Gregory girls, and Bev and all the Penguins for their help, support and patience while I was writing this book.

Also thanks must go to Mary and Karen, who try hard to organize me and never seem discouraged by their failure. And of course thanks to all at work for the sneaky days off and, in particular, to Annette for knowing how to work a computer ... properly.

And to Ma, Pa, Emily and Pi.

Special thanks and acknowledgements should go to my pals in Strathclyde Police, especially Superintendent Donald McCallum, not forgetting the legal expertise of R. J. P. Kerr and my medics – Dr Penelope Redding and Dr Tara Singleton.

Thanks to you all, hope you enjoy it.

Caro

Tuesday,
19 December 2006

He was supposed to have been at school, but his ma couldn't be bothered to walk that far. She couldn't be bothered most days now.

She'd been in such a hurry to get out the flat he'd not had a chance to put his jacket on. Once he'd gone back to get it and she'd locked him in and left him all night. So all he had was a wee fleece from the Oxfam shop, and that was soaked through and sticking to his back.

Shite, he was cold. He was always cold.

Christmas shopping at Woolies, she'd said, but she never made it further than the offie. So there'd be nothing left to buy presents.

It was getting very dark now; soon they'd be turning on the big light at the end of the playground. He sat on the swing, shivering in the slow-falling sleet, not daring to touch the freezing iron chains with his bare hands. If you work a swing up high enough, his dad said, you can kick the clouds up the arse. But that was two Christmases ago; a long, long time. He was only five then. If his dad was here now he'd give him a push, but he didn't know where his dad had gone to, and he was too cold to swing himself.

So Troy McEwen sat watching the lights come on one by one in the tenements, a growing patchwork of comforting brightness, and played a game with himself, betting which window *would light up next. The playground was empty. Everyone else was somewhere warm and bright and happy.*

He watched his ma wiping the rain from the bench seat, using her sleeve like a big paw. She'd a huge coat on, made from a dead sheep; she'd got that at the Oxfam shop too. Now she was taking a bottle out the bag at her feet, unscrewing the cap. She always came to the same bench, her favourite place for a wee drink.

There was that old woman again, the one with the scruffy white dog. He waited to see if she had a go at his ma. It wouldn't be the first time. They hung about for a bit, the wee dog crapped on the path, then they buggered off up the road.

He wanted to see if he could give the clouds a kicking even though it was too dark to see them. So he shouted to his ma to give him a shove. But she wasn't listening. She didn't look up. She was taking another swig from the flat bottle with the stag on it.

He wanted to go home now. Maybe there'd be something to eat. So he slid off the swing and went over to his ma. He tugged on the sleeve of the dead-sheep coat, and she slumped sideways, her eyes hazy, unable to focus. Pissed again. She looked older than everybody else's ma, and he didn't like the way she pulled her hair back in an elastic band. It made her look like the dead cat he'd seen floating in the canal last summer. He could smell her whisky breath through the rain.

He wasn't allowed on the roundabout in the rain ever since he'd fallen and broken his arm and they'd tried to take him into care — again. But she wasn't watching, so he'd not get a skelping. He pushed and pushed, went round once, twice, and got the wheel going really fast, all by himself.

Suddenly the floodlight came on. In the brightness he could see a syringe abandoned, close to the roundabout. Next time round, he'd kick it right on to the grass ... But he stretched too far, his numb fingers slipped, and suddenly he was on the ground.

He lay there for a little while, whimpering, frozen hands stinging with pain. Then he rolled over and sat up wearily. In the floodlight he could see his knee skinned raw and tiny red bubbles of blood welling up. He'd ripped the knees out of his leggings. His ma would kill him.

Out beyond the light it was really, really dark. His knees and hands were hurting. And he was so cold.

Then a tall shadow fell between him and the floodlight, a grown-up wearing a long black coat, carrying a newspaper packet. The salty smell of the local chippie enveloped him.

'You've hurt yourself,' a kind voice said. 'I've just got some pies and chips to take home. Why don't you come and have some?'

He sniffled and wiped his nose on his sodden sleeve. All he wanted at that moment was for somebody to pick him up, cuddle him and take him somewhere warm.

And feed him a nice hot pie. With chips.

Wednesday, 20 December

I

Detective Inspector Colin Anderson held a handkerchief to his nose, trying not to breathe, his eyes watering in the acrid smoke, and looked at the remains of the ground-floor flat, 34 Lower Holburn Street. The fire had been out for half an hour but the whole place was still humming with the intense humidity of a tropical rainforest. Two firemen, boots squelching, emerged from the smoke-filled kitchen and stood for a moment in the sanctuary of the hall, sweat tracing veins of white skin in the soot on their faces. The younger of the two stared at the sagging ceiling, looked troubled and sighed. A close call but too late.

The older one gesticulated tiredly with a heavily gloved hand – Anderson could have a look if he wanted.

DI Colin Anderson tiptoed forward and squatted beside the black plastic sheet as Woodford, the senior fire investigator, lifted the corner. What lay beneath was only vaguely human. The crouching pugilistic pose, limbs contorted into flexion, clenched hands pulled up to the face, the muscle contraction – all were typical of a body caught in intense heat. Anderson leaned in for a closer look, coughing into the back of his hand, and Woodford pulled the plastic away further. They knew it was the body of an old man – they surmised he was 76-year-old John Campbell – but the mass of charred flesh could have been anyone, anything. The body was black and yellow, darkened with dried blood, devoid of hair and eyebrows, clothing either melted on or burned away. Small patches of coloured fibre with frazzled strands were dotted around the shoulders. Had he been wearing something woollen? A cardigan, maybe dark blue? Anderson looked more closely and saw a melted button. He remembered his own granddad wearing those cardigans – Fair Isle with metal buttons like little medals. He picked this one up on the end of his pen, and looked at it closely. The lion rampant was still recognizable, its stance a cruel parody of the deceased. He slipped it into an evidence bag.

'What time was it called in?' he rasped.

'A few minutes past ten, so an hour and a half ago,' Woodford replied. 'We were here in minutes, but too late is too late. There's no debris underneath him, so he was already on the floor when the fire took hold.' Woodford gesticulated with the back of his hand.

'Is that suspicious?' Anderson started to cough again.

'Probably not. He was old, the smoke would have knocked him out quickly; or he could have had a coronary, collapsed, and that's why the pan went up in the first place.' Woodford pointed to where an open can, a blackened cracked plate, and the remains of a knife lay on the floor. Part of a worktop remained, sticking out like a jetty. An oval-shaped biscuit tin with a picture of a green Bugatti on the lid sat waiting, incongruous, as if it had been kissed by the flames and rejected. Close by was a twisted plastic strip of tablets, and a seven-day dispenser melted into the shape of a blackened flower. 'Signs he was on medication, would you say?'

'Maybe. There's no indication he tried to put the fire out?' Anderson asked.

'No extinguisher, no fire blanket and the smoke alarm was bugger-all use. The place went up like a . . .'

'House on fire?' smiled Anderson and nodded, signalling for the body to be covered up; his eyes were streaming so much he couldn't see any more anyway, and the noise of the generator starting up was deafening. He retreated, looking at the firefighters in the kitchen, their boots tramping everywhere, contaminating the scene. *Site*, he corrected himself. Nothing so far to indicate that it was a crime scene.

He gingerly dipped his head under the door lintel, now supported by an inner metal frame, and felt the vicious heat eating through the soles of his boots. Even Anderson's inexpert eye could tell the ceiling was sagging like a hammock.

One of the firefighters tapped along the wall none too gently with a hammer. 'Do you think this is weight bearing?' he shouted, keeping his eyes on the crack in the plaster that ran the length of the room.

'Tap it any harder and we might find out,' answered some smart-arse through the smoke.

Anderson knew they were on the ground floor of a four-storey tenement and felt his stomach sink.

Somebody handed him a hard hat.

Great.

He shuddered, casting his eyes round the room, as Woodford shouted and the generator was cut. The hammering died abruptly and all was quiet apart from the walls cracking and sighing as they relaxed after the intense heat. Anderson stayed still, thinking they were listening for further signs of life, but they had stopped only because somebody more senior was taking a phone call.

In the relative silence, Anderson turned back to look at the kitchen. Everything, in the aftermath of the rage that had passed this way, was consumed and blackened, warped and twisted. The lino on the floor had shrivelled into leaves that floated now on little pools of water. He could hear something still sizzling. Yet, amid all this destruction, this was still recognizably a kitchen. Two hours ago somebody had been cooking a leisurely Wednesday morning breakfast. Anderson noticed that the fridge, the same model as his own, had buckled under the pressure of sheer heat. The focus of the rage, the cooker, was a dark tangle of metal, with the odd bit of chrome stubbornly shining through.

A fire officer appeared with a video camera, nodding to DI Anderson for tacit approval to keep filming. Anderson gave him the thumbs up, pulling the hard hat further down over his blond hair, trying to ignore the savage heat that gnawed at the exposed flesh of his neck and face. He knew a fire investigation officer could read a fire in a way a run of the mill SOCO never could; best leave it to the experts. The camera whirred into life, the operator complaining about the lack of light. Anderson felt the smoke irritating his throat again, and coughed deeply. No amount of money in the world could persuade him to do their job.

'You OK?' asked Woodford, holding his hand out. 'You were a bit late for the barbie.'

Anderson smiled wryly and reversed out of the flat, keeping his fists clenched and his arms folded; it was easy to forget, to put a hand down and get a palmful of burns. The soles of his feet were complaining loudly; he was going outside to stand in a puddle. He started to cough in earnest, a dry hacking at the back of his throat. Then he retched.

'Yip,' Detective Chief Inspector Rebecca Quinn snapped down the phone. Its high-pitched ring tone made the fillings in her teeth hurt. Twice she had asked for a new one but she might as well ask to be made the next Queen of England. '*Yes?*' she said again, but whoever was at the other end totally ignored her and said, 'Left a bit, left a bit,' to some unidentified other. 'Wyngate!' she shouted. The incoming code said Reception and there were only two people at Reception — Costello and Wyngate. The latter, she knew, was unkindly but accurately known as Wingnut because his ears stuck out. At least *he* was easy to remember. DC Gordon Wyngate? The skinny computer geek, clever with no common sense.

'Yes, ma'am. Wyngate at Reception, ma'am.'

'I know that. What is it?'

'You asked me to let you know if anybody else called in sick. Well, DC Burns just has. He's got this throat thing,' Wyngate added helpfully.

Burns? Burns? She flicked through the file in her mind. Burns? The big, softly spoken islander. So, they were another good man down. 'Might be quicker to send me a list of who's actually coming in,' Quinn said in resignation.

'Well, Vik Mulholland has a rest day but he's promised to come in later.' Wyngate gauged the pause at the end of the phone and added, 'He's the one who looks like . . .'

'Yes, DC Wyngate. I know who he is.' Any cop who looked like Johnny Depp's better-looking brother was not easily forgotten. 'Thanks for letting me know,' Quinn said with slight sarcasm and put the phone down. Over sixty per cent of the squad was now off with either the flu or a throat infection, and it was Christmas next week. Just as well things were relatively quiet.

She glanced at the clock — quarter to twelve. The briefing was scheduled for noon but she'd start five minutes early, just to unnerve the bad timekeepers. She could hear the remnants of the squad gathering on the other side of the blind. As usual, she was immaculately dressed in the navy-blue classic suit that she considered her uniform; her red hair was precisely pinned back, but her lips were pale. She opened her make-up bag, and applied her deep-burgundy lipstick carefully, pursing her lips, watching the coloured lower lip blot the stain on to the upper, checking her reflection in the mirror in the lid of the bag. It was one of her little rituals; just as Beryl Reid used to say that if she got the shoes right she got the character right, so DCI Quinn relied on her lipstick. Without it she was a human being; with it she was a cop. And a good one.

She checked there was no lipstick on her teeth, no loose hairs on her collar, and turned back to her desk. The pile of files added up to nothing much.

A seven-year-old boy called Luca Scott had disappeared thirty-six hours ago. The boy had more or less lived on the streets and it wouldn't be the first time he had done a runner. The family, such as it was, belonged to that inner-city underclass which was of no fixed abode but always seemed able to afford the latest mobile phone and a bad-tempered pit bull. Quinn sighed. She'd hoped to have rather more than this for the briefing update.

The next file was forty pages thick, a document circulated to all Strathclyde stations. Rock legend Rogan O'Neill was flying back into Glasgow airport, and a brief itinerary of his castle-hunting plans was attached, plus details of the Hogmanay concert which had been rumoured but was now definite in the light of the Pakistan earthquake appeal. Nothing like a good disaster to jump-start a flagging career. There was page after page about the security involved, with special notes for Partickhill Station. No special budget or manpower, Quinn noted, just more work. Why did they not go to the old divisional HQ at Partick rather than this tiny station, built to fill a gap in the tenements where the Luftwaffe didn't miss? Partick Station was big enough and modern enough; it had the staff and resources. So, why had this landed at Partickhill? In fact, why had she been landed at Partickhill? All because some aging rock star was staying at the Hilton round the corner, with – rumour said – the compulsory blonde model girlfriend, or at least the latest in a long line of blonde model girl-friends. Quinn looked at the press photo of him. The years of Californian sunshine and Botox had not been kind; O'Neill was verging on the ridiculous. The memo gave his age as 'early fifties'. Quinn did a quick calculation – by that reckoning she was still in her late thirties. If he could take a decade off his age then so could she. Quinn lifted the lid of her make-up bag, and looked in the mirror, pulling at the folds of skin under her eyes. Maybe not.

She opened a few more bits and bobs, determined to make her way to the bottom of her in-tray before the briefing – she wouldn't put it past this lot to leave something really important right at the bottom, then ask her about it. The usual pile of memos, her expenses form (last month's) ... She pulled out a piece of stiff white card: *Alan McAlpine, 1960–2006.* His picture on the front of the funeral Order of Service looked back at her, a relaxed and handsome man with melting eyes and a smile that was more intriguing than friendly.

Eight weeks before, only eight weeks. Her predecessor, DCI Alan McAlpine had died a hero, and since then Quinn had sensed quiet smiles of support between DI Anderson and DS Costello, had witnessed the pinched words and understanding silences.

Before Quinn arrived, Partickhill had been their perfect enclave. DCI McAlpine in his mid forties. Colin Anderson, his favoured inspector, a few years behind and Costello a few years younger again. Their careers had flourished in McAlpine's wake but, with McAlpine gone, Anderson had been severely tested and he had stood firm. Very firm. And tight-lipped. Quinn knew there was a lot to the story of DCI Alan McAlpine – more than she would ever be told. As their boss, she was on the outside. As a woman, she preferred to remember McAlpine the way he was; handsome, complicated, vulnerable. She looked into his eyes again, those brown almond-shaped eyes, remembering the quiet hiss of the crematorium curtains closing, the subdued whirr of the coffin sliding into darkness. It could have been yesterday.

She looked at the photograph for a minute longer, pleasant memories stirring, and stuck it at the bottom of the pile.

She jumped as the shrill ring of the phone reprimanded her.

'DS Costello here.' Female, clipped, abrupt, only just this side of insolence.

'Yes, DS Costello.' Quinn spoke with pointed politeness.

'Any news on Luca Scott, ma'am?'

'Am I not supposed to be asking you that?'

'Well, I've been trying to get access to his mum at the hospital, but no joy. There's something else, ma'am – a Miss Cotter of Havelock Street ... that's near where ...'

'Yes, I know ...'

'Well, she's reported that her neighbour came home last night without her son and he's not in the flat this morning. The mum is too drunk to remember where she's left him. I checked on the database and it's not the first time *this* boy, Troy McEwen, has been reported missing either, so in light of Luca Scott ...' Quinn heard Costello flick over a page of her notebook, '... both seven years old, living within half a mile of each ...'

'Send me up anything you have.' Quinn pulled Luca Scott's file from the small stack on her desk. 'And get DI Anderson back here, as soon as.' She hung up. She shut her eyes for a moment, willing the two little boys not to be connected. Not *two* missing children, just before Christmas, not for *her* first case with this team – McAlpine's team.

They were good – Anderson and Costello – McAlpine's hand-picked little squad, a tough team to crack. But the king was dead, long live the queen. *Long live the Quinn* – she allowed herself a little smile. DI Colin Anderson was the one she had to break. The tall fair-haired intelligent one, who thought before he spoke, each action considered. She had expected some resentment from him that she'd taken over from McAlpine, but there was nothing. Well, not exactly nothing – more of an indefinable something, as if he were merely going through the motions, like a clever pupil with a slightly dense teacher. Quinn had been hoping he would blow, say what he had to say and get it over with, but so far, nothing. Anderson was respected by the whole squad; he would accept the hand he was dealt and get on with it. But Costello wore her resentment of Quinn like a badge of honour. No way she could get between those two.

But Mulholland, the good-looking fast-track boy, was anybody's slave for promotion. He hadn't been at Partickhill long enough to be bonded to the other two. She had heard nothing but excellent things about DC Mulholland from Divisional HQ. Maybe dangling the carrot of promotion was the way to cut the Partickhill pack.

Quinn smiled – they were McAlpine's hand-picked team no longer.

They were hers.

Annoyed, she saw the picture of the old DCI looking up at her with some reproach; he had worked his way back up to the top of the pile, just as he had in life. *Bastard*, she muttered to herself, picking up the Order of Service and wondering where to put it. The bin seemed disrespectful, and in any case someone might find it there.

She knew she was not the only one who had succumbed to McAlpine's charms more than once in the last twenty years, not by a long chalk. She spun her leather seat round, away from prying eyes, and stroked his picture against her cheek before feeding him slowly into the shredder.

She sat for a moment, watching him go. Then she stood up.

Five to twelve. In-tray empty, desk tidy, lipstick in place – she was ready.

2

The mouths of the tartan-clad observers swelled into perfect pink Os as Squidgy McMidge broke the ranks of the massed pipe marching band, picked up Callum the Caber and prepared to fling him in the great Scottish tradition, scraping his front two legs into the ground like a bull ready to charge.

Squidgy tottered and teetered, his eyes scrunched into walnuts, as he began his run-up. As the midge's six little legs gained speed, they whirled like Formula One wheels, first in mid-air and getting nowhere then, as they made contact with the ground, he hurtled along and punted the Caber high into the air.

As Callum upended, so did Squidgy.

Completely airborne, Squidgy McMidge posed in a vast expanse of cloudless powder-blue sky. A fat little insect with a cheeky grin, six legs akimbo, his wings as useless as a neatly folded parachute, he drifted and ran out of pages.

Eve Calloway eased her body weight to the back of her wheelchair and smiled. She was pleased. It worked – *Squidgy* worked. On each page of a series of little notebooks shoplifted from the local supermarket was a simple drawing, almost identical to the ones before and after, but as she ran her thumb down the free edge and flicked them Squidgy McMidge, with his evil beady little eyes and his dangerous grin, came alive. Squidgy McMidge, the new face of Andy's Appeal for the victims of the earthquake in Pakistan. But the midge needed a little more colour. Maybe a little purple kilt ... She ran her thumb a second time across the ends of the pages, and as Squidgy took the run-up again and tossed Callum the Caber high in the air, the faces in the crowd left the page in a series of hurried lines.

Eve rubbed the tension from her eyes and glanced at the clock. Midday. She had been drawing for over an hour, losing herself in giving life to her cartoon. Squidgy was a difficult child, demanding his life on the page. She picked up the furry purple midge, a prototype for a kiddie's soft toy, and looked into his beady little eyes. He looked happy – well, as happy as he ever looked.

Eve arched her back; she was sore, and her bum was numb. She needed sugar. She reached forward and made an assault on a family bag of Maltesers. Stuffing her mouth full of chocolate, she caressed the midge gently with the fleshy part of her thumb, saying goodbye for the moment, and sighed. The vinyl cover of the chair squeaked beneath her weight as she pressed the remote control, turning up the sound as the TV returned to the news coverage.

A UN spokesperson was talking about the threat of hypothermia hanging over the victims of the earthquake. *'The death toll is rising every hour, and will rise with every further hour that passes,'* she declaimed. *'Many of these deaths are preventable, but there's a desperate need for blankets, tents and warm clothes –'* Eve picked up the remote ready to kill the sound, but paused. *'Eight-year-old Andy Ibrahim, who flew from Glasgow to stay with his cousins two days ago, is known to be among the survivors ...'* A news agency photograph of a traumatized child tied up in a filthy blanket appeared on the screen. *'... his grandparents are still listed as missing. His friends in Scotland have set up an appeal in his name to help all those affected by this terrible human tragedy. If you want to help, donations can be –'*

Eve zapped the sound impatiently. 'Ah, bless them; it fairly brings it home, Squidgy, doesn't it? One minute the wee guy is on the terraces watching Rangers getting gubbed, the next he's under a pile of rubble with his dead granny. There but for the grace, et cetera.' Squidgy's piercing black pinhead of an eye watched as Eve stared into the middle distance, whispering to him. 'And while our hearts bleed for them, Squidgy, we can't deny it has propelled us into the big time. You were in the right place at the right time.'

Squidgy remained silent in the belief that his genius would have taken him to the top anyway.

'You'll be worth a bloody fortune if we play our cards right – one hundred thousand Squidgy McMidge car aerial decorations are hitting the shops tomorrow, at a quid a time ... *A quid a midge* ... and if you want to fork out a fiver, you can have a Squash-a-Squidgy.'

Squidgy's eye caught her own, demanding an explanation.

'It's a soft midge that you throw at the wall and it squeals with demonic laughter.' She tossed a Malteser in the air, catching it expertly in her mouth.

Unimpressed, Squidgy remained silent.

'And by the time Madam Tightarse has finished her interview at Radio Scotland, you might be heading up the *entire* appeal.'

Squidgy showed his total lack of appreciation by falling off the table, and bouncing silently on the carpet. Eve sighed, wondering whether to pick him up with her grabber, or leave him lying there with his purple legs in the air until Lynne-the-Tightarse came home. She turned back to the TV, her attention pricked by a face she knew. And there he was, Rogan O'Neill, flying into Glasgow with his perfect smile, with his perfect girlfriend and their perfect life. She grabbed the remote to turn up the sound, and the slow seductive strains of the opening bars of 'Tambourine Girl' underscored the emotional tableau as Rogan kissed his super-young bimbo supermodel before kneeling down to kiss the tarmac of the runway.

'Arse!' muttered Eve, leaning forward in her seat slightly, listening intently as Jackie Bird's voice-over announced, '... *Rogan O'Neill is donating all the profits from his New Year concert at Hampden Park to Andy's*

Appeal. And, twenty years after it was first recorded ...' she paused for dramatic effect, *'... the re-release of "Tambourine Girl" is storming up the charts and is hotly tipped to be the Christmas Number One. So, go out and buy your copy now. It's all for a good cause.'* The CD cover appeared on the screen, with the image of his girl-friend Lauren McCrae, lying in a tambourine. Eve pointed the remote at the screen, pressed Off with her podgy thumb, and watched Rogan fade to black. For a minute she was quiet. She stared out the window at the ever-falling rain, her pretty face frozen in thought.

'Bastard,' she said quietly.

3

Vik Mulholland was sitting on one of the bench seats outside Marks and Spencer's, absent-mindedly forcing his fingers into his leather gloves, watching the kids on the carousel in the middle of the Sauchiehall Street precinct. Frances was late, she always was. A quick check up and down the street, but he couldn't see her through the Christmas crowds. Vik went back to looking at the carousel; each of the animals had a collar of tinsel and a Squidgy McMidge stuck on an ear or an antler.

He took a small tube of lip salve from his pocket, removed his gloves and dabbed his lips slightly, twisted the tube closed and replaced his gloves. He checked the street again. Still no sign of her.

He watched a man in a fine woollen Crombie kneel at the feet of his overexcited little daughter and fiddle with her red wellington boots with their border of yellow flowers. The fair-haired girl then kicked up her heels, admiring the red flashing lights that ran in sequence down the sides. Mulholland was impressed; he might get a pair of those for his wee cousin. The man lifted his daughter on to a fearsome-looking pink bird and stood back, ready to line up a photograph, as the carousel took off again. The festive mood was spoiled somewhat by the music – 'Tulips from Amsterdam'.

Mulholland sighed, his breath billowing as he watched the large pink bird sail past, the little girl giggling with delight, the lights on her red wellingtons flashing as she stuck her legs out.

Still no Frances; she was twenty minutes late. It puzzled him that he wasn't put off by her tardiness. But soon she would appear, strolling along Sauchiehall Street, ignoring the looks of admiration from passing men, and Vik would feel a thrill that she was there, for him.

He leaned back, letting a few falling raindrops kiss his face, recalling the first time he'd set eyes on her, standing on the pavement with her arms round a small boy. There had been a mild RTA – an old Jag had slid in the sleet and rear-ended a Honda – and the drivers were having a bit of a set-to. Vik Mulholland had never been known to intervene if off duty but when he saw the long-haired beauty protecting the child like some dark guardian angel, he was hooked. Once he had made sure both drivers were unhurt he was surprised to find that she hadn't been in either car. She had looked up at him, the swathe of dark hair falling to one side, and he was lost for words. She was so beautiful.

But he'd regained enough sense to ask her name.

'Coia,' she said. 'Frances Coia.' Her voice was low, slightly husky. She had the most amazing eyes, huge and brown, her irises flecked in gold, yet her skin was ivory, like porcelain. She was older than she had appeared at first sight. He asked her to repeat her address, even though he'd got it the first time, just to hear her voice again. Beaumont Place was a small cul-de-sac of once-splendid but worn apartments, just round the corner from the station.

Then of course, having seen her once, he had spotted her again the very next day, going into the Oxfam bookshop in Byres Road. He abandoned the Beamer and sneaked up on her as she lost herself in a battered copy of the *Oor Wullie* annual, one of his own childhood favourites.

He'd said hello, she'd looked right through him. He had ploughed on regardless, telling her that the wee boy in the Honda was fine and that the mother wanted to pass on her gratitude.

Then she had smiled, and he had asked her to join him for a coffee outside Peckham's. They had ended up sharing carrot cake. And then a bed in the Grosvenor.

And now his heart was in freefall.

He sensed her slip on to the seat beside him; he caught a waft of her patchouli oil. He opened his eyes, looking at her profile as she gazed up at the heavy sky. He watched a tear of rainwater meander slowly down the arc of her cheek. She winced slightly, opened a bottle of mineral water and swallowed a tablet.

'Is your face still sore?' he asked, resting his hand on her shoulder.

Eyes closed, she nodded almost imperceptibly. She never complained.

'See that wee lassie with the lights on her wellies?'

'Yeah,' said Frances, but she didn't look.

'What's she riding? A pelican or a half-cooked turkey?' he asked as the pink bird flew past, its tinsel scarf flowing behind.

She answered without opening her eyes. 'It's a flamingo.'

He squeezed her shoulder gently, and she smiled.

'You know, Frankie . . .?'

'Don't call me Frankie,' she whispered. 'It's Fran.'

'Fran, I'm about to say something to you that I have never said to another woman.'

She arched a perfect eyebrow.

'Let's go to Marks and buy a nice curry.'

But Frances wasn't listening. She was looking at Santa pushing a garish tinfoil-clad wheelie bin with sodden earthquake appeal posters on its sides and reindeer dancing round a makeshift Squidgy McMidge holding a golden trumpet, a red balloon issuing from his mouth saying: *Gie's yer cash!*

'Look at that – DEATH TOLL 76,000 AND RISING – It even has that boy's picture on it, that wee Andy, out there with no shelter . . .'

'One specific face to tug on your heartstrings, Fran, that's all it is,' Mulholland added.

But Frances seemed not to hear him; she was busy scrabbling coins from her purse, her eyes welling up as they settled on the picture of Andy Ibrahim.

'You give them your last penny,' said Mulholland, knowing there was no stopping her. He planted a kiss on her cheek. 'And I'll buy the curry.'

Detective Sergeant Costello was sitting uncomfortably on the huge leather settee in Sarah McGuire's cream and beige living room, her feet sinking into the deep-pile carpet. She sipped her tea, trying to ignore the strong perfume of the Earl Grey, Typhoo being her own preference. It was half past twelve, at the end of a fourteen-hour shift, and her headache was getting worse by the minute. Sarah, an intelligent, attractive woman in her mid-forties, was leaning forward slightly, listening intently, legs crossed at the ankles. She was wearing black mules and pristine woollen slacks – John Campbell's daughter was the effortlessly groomed type. Beside her, her darker-haired, chubbier teenage daughter Karen, even though still dressed in the blue uniform that she had been wearing when the cop car picked her up from her private school, displayed the same faultless veneer as her mother. Sarah McGuire's handshake had been firm and accompanied by the discreet rattle of good jewellery. Costello noticed the band of pale skin where until recently a wedding ring had been.

Costello pulled her short blonde hair tight behind her ears and sneaked a glance at her mobile – no message yet. She had been furious at Colin Anderson for pulling her off the Luca Scott enquiry and even more furious when she heard that Quinn had told him to do it. The minute Luca's mum was capable of coherent thought she wanted to be there. The doctor had been firm to the point of obstructive, his patient was to remain under sedation until they could ascertain the nature of any injuries sustained during her fit. Costello's argument, that the woman must have some idea where her son would go, was met with a sympathetic shrug and a closed door.

Costello looked out the window at the manicured garden, the electric gates. Luca Scott had nothing, he was little more than a street kid. The girl sitting opposite her on the settee, Karen McGuire, had everything. But money wouldn't bring Granddad back.

'Do you know what happened yet?' Sarah toyed with the single strand of pearls at her throat, one mule swinging from her toe with an incessant rhythm that was getting on Costello's nerves.

Costello noted that Sarah's tone of voice was careful, not accusatory. PC Gail Irvine had already backed off to stand by the window; Costello knew she was on her own. She decided on finely edited honesty. 'We're still trying to piece it together. Did he have problems with his heart or anything?'

'No, he had painkillers for his knee. He'd been on them for as long as I can remember,' said Sarah, still pulling at her pearls.

'And were they in some sort of daily dispenser?'

'Yes, he had a dosset box so he would take them

with his meals.' Sarah nodded. 'Oh, and a tablet to stop them affecting his stomach.'

'So, Karen,' Costello turned to Sarah's daughter, who was now visibly calmer. 'Did he seem his usual self when you saw him on Saturday? He wasn't complaining of feeling ill?'

'No. Well, he had the previous week, but just a headache. The tenants upstairs had been playing music all night and he'd run out of his headache tablets.' She rubbed her eyes with her fists, suddenly childlike. 'He asked for some more, Mum, remember?'

'Yes. I bought him some more on Friday on the way home from tennis,' Sarah put in. 'Headeze they were, but he'd had them before. They didn't upset his stomach or anything.'

'So, he seemed his usual self?' Costello moved to the edge of the settee, before it swallowed her.

'He was going on about his Christmas dinner, how he wanted the sprouts cooked properly. And the weather. And he was reading the *Radio Times*, complaining that they were moving *Top Gear*.' Karen recalled the memories in a single rush. 'He was complaining about everything – *The Great Escape* being on again, the team Celtic have chosen . . .'

'Him and every other Glaswegian bloke, eh? Did he live on his own?'

'Since Mum died,' said Sarah, a faint smile through the tears. 'He was very independent – too independent at the wrong time, but what can you do?'

'How often did you see him?' Costello kept her voice friendly.

'Oh, I'd hand in the shopping on Saturday lunchtime. On a Wednesday night we would go round and ...' The tears started again, '... play Scrabble.'

'He always cheated,' said Karen, folding her arms. 'He'd put in words that nobody else knew.'

'My dad used to do that as well,' lied Costello, trying out a slight smile. 'Well, either that or he couldn't spell.' She paused. 'Mrs McGuire, I believe your husband is coming over?'

Sarah nodded. 'Tom? Yes. We're separated now, but he always got on great with Dad. They'd have a pint together on a Thursday – the Clutha Bar. Dad always had a whisky chaser; it would last him all night.'

'He had a load of old pals,' said Karen. 'And they'd sit around the bar and talk about the war. Granddad's got lots of books about it; he's lent me some for my modern history project.' Karen indicated a pile of books, lying on their sides in the bookcase. Costello tilted her head to read the titles, but she only recognized one.

'Karen has her prelims just after Christmas. It's a very important time,' Sarah confided, as her hand reached out and covered her daughter's. 'We've invested a lot in her education.'

'Of course,' Costello agreed, before asking, 'This might be a strange question, but was it usual for him to have a chip pan on at breakfast time?'

It was Karen who answered. 'Yes, he liked a chip buttie, with brown sauce. It had to be HP,' she said with a hint of scorn. 'He would have got up late, especially if the folk upstairs had kept him awake.'

'Mrs McGuire,' said Costello, concentrating hard. The heat in the room was making her eyes pound, she could feel her lids dropping, and she wanted to take her jacket off but couldn't because of the stain on her jumper. 'It's just possible, and I emphasize just possible, that he had a heart attack and collapsed. He was definitely unconscious when the fire took hold.'

Sarah latched on immediately. 'So, he didn't suffer.'

'No, he didn't suffer at all,' said Costello, hoping it was true.

Sarah nodded, as if finding a little comfort in that. 'I don't understand. He saw his GP only last week. He said he was fine,' she added lamely.

'Can you give us the name of his doctor? And his dentist?' asked Costello, glad to see Irvine was scribbling down the details. 'We'll need to do a post-mortem to find out what exactly happened.'

Sarah's mouth opened but she did not speak. She glanced at her daughter.

'Maybe we could discuss this at another time?' Costello offered.

'No, no. It's fine. I thought you only ... I wasn't expecting it.' Sarah shuffled slightly on the settee, smoothing down the legs of her trousers. 'The doctor told him he was fine,' she said again vaguely. 'But you say you still need to do a . . .'

'To establish a precise cause of death. But there's no sign of foul play – that was the first thing we checked.' Costello could sense her sight starting to drift. 'Do you have a recent photograph of him? It's always useful.'

'Help yourself.' Sarah indicated the array of pictures on the sideboard.

'I'll make sure you get it back,' said Gail Irvine, stepping away from the window and choosing one.

'I've just remembered – I didn't see him on Saturday. I dropped Karen off with his shopping, because I had a call to make from the car to rearrange a tennis match . . .' Her voice broke, suddenly guilty.

Costello let the silence drift, then when she spoke her voice was firm. 'Did your father have a cardigan? A Fair Isle cardigan, blue with a white pattern round the neck?' She patted the collar of her own jacket.

Karen thought for a moment, white teeth biting into cherry-red lips.

'Wee silver buttons with the Scottish lion on them?' prompted Costello.

It was Sarah who answered. 'Yes, he's had that cardigan since Karen was a baby. He had new ones in the cupboard, presents.' She tutted. 'But he would never wear them. Why do you ask?'

Costello shrugged vaguely, glad that she had not seen the body, glad that no memory of it could show on her face, glad she wouldn't have to take out the silver button in its sterile little bag and ask: *Do you recognize this?* She knew Sarah was looking at the gap on the sideboard where the photograph of her dad had been.

'I can come down and identify him, if that would help.'

'I don't think there'd be any need. It's not something we do a lot nowadays – visual ID is a bit old-fashioned.'

'I would like to see him.'

'Better not,' said Costello, as quietly as she could, shuffling right to the edge of the settee as a precursor to getting up and leaving.

'Oh ...' It took Sarah a moment to absorb what Costello had actually meant. Then she sat up briskly. 'What about the flat?' she asked.

'The flat?'

'Yes, Dad's flat and the three above. How badly were they damaged?'

Bloody hell, your dad's just burned to death, Costello thought, but said, 'That'll all be in the Fire Master's report.' Then she added, 'If you can wait till then.'

Outside in the rain, Frances stood looking at the Virgin Megastore, its windows covered with posters for Rogan O'Neill's re-release of 'Tambourine Girl'. The posters showed his Canadian supermodel girl-friend, all blonde hair and endless suntanned legs, coiled inside a tambourine as if she were swinging in a hammock. Vik went over to Frances and put his arm round her.

'I bet you didn't know the original cover for that was designed by a graduate of Glasgow Art School,' he said, wondering whether those were tears or raindrops on her face. 'Must be worth a bloody fortune now. And did you know ...' he paused for effect, '... that nobody knows who the girl is who actually says that husky *goodnight* at the end of the record?'

'That's because only the really sad listen to it right to the very end,' she said quietly, a slow tear falling on her cheek. 'It was explained at the time as a mistake in the master tape but the mystery did the sales no harm. Who was the poor little tambourine girl? That's what they all wanted to know. It made his career, that song.'

'I just want to know what the bloody song is *about*, that's all.' He glanced at his watch. Work was calling. 'I'd better get a move on.'

But Frances was staring at the blonde model, coiled in her tambourine. 'Nice, isn't she?'

'If you like that kind of thing. But I'll make do with you.' He kissed her cheek, tasting the salt of her tear. 'Come on. Where are you going? I could drop you.'

'Just up to the Western. I have an appointment for my face.'

'Your face looks fine to me.'

Her good mood had passed. 'I'll catch the bus and walk the last bit, get some fresh air.' Her eyes narrowed as she looked into the dreich damp of Sauchiehall Street. It was miserable. It was catching.

'Well, if you want to die of hypothermia, go ahead. But I'll take the grub and bring it round after work.'

They both had their hands on the handles of the bags, standing face to face. He hesitated, thinking about kissing her, but contented himself with looking into her brown eyes with their little gold flecks, her face framed by a black pashmina.

She blinked slowly, a last raindrop fell from her long lashes on to her cheek, then she smiled. 'I'll manage,' she said, tugging the bags towards her.

As he hugged her goodbye she looked over his shoulder catching her own reflection in the shop window; the scarf round her head, her tall thin figure clothed completely in an ankle-length black woollen coat, made her look like an image of a medieval saint. Beyond her reflection, two tinselled Bang & Olufsen widescreen TVs were silently chattering away: the Scottish news headlines, footage of rescue teams scrabbling over rubble in Pakistan, a factory conveyor belt dense with jostling Squidgy McMidges, a school picture of Luca Scott, and then a shot of the Joozy Jackpot amusement arcade. She pulled free from Vik and walked up to the window for a closer look but the screen was already back at the studio. The polished lips of the redhead reading the news moved with animation. Her ginger eyebrows were raised in a pleasant arc, not frowning with professional sincerity. Good news then. Both screens changed to a picture of clouds and more clouds, the dark rain-filled clouds of a Scottish winter. A subscript announced that Rory McLaughlin was reporting from Glasgow Airport.

Frances screwed her eyes up slightly as a plane shimmered through the clouds and disappeared, only to reappear closer, much bigger.

The image switched to a crowd of young fans and some not so young. The badges, the scarves, the T-shirts and the hats all said one thing – ROGUE. Somebody's granny in a wheelchair was wearing an 'I love Rogan' badge; she held it up and kissed it for the cameras. Then the picture moved quickly to the plane door opening, and there he was, Rogan O'Neill, standing at the top of the steps in black leather. He lifted his sunglasses, waving, lips to his fingertips, kissing the air of his homeland. Then he turned to smile at the beautiful blonde woman, who followed him down the steps. Lastly he knelt down to kiss the tarmac.

Frances placed the palm of her hand flat on the window – separated from him by a pane of glass and twenty years.

Never really separated at all.

'Look at that bloody rain,' Costello said, peering out through the glass panes of Sarah McGuire's front door. 'And it's cold enough for snow.' She tightened her jacket round her in readiness for a quick dash to the car. 'Gail, you hang on till the husband gets here.

Find out how the land lies.' Costello looked at a wedding photograph of Sarah's parents on the wall in the hallway, her father looking uncomfortable in a dark suit and Brylcreemed hair, pencil tie, a single flower in his lapel, and her mother, in a boat-necked wedding dress, ballerina length, smiling shyly. The similarity of daughter to mother was striking.

'What do you mean, how the land lies?' asked Irvine.

Costello lowered her voice. 'If she gets talking, find out how amicable the separation and divorce really are. There's a GSPC magazine on the coffee table, lying open at the West End property pages. Look at this place – would you want to move from here? Posh Newton Mearns postcode? Brand-new Porsche outside? Electronic gates? And Karen's at private school.' She mimicked Sarah cruelly: '*We've invested a lot in her education.* And those are not fake pearls round her neck.' Costello added as an afterthought, 'If your dad was burned to death, would you be worried about the state his bloody flat was left in?'

'Are all those statements connected?' asked Irvine, slightly confused.

'Call it instinct, call it snobbery, but that magazine is open at a page of properties far inferior to this, and she doesn't strike me as an inferior sort of woman, that's all. If her dad owned all of 34 Lower Holburn Street, then he'd be worth a bloody fortune.'

'How can you be so suspicious?' asked Irvine, horrified. 'She's just lost her father . . .'

'My point exactly. The suspicion goes with the territory; we're cops, not bloody agony aunts,' Costello said. 'Find out the story with the husband and the break-up, and be a bit nosy with regard to the finances. I've a feeling something is wrong here. Those tears didn't convince me.' She pulled her mobile from her pocket and called a memory-stored number.

'You might be right. I was in pieces when my dad died.' Irvine looked as if she were about to cry, right there and then.

'Didn't know my dad, and what you never had you can't miss.' Costello smiled at her, phone clamped to her ear. 'Wingnut? Is Quinn the Eskimo not in her igloo?' She pulled a face at the answer. 'Look, I'm feeling rough, I think I've a migraine coming on, so I'm clocking off before it gets worse. Leave a message for her, will you? It's just gone one now. I'm leaving PC Irvine here to wait for the hubby, then she'll get back to Partickhill asap for the update at two . . . No, I'll be blind and unconscious by then.' She closed her phone.

'But you're going to miss the update? You really feel that bad?'

'Yes, but if I get a good kip, I'll be in tomorrow. Luca's mum should be available by then; I can get moving on that. Can you get in touch with the dentist?' Costello ripped that page out of her notebook.

'Leave anything you get on my desk and I'll deal with it tomorrow. Don't bother to type it up. We'll do it all in the one report.'

She walked towards her car, her head thumping, and put the rest of her notes into her handbag. Like she said, she would deal with it tomorrow.

4

Colin Anderson's first impression of the new DCI had been of a hard, brittle woman. A month of working with her had not changed his opinion. When Costello commented that the SS had lost a good recruit when Quinn joined the force, he had laughed. He wasn't laughing now.

'Do come in, DI Anderson.' A tight smile snapped across the face of Rebecca Quinn. As usual, she was dressed in her classic navy-blue suit, red hair pinned back. The smattering of pink freckles on her nose reminded Anderson of those red ants that burrow under your skin and eat you alive.

He walked into the DCI's office, now painted white and furnished with a state-of-the-art water cooler for her own personal use. The windows had been cleaned, the squeaky leather chair replaced, and the breath of life had miraculously returned to the fern on the window ledge which was now luscious and verdant. It jarred with Anderson. So did the tanned length of lean thigh being displayed by the leggy brunette perched on the window ledge. He nodded at her face and pretended not to notice her legs.

'DI Anderson, thank you for joining us –

eventually.' Quinn looked pointedly at the clock. Anderson wasn't aware that he was late, so he didn't apologize. No introduction was offered with regard to the brunette and he wasn't going to be the one to ask. Rumours of the new DCI's mind games had gone before her.

'Hello, ma'am,' he said to Quinn, then said it again to the brunette who flashed a quick smile in response. Quinn ignored him and sat down behind her desk, slid up the sleeves of her jacket and adjusted the small clasp that contained her hair. Satisfied, she opened a brown file and ran her thumb along the fold, up and down, up and down. Anderson bore the silence, still trying, with increasing difficulty, to ignore the length of leg behind her. Both women were of a type – slim, well dressed, well groomed, assertive. He detected a little attitude problem coming from somewhere. He wished he had a map of the situation.

Quinn looked up and handed him a manila folder. 'Are we any further with Luca Scott? Have the hospital given Costello permission to interview his mother yet? I arranged an update on the basis that there'd be more news.'

Anderson decided to tread carefully. 'Sorry, but the last time I spoke with DS Costello, it was still no go.' He opened the folder. 'I think we need to be careful to emphasize that she was not an "unfit mother", she was a *medically* unfit mother.' He fell silent as he looked at the three photographs, so recently developed they still smelled strongly of chemical fluid. The first showed a blond-haired boy, Luca, smiling at the camera, his hand holding out an apple for a police horse. The huge head of the horse was down, the grey velvet muzzle engulfing the apple, narrowly missing the fingers. The next picture was a close-up of the same, the third even closer, just the boy's face. Anderson covered Luca's smile with the palm of his hand. 'He's terrified of that thing,' he observed. 'It's only his mouth that's smiling. His eyes are scared.'

'But he's being brave,' said Lovely Legs on the window sill, nodding thoughtfully.

Anderson handed the photographs back. Briefly, he remembered how apprehensive Peter had been not so long ago, faced by a truculent goat at the zoo. 'I think you should make it clear that all Lorraine Scott's drugs were prescription. She has some mental health issues, and she'd just come from having an injection at the hospital, as she does weekly, regular as clockwork. She then had a . . .' he paused, looking for the right word, '. . . fit in the Joozy Jackpot.'

He saw the brunette raise an eyebrow.

'It's a small amusement arcade in Byres Road,' he said in answer to the unspoken question.

She nodded as if she knew it well.

'It was in the ensuing confusion that Luca went AWOL. Wyngate will put it in an update for those who missed your full briefing. He's good with computers,' he added for Quinn's benefit.

'Medically unfit mother? Was she fit to look after her child?' Quinn looked up. 'No, she wasn't. I don't particularly care why. We have to keep our own noses clean on this one. If the social work team have messed up, this station is not taking the blame.' She looked Anderson straight in the eye.

'We run a tight ship,' he said evenly. 'No leaks.'

Quinn pursed her lips. 'But if the boy was on the street unattended, why did we not act immediately on the basis of it being a possible abduction?'

Anderson phrased his answer carefully. 'We acted on the basis of him being a runaway, because it's not the first time it's happened. As a team, we agreed that since his mother had reported him missing six times before, we could assume it was probably another false alarm ... and then time passed, and we're so short-staffed ... we did what we could ...' His words sounded like an excuse even to his own ears.

'And what would happen if the press got hold of that?'

'Well, they shouldn't. We had credible support for our assumption from Patsy McKinnon, the cashier in the amusement arcade, and the security chap. The medics were slow to give us details of the mother's depression, paranoia and epilepsy.' The brunette perched on the window ledge smiled, offering understanding. Cautiously, Anderson smiled back. 'But you'd know that if you had read the file. Luca was last seen with his mother about four, but he wasn't reported missing until gone seven. And that was only when his mum was coherent enough to ask about him.'

'Spare me the sentiment,' said Quinn, her pen tapping on the desk. 'So we have no idea where the wee sod is? We've checked all known contacts?'

'Yes. And he's not at his home, not at his friends'. We're still trawling through all the places he might be. And now Troy McEwen's been reported missing.' Anderson shook his head.

'Poor wee Luca, with his mum being so poorly,' said the brunette, swinging her heels. It was said casually, and Quinn nodded in agreement. The best of friends then. 'Do these boys know each other?'

'Still working on that one, ma'am.' Anderson was careful to direct his answer at Quinn.

'Where is DS Costello at the moment?' asked Quinn, her tongue flicking round her lips like a serpent's.

'Well,' Anderson began cautiously. 'She was on the blower to the hospital earlier, trying to interview Lorraine Scott, then I sent her out to see John Campbell's family to get a positive ID without anybody having to look at his burned remains. Is she not back yet?'

Quinn shook her head. 'Costello left the McGuires ages ago. She has not phoned in.'

'Not like her, ma'am. Maybe . . .'

'And there is no report on her desk. And PC Gail Irvine – was she there too?'

Anderson silently cursed Costello. 'Yes, she was.'

'So why did you send Costello?'

'You wanted me back here and she's good with women.'

The brunette smirked. 'I'm better with men.'

Quinn allowed a smile to curve her lips. 'So, you don't know where Costello is, and the report has not been done?'

'No.'

'The deceased's daughter has already been on the phone asking about it and wasn't happy being fobbed off with *the officer in question has not yet returned to the station*. I want the report on John Campbell's death first thing tomorrow.'

'It's his PM tomorrow.'

'So, get Costello in early. What do you call this tight ship of yours? The *Titanic*?'

Anderson looked at his watch. 'She only left there at the back of one, and given the Christmas traffic coming through the Clyde tunnel ...'

'Well, let's hope it doesn't turn out to be important.' Quinn glared at Anderson who failed to respond. 'So, DS Costello did not actually attend the fatal fire?'

'No.' Anderson glanced to the brunette at the window, looking for some clue as to why he was being asked this. But the young woman stayed silent, merely giving him the full benefit of her luscious smile.

'And was it just a fatal fire?'

'No sign of foul play with regard to the fire.'

'But with regard to his death?'

'I'd like to wait for the postmortem.'

'We are very busy.'

Anderson stood his ground. 'I know.'

'You have twenty-four hours.' Quinn swivelled her seat back round to the desk.

Thinking he'd been dismissed, Anderson got up to go to the door when Quinn's voice whiplashed him back.

'We are not finished yet.' She turned to the other woman. 'Lewis?'

'About Luca Scott – I thought it might be useful to do a re-enactment,' the brunette said. 'It must have caused a commotion, a forty-year-old woman losing the plot in the arcade. The street outside would have been busy, so somebody must have seen the boy come out. It might jog a memory if we stage a photo opportunity – give the press something to latch on to.'

'Good idea. It also might draw out the perpetrator, if he or she exists. So, if you do it, better send our photographer down there, get him snapping the crowd,' Anderson said.

Quinn tapped her fingernail against the desk. 'So, it's agreed. But when? This is the twentieth. By Friday everything will be breaking up for Christmas. Best get it done tomorrow, Lewis, as close to four o'clock as you can. Go and speak to Patsy McKinnon or the manager of the joint and get the same staff in the same place. Get hold of Irvine, she'll do the legwork for you. Mulholland will get a press release done; and get him on film, the camera loves him. I presume you know where DC Mulholland is?'

Trick question? Anderson glanced at the figure on the window sill in a subtle search for clues. 'He's off duty today. But I think he said he'd be back in later so we can catch him then.'

'We need more media coverage. With Rogan O'Neill flying in, the way they're carrying on you'd think it was the Second Coming of Christ. We didn't get much on the TV about Luca, and in the papers all we got was a single column and a small picture. The evening papers are picking up more.' Quinn's catlike eyes moved across Anderson's face, not exactly accusing but not approving either. Then, in a moment, her whole demeanour changed.

'Detective Inspector Colin Anderson, this is Detective Sergeant Kate Lewis. Pitt Street have transferred her here from Aikenhead Road. She's a very experienced officer. I'm sure you will welcome her as part of your team – you are more than a little short-staffed.'

'Are we?' Anderson enquired, trying to ignore the flash of thigh as Kate Lewis crossed her legs.

'For what we have to do, yes.'

'Well, you'd know more about that than me,' Anderson said pleasantly. 'Were you not transferred here from Aikenhead Road yourself, ma'am?'

'I'm sure they can manage without the two of us,' Quinn replied curtly.

'But only just,' said Kate Lewis as she slid from her window seat on to fine tippy toes. She smiled again, displaying a full set of too perfectly capped teeth.

'Their loss our gain, I'm sure. Welcome aboard,' said Anderson, reaching out a hand.

The grip that returned was soft, long fingers stroked their way into his, and he thought he registered a flirtatious scrape of her nail on the palm of his hand. Her smile stayed wide and seductive before a veil of silky brown curly hair fell across her eyes.

'Maybe you could arrange for DS Lewis to be teamed with DC Mulholland. We'll let the young good-looking ones charm the press.'

'Things seem very cosy here,' Kate Lewis said to Colin.

'It's a small station,' he said, again aware of an undercurrent but not of where it was flowing.

'It may be a small station but it's too big to find DS Costello,' Quinn said to Lewis who was posturing like a young foal, all wide-eyed innocence and very long legs. 'DI Anderson, while you're looking for Costello you can find DS Lewis a desk. And,' Quinn paused for effect, 'I want everybody – *everybody* – back in the Incident Room at two p.m. Lewis, have the arrangements for the re-enactment ready. This other seven-year-old, Troy McEwen, wandered off to God knows where while his mum was pissed. The house-to-house team is out already and I'll call in the search team again. No assumptions this time – I want it done by the book right from the start.'

'It *was* by the book . . .' Anderson began to argue, but Lewis interrupted, slipping her arm through his elbow.

'Come on, you can introduce me to the squad.' Once again, he got the full power of that smile face on.

'Of course.' Anderson released himself from her grasp on the pretext of opening the door for her.

Kate Lewis had a voice to match her smile, low and gravelly, like a porn star's. 'Is DI your first name?' she asked, preceding him through into the main office.

'My wife calls me Colin.' Hoping she would note the *wife*, while reflecting that he should be so lucky that a girl like that would notice him. Costello once told him that he wore being married like a pair of old slippers. At the time he had thought it a compliment.

Kate Lewis stopped in front of DS John Littlewood's desk. 'And this is . . .?'

The old detective looked up and held in his beer belly, a slow smile moving like honey across his razzled face. 'Well, hello,' he said. 'We could sure use you to brighten up things around here. Detective Sergeant Littlewood – call me John.'

'You must have made an impression; we never get to call him John,' muttered Anderson, loud enough for him to hear. 'We call him many things but none as friendly as that.'

'Well, John, I'm sure we will be great friends.' Kate Lewis winked at him and lifted her ringing mobile from her jacket pocket. The ring tone was Tom Jones's 'Sex Bomb'. 'Personal phone,' she said in explanation, and walked away to take the call, leaving Littlewood and Anderson watching the undulation of her narrow hips as she went.

Something about the way she moved, straight-backed with a long stride, her skirt shorter than it should be and her heels higher, made Anderson think of a pole dancer. Or what he imagined a pole dancer would look like. One thing he knew: women who moved like that were trouble.

She smiled at the whole squad as she went past, and a few of the men smiled back. DC Wyngate forgot he was speaking down the phone, his jaw hanging open in mid-air, making him look more glaikit than ever.

'Rabbits in a sack, rabbits in a sack,' said Little-wood, staring at Lewis's retreating rear end. 'So, *that's* Kate Lewis.'

'From Aikenhead Road? You know her?' Anderson leaned over, speaking softly. 'Pray, do tell.'

'DCI Quinn and DS Lewis. You don't get one without the other. Quinn got Pitt Street to send her up here the minute the Scott boy went missing.'

'And how do *you* know all this?'

'Make it my business to keep my eyes on an arse

like that,' murmured Littlewood. 'Lovely to look at, this Miss Lewis, but I'd trust her as far as I could spit on her.'

'Yip, I'll give it three weeks before she sues for sexual harassment,' said Anderson. 'If Costello doesn't have her for breakfast first.'

Littlewood said, 'Yeah, but still a nice piece of arse.'

Eve Calloway took her mobile phone from the side pocket of her wheelchair as she heard her sister come in the front door. She found the stopwatch function and pressed Start. Lynne's record for basic farting around was six minutes ten seconds, obsessive-compulsive cow that she was. Eve listened, creating the scene in her mind – Lynne taking off her coat, shaking it, sniffing the air to see what Eve had been eating without her permission. Lynne faffing around with her mousey blonde hair in the hall mirror – that could take another two minutes. Then she would be pulling her narrow features into some kind of prettiness – that could take for ever. Then Eve heard the bathroom door open – this was the big routine, eight minutes at least. The beige coat would be put on a quilted hanger, and hung over the shower, the collar pulled straight, every second button fastened, belt buckled, the hem of the coat tucked inside the shower tray. Then the heated towel rail, squaring the towels, folding them so the corners were perfect right angles. On and on it went.

Eve turned to Squidgy and whispered, 'What do you think it'll be? Using her towels or turning on the heating?'

Squidgy refused to pass judgement.

'*Eve?*' shrieked Lynne from somewhere down the hall. 'Have you been using my towels?' The voice was insistent. 'Eve?'

Eve pulled a face at Squidgy; she had to hand it to her sister – Lynne missed nothing. She heard her pad down the hall, back to the front door, and pick up the mail. Then Eve heard the rustle of newspaper pages opening and closing; that would be Lynne feeding her obsession with property prices again. The feet padded back up the hall with some speed.

'Look, Eve, this flyer advertising the Christmas Fair at Rowanhill School – listen! *Guest appearances by Rogan O'Neill and bestselling author Evelynne Calloway.* That's me.'

'That's me actually,' corrected Eve.

'No, it's me. Don't think any decent publisher would let you near any children, with your foul language. God knows you're disgusting enough in here, never mind out in the big wide world.' Lynne scrutinized the flyer as if it were a near-miss lottery ticket, her pinched face screwed up. 'Did you get the drawings done? You've had all morning.'

'I devoted all of five minutes to them. That's all I need, me being the creative genius I am.'

Lynne dismissed her. 'Good. Rogan O'Neill has

confirmed he'll be at the fair. And look at this – Helena Farrell has the billing *below* me.'

'Below *us*,' corrected Eve. She picked up the pad on her lap and sketched a few deft pencil strokes – Lynne being strangled by Squidgy.

'You just remember that your name is not Eve, not when we're together. I am Evelynne and you are a nonentity.'

Eve's voice was silkily sweet as she took her revenge. 'Just think, Lynne, Douglas won't be able to resist you now; you'll be moving in the same circle of pretentious wankers that he moves in. Problematic, as you'll keep bumping into his wife.' Eve hit her chest hard with her fist, noisily clearing a ball of phlegm. 'Because it's the wife's money, isn't it? You'll need a few bob more to prise him away from her. Or bigger tits.'

'He's branching out into property development now, for exactly that reason. The money, I mean. Money for us.'

'But he must have made good money in criminal law. Defending the guilty.' Eve let the words hang in the air.

Lynne changed the subject before Eve got started on her rant. 'Can I see the drawings you sent?'

'You'd better, seeing as you did them, supposedly. They're on the system.'

Eve wheeled into the hall, taking another chip out of the skirting board as she went, before stopping at the kitchen door. 'Do you want a cuppa?'

'Yes, please,' Lynne answered, the flyer held tight to her chest.

'Get us one while you're at it.'

Lynne turned, and walked smack into the wheelchair. She growled, 'Could you not have parked yourself somewhere else?' She twisted sideways to get through the narrow gap. 'And who has been here?'

'Nobody.'

'Well, somebody was tall enough to knock the picture in the hall.'

'Must have been you on the way out.'

'Oh, and I ripped the wallpaper, did I?'

'No, I did that, but it's so low the only person who would notice is a dwarf with a squint. Hurry up, I'm gagging for a cuppa. I'm drier than an Arab wrestler's jockstrap.'

Pained, Lynne closed her eyes and went into the kitchen, where she started to swear. Eve smiled; her sister never swore. She wheeled after her. The kitchen was a bombsite, littered with Crunchie and Kit Kat wrappers, and a Battenburg that had been relieved of its marzipan, the toothmarks still in evidence. Two empty Coke cans had been flung in the general direction of the bin. 'What did you have to eat, Eve?' asked Lynne sarcastically.

'Not enough.' Eve started rolling her head as if her neck were stiff, and the gelatinous fat on her neck swelled first on one side then the other so she looked deformed.

'And did you actually post the images of Squidgy to the paper? They need them for tomorrow.'

'Yes; as I said, my genius never sleeps.'

'Nor does your modesty. I hope you drew him sweet and festive.' Lynne placed her bony hands on the taps and looked out the window, aware of Eve sniggering behind her. 'What am I saying? You did something horrible, didn't you?'

Eve just winked. 'They loved it. Santa being mugged by Squidgy. I thought him shagging a reindeer might be a bit much.'

'I really don't believe you at times. This is our income, you stupid cow; this is what pays the bills. This is what keeps the roof over our heads.'

'My roof. Your head,' corrected Eve.

Lynne gritted her teeth and glared at the mess on the worktop. 'And how come you can manage to get all this stuff out, but not quite manage to put any of it back again?'

'I guess I'm just talented.'

'Oh, be quiet,' said Lynne, going off in search of the computer.

Alone in the kitchen Eve turned on the radio, and a moment later the gentle strains of 'Tambourine Girl' drifted out. She leaned her head back, and hummed along – *Say hello to the tambourine girl* – staring out the window. It was still thinking about snowing. She began to reverse her chair, silently, positioning it in the hall so she could see Lynne. She half shut her eyes and watched as her sister pressed Enter to call the screen from hibernation. The email from the appeal office at the newspaper came up instantly. *We love them, can we use them all? Squidgy's a superstar.*

Lynne looked around. Eve appeared to be dozing in the kitchen doorway, listening to the radio. She sat down and began scanning the rest of the emails. Eve had been busy. She had been in touch with a few comics, and had ordered some artist's materials. Then she noticed a folder of emails named *Sheriff Court; Records Department.* Lynne felt her heart begin to thud, realizing what Eve might have been researching. Indeed, *who*? She hovered the cursor over the icon and left-clicked the mouse. As the folder opened a message flashed up. *'Get off my computer, you nosy cow.'*

5

A sodden poster of Luca Scott was hanging by a tattered corner. Costello leaned against a lamp post, checking the time on her mobile. Half one: she should be back at work, trying to find him, but she was blind in one eye, and the pain in her temple was intensifying. The Sanomigraine had been too little, too late.

She stood on the kerb, wet hair sticking to her scalp, Christmas music cutting through her head like cheesewire. The cars on Byres Road were queuing back all the way up to the lights at Queen Margaret Drive. The headlights seemed to be dancing in pairs under the parabolas of the Christmas lights above, merging into one and separating again. She couldn't even see straight; there was no way she could drive like this. She was frozen, sweat making her clothes damp, chilling her to the bone. She started to walk along the pavement to keep warm, one foot in front of the other, one foot ... then the other ...

'Oi, Costello?' a voice said. As she put her hand over her bad eye, a figure came into view ... anorak, blond hair, tall ... 'It is you, isn't it?'

Yes, it's me. Who else would I be? 'Colin?' She felt the blood drain from her head, her knees started to buckle, and she gave up every pretence of being well. She felt a strong arm round her, folding her into the passenger seat of a battered blue Astra, and was aware of a furry dragon being retrieved from under her before she sat on it.

'You look about as good as I feel.'

She heard the seat belt being clicked home and she leaned her head against the cool headrest, and closed her eyes. 'Why, what happened to you?'

'I've been Quinned. And you're for it tomorrow. I think she's going to get a tracking device put on you,' said Anderson, smoothing Costello's jacket collar underneath the seat belt.

Costello realized she was slowly stroking the fur of the dragon, now on her lap. 'Who cares?'

'Are you going back into work?'

'No, I'm going home. It took me bloody ages to get through the tunnel and I didn't get my migraine tablet in time.'

'Accident on the Kingston Bridge, that's why the traffic's so heavy.'

'My sight isn't good enough to drive now. I was trying to find a taxi.' She swayed a little in her seat. 'I told Irvine. I'm sure I told Wyngate. Might as well talk to a brick wall. Look, it's just a migraine. I'll be fine tomorrow. It's because I'm overtired.'

'Tell me about it.' Anderson shut the passenger car door and walked round to the driver's side, holding a hand up in mid-air in an apology to the traffic queue. The slam of the driver's door bagatelled around in

Costello's head. She leaned forward, eyes closed, and held her head in both hands, concentrating very hard on not being sick. 'The problem with this squad is,' Anderson went on, 'the right hand has no idea what the left is up to. Kate Lewis is doing a . . .'

'Who?' Costello screwed up her face.

'Some high-flyer – great legs and not enough skirt – she's organizing a photo shoot with a blond boy standing on the street in the rain and . . .'

'If you want somebody to act as his mum and headbutt a puggie, you can count me out.'

'As subtle as ever. For Christ's sake, the poor woman had a grand mal fit. Lewis won't re-enact that, I hope,' he added. 'But yes, that's what we're arranging. Costello, you look terrible, if you don't mind me saying so.'

'Yeah, well.' For a minute Anderson thought Costello was going to cry. 'It's been a difficult few weeks. It's been hard. '

Anderson lifted his own hand from the gear stick and patted the back of her hand, then asked quietly, 'How did it go with Sarah McGuire?'

'I wasn't happy. Couldn't exactly tell you why, though. With McAlpine I'd have said straight out: *I don't like her, she's up to something,* and he'd have understood. Can't do that with Quinn, eh? I'd have to submit it in a bloody report in triplicate.'

'We have until tomorrow to make something of it. But apparently Sarah McGuire has already phoned to track down the Fire Investigation report.'

'She's entitled to ask, I suppose.'

'But not to see it, if she's a suspect. Is she a suspect?' asked Anderson.

'Could be; she's very quick off the mark for one so grief-stricken with bereavement, don't you think?'

'And Quinn went apeshit because you hadn't filed your report and weren't around.'

'Tough.'

Anderson watched as Costello's head lolled alarmingly. 'Do you want to go to the doctor?' He glanced at his watch, as if he had somewhere important to go. 'It would give Quinn a whole load of paperwork if you snuffed it somewhere official.'

'No, just home.' She ground her teeth; she *was* going to be sick.

'I'm supposed to be out picking up Peter's Puff the Magic Dragon outfit for his nativity play. Poor Brenda's stuck at home with Claire moaning about a sore throat. Although you can never tell with her; she might just be jealous of all the attention Peter's getting, with his starring role. But I'll nip home later,' he sighed. 'Should I cut on to the expressway? I really need to get back to the station asap.'

'Expressway is quicker.' Costello's voice was staccato. She tried to open the window with clumsy fingers, trying to find the handle without moving her head or opening her eyes. 'Puff the Magic Dragon . . .?'

'Don't ask.' As the car stopped at the lights on Great Western Road, Anderson reached across and wound down the window for her, knowing that Brenda would go ballistic if Costello threw up in the car. 'And I should really do some Christmas shopping at some point. You're a woman – any idea what Brenda might want as a present?'

'A divorce?'

'Not thinking of spending that much.' Anderson sighed, 'But, as you say, the last few weeks have been difficult for us all. I've not been much use at home at the moment; Brenda has had a lot to cope with ...'

'You lost your best friend.' Costello looked out the window, then closed her eyes, as if the daylight itself were painful.

'*We* lost our best friend.'

'We certainly did.' Costello sat forward, holding her head, trying to anticipate the movement of the car as it weaved through the narrow streets of Rowanhill to get back to the river. Her heightened senses picked up the smell of petrol. She could sense the sweet chemical scent of fresh newspaper somewhere in the car, the stale grease of yesterday's chips ...

'Can you stop the car?' she said urgently.

Anderson pulled over, the tyres bumping on to the raised coping stones beside a grass verge. Costello opened the door and suspended herself by the seat belt, as her stomach emptied out three cream crackers and two cups of Earl Grey, as vile coming up as they had been going down.

The thumping intensified until it felt as if her brain would split, and for a moment she thought she was going to faint. The concrete came dangerously close, then she felt a hand close gently on the back of her collar and herself slowly being pulled upright, back into the seat. She put her head in her hands, wanting to die. She knew that something very unpleasant was dangling from her nose and something even more unpleasant was dribbling from the corner of her mouth. But Anderson, the doting father of two, had a whole boxful of tissues in the glove compartment. He had to pull a few used crusty ones out of the box first, apologizing for his disgusting son. 'Better now?'

She clamped a clean tissue over her mouth and nodded carefully.

He reached across her, closing the door against the cold wind, and she felt the car pull into the traffic, heard the constant drum of rain on the windscreen, the gentle tick of the wipers, back and forth, back and forth. She opened her eyes, and saw droplets of water, each with a little comet tail behind, being swiped by the blade of the wiper against the glass, only to be replaced by more ... and more.

Then she realized she was home.

There was a gentle nudge at her shoulder. 'I think that's your mobile. It's the station. I'll get it. I'll tell them you'll phone in when you're fit.'

'It'll pass now I've been sick,' Costello croaked. 'I'll be fine tomorrow.'

Anderson flipped the phone open. 'DS Costello's mobile, hello.'

'And when did you start answering her phone?' snapped DCI Quinn.

By five past two the meeting was still only half full. A picture of a second boy with a stud earring now hung beside the new photograph of Luca with the police horse. Troy McEwen had disappeared from the playground off Horselethill Road sometime the evening before. The incident board told its own story.

The DCI had reapplied her red lipstick, removed her jacket and rolled up the sleeves of her white blouse, ready for business. She consulted a list on a battered clipboard and surveyed the room. 'Is this it? Where is everybody?'

PC Gail Irvine peered at the list over Quinn's shoulder. 'Yip, this is your lot. It's this throat infection, Christmas leave . . .'

'Has DS Costello called in sick?' There was silence. 'DI Anderson? Has DS Costello called in sick?'

'You know she did,' growled Anderson. He caught a sly smile from Kate Lewis, and smiled back just to confuse her. 'And so has DC Burns, in case you missed that too.'

'So, I may as well start then.' Quinn tapped the photograph. 'The first thing I have to say is that, no matter what happens with the missing children, no matter what Rogan O'Neill gets up to – this squad has to cope with it. There will be no more in the budget, no more personnel. So, what have we got to work with here? We've learned very little since the earlier briefing, but we'd better recap for the back shift. Troy McEwen's disappearance is far too similar to the disappearance of Luca Scott for it to be a coincidence. So, it now looks like abduction. And, following that theory, abduction involving some planning and some kind of surveillance. So,' Quinn continued, not bothering to hide her irritation, 'let's see if we can brainstorm and find some point of connection between the two. Mulholland and Costello had traced Luca as far as the amusement arcade in Byres Road, and we all know what happened when his mother had her fit. There was a biting wind that afternoon, it was dark, it was busy. The ambulance had to double-park and the usual gore-seekers had formed a crowd. In the confusion, Luca was forced or jostled on to the pavement, or perhaps he made his own way there. Everybody was looking in the opposite direction. Kate is organizing a re-enactment of the whole thing tomorrow at four p.m., with the press there.' DS Kate Lewis rippled her fingers at the squad in a childlike wave, beaming. Quinn continued, 'We'll dress up a boy of the same height, and photograph him. Hopefully that will jog a few memories.'

Anderson caught Gail Irvine glaring at Kate Lewis and muttering something rude which sounded like *stupid cow*. 'What was Luca wearing?' he asked, moving the conversation on.

'A parka from Primark. With a snorkel hood. And

yes, they do hide the face, which will afford some anonymity to the stand-in.' Quinn continued, 'The mum, Lorraine, is still under observation in Leverndale and can't really remember anything. No matter which way round we go, we can't get past her doctor. So, we have to accept that there's not much more to be gained from her. Nobody knows who the father is, there's no ongoing custody battle, and Luca has not appeared at any of his local haunts, so ... It looks as if he just wandered up the road and vanished into thin air. DI Anderson?'

Anderson shrugged. 'All procedures for a lost child have come up blank, so we're now considering it an abduction. The CCTV backs up Patsy McKinnon's statement, but we can't see much what with the weather, the poor light and a whole load of people milling around.'

'In the light of Troy's disappearance, we must re-examine,' Quinn took over. 'Troy McEwen was wearing only leggings and a lightweight fleece – so, if he is out there, he will be cold, very cold. He was last seen around half past four yesterday. We have a sighting of him here on the swings up in Horselethill Park ...' She tapped the map, '... with his mum. The woman was described as sitting slumped on a bench in the playground. The sightings are not confirmed as it was dark, and nobody had a look at her face, but our witness – Mrs Moxham, who was out walking her wee dog – says it's not the first time she's seen them both. Troy's mum has a distinctive Afghan, coat not dog. Mrs Moxham noticed the boy didn't seem to have a jacket on. You know what the weather was like yesterday; rainy, murky, turning to sleet. The temperature went down to minus three. And Troy wasn't reported missing until this morning, and that was by a neighbour. Forensics can pick up a whole mishmash of footprints up as far as the rubber matting of the playground, but any shoeprints we got are of doubtful value. We did get a scrape of blood which we're looking at; however, it is only a scrape, not enough to indicate any real violence.'

'Doesn't rule it out, though,' said Kate Lewis, reasonably.

'Did his mother go home without the wee lad then?' Irvine asked, in disgust.

'The neighbour who reported him missing, Miss Cotter, has already given us a good statement. She's a nice old dear, lives on the same landing as Troy,' Lewis said, handing out photocopies of the statement. 'You can see from this that it wasn't unusual for Troy to go home on his own. He lived round the corner from the park, across busy roads but still close. The park was his mum's favourite drinking den, so he was used to walking home, and if his own flat was locked, Miss Cotter would take him in. She noticed he wasn't there this morning – the McEwens' flat door was open, apparently – and that Troy's mother, Alison, was dead to the world on the settee, clutching a bottle of pills in her hand.'

'So, why did she not think Troy had just gone out?'

'If his mum was having one of her little episodes, i.e. she was pissed, Troy would go next door to Miss Cotter for his breakfast. But he didn't this morning . . .'

Anderson read through Miss Cotter's statement and could see it all in his mind, a modern-day tale of *Babes in the Wood* but without the happy ending. Troy McEwen, at seven years old, had enough savvy to find his way through the maze of dark streets that nestle between Horselethill Circus and Byres Road. He knew his own close, and he knew his own door would be on the latch if his mum was in, or to bang Miss Cotter's letter box if his mum was out. And in he would go, and have chips. Anderson would bet his bottom dollar that had been the pattern of Troy's life ever since the dad walked out. He thought of Peter, his life full of dragons and pet goldfish. The way a wee boy's life should be.

Gail Irvine tentatively raised her hand. 'From the door-to-door reports, it looks as though Troy wasn't the only one in and out of Miss Cotter's flat. She entertains quite a few of the wee kids round there.'

Quinn nodded. 'Might be of interest.' She turned to the wall and ran through the grid search that had already been covered, her finger indicating the ever-increasing circles on the map that centred on the last sighting of Troy. With each hour that passed, the circle was expanding. The abduction sites were less than half a mile apart, so by the end of the day the search teams would be going through the same premises for Troy as they had for Luca the previous day. Even as Quinn resumed speaking, they could hear doors opening and closing downstairs, a constant tramping of boots along the corridor as the search team reassembled, grabbed a cup of tea, warmed their feet and went back out again.

'I'm afraid the search of the McEwens' flat gave us no leads and, as far as we can tell, nothing else is missing. I want somebody to have another look at it before we talk to the mother, try and get a bit of a feel for the boy. What made him go away just in the clothes he stood up in? He'd no coat, no thick anorak, and it's going down to minus three again tonight. There was nothing in the fridge – you all know what that means. I don't think the mother quite grasps the gravity of the situation. She thinks Troy will just turn up . . . We need to be careful not to interview her without her social worker's knowledge; need I say more?' Quinn cracked her fingers. 'And I don't need to remind you that family members are responsible for eighty-five per cent of child disappearances. So, are both boys safe and sound somewhere that we have yet to hear about? Do they know each other?' She kicked a table leg with her heel. 'But we'll go with the theory that they have both been abducted. What about the CCTV at the park? Was it any use?'

'There are no cameras at the park itself. We can see the woman and the dog on the way there, but the tape is so bad, they look like snowmen in a blizzard.

We don't actually see Troy. Or anybody else,' came a mumbled reply.

'The camera would only pick them up if they came out to go to Byres Road or up on to Great Western Road. There's a whole maze of side streets and back lanes in between, it's a bloody rabbit warren. Look at the geography – the two main roads form a right angle and the park is dead centre, if you'll pardon the phrase. So is this station, in fact,' Anderson pointed out.

Quinn sighed. 'So, cast the net a bit wider.'

They groaned.

'Both boys disappeared in public places. They must have gone somewhere.' She gestured vaguely at the four corners of the map. 'Go through all the statements again. Examine what we have, compare it with the door to door, see if we can match anything up. Look again at the lower end of Byres Road, the pubs, the back alleys. We know Troy was wearing a fleece when he went missing, but somebody might have put a parka on him. So, look for a boy with a hood up. DI Anderson ...?'

He nodded.

'... Any discrepancy, I want to know; especially close to the location of the last sightings by the dog walker Moxham and the cashier McKinnon. Vehicle alerts have gone out, all with these photos.' Quinn indicated the blown-up photos on the incident board. 'I've asked both boys' social work teams to liaise with each other and to note any point of contact between them, so I daresay we can expect them to report back sometime before the next millennium. If anybody has a friend in that office, call in any favours you can. Littlewood, does that MO cast anything up on the sex offenders register?'

Littlewood shook his head, scratching his beer belly through his white T-shirt. 'Nothing as yet, ma'am. I'm going to Stewart Street HQ to look at that myself, chat up a few contacts, see if anything has come down the wire yet. I'll report to the DI, ma'am.'

'Good. Wyngate, get on with tracing all Troy's relatives, recheck his usual haunts, press them to think where else he might be. Lewis, get on with the reconstruction. And Mulholland, get something ready for the cameras; they're parked downstairs. Irvine will help you. Bear in mind we'll only have one shot at this. Anderson, you're checking statements and collating the results of the door to door. And Costello can join in when she deigns to grace us with her presence. The rest of you, get on with the grid and the door to door, and stay in touch with DI Anderson. I want those photographs everywhere. Somebody saw those boys, with somebody, going somewhere. And, I expect you – no, I am telling you – to man this office 24/7. No leave until you are all dead on your feet.'

'Dad, is that you?' A bout of coughing came from the back room.

'Yes, sweetheart, I'm home.'

'Daddy's home! Daddy's home,' squealed Peter in delight. 'Did you get my dragon suit?'

'No, not yet.'

'Why?' Peter managed to stretch the word out to three syllables of outrage.

Colin pretended to cuff him, and said, 'Because. Let's go in and see your sister; she's not well.'

They went into Claire's room. She lay on the bed, her favourite Paddington Bear beside her. She looked hot, with a sheen of sweat over her pale face.

The Barbie-themed room smelled stale. 'I'm poorly,' said Claire, impersonating a dying swan, her voice dry and croaky.

'She said she felt like shite,' added Peter, with some enthusiasm.

'I didn't say that, Dad, honestly, I didn't.' Her large eyes looked as black as coal and her hair, wet with sweat, lay sleek against her skull. 'My throat's really sore. See that big lump?' She opened her mouth. 'That's my gland. The doctor said it was swollen.'

'Did the doctor say that today?' asked Anderson.

'No, yesterday. You were supposed to get my stuff last night but you didn't come home for ages.'

'Sorry, pal, I was busy.' Colin kept his tone light while mentally wanting to strangle Brenda. She could have gone for the prescription; it would have taken her ten minutes. He bit back his anger and made up his mind. 'Right, this is what is going to happen.' They both listened. Dad was always easier to get round than Mum and they could sense weakness. 'I'm going to go out and get your medicine . . .'

'Wouldn't some ice cream be better? My throat's really hot.'

'I think it would help, Dad,' Peter agreed. 'My goldfish died today.'

Anderson tried to see the connection but failed. Not for the first time, he got the feeling that his son would end up either running the country, or in jail.

Brenda was doing her teeth in the bathroom. Anderson could see a new outfit spread out on the bed, the TK Maxx label still on it. A glittery top and a pair of silk trousers in powder blue. Then he realized he had no idea where she was going. Or who with.

He turned back to the kids. 'Right, here's the game plan. You,' he looked at Claire, 'stay in your bed and do not move till I get back.'

'What if Mum goes out and you don't come back?' asked Claire, pointing a finger at him.

Colin met her fingertip with his own. 'She won't. You stay here with Pooh and Paddington, and don't move.'

She tutted in annoyance at being treated like a child, but her arms went round both bears just the same.

'Peter, you come with me. We will get the medicine and get some . . .'

'Ice cream,' they both said in unison. Colin raised a finger to his lips.

He went into the bedroom. Brenda was peering in

the mirror, rubbing foundation over her face. 'Can you stay in for now?' he asked her. 'I'm going to nip out for the prescription, I know you've been busy today.'

'Did you get his dragon suit? No, I bet you didn't.' She didn't look at him. 'As usual, my life depends on what you are doing at your bloody work. But I'm being picked up at half six, and I am *leaving* at half six. So you'd better be back.'

'If I'm not, you can follow in a taxi, or ask them to wait. I'll only be a few minutes. Pour some wine down their throats. It'll be cheaper than going ... where are you going anyway?' He placed his hands on her shoulders and squeezed gently. He could smell a perfume he wasn't familiar with.

'Out. I'm going bloody stir crazy in this bloody house with those two,' she said, shrugging herself free of his touch.

'Keep your voice down,' said Colin calmly, aware Claire's bedroom door was opening. 'I'll call if I get held up. If you really need to go, get Caroline in from next door to babysit. I'll be as quick as I can.' Anderson softened his voice and tried again. 'You going somewhere nice?'

'Christmas night out, with the girls.'

'When will you be back?'

She sneered. 'You're never back when you say you'll be. Why should I?'

'Because you are going out with your pals and I've spent the day looking at ...' He felt Peter swinging at his elbow. 'Never mind how I spent the day. Do you think you will be late? Will I wait up?'

'Do what you want,' Brenda said, rolling her eyes as she pulled the mascara brush through her lashes. 'You normally do.'

He retreated into the hall as the bedroom door slammed shut. Peter hesitated for a moment before following his father downstairs.

It was the number plate Anderson noticed first. The blue BMW 5 Series was common enough but the plate – HF 113? He would have recognized it anywhere. The car was pulled hard against the kerb, its hazard warning lights flashing like fairy lights in the rain. Helena's car. Helena Farrell, Helena McAlpine – Alan's wife. Alan's *widow*, he corrected himself. He felt a rush of familiar pleasure, as though the old Boss himself had come back to help out his former squad. But then he remembered – and the memory was almost enough to crush him.

Helena was crouching on the pavement, wielding the handle of a jack ineffectually. Anderson put on his own hazard lights at the last moment before pulling in front of the Beamer, while the car behind tooted in annoyance.

He looked in the rear-view mirror while Peter turned in his booster seat to look through the back window, holding his Monkey Meal with Cheeky Chips to his chest like a pensioner clutching a hand-bag full of Bingo winnings.

Helena Farrell got to her feet, hand up to protect her eyes from the rain, and looked at the tyre. She was thinner, less substantive, but it was definitely her. She had had her auburn hair cropped short. Colin preferred it long; he always had.

'Stay here,' he said to Peter, and added as an afterthought, 'and don't touch *anything*!' He got out of the car. 'Trouble?' he shouted.

'Colin! My knight in shining armour!' Helena smiled through the rain, which was rapidly turning to sleet, flakes settling on the shoulders of her coat. 'I've got a flat, and I can't even get the nuts off the wheel.' She kicked the jack with an elegant boot. 'The AA said they'd be another two hours or so.'

He took the wrench off her, feeling like a man doing a man's job. 'I'll do it.' He crouched, running his hand under the sill of the car, pressing his thumb into the tyre. 'Go and sit in my car. You'll get soaked.'

'I'm soaked already.'

'Can you keep an eye on Peter then? I wouldn't put it past him to drive off. I'll shout if I need a hand.' He watched her walk away, head down, into the rain. He wondered how her expensive cashmere coat would survive in his car, with its deep litter of Ribena cartons, and Peter's Cheeky Chips fingerprints.

Six minutes later, with the Beamer standing on three alloys and a spare, Anderson put the jack back in the boot of Helena's car. He put the flat tyre in the boot of his Astra, then he flicked the door open and dived into the driver's seat. 'How are you getting on?' he asked.

The answer was surprisingly well. Helena had made herself at home in the back with Peter, and both were involved in a grave discourse on dragons and how to draw them. Helena looked up and smiled as Anderson twisted round in the driver's seat, but she made no move to get out of the car. Her arm was round his son, her index finger pointing to the back of the Monkey Meal box – they both looked totally at ease.

'A long, long tail,' she was saying.

'A long, long, *long* tail,' Peter repeated, the pen going along the top of the box and down the side.

'If you'd drawn him a bit smaller he would fit.'

'Yeah, but he's wagging his tail,' Peter said in all seriousness, rotating the box so Helena could see.

'I can't thank you enough, Colin, rescuing a damsel in distress and all that.'

'I'll get the tyre repaired for you.' How easily it would have rolled off his tongue – *seeing as Alan isn't here to do it.*

Helena smiled again and shook her head. 'If you have time, that would be great. I've a lot on my plate at the moment.' She changed the subject abruptly, and turned to Peter, saying rather formally, 'It was a pleasure to meet you again, Peter. Come and see me sometime soon, and we can finish your dragon.'

'You keep my crayon and you can help me colour it in.'

'I'll be on my way, Colin.' She began edging her way towards the door.

'What are you doing out in this? Should you not be . . .? I mean, how are you and everything?'

Helena bit her lower lip. 'I get up in the morning, I miss my husband. I eat my breakfast, I miss my husband. I go to work, I miss my husband . . . you get the picture?'

'We all miss Alan, but I can't imagine how it must be for you.' He rubbed the heel of his hand round the arc of the steering wheel. 'But I asked how *you* are.'

She caught the meaning in his voice. 'I have a meeting with a surgeon tomorrow at the Western.' She reached to open the door but paused slightly. 'Just my pre-op check thing; the big op won't be until later in the week. It's a small lump, it's not been there long, but they'll only know how much to take out when they are in there digging around. The only problem I really have is that I feel so cold all the time.'

'Maybe because it is cold,' Anderson smiled, flicking the windscreen wipers from normal to fast to clear the build-up of sleet, then switching them back to normal again. 'If there's a problem, phone me. Getting there? Getting back? Flat tyres?'

'I will.' She was looking at him thoughtfully, the streetlight casting raindrop shadows on her cheekbones. She looked stunning.

'Hope it all goes OK,' was all he could think of to say.

She sighed slightly. 'I'll be fine, Colin.' Her hands still did not release the door catch. 'Colin?'

There was something in her voice that made his heart jump. 'Mmm?'

'I'd booked our usual two tickets for the Christmas concert, Carols by Candlelight. Alan and I used to go every year. He said he hated it, but I think he enjoyed it all really.'

'I know; he said he had to dress up like a penguin to see a lot of fat women shouting at each other in a power cut.'

Helena laughed. 'That sounds like Alan.' She stopped laughing. 'And that's my point.' She pursed her lips and gave him a wry smile. 'Well, this year they're fundraising for the Pakistan earthquake and I feel I need to go. And I'd like to go with someone who remembers Alan, as he was, if you know what I mean. I want to talk about him, with somebody who knew him.' Her voice was barely a whisper.

'If that's an invite, you're on,' said Colin, thinking that even if Brenda killed him, he'd die happy. 'But in return you have to come and listen to Peter singing "Puff the Magic Dragon" as part of his nativity play at the fair. Are you not judging the drawings or something?' he asked, belying the fact he had noted the time and date in his head the minute he'd seen the flyer.

'I'm judging the kids' art competition.' She poked

Peter's Squidgy in the stomach. 'They're drawing this horrible wee guy that's everywhere nowadays ...'

'My goldfish died,' he said, prodding Helena with the rubber end of his pencil. 'He's in heaven now.' Peter pointed to the roof of the car. 'It's a very special place,' he said carefully.

Anderson sighed. 'As in P.L.A.I.C.E ...' he explained.

'The best place for a goldfish's soul – as in S.O.L.E – to be.' Helena ruffled Peter's hair again, smiling at Colin, before she got out the car and walked back out into the rain.

He watched her in the mirror as she got into the BMW and raised a hand to him. He started the engine of the Astra, thinking. She had said something at the funeral about wishing she had had Alan's children, something to comfort her, a little piece of him to remind her. And she had looked so natural, sitting in the back of the car with Peter ...

As if reading his thoughts, Peter said, 'She's a nice lady. She's going to finish my dragon.'

Anderson realized he was smiling, but whether at Peter or the thought of seeing Helena McAlpine again, he wasn't quite sure. But he was sure of one thing; the woman had not looked well.

6

'Ma mum'd go mad if I did that,' Luca said, watching Troy as he tugged at the mattress standing up against the wall until it nearly toppled over on top of them.

Troy giggled. 'Stupid place to have it anyway. Let's lean it against the bed and make a tent and hide. We can put the light out. Then if someone comes we can jump out! Come on – gie's a haun.'

Luca didn't want to refuse, so he grasped the edge of the mattress. He'd ask his mother later why anybody would stand mattresses up against the wall when the bed was narrow and all knobbly and jabbed you in the back. But then, when he slept at his foster parents' – when his mum was sick – he often made a tent from the furniture and slept in that. It made him feel safer.

Gravity eventually had the mattress keeling over, Troy shouting 'Caber!' as it went. With a lot of pulling and shouting they got the end up on the bed, and it became a tent, or a slide, or a squinty trampoline.

Luca placed a hand on the wall in the gap where the mattress had been, between two others. The wall was cold, wet even, and made his fingers smell funny, like somebody else's granny.

Troy went to the wall to put out the light, and they hid under the bed, behind the mattress, giggling and making *shoosh* noises, forefingers to lips. The footsteps outside grew louder, then receded. Nobody came in.

'Let's go sliding,' said Troy.

'You'll hurt yourself,' cautioned Luca.

'No' me.'

Troy hopped up on the bed and jumped up and down experimentally on the twanging bedsprings before bouncing on to the mattress. He slid chortling down the mattress, again and again, first on his backside, then on his back, and finally head first.

But he got too cocky, bounced too hard, and the mattress bounced him right off again so he landed on hands and knees on the hard floor. He sat up, rolling his legging up, crying a little with the pain. He'd opened up the raw scab on his knee, only it was worse now, the blood bubbling and weeping down his leg.

Luca went across to put the light on. He prodded at Troy's knee carefully, his dirty fingers leaving livid marks on the hot and angry skin. 'You need a plaster on that. Ma mum always has Mr Men plasters – she's always cutting herself.' He went to the big door and pulled the handle down. The latch clicked but the door didn't open. He pulled again, harder. Nothing.

He looked at Troy. 'But it's always open.'

'We were told to go to our bed,' said Troy, still squeezing his knee.

Luca lifted his feet from the ground and pulled on

the handle with all his weight. Then the solitary light bulb popped and died, and darkness came down like a shutter.

The lone figure trudged up Rowanhill Road, his breath clouding the air with effort. Every lamp post he passed had a poster of Luca Scott on it. Every third one or so had a poster of Troy McEwen. The railings of Rowanhill Primary School were adorned with pictures of the missing boys in clear plastic coating, and pictures of wee Andy Ibrahim out in Pakistan. All were covered in tinsel, garlands, messages of hope and scribbled prayers. The school was non-denominational but in the corner, inside the protection of the railings, was a small nativity scene. A few flowers were scattered around, having been thrown in from the road through the railings.

On the classroom windows, fluorescent posters announced the forthcoming fair.

Constable Smythe quickened his pace, hurrying towards Byres Road and the subway at Hillhead. He had been drafted down from Partick Central Station the minute Partickhill had put a call out to all surrounding stations for help with the search for the missing boys. He didn't know why, but he could guess. His DI had taken great delight in sending him on the new detail – to go out and search every bloody wheelie bin and piss-soaked alley in the West End on a freezing cold night to look for two children who would not be there.

Smythe knew he was unpopular; he also knew he was good. He was resented because he was good. Appraisals were coming up and he could sense promotion in this, now he was away from his own squad. He walked on past the terraced houses of Crown Avenue and Crown Drive. All were within the Red Triangle, so they should have been searched already, with the exception of the properties the day shift couldn't get access to. He stopped on the corner of Rowanhill Road and looked up, behind him, recalling the grid plan he had spent all afternoon working. It was logical to him that if no access had been gained at three p.m., they'd have more of a chance now at eight thirty. Yet here he was, walking past these houses again, and there were no cops in sight, no search team. No doubt they would be back at the station with a hot cuppa and a bacon roll.

Smythe pulled his glove from his hand with his teeth, got his pen and notebook from his pocket and started scribbling. If need be, he'd go over the whole bloody lot on his own. He glanced at his watch and headed towards the tube station. He wanted to get home, it was his turn to bath the kids.

Frances looked as though she had only just got home – she still had on the long woollen coat, to which the rain had attached itself in perfect droplets, and her hair was soaked, stuck flat to her head, making her long pale face look like a white shield.

Vik thought she looked a little red round the eyes, as if she had been crying.

She eyed him blankly at first and then leaned forward to kiss him. 'I'm sorry,' she said. 'I didn't realize it was so late . . .'

'Look, Fran, if it's too early I'll . . .' He leaned on the wall as a sign that he had no intention of going anywhere.

'No. No.' She drummed her fingers along the door jamb as if making up her mind about something. He stayed against the wall, hoping he looked relaxed but sexy, watching her eyes narrow as she frowned in concentration. She said again, 'No, no. Come in.'

'For you,' he said, handing over the huge bouquet of flowers he was holding.

And he got her hundred-watt smile.

She led him into the dark hall, pulling the coat from her shoulders and dropping it over the out-stretched arm of a window dresser's dummy that stood in a recess by the door to the bathroom – the recess that would have held the cloaks of the cloak-room, its row of tiny pegs still visible behind the fedora the dummy was wearing at a perilous angle. He followed as she walked in front of him. Her jeans and jumper were both well worn, shaped to the contours of her body, and her fine-boned elbows were clearly visible through the thinning wool of the overlong sleeve. He thought about buying her one of those nice cashmeres. He jumped a little when Frances flicked something with her boot on the way past – something she didn't want him to see. His Christmas present, he hoped.

The dummy, bald and naked apart from the fedora, had its right hand held out at shoulder height, palm up as if expecting a tip. A tambourine dangled from its badly chipped fingers. Vik gave it a high five. Frances turned to look at him.

'I guess everybody does that,' he said sheepishly.

'Who's everybody? It's my hall, isn't it?' she asked without humour. 'Come through to the fire; I'll take your coat.' She ushered him into the living room.

This was the first time he had been in her flat properly. Normally he was kept at the door or went straight into her cramped, dark bedroom. He had expected a front room out of Ikea – all feng shui and laminated floors. He could not have been more wrong; her home was old, neglected but well loved, and Frances wore it like a glove. The room was a 1950s time warp, a mass of different shades of dark red. The thick burgundy carpet, which had seen better days, had a trim of grey dust at the skirting board, and was covered in patches of pale silky hair, belonging to Yoko the Siamese cat, he presumed. As he set down the shopping bags, the wine bottles clunked noisily together, and he rested them against his foot as he slipped his arms out of the sleeves of his coat.

She took it from him, smiling her enigmatic smile.

'Make yourself comfortable,' she said as she left the room, her heels clunking on the bare floorboards in the hall.

He sat on the floor, warming his hands at the coal fire which was beginning to catch. It spat and crackled a little, a living thing. That explained the coat; she had been outside to get the coal that stood in a basket, still dotted with rain. Then he sat back, looking up at the ceiling. A glass amber-marbled ceiling light hung suspended on three chains. Several dead flies lay like the spent heads of matches in the bowl. On a high black mantelpiece stood two sepia photographs in oval frames; in both the couple looked old enough to be Frances's grandparents. Her granny, a brown-eyed benign witch, had had the same long dark hair, the same perfect features. No photos of her parents, he noticed. The hearth and fireplace were covered in wine-red tiles, many broken, with white scars between the tiles and the black plaster beneath. Somehow the vinyl record collection, stacked on makeshift shelves along one wall and standing in piles on the floor, seemed completely in keeping; the pile in front of the window had a plant on top. There must be two thousand records in here, he reckoned, and only a few CDs, all with bargain-basement yellow labels. Pride of place in the room was occupied by an old Dual turntable standing on top of a shock-absorbing mat. Vik was impressed by the range of Frances's record collection; she had lots of rare editions in multicoloured vinyl, and the black version too for sound quality. He noticed there was no DVD player; he would have to buy her one. He had already got her a DVD boxed set of Rogan's *Greatest Hits*. With a bit of luck he might be able to get it signed if O'Neill was making an appearance at the Rowanhill School Fair.

He found a vinyl copy of *Tubular Bells*, kept in pristine condition in a plastic envelope. He pulled it from its protective sleeve and placed it on the turntable, watching the arm drop. He leaned back against the front of the settee and closed his eyes, letting himself float away on the haunting, staccato melody.

An hour later, he was still sitting there leaning against the settee. In the glow of half-light, the empty containers of their meal were stacked up on the floor, dirty plates beside them, and the empty bottle of red had rolled against the hearth. Frances, who had changed out of her wet things and was wearing a black towelling dressing gown, was lying on the settee behind him, long limbs half curled round him, slender fingers caressing Yoko who was purring quietly like the engine of an Aston Martin.

Vik couldn't quite figure out all the contradictions that were Frances. So much attention to detail, to good music, yet she lived in a flat with a Stone Age kitchen. She was an attractive woman – a beautiful woman – who didn't care about clothes. She was bright, well read, but didn't work. She didn't seem to need money. She didn't even seem to need company apart from the cat. Yet she was a breath of fresh air.

'Was this flat your mum's?' he asked.

Frances half smiled, and her hand came to rest on his shoulder. One touch. So sensuous. But she didn't answer.

'So, did you buy it then?' Vik persisted. He had known the flat was big, but he had no idea it would cover the ground floors of both sets of flats above. 'Surely you didn't buy somewhere this size on your own.'

'I inherited it from somebody,' she said. 'Well, they didn't die – can you inherit if they don't die …?'

'It's a huge flat for one person.'

'I have no one to share it with.' And that was the end of that conversation.

He closed his eyes again, just for a few seconds, breathing in patchouli. When he turned to look at her, she had fallen asleep.

He shifted himself round to gaze at her, at the faint smile on her lips as she slept. Sleep had eased the pain from her face, and she looked young again. She was someone who had almost forgotten how to smile, he thought, how to laugh. That glorious smile so rarely lit up her gravely beautiful face. The flowers – he glanced at them briefly – had ignited it for a moment, and the memory of it warmed him. One day, he promised himself, one day he would know her secrets.

He leaned over to kiss her, and her eyes opened.

'Bed time?' he whispered. She stroked his hair and nodded sleepily.

He smiled back. As he got to his feet he realized that he had not thought once about the stains on the carpet, or the fact that he had touched the cat without washing his hands. And he realized too that he had not given a thought all evening to Luca Scott or Troy McEwen. He lifted Frances's hand, caressing her fingers with his own, then slowly pulled her to her feet.

There had been a little icon blinking at the top of her mobile phone and Lynne had pressed Playback carefully, trying not to smudge the white tip of her new French manicure. The message had been received at 7.50 p.m. Douglas's voice was seductive but furtive, words spilling out before somebody overheard. 'I'm sorry, love, I can't make it tonight. Eleanor's not feeling too grand ...'

Lynne had snapped her phone shut.

But she was already dressed for her evening out, in a plain grey cashmere dress, a present from Douglas himself. She had twisted in the mirror; the soft wool clung to her body, giving her stick-thin figure some contours. She was elegant, colourless, almost ghost-like. She hadn't changed one thing about herself since she had met Douglas that day in court. He had been dressed in his designer suit, she had had a black coat on. Eve had come to court from her hospital bed, still in plaster from corrective surgery, still in pain. At some point in the proceedings Eve had been sick down the side of Lynne's coat and Douglas had witnessed it, hurrying past, embarrassed. Later, he had apologized. Over an Earl Grey.

Douglas, Earl Grey, designer suits. There was no way she could go into her living room now and spend the evening looking at Eve squatting in her chair with her legs apart, feeding crisps and chocolate into her face as if eating were an Olympic sport, wiping her nose noisily on her sleeve and swearing at the telly.

Lynne pulled on her long black coat, and belted it tightly. She put on her hat and tucked her blonde hair under it, wound a scarf twice round her neck and folded it tightly under her chin. Her boots were waiting ready in the hall. She slipped them on silently and then went out into the calm moonlit night.

Across the way she could see Stella McCorkindale, Douglas's faithful secretary, still in her kitchen, a faint shadow moving back and forth behind the blind. Their two houses had been the same at one time – well, nearly. But Stella had sold hers to be converted into two flats and had bought the top one back. It had freed up a lot of capital. Douglas had overseen it all for her and kept telling Lynne that was what she should do with her own at number 66. Except number 66 wasn't hers. She had never exactly lied to Douglas. He had assumed the house was hers and she had never got round to telling him otherwise. The house was Eve's. Lynne looked behind her at her old family home, set back from the road on a quieter part of the hill, and cursed her mother from the bottom of her heart.

She walked past the park. The grass had a faint dusting of icing sugar; the rain was turning to sleet. The air was still and silent. The park was devoid now of police activity, and the tape had gone. She only hoped the abduction wouldn't cause a dip in property values.

She walked on, staying close to the hedge where the sleet had settled deepest, listening to the sound of her feet crunching. It was less than a ten-minute walk, though a world away socially, to Kirklee Terrace where Douglas lived. With his wife.

The sleet drifted silently through the bare branches overhead as Kirklee Terrace came into view. Flood-lights gently bathed four storeys of white sandstone in a soft hue of rich magnolia, and the three-faceted bay windows showed an array of tinsel and glitter, bright light bulbs crystallizing and kaleidoscoping behind the glass.

It was so beautiful, so quiet up here. Lynne turned to look at the cars slowly moving up Great Western Road, at the city lights spanning out below her. She wanted to live here, more than anything. This was where she belonged. Douglas had one of these houses, Helena Farrell the artist had another, and that took serious money. And she, Lynne Calloway, was now acquainted with them both. Maybe not a world away after all.

Lynne shivered. Thick baubles of rain were settling on her shoulders and soaking through her coat, and her woollen dress seemed very inadequate now. She paused at the sound of a car coming up the hairpin at the far end of the road, and ducked into the shadows. The Jag drew to a halt, the back door opened, and three young children spilled out on to the pavement, each with a half-opened present, the wrapping paper still attached. They ran up the steps to their front door, the smallest child, a girl wearing red boots with flashing lights, holding her present over her head in an attempt to keep dry. As the door opened Lynne caught the fragrant aroma of hot cakes, baking apples and cinnamon.

Lynne watched the Jag as it pulled away to find a parking place, and noticed Douglas's Audi, carrying a fine dusting of snow from some outskirt of the city. She put her hand out, wanting to stroke it, caress it, but then saw the new XK8 Jag behind it, dark blue, convertible, with a private plate. EM 022 – Eleanor Munro, she presumed. Lynne felt for the house key in her pocket and squeezed it between thumb and forefinger. She could hardly resist the temptation to scrape metal against metal.

The message was short and unequivocal – *Your dinner is in the bin*. Brenda hadn't even bothered to take the microwave Fisherman's Pie out of its cardboard sleeve. Colin Anderson swore gently and wished he had got some chips for himself at the Hungry

Gorilla. He found the late-night news on a cable channel; it showed footage of the ruins of the earthquake in Pakistan, with the inevitable makeshift tents and queues for aid. Then the news moved on to a castle in Scotland, nowhere Anderson recognized, but Rogan O'Neill was buying it. Out of interest he flicked the sound up. '*And Glasgow's own Rogan O'Neill is reissuing his classic single, "Tambourine Girl", in aid of Andy's Appeal,*' the irritatingly cheery voice announced. '*So, if you're stuck for that stocking filler for the lady in your life ... "Tambourine Girl". It's Christmas, and it's for charity ...*'

'It'd bloody have to be,' muttered Colin, pulling a piece of toasted cheese apart with his teeth and zapping the news to silence before opening the police file.

Two minutes' reading told him: Luca – nothing; Troy – nothing.

Anderson's heart sank. It was all looking a little too familiar. The vehicle patrols had all drawn a blank, the social work teams seemed content to blame each other as usual, and the area of waste ground beyond Maryhill was earmarked for a dawn search the next morning. But the boys wouldn't have got that far on their own without being seen. So, that meant DCI Quinn was looking for a body now, maybe two. Why did she not come out and say so? He glanced at the poorly photocopied images of the two boys with such similar faces, the main difference being the faint outline of Troy's gold stud earring. Anderson knew the old DCI would have ordered colour images. Making notes, he reread the statements; all were consistent with what they already knew. Then he read again the statement from the dog walker, Mrs . . . he looked for the name . . . Moxham? She had given a statement to the uniform at the time of the door to door, and then another to Mulholland. He looked closely at the wording in Mulholland's notes – he wasn't there. *He* wasn't there. *They* weren't there on the constable's – Whittaker's? – notes. So that meant Mrs Moxham had seen Troy as she walked out, but not when she came back. Alison McEwen was slumped on the park bench, *alone*. It was confirmed later in Mulholland's report. And for all his irritating ways, Vik Mulholland was normally efficient about note-taking. Anderson was inclined to rely on him in this. So, they could now narrow down the time frame, they could enhance the CCTV, steal Lewis's idea and do a time-relevant reconstruction, and refocus attention. Yawning, he made a mental note to phone the witness and make absolutely sure. *If you want something done properly*, he told himself, *do it yourself*.

He read the notes contributed by Littlewood. No new paedophiles were known to be active in the area. None had been released on parole for Christmas – well, none that Littlewood and his former colleagues saw as a threat. All the known ones had been talked to, questioned as a matter of routine. None of them had been behaving suspiciously, all had alibis. Then Anderson noticed Littlewood's chilling memo to himself, scribbled in thick black biro – *Somebody new on the scene?* Somebody who had come from nowhere? Anderson prayed that he was wrong. He wondered whether, if he was faced with the situation, he'd have it in him to thump the shite out of a pervert and keep thumping until they divulged something – anything. Then he remembered: that was exactly why Littlewood had been bumped down to sergeant, for beating the crap out of a suspect. And good luck to him. Colin didn't think he would have the nerve to do it himself; his pension meant too much to him, his kids meant too much to him, to be drummed out of the force on a disciplinary charge. He looked at the pictures of his kids on the mantelpiece, Peter with his front tooth missing, Claire with her fringe blunt cut, framing her freckled face; she was like Brenda to look at, but had his own stolid persistent personality. Peter, mercurial and none too focused, looked like his father, but in character took after his mother.

It was getting on for ten, and he wondered where Brenda had gone for her night out, and who with; he had noted her vague 'the girls'. She had been out a lot lately, with friends from the PTA, friends from the Sunday school, women she had been friends with since Peter had been at the toddlers' playgroup.

He switched off the living room's main light, leaving his dirty dishes on the settee along with Brenda's, Claire's and Caroline the babysitter's, and went to the bottom of the stairs, deciding to leave the light on for Brenda.

He became aware of a strange grunting and wheezing noise from upstairs. Peter doing his impression of the Little Engine That Could, no doubt. At least it would be a respite from Puff the Magic bloody Dragon.

But Peter was in his cabin bed, dead to the world, his bum up in the air, his PJs exposing a wide expanse of bare flesh. The noise was coming from Claire's room. He rushed in. His daughter was lying there red-faced, sweating, glassy-eyed, her finger-nails scratching at her throat. She was gasping for breath.

They said the ambulance would be a quarter of an hour at least, and Colin Anderson knew he could drive it faster. Christ, he could see the Southern General from his own back garden.

At the entrance to A&E, he dumped the car and walked through the sleet to the sliding doors, Claire in his arms, wrapped in her duvet, her head lolling. He tried to walk steadily but Peter, frightened and crying, was clinging tightly to his trouser leg. Colin looked around, waiting for his eyes to adjust to the bright lights. They'd said they would be waiting for him but there was a long queue for registration.

Claire was unconscious now, her eyes rolling, her body totally limp. Weaving in and out of the queue, Anderson carried his daughter through a throng of drunks vociferously demanding attention for the usual collection of cuts and contusions. He'd found himself muttering, 'Keep breathing, keep breathing,' in the car. He was still doing it now.

And there they were, waiting for him. The door to an examination cubicle was being held open for him by a female doctor who looked only slightly older than Claire. 'Sorry about that lot out there,' she said. 'Party season. No party for us, though.' She patted the bed. 'Could you just lie her on the bed, Colin?' But he couldn't; his brain was only half listening and he couldn't let her go.

'And how old is Claire again?' the doctor asked, wresting her gently from her father.

'She's nine,' Peter sniffled. 'I'm five.' Anderson nodded agreement.

'You're both tall for your age, aren't you?' said the doctor, pulling the stethoscope from her neck. She turned to Anderson. 'Do they get that from you?'

Colin knew what the doctor was doing – that thing Costello did: *Keep bloody talking and sooner or later they respond.*

'Has she been complaining of a sore throat?' Claire's mouth was opened, her tongue held down. A nurse steadied her head. Then with the ophthalmoscope, the doctor gazed into her eyes, a white latex thumb gently pulling her eyelids back.

'Yes, she's on antibiotics.'

'Since when?' The doctor was feeling the glands in Claire's neck, probing the flesh under her chin. 'She's still very swollen. Has she been lethargic? Complaining of being hot?'

Anderson shrugged his shoulders and sighed. 'I'm sorry, I've not been around, I mean, at home much lately. I don't know.'

'Mmmm, when did she actually start taking the antibiotics?'

'Eight o'clock ... no, a bit later.'

'This morning? Or tonight?'

'Tonight.'

'And that was her first? But she saw her GP, surely? Yesterday? The day before?'

Colin confessed, 'Yesterday.'

'So, there was a delay in her getting the meds.' The doctor made a decision. 'We might need to tube her.' She stood back and rattled off some figures to the nurse. In one easy movement a fine plastic tube was stripped from its sterile backing then Claire's head was whipped back, her throat sprayed and the tube slid in from the side of her mouth. Claire convulsed, her spine arching from the bed, then she relaxed, her body sighing to rest. The doctor looked at the nurse, and Anderson read it as *not a minute too soon.*

'She'll be fine.' The doctor stood back, the job done, and pulled off her gloves. 'Her antibiotics were far too little far too late. I'll give her a dose of IV antibiotics right now, and she needs the rest every four hours. And I mean exactly that. If she is asleep, wake her up; don't allow the time to pass. A child's immune system can't really cope with this infection. It can be very serious indeed; in fact, it can be fatal.'

Anderson watched as she drew up the injection, accompanied by strident singing from a drunk out in the corridor. The doctor turned to the nurse. 'Get somebody to shoot him, will you?' A look passed between them as the rabble of raised voices, effing this and effing that, was followed by a smack and a crash.

She clicked her pen and slipped it into the breast pocket of her white coat, as the swearing and crashing of a full-scale fight echoed down the corridor. 'Can you call Security?' she shouted to someone outside.

'Forget it, I'll do it myself.' Anderson strode out of the room. 'I'm just in the mood for this.'

Thursday, 21 December

7

The orchestra inside Costello's head had at last fallen silent, but a single campanologist was now practising his bell-ringing. In her mind's eye, she could see him swinging up and down on the rope, the huge clapper clanging against the inside of her skull, its intensity increasing with every stroke. She turned over, pulling the duvet up round her ears, trying to blank it out, but the noise was incessant, echoing round her skull, deafening, and the pain wasn't much better than it had been the day before.

And buzzing. As if a wasp had got caught in her ear. Something pricked her brain, and the buzzing stopped, giving momentary relief. She sighed and pulled the duvet up again.

The buzzing resumed.

Stopped.

Then started again.

'*Costello.*'

Her own name echoed round inside her head.

'Costello? Are you there?'

She heard the letter box rattle, and rolled over again, covering her eyes against the dull December daylight.

'*Costello!*'

The inner cover of her duvet was soaking, she was stinking with sweat, and the sweet smell of cloistered sick hung in the room. She still had on the grey trousers she had worn at work. She had managed to remove her tea-stained jumper, which was lying where it had landed on the floor, but was still wearing the pink T-shirt. A brief memory of Colin Anderson picking her up in his car flickered across her mind, and a memory of being very sick in a streaming gutter. She didn't want to think about it.

The doorbell sounded again.

'Hang on,' she muttered vaguely, trying to disentangle uncooperative feet from the duvet.

A familiar voice said, 'Are you still alive?'

She opened the door, one hand on the lock, the other holding her head. 'Only just.'

Vik Mulholland walked in purposefully and uninvited.

'Come in, why don't you?' She closed the door, wincing at the noise as it slammed shut. 'Obviously I'm very pleased to see you, but what the hell are you doing here?'

'It's Thursday morning. John Campbell's PM. You were supposed to be on duty at eight. Colin's daughter was ill last night, he got in late and Quinn the Eskimo is raging.' He looked over at the answering machine; its little red light was flashing repeatedly. 'You haven't listened to that?'

'Thursday,' Costello repeated slowly, as if she recognized the word but had no idea what it meant.

'Thursday?' She walked to the mantelpiece and picked up the clock. 'What time is it?'

'Half past nine.'

'I've just woken up. What was up with Claire?'

'She had that throat bug. Very nasty but she's OK now.' Mulholland sniggered slyly. 'His missus was out and he didn't know where she was, so he had to do the hospital run. Which meant he was late getting back to Quinn about a discrepancy he thinks he might have found in Mrs Moxham's witness statement. If he's right we might have nailed a time for Troy's last sighting. And of course, Sarah McGuire phoned again asking for that report which Colin was supposed to get you in early to do. Quinn couldn't find it – or you – and went off on one. There was a briefing at eight. You weren't there. Then Colin got worried when you didn't answer the phone. Quinn thought it was interesting that he was with you yesterday … a brief encounter as he nipped out for lunch. I think she thinks you and he are at it like bunnies.' He looked at Costello standing, pale faced and with her hair dishevelled, in a yellow dressing gown that had seen better days. 'Maybe not.'

She held her forehead with both hands, face flushed with embarrassment. 'Oh God, I was ill. I nearly threw up in Colin's car.'

Mulholland shuddered. 'Probably used to it, with those kids of his.' He tapped his watch. 'We have to get a move on. The Prof is waiting for us before he can do the PM. The Fire Master's report will be in when we get back. If we can tie that up, we can get on to tracking down Troy. The mother sobered up yesterday for five minutes then promptly got pissed again. And Gail Irvine was telling me about the reconstruction outside the amusement arcade – they still haven't found a boy to act the part of Luca. She reckons Peter Anderson will be called in at the last minute.'

'How hard have they been looking? This is the first I've heard of it. So, who's in charge of that then?' Costello rubbed her eyes, the fog in her head starting to clear.

'The gorgeous DS Kate Lewis . . .'

'Oh yeah, Colin mentioned her. Where's she from?'

'New cavalry thrust upon us by Pitt Street, from Aikenhead Road.'

'BOGOF? Buy one get one free? I think we could do better without either of them.'

'Maybe, but poor Irvine is mortified that she's going to be left to ask Colin if they can use Peter. I don't see why not.'

'Over Colin's dead body might be a reason why not,' said Costello.

'Oh – by the way – Irvine said to tell you that you were right about Sarah McGuire . . .'

'John Campbell's daughter. Really?'

'So, what were you dead right about?'

Costello blew her nose really loudly just to annoy

him. 'Motive. I asked Gail to check out Sarah's finances ... and her finances with regard to the soon-to-be-ex-hubby in particular. Pretty women can be dangerous, you know,' she answered cryptically.

'So, I'm safe from you then.' Mulholland smiled sarcastically. 'But do we have a crime?'

'I don't know, but we might have a reason for one. I suspect Sarah McGuire's having to move out of her million-pound house because divorce is imminent and hubby wants his share in cash. And what do you know? Dad conveniently drops dead and leaves a property worth half a mill even burned to a crisp. Her half of the house plus her dad's estate would keep her comfy.'

'Now that's a motive,' said Mulholland, wondering, not for the first time, what depths Costello's mind would sink to.

'Did you check up on the old guy's health? Prof O'Hare might ask while he's dissecting.'

'Irvine did a check with Campbell's GP; he had a bad knee and a sensitive stomach. So it's looking less likely he had a heart attack.'

Costello sniffed loudly, her brain slowly crunching into gear. 'Stick the kettle on, will you? I need a shower.'

'You certainly do. You smell like cat litter. And put some make-up on. Go into the mortuary looking like that, they'll keep you in.'

'So, what's the script with your hickey bites?' Costello shouted from the hall.

Mulholland raised his hand to his neck, feeling an area of tenderness, remembering – smiling – Fran. If only Costello wasn't so thrawn, he would have asked her for a dab of make-up to cover it but that would be like telling Radio Partickhill. He wandered into the kitchen, and found the kettle half buried among notebooks and old newspapers. He switched it on and tried to look at his neck in the distorted reflection. 'Oh, but wait till you see the new Aikenhead Road cavalry,' he called back. 'The new DS. Very tasty, legs right up to her arse.'

'And what would the lovely Frances think about that?'

Costello heard the change in Vik's voice, even over the noise of the shower. 'Fran's fine, she's cool.' He sounded affectionate, as if genuinely fond of her. 'She's a funny girl. I saw round her flat yesterday. It's really strange – right out of the 1950s, no central heating and a bloody great dummy with a fedora meets you when you go in the door. She doesn't watch the telly, never reads the papers. Unworldly really.'

'Doesn't sound your type at all. Probably do you the world of good,' said Costello as she kicked the bathroom door shut.

After her shower she wrapped a huge towel round her and went back to the bedroom to dress. 'Has Quinn got me on her hit list now?'

'Yip,' Vik shouted through from the living room. 'Twice.'

Costello paused, pulling on a clean T-shirt. 'Bugger. I mean, I *told* Gail Irvine and bloody Wingnut that I had to go home, that I had a bad migraine. Why did they not tell Quinn? Why didn't Anderson?'

'They all told her, they all got a bollocking. Then this morning, somebody called Karen McGuire phoned and insisted on talking to you and you were nowhere to be found.'

'Karen? The granddaughter? What did she want?'

'No idea; she hung up on Quinn, which made her mood a thousand times worse.'

'I'll sort it out when I get there,' Costello grumbled, slipping her jacket on, raking a hand through her hair and walking back down the hall. It was cold; the heating had gone off ages ago. 'Something's up – Karen wouldn't phone me for nothing. No news on the wee guys?'

'Just this reconstruction. Bet you a fiver they're both dead. We've moved from searching empty, unsecured buildings to searching empty, *secure* buildings. That's never a good sign.' Mulholland pointed at his watch. 'We were due at the mortuary ten minutes ago.'

'The dead will wait.'

'But the Prof won't.' Mulholland presented her with a cup of sweet black tea. 'Don't even think about chucking that up in my car.'

'Here.' She handed him a stick of concealer. 'Dab that on your neck; it won't come off on your shirt.'

'Thanks, Costello,' he said, surprised.

'Ripping the piss out of you is my prerogative. I don't want the whole bloody station doing it.'

Eve was sulking. In silence. No breakfast TV, no radio. The remote was on top of the mantelpiece; it might as well have been in Timbuktu.

She heard the front doorbell ring, heard her sister say, 'Oh, do come in,' loudly, and then a few moments' silence. No footfall, no talking. Did they think she was stupid?

'Oh, hello,' she said amicably. 'Finished snogging? Mr Munro, how are you?'

'My friends call me Douglas.'

'Yes,' she said sweetly. 'That's why I call you Mr Munro.'

'We really are in a bit of a hurry,' warned Lynne, her eyes flashing at Douglas. 'Don't make a mess, Eve.' She picked up some invisible crumbs off the floor. 'It encourages mice, leaving food about like that; you tell her, Douglas, she doesn't listen to me.' Lynne tipped the crumbs artfully from one palm to the other.

Eve smiled up at Douglas. 'Lynne's more used to encouraging rats.'

'Take your medicine, Eve,' said Lynne, with quiet malice. 'We'll be going soon.'

Eve palmed her capsules to her mouth and slurped them down with a generous mouthful of water, pulling a series of Quasimodo faces.

'The stage lost a great actress when you took up

drawing.' Douglas looked at the print on the wall, before asking innocently, 'How's Squidgy?'

'How's your goldmine, you mean?' She wheeled her chair closer to Douglas, trapping him mid-thigh. 'Would it bother you, dreadfully, if I didn't sign this contract thing, due to artistic integrity and all that? I mean ...' She smiled sunnily at him with mock politeness. She really was a very pretty girl when she wanted to be. 'I mean, I have my personal integrity to think about – all those lovely little children thinking these books are written by my tight-arsed cold-blooded control-freak sister, when in fact, they were written by lovely wee me.'

Douglas leaned down and spoke in her ear. 'Do you really think you have any personal integrity left, Eve? It's that warped thinking that forces us to keep you out of the public eye. If you don't sign, you will be here, in Lynne's house, dependent on Lynne's good nature, all your life. You're not stupid. You'll sign. From here on in you and your sister will be one legal entity. You know we have been careful to use Lynne as the public face of Squidgy right from the start.'

Lynne snapped. 'We had to with your past of ...'

'Exactly, Lynne,' interrupted Douglas before a long and familiar rant started. 'But you do have to sign it, Eve, to create this single legal entity; we have discussed it a hundred times.'

Eve gazed at him levelly, savouring her own knowledge like a fine wine. She had heard the lie and let it pass. Of course Lynne would lie to Douglas Munro of Munro Property. She'd do anything for money, anything to be seen to have 'class'. Eve picked up the copy of *Bonjour* magazine that was lying on the arm of the settee. She turned the page over to the Rogan O'Neill centre spread. 'My sister used to be a big fan of his, you know. That was before she took up with pathetic old bastards like you who have to dye their hair.' She thrust the magazine at him. 'Except your bald patch of course – is that natural?'

Douglas screwed his eyes up as he tried to examine the pictures of Rogan, and moved the magazine in and out to gain focus. 'What's he saying in today's interview? Yesterday's was about saving the planet, saving the children of Pakistan, global harmony. The tabloids today are full of his "sexploits", as if we're interested.'

'He says he doesn't do drugs. Well, he did when I knew him – and he was no spring chicken then – but now I expect the only drugs he's into are Botox and Viagra.'

Douglas looked at Lynne and tapped his temple. Lynne smiled and left the room. 'When *you* knew him?'

'Yeah, we were an item once.' Eve placed a podgy hand over her heart, and fluttered her eyelashes. 'I could sell my stories about him for a few grand, I can tell you. In fact, I still might.'

'And it's that dubious past of yours which means

you'll never be the public face of Evelynne Calloway,' said Douglas in all seriousness. 'And, not to be too harsh about it, look at the girlfriend he's got now.'

'Yeah, he's gone downmarket a bit, but all men do as they get older,' Eve said, flicking a glance at her sister.

'Stop it, Eve,' snapped Lynne, coming back into the room and handing Douglas a glass of water.

'She's a supermodel; she was a bit tasty in that bra campaign.'

'If you'd put your specs on you'd get a better look at her tits. I thought she had a black eye in the *Daily Record* this morning.'

'Surgery for laughter lines, I expect. It happens to us all,' said Lynne.

'Not to you, it won't,' retorted Eve. 'Look round her eyes; look at how swollen and puffy they are.'

'She happens to be pregnant, which is why she's not working. At least, that's the rumour,' Lynne pointed out.

'She's backed out of all kinds of deals, apparently. A shame. Still, she's a very attractive girl, with those endless legs,' Douglas said admiringly, holding the magazine right up to his face.

'*Functioning* legs – that always helps.'

Douglas ignored Eve's barb. He handed back the magazine and took a sip of water, then palmed a capsule down his throat and swallowed.

'You should wear your specs, you know. It's eye strain that's giving you all those headaches and you'll end up with gut-rot from those painkillers,' said Eve, her nose back in the magazine.

'It's stress headache,' fired Lynne. 'His job is very high-powered.'

Douglas changed the subject. 'So, if you knew him, what do you know about this rumour in today's paper that O'Neill didn't write any of his greatest hits?'

'I know lots and lots ...' Eve rolled her eyes and sighed. 'But my lips are sealed. Put it this way: his *two* greatest hits, "The Lost Boy" and "Tambourine Girl", are hauntingly beautiful, genuinely melodic songs. Everything else sounds like a pathetic rehash of any Beatles song you wish to mention. He thinks we've forgotten the twenty years he spent singing crap on the Scottish pub circuit. Then one day he suddenly hit it big – one day he got talent. Work it out for yourself.'

'Did the real tambourine girl write them?' asked Douglas.

'Got it in one. Then Rogan did a runner with the dosh. Did a runner on her as well, in fact. She's penniless now and starving in a garret. And you want me to do the same thing with Squidgy? Sign him over and then starve in a garret while you and Lynne live off my talent?'

'It's not the same thing,' Douglas said patiently. 'Not the same thing at all. I do actually have your best interests at heart.'

Eve grinned, delighted to see him hooked. 'Oh,

Doogie, don't you worry about me,' she said. 'I have many talents, including a marvellous memory. I don't forget much.' She looked at him almost adoringly. 'In fact, I don't forget anything at all.' Her left hand had slipped below the tabletop to rub the side of her hip, right at the point where the bonnet of a green Mitsubishi had staved in the door of her car, pushing the head of her femur three inches into her abdomen, before the bottom of the door smashed the lower part of her leg.

'I can believe it, Eve, I can believe it,' Douglas said, not without sympathy.

'Hello, hello, better late than never.' Professor Jack O'Hare couldn't resist glancing at the clock through the lock of grey hair that had a habit of falling over his face.

'We had difficulty rousing the Sleeping Beauty here,' said Mulholland. 'John Campbell's PM?'

'You're lucky; you nearly missed it. Costello, how are you?'

'Bloody awful, thank you for asking, Prof,' she said, amicably. The place stank more vilely than usual. She wondered if the rumour that the mortuary was full was true.

'Never mind, you still look better than most of my clients.' Then O'Hare looked at her more closely. 'But only just. I think the term Sleeping Beauty might get you done under the Trade Descriptions Act. Have you seen a doctor?' He advanced on her, then realized, as she pulled away, that he had a scalpel in his hand.

'I'm OK,' she answered tetchily. 'I had a migraine. I get them when I'm overtired. Things just take a wee bit of getting used to, you know.'

O'Hare frowned slightly. 'Well, make sure you get enough sleep. And take time for a meal every now and then.'

She tried to be light-hearted. 'In our station? That would be asking for food poisoning.'

O'Hare's voice was serious. 'Bereavement takes us all in different ways. Throwing yourself into work is commendable, but not always wise. I don't want to be doing a PM on you.' He looked at her, noting the defiant set of her mouth. 'Haven't seen you around; I thought you might have taken some time off.'

'Yeah, I tend to hang around the morgue when I am at a loose end. Dead end even?'

O'Hare raised an unamused eyebrow. 'You eating OK?'

'I'm fine,' she insisted. Kindness always made her feel vulnerable. 'I'll have something to eat later. My stomach's still a bit sensitive.' She looked round for a pair of latex gloves.

'Only really intelligent people suffer from migraine, you know,' the pathologist went on. 'As I know to my cost. I get them too.'

Mulholland coughed and pointed at the charred remains on the table. 'Is this our man?'

John Campbell – what was left of him – lay on the

slab covered by a blue plastic sheet. O'Hare pulled it back, revealing a body where the exposed flesh had turned black then grey. The burned skin on the forearm was split open, the edges drawn back like lips baring teeth of blackened charcoal bone underneath. On a stainless-steel trolley beside the slab lay the cremated remnants of a pair of trousers, a leather belt with its buckle still intact, and a tiny piece of dark-blue cardigan, burned and crisp, with a few twisted strands of Fair Isle wool sticking out like half-cooked vermicelli. On a kidney dish, with a pair of green plastic tweezers, lay five metal buttons, still gleaming. Somebody had taken the trouble to turn them face up, lining up all the little lions rampant.

Costello took the sixth, still in its sterile packet, from her pocket and placed it on the tray. 'You'll see from Anderson's report that he took one of these from the scene. That's me returning it, OK?' She paused to line up the button so that even inside its little plastic bag it matched its fellows.

'Noted, DS Costello,' said O'Hare formally. 'I hear another child has gone missing.'

'Some drunken bint lost her son in the playground, but we don't know if it's connected with anything else.' Mulholland was impatient and could barely be bothered to conceal it.

'Well, this one should be a nice straightforward accidental death, then you can get on.'

O'Hare called out for his colleague, Dr Cathie, getting a hurried *I'll be along in a minute* in response.

'Have you an established cause?' Mulholland, flicking over the report sheet, spoke with the slightly superior tone of one who has better things to do. 'A specific one, I mean, apart from being toasted. We need ...'

'I know what you *need*, DC Mulholland,' said O'Hare frostily. 'And I know I'm good, but it is customary to open the body first and have a good look around; it tends to give a better idea of what might have happened.' The sarcasm was thinly disguised.

'He did have a history of arthritis in his knee and a bit of tummy trouble,' said Costello.

'Really? And do you know the daughter is in the High Dependency unit at the Western? She collapsed this morning, and young Karen found her on the kitchen floor. Quinn couldn't find any paperwork at all pertaining to your visit to her home, DS Costello.'

'When did that happen?' asked Costello. 'And why? She was OK when I left her yesterday.'

'I think she was admitted about nine this morning. As yet they do not know what the problem is.'

'Shit,' said Costello, adding, 'Sorry, Prof,' at his glance of disapproval. 'So, are they connected then? Could it be a hereditary thing? The daughter's only in her mid-forties, and she didn't mention anything. She didn't seem too distressed about her old dad either.'

'It seems too close to be coincidence,' said O'Hare. 'Rebecca and I have already discussed it.'

Rebecca and I! Costello opened her mouth to ask

but O'Hare had already moved into professional mode. 'However, John Campbell's heart doesn't look too bad; it's within normal limits on X-ray. We might find some kind of sudden blockage in the coronary arteries, but I doubt it . . .' He walked down to the end of the table. Costello followed him while Mulholland stared at the ceiling, bored. 'His left foot largely escaped the attention of the flames, which means it might have been underneath him when he fell.' He touched John Campbell's toe, the skin matching the latex of the glove in colour and texture.

'His other foot looks like a rotisserie chicken,' said Mulholland.

'All flesh is meat, chicken or human, and cooks likewise.' O'Hare lifted up a magnifying light and peered through it at the toe. 'His nails are in very good condition, and he still has hair on his big toe.'

'So, what does that make him? The missing link?' said Mulholland, his eyes on the clock, looking anywhere but at the body.

'It means, young man, that his circulation was excellent for a man of his age. Probably better than yours.'

'Definitely better than his,' said Costello. 'Mr Campbell had a heart – Vik here has a swinging brick.'

Dr Cathie appeared through the door, gowned up, her short brown hair sprouting from its clasp like a thistle. She was clinging on to a large glass of water, as if clinging to life itself. 'Sorry.'

'Hard night, was it?' asked Mulholland.

'Had to represent the department at the Christmas do,' she croaked. 'It was a huge sacrifice.'

'Come on, children, better get started,' O'Hare said, handing the file to Cathie. 'I presume you can still write.'

Costello watched as his fingers spanned the distal clavicular notch, pulling the skin tight as he dipped the blade of the scalpel firmly downward with the precision of a sculptor. This was the only time Costello ever looked away; the first prick of the blade was the one cut that made her queasy. When metal first punctured skin, even with no blood seeping and the flesh lifeless, no matter how dead they were, how decomposed, how blue, how bloated, she somehow felt it must still hurt.

She was glad O'Hare was covering the blade with the curve of his hand, as they watched the chest, then the abdomen, open under the scalpel. The two police officers stood in respectful silence, listening to O'Hare's more technical mutterings to his assistant and understanding every second word.

O'Hare, his fingers like rubberized octopus legs digging inside the chest cavity, paused; his eyes were on Costello. 'You OK?'

'Fine.'

'When *did* you last eat?'

'Anything that stayed down? Tuesday night.'

But O'Hare was already ignoring her; he was peering into John Campbell's chest, easing the ribs out of the way. 'You know, it's very red in here. That's not usual.'

'And it smells foul in here, worse than usual,' said Costello, wrinkling her nose. 'Something smells bitter, sweetish. I don't know. Not the normal niff you get in here anyway.'

'Do you get a hypersensitivity syndrome with your migraine, DS Costello?'

'No, I get a terrible headache and I throw my guts up,' she answered sweetly.

'I mean,' he tried again patiently, 'do you develop a sensitivity to light, smell and sound?'

'Oh aye, I do that. That's what makes me sick.'

O'Hare said carefully, 'This smells the same to me as any other burned body, but it doesn't smell normal to you?'

Costello shook her head gingerly.

'And you, Dr Cathie?'

'Hang on, I've just done my teeth so all I can smell from here is toothpaste.' She walked forward and sniffed the air above the body. 'But DS Costello is not mistaken,' she said, looking meaningfully at O'Hare who grinned with satisfaction.

'One of the many areas of female superiority is the sense of smell.' He stood back, his fingers in the gap made by the rib separators, spreading the contents of the chest cavity, looking intently at the colour. 'He was in the kitchen, you say, cooking chips? Was there any upholstered furniture in the kitchen? Anything containing foam?' O'Hare went over to the bench, slipped one glove off to take the notes from Cathie and proceeded to flick through them. He read for a minute, the silence interrupted only by the whoosh and hum of the door as Dr Cathie left, rubbing her temples. O'Hare repeated the question without looking up. 'Anything containing foam?'

Costello shrugged. 'I don't know. Is it important?' O'Hare went back to the body after he had re-gloved and she watched closely as he opened John Campbell's mouth and shone a little torch around inside. 'OK, we stop the PM right now. I'll do some tests. We might need a clean cabinet.' He signed off on the first two pages of notes. 'And leave me your mobile number, Costello; I'll want to talk to you shortly. But first I need to speak to the hospital and alert the Poison Unit. I'll get the team looking after Sarah McGuire on it as well; it might answer a lot of their questions. It could be that father and daughter were poisoned by the same substance. Do you know what he was on for his stomach?'

'It's in the notes,' said Mulholland. 'Began with an L.'

'Lansoprazole, probably. So he had a thin stomach lining – interesting. If they ingested the same thing ...' O'Hare was thinking out loud. 'He might have been more vulnerable because of his stomach condition, and she would have gained some protection if her stomach was full, so find out if she'd eaten. I'll get Garrett from the Poison Unit to phone you.' With that O'Hare was out of the door, the air pressure hissing slightly as he went through.

The two of them were left standing over the body.

'I suppose this is what you call a deathly silence,' said Costello.

Costello pressed the End Call button on her mobile phone and tapped it gently against her lips. Colin Anderson was flicking through statement after statement about Luca Scott and comparing them with those about Troy McEwen. Every so often his eyes would float to the pictures on the wall – Luca with his mop of blond hair, Troy with his blond spikes, freckles and earring. He sighed as he typed something into his computer with his index finger. He then sat back, closed his eyes and waited. He looked dog-tired.

Costello glanced over her shoulder, checking that DCI Quinn was head down in a pile of paperwork. She stood up, picked up a file and shooed Wyngate from the seat beside Anderson but didn't get a chance to sit down as a long-legged brunette beat her to it.

'Kate Lewis,' she introduced herself to Costello, while managing to flutter her eyelashes in Anderson's direction.

'Enchanted,' said Costello dryly.

'Guess what?' Lewis asked huskily.

'They've arrested Santa for housebreaking?'

'I had a little boy lined up to wear a parka for the photo this afternoon.' She shrugged her shoulders. 'And I've been let down.'

'Story of my life,' said Costello, now perched on the desk and looking at her fingernails.

'I know it's a big favour, Colin, but could we use Peter?'

'Peter? He's too young, he's only five . . .'

'But I hear he's tall for his age. And he's a dead ringer. I saw the piccy in your wallet; it's soooo sweet.'

Costello looked heavenward in disbelief.

'Can't. Claire's not keeping so good and Brenda has to look after her. The wee guy's at home as well; he got no sleep at all last night.'

Lewis was not to be put off. 'We'll send a car. Irvine will look after him; he'll be fine.'

Anderson looked at Costello, trying to find a way to say no.

'I don't think the DCI would like it,' said Costello.

Lewis didn't move her eyes from Anderson. 'Actually, it was Rebecca's idea. We'll keep the hood of the jacket up, so nobody will see his face.'

'I'll have to ask Brenda.'

'I'm sure you can persuade her,' Lewis purred. 'I'm sure you can tell her how important it is, those two wee boys out there . . . it's going to snow, you know.'

'Just keep him anonymous,' growled Anderson, picking up the phone to call home.

Lewis gave him a beaming smile. 'You're a star.' They watched her wiggle away.

'You know, women like that remind me how long it's been. I'd need a map these days,' Anderson said, ear to the phone, waiting. Costello drummed her fingertips on the desktop as Anderson rang off and then tried his wife's mobile.

'Still no answer?'

Anderson looked puzzled and left a curt message for Brenda to get in touch. He closed the phone but looked at it, reading the time. 'Where is she? I hope Claire's OK.'

'She would have phoned if there was a problem. Do you want me to check the desk downstairs? See if any messages have been left for you? They forgot to pass on my message to Quinn the Eskimo.'

Anderson shook his head. 'She would have left a message on my mobile. But I guess they will have to use Peter. It's too late to find another kid ...'

'... who looks so like the other two,' finished Costello for him. 'But if I were to bet on how much effort the delectable Miss Lewis had put into finding a stand-in? Fuck all, would be my guess. How's Claire now?'

Anderson rubbed the tiredness from his eyes. 'She's fine. It was one of the more frightening experiences of my life. But one injection at the hospital and that was that.' He sighed slowly through pursed lips. 'This morning she was up and demanding breakfast, so she can't be all that bad.'

'I was surprised to see you in today,' said Costello.

'No reason to stay at home,' said Anderson.

And every reason to escape, Costello thought. 'Anyway, I've just heard back from O'Hare,' she said. 'John Campbell has tested positive for sodium cyanide.'

Anderson looked at her eager face, animated. 'From where? Burning ceiling tiles? His settee? Something like that?'

Costello shook her head. 'No, he ingested it, not inhaled it. No corrosion in his airways, no soot – he was dead before he hit the deck. Because he hadn't eaten much and he had a thin stomach lining, it went through him like a stone through a wet paper bag. He had no chance.'

'Why do I get the feeling you're on to something?' Anderson folded his arms on his desk and dropped his head on top.

Costello pulled her chair closer, opened the file and took a magnifying glass from her pocket. 'Well, you can't eat cyanide and not notice. O'Hare told me that. So, how did it get into his stomach?'

'No idea.'

'Rhetorical question. Look …' She pushed the photographs of John Campbell's flat underneath Anderson's forearms, forcing him to look. She tapped her fingertip on the scorched counter. 'What do you see there?' She placed the glass on the photograph. 'Right there, beside that tin?'

Anderson sighed and leaned over, closing one

eye to look. 'That's a strip of tablets of some kind.'

'Did you see them there? What were they?'

'Sorry,' Anderson said sarcastically. 'I was busy concentrating on not stepping on a dead body while being asphyxiated. But I remember thinking that Bugatti biscuit tin looked as though the flames had just swept over it. And the tablets are right beside it.'

'But John Campbell kept his tablets in a seven-day dispenser – one of those dosset boxes.' Costello stabbed at the photograph with her pencil. 'I'd say this is it here. So, what was in that strip? Karen said he had a headache, and that she took him some Headeze. He would have been careful what painkiller he used so as not to upset his sensitive stomach, and Sarah made the point that Headeze didn't. The Prof said Campbell only had cyanide and his stomach tablet in him drug-wise, and a few bits of food he's sent for analysis. Which means we could be talking poisoning, in error or by product tampering. I'll check the contents of his fridge, see what he and Sarah might have eaten in common. But I'm looking at that strip of painkillers first.'

'What about Sarah?'

'She's still in the High Dependency unit. I'd like to look round her kitchen.'

Anderson could read her like a book. 'On the pretext of . . .?'

'Well, if there is a toxic substance in that house, I'd better go and find it. In case poor Karen eats it too,' she added lamely.

'As long as you've alerted the Poison Unit ...'

'O'Hare's seen to all that. Look, maybe Sarah took a painkiller from the same batch. If the stuff's out on general sale, we need to get moving.'

'Yeah, but not you. Get a uniform round to Sarah's to search the kitchen and bring back any tablets or meds. In fact, run it past Quinn to send Irvine; she'll be out that way in any case to pick up Peter. If a faulty batch of headache tablets is out there, they'll be dropping like flies after Hogmanay's hangovers.'

'It *might* be a faulty batch. Or they might have been tampered with. Deliberately. I think I'll have a word with the ex-husband.'

'Just make a start somewhere. I'm busy,' Anderson's eyes went back to the screen, checking a more recent map of the Red Triangle, as the area of abduction had become known, an isosceles triangle with Byres Road, Great Western Road and a bottom line that varied with every false sighting. His phone rang, and he answered it without moving his eyes from the black cross that indicated the Joozy Jackpot on Byres Road. A shiver chilled him to the core as he said, 'Yes?'

'Daddy, will you take me to the place tomorrow for my dragon? You said!'

'Where?'

'The place for my dragon? To wear.'

'Peter, is your mum there?'

'Mummy's busy, and I have to do my Puff the Magic Dragon.'

Anderson sighed and looked at his watch. 'I'll get your outfit if you do a big favour for Daddy.' As he told Peter about the re-enactment, his eyes drifted back to the photographs of the two missing boys.

Costello listened to him carefully explaining to his son what he had to do, sounding calm, comforting. She sat back, thinking about Sarah McGuire, so keen on Karen's education at one of the most expensive private schools in the city. The gap between granddad and granddaughter was a social chasm. Giving Anderson a comforting pat on the shoulder, she went back to her desk and began to type a formal request to look into the estate of John Campbell, and the financial affairs of Thomas Patrick McGuire. And, to a lesser extent, his daughter Karen Lisa McGuire. Costello flicked her pen against her cheek. The girl was doing a school project about the war, and her granddad was helping with it, lending her books. She recalled seeing some of them in their living room, marked with fluorescent page tags. She twisted in her chair and called across the room to anybody who would listen. 'What do you lot know about cyanide?'

'It kills you. It tastes bitter,' Wyngate volunteered. 'It's found in apricot kernels.'

'The Nazi war criminals killed themselves with it, Goering for one,' offered Littlewood. 'You seen that film, *Downfall*? The big scene is Magda Goebbels killing their kids – one cyanide capsule in the mouth then …' Littlewood snapped his teeth together, '… goodnight, Vienna.'

'Or goodbye to Berlin, in that particular case,' said Wyngate and smiled. 'Why do you want to know about cyanide?'

'Just an idea,' said Costello bluntly.

Littlewood asked, 'Do you know when Lewis plans her little showpiece to kick off?'

'About four, I think,' answered Costello. 'Why, don't you know?'

'She's playing it close to her lovely and ample chest. Not a good idea.' Littlewood rolled his shoulders and turned away. He stood at the open window, arms folded, his thick neck red with a nasty rash, concentrating on the street below, thinking. DS Littlewood had spent more years in the dirty squad than Quinn had spent on the force, and he was clearly not happy about Lewis's plan.

Costello didn't like the implications of that.

'How is she doing?'

Thomas McGuire didn't turn round, not that he was looking at the figure lying in the bed in front of him. He was staring into space, holding a forgotten cup of tea in mid-air. 'As well as can be expected, apparently,' he answered. 'They seem to be pleased with her so far. Who's asking?'

McGuire was a small fresh-faced, casually dressed man, with pointed but attractive features. His grey hair was pulled into a small ponytail. He was not at all what Costello had expected.

She flashed her warrant card at him. 'DS Costello. I was chatting to Sarah only yesterday, about her dad.'

He nodded. 'Karen said. Yeah, old John, bit of a shocker that one, rather a tragedy.' He said it in a way that implied his wife lying in a coma wasn't so much of a tragedy.

'I'm sorry I didn't get back to Karen when her mum collapsed but I wasn't in the station. You'd think somebody would have had the sense to pass on the message to me.'

'Would it have made any difference? Her mum would still be in here.'

Costello shook her head. 'But I gave her my card in case they needed their hands held. And she phoned and I failed to get back to her. I feel bad about it,' she lied. 'Have they told you anything?'

He laughed slightly. 'Do they ever? What do you want, DS Costello? What's going on here?'

'We're following a line of enquiry.'

'I know they're testing her for cyanide. It's not the sort of stuff you leave lying around, is it?' He downed the dregs of his tea and placed the empty cup and saucer on Sarah's bedside table.

'Can I ask you a few questions? If it's convenient?'

'Fire away.'

'Where's Karen? I don't want her overhearing.'

'Outside, texting her pals.' He didn't sound impressed. 'So, what have you dug up? Both Sarah and old John – that can't be coincidence.'

Costello agreed, making a mental note to find out when Thomas McGuire had been told. 'Please keep it to yourself. They might not have been targets; both might have been accidental, purely random events. But in case they weren't, we need to investigate.' Costello leaned against the wall, ignoring the figure on the bed. Somebody wheeled a trolley past the open door, singing 'Hark, the Herald Angels Sing' very badly. 'I'm out on a limb here; I need a bit of help.' She tucked her blonde hair behind her ear in a way that made her look unthreatening; it always got men to say more than they intended. 'Is your wife in any financial trouble?'

'You lot are quick, aren't you?' he smiled. 'Not yet, she isn't, but the minute the house goes on the market she will be. She has been dragging her feet over the sale. I'm supporting Karen for now but she's growing up, and God forbid Sarah might have to get a job and support herself. Sarah got half my mum's estate in her settlement and she's already gone through that. I'll get none of John's – not that I want it. And if you were to ask me if everything in our marriage comes down to money, the answer is – latterly, yes. Sarah is a leech and a bitch.' He took a deep breath. 'I couldn't take the dog when I left her. Next thing I knew, Treacle had been put down. She said he was ill, but I doubt it. I don't know how you can tell somebody their dog's been put to sleep, and smile.' He shook his head. 'But that's the way she is. And Karen's turning out the same. She said she wanted a gap year to go round the world. So, I told her to get a Saturday job to save up; in fact, I made a few phone calls to a few contacts, to see if they could put a few hours her way. I was curious to see what excuses she'd come up with not to work.' He rubbed his eyes. 'My wife was bleeding me dry, and my business would have been brought down too, if I hadn't escaped. But if I was going to do away with either of them, I'd have done it before we separated and saved myself a fortune. Sorry to be so blunt.' He looked down at the face behind the oxygen mask. 'I got a call on her mobile this morning, asking why she wasn't at the tennis. She'd arranged the match last night. I ask you, playing tennis the day after your dad's died?'

'It takes all sorts,' Costello said evasively. 'Tell me, did your wife generally eat breakfast?'

'No, she always made do with a fag and black coffee.' He thought for a minute and then added, 'But she and Karen were both on a pre-Christmas diet, some carbohydrate nonsense.'

'The GI diet?'

'Something daft like that.'

'And did she normally suffer from headaches?'

'All during our married life,' he said caustically.

'Thanks.' Costello couldn't think of anything to say so she slipped her card onto his saucer. 'If you need anything, or think of anything, let me know.'

'Will they pass the message on, though?' Tom McGuire smiled and then looked her straight in the eye. 'I'm sorry about John. He was a nice old bloke. And she was his eternal disappointment,' he said, and his voice cracked slightly.

Costello nodded, understanding. 'Well, you can never choose your family, can you? Bye.' She left the room. Outside she had to sidestep a wheezy old dear who was manoeuvring a WRVS trolley with a cargo of fruit and newspapers, bottled water and Lucozade, and a wicker basket of home baking, scones, pancakes and Empire biscuits with the Scottish flag on the front in wobbly white and blue icing. Costello took a deep breath as she passed, and the smell was wonderful. She stopped the woman and bought a can of Diet Coke.

She needed to find a quiet corner and think about the money. She made her way out to the car, parked in the loading bay behind the Pathology lab of the hospital. She sat in the front seat, her yellow notebook resting on the steering wheel, sipping her Diet Coke. She wrote the word *Money* in the middle of the page, then thought. Who'd made it, who had it, who wanted it? Thinking was what DCI McAlpine – the Boss – always did. First rule of detection, he used to say . . . *follow the money*.

8

Anderson was still studying the pictures of the two boys on the white wallboard. Blond-haired Luca, blond-haired Troy, so like each other. So like Peter. It made him uneasy. He looked at the map. The Red Triangle was becoming a mass of stickers and pins. Somebody had scribbled *Large scale map on order* under it. Anderson looked at the names on the rota for the search parties –he didn't recognize any of them. That made him uneasy too. He glanced at his watch – it was going on half one – and coughed. 'Is Costello back yet?'

'Saw her a minute ago, guv,' said Wyngate.

'And DS Lewis?'

'Haven't seen her,' shouted somebody wistfully.

'She's running around doing her thing for the press. Irvine will be heading out to get Peter soon, once Costello has finished nattering to her about Sarah McGuire,' said Wyngate. 'She's got a bee in her bonnet about that woman. She's had Gail Irvine go right through that house.'

'I thought that was to wait until Quinn had agreed it.' Anderson turned round and, sure enough, Costello had collared Irvine for a chinwag that he was glad he could not overhear. If whatever they were hatching sent Quinn ballistic, at least he'd be able to say honestly that he had no idea what it was about.

'Well?' demanded Costello.

Irvine pulled out her notebook. 'There was an open strip of tablets, Headeze to be exact, on the kitchen worktop, and a glass tumbler upturned on the draining board and a plate and a spoon lying in the sink, rinsed. I brought them in with me . . .'

'For public safety, not because they're evidence,' prompted Costello.

'Indeed. And I still have them in my desk. Locked. I made a list of the contents of the fridge and put stickers all over the place.'

'The ex-hubby said Sarah was on some daft carbo-hydrate diet. So, what would breakfast be? Porridge? Weetabix?' Costello looked thoughtful. 'Look, Gail, I'll stay on here for the briefing, as I missed this morning's. I know Lewis has you running around like the proverbial blue-arsed fly, but can you do this for me?' She handed over the final list that had evolved on the yellow notepaper. 'I don't want DCI Quinn to see the results yet, so just leave it on my desk marked for my attention, OK?'

Irvine's eyes opened as she looked at the length of the list. 'Will I have time?' she queried.

'Find time.'

Irvine hesitated.

'If you don't do it, somebody else will, and I'd

rather you got the credit,' said Costello quietly. 'Rumour has it Quinn is putting names forward for promotion on these appraisals; that's why Vik is being such an arse. I'd like to see you on the list as well.'

'Cheers, Costello.'

They both turned as the brisk clip of high heels along the corridor heralded the arrival of Kate Lewis with John Littlewood, Kate's wide lips turned up in a hundred-watt smile as she gazed at him.

'I get your point,' said Irvine out the corner of her mouth, folding up Costello's list. 'You know, Costello, I've never seen that before, a woman smiling at Littlewood.'

'She'll be trying to borrow money.'

'She doesn't need it; the rumour is her man's loaded.'

'I'd heard he was a cop.'

'A loaded cop? My God, Littlewood is smiling back.' Irvine tapped Costello with the yellow paper. 'I'll get on with this then. I take it no one's supposed to know?' Costello nodded, and Irvine slipped out the room.

Anderson banged a spoon against a mug for attention. 'Right, you lot – briefing. We know two children are missing. DS Lewis's reconstruction is based on the definite facts, not the maybes. Luca Scott was in the Joozy Jackpot amusement arcade with his mum, Lorraine.' He pointed at a picture of a pale-faced, black-haired woman of indeterminate age, her face drawn and eyes dead. 'She went into a … *status epilepticus* …' he stuttered over the word, 'a constant fit to you and me, and they called an ambulance. In among all the confusion and mayhem, the wee lad disappeared.' Anderson pointed to the other board. 'Troy McEwen went missing on Tuesday; the window of opportunity is now from four thirty to four forty-five. You all know the site? It's not a park; it's a big public garden, overlooked on all four sides. The trees are bare, no buildings, no cover, and the boy wasn't airlifted out by aliens. Somebody, looking out their window, must have seen something. So, we go back through all those flats again. We are now working on this bigger grid.' He indicated the area on the map with a quick sweep of his forefinger. 'Let's look at the neighbour – Miss Cotter,' he continued. 'She noticed the McEwens' flat door was open, and that Troy wasn't there. She phoned the police, as she already knew about Luca. So, we have another seven-year-old boy, this one wandering around in a bright-blue fleece and baggy leggings, and again, nobody saw anything. There are no forensics at the park, just a speck of blood, and that's being tested.'

'No word back on that yet,' said Wyngate.

'Can you ask them to do it before Christmas? This Christmas! Any other ideas? Mulholland, am I boring you?'

Vik turned, woken from his dwam. 'Sorry, what?'

'Any other ideas?'

'Oh, Miss Cotter, obviously; she's the batty neighbour, killing the children and putting them in the back of the wardrobe,' said Mulholland. 'Case solved. Can I go home now?'

Anderson ignored him. 'Anything else? Has anybody found any tie-up with Luca Scott? However tenuous?'

Lewis shook her head. 'Nothing that we can find.'

Anderson said, 'OK, interview Miss Cotter. And Alison McEwen, and Lorraine Scott – just in case there is a connection. Both boys are seven years old, cute, angelic-looking, both have dysfunctional mothers, and both are under social care orders. Both boys disappeared at roughly the same time on consecutive days; is that a connection? Anything else? Come on, you lot.'

'We've checked the central record, cross-referencing these abductions, if that's what they are,' said Lewis. 'There are no matches, and nobody jumps out as a suspect.'

'Which leaves the possibility that there's somebody new we don't know about,' said DS Littlewood. He added darkly, 'Or somebody we don't want to know about – a new perve on the block.'

Anderson ran his fingers through his hair. 'I really don't want to think about that. And Rogan O'Neill's presence in the country means the papers are paying these abductions a lot less attention than they normally would at this stage. The media are more interested in his sex life than the fate of two missing children.'

'No change there then,' muttered somebody from the back.

'So, let's hope that Lewis's photo shoot gets us some good coverage. Christ knows we could use it. Meeting over,' Anderson announced. 'Such as it was,' he muttered to himself.

9

Anderson took a deep breath out in the close, as though not sure when he'd get another. He immediately regretted it, as he took in a heady mixture of pakora, vomit and cat pee. Costello looked at the panel of hardboard on Alison McEwen's door.

'Violent entry?' Anderson suggested.

'Alcoholics don't always remember the keys, or to feed their children, or indeed bloody notice them – otherwise we wouldn't be here,' Costello pointed out dryly. 'Let's get on with this.'

The first search of Alison McEwen's apartment had been carried out immediately after the alarm had been raised. They'd looked in the usual places children always hid – under the bed, on top of the wardrobe, in the attic behind the water tank. Now they pulled on protective gloves before starting to search for the second time.

Troy's bedroom, a small room at the back of the flat, held a narrow single bed under a cracked window which let in a bitterly cold draught. The room itself smelled awful, a damp cloying reek. A growth of mould crept across the floor under the window. A dehumidifier sat idle in the corner, and Anderson nudged it with his foot; it was full. The radiator was cold, and felt as though it had been that way for a while.

Colin Anderson pulled his anorak round him and opened both the window and the door to allow a breeze through. It was a typical boy's room, not unlike Peter's, with posters on the wall, he noticed, pinned up only as high as the boy could reach himself, higher over the bed, lower round the walls. The duvet was still pulled back where Troy had shrugged it off. Lying against the skirting board were a discarded T-shirt and a pair of socks. Oddly, the other dirty clothes were piled neatly in the corner. Colin opened the single wardrobe to find a few clothes, hung up neatly but smelling slightly stale. He found some DVDs and a small collection of videos, mostly Wallace and Gromit and a few Disney classics. He recalled that no DVD player had been found in the living room, where gaps in the usual detritus of living indicated that things had been pawned, never to return.

Anderson opened the little chest of drawers, and found a few more T-shirts, and a tinfoil bundle. Carefully he opened the package to find a home-made Empire biscuit, the blue and white Scottish flag on the top knocked sideways. At the back of the drawer he found a selection of brightly coloured paper umbrellas, the type used for cocktail decorations. His eyes went round the room, falling on a black shoebox in the corner, with a folded jumper on top, a video, and a pair of socks that were almost threadbare. Troy had begun to write the label – *for my frends in Pakistan* – pointing out in very bad spelling that there were '*no earthcakes in Scotland*' and '*we was luki*'.

'He seems to be a sweet kid, this Troy,' he observed.

'Hey, look at this – a prescription slip,' said Costello, waving a piece of paper. 'For something called Penicillin V. But it isn't for the mum. It's for him. Do you want me to phone and find out what it's for?'

'I know. It's what they gave me for Claire.' Anderson's face paled and he sat down on the bed. 'It's dated a week ago. If we show that to O'Hare, he'll tell you we're looking for a body.'

'I think it might be worth asking him, though. A sick kid would give us more leverage with the press.' Costello pulled her mobile from her pocket. 'I should have his number stored somewhere. What gets me is that Alison made the effort to get her own script filled – that bottle of capsules she had in her hand was dated Tuesday. So, why did she not pick up his stuff at the same time? Unless she knew he wouldn't be around to use it . . .'

'Or was too thick to realize how important it was. That sore throat thing can be fatal.' He thought about Brenda. She wasn't stupid but hadn't she just done the same thing?

Costello scrolled down to O'Hare's number and pressed it. 'How could she not say? She didn't even mention it. He might be lying dead somewhere behind a wheelie bin. If he collapsed, this bloody weather would be enough to do him in. Oh, it's ringing …' Costello paused, then smiled. 'DS Costello here, can I pick your brains?' She related the contents of the prescription, then said *yes, yes, yes* and a quiet *oh, no*, before saying thanks and closing her phone.

She looked at it thoughtfully for a while, prompting Anderson to ask, 'Well?'

'If we accept he's badly nourished, he might have been given that script just because he has a weak immune system. But if he's out in this weather, any secondary infection – food poisoning or anything – will just rip through him.' She drew her finger across her throat.

'Cheery bloke, that O'Hare.' Anderson held out the Empire biscuit in his open palm. 'What do you make of this?'

'I bet that will be his little stash of treats. Troy never knew where his next meal was coming from. You know, I saw an Empire biscuit just like this not two hours ago.'

Anderson passed the biscuit under his nose. 'It smells fresh enough. You think he might have gone hungry?'

'Kid of an alcoholic mother? No dad? Bloody right he'd go hungry.'

Anderson busied himself with wrapping the biscuit up again. 'Right, we'll go next door and speak to Miss Cotter. See how ill she thought the boy was.

And if she's in the habit of handing out Empire biscuits.'

'The issue is: were they his treat?' Costello took the biscuit from Anderson and turned it over in her hand. 'Or her bait?'

'Hello?' said a voice, cracking with age. The other door had opened a few inches, caught by a thick chain, a fine polished wood door with a spyhole.

Costello looked at the nameplate. 'Mrs Cotter?'

'Miss Cotter,' the voice corrected.

'I'm DS Costello, Partickhill Station. This is DI Anderson.'

The door closed slightly, then opened, the rattling of the chain echoing up the stairwell. Miss Cotter, a tall woman in a beige cardigan that had seen better days, did not invite them in, but stood there expectantly, her blue-veined twigs of legs sagging under her weight.

She took a deep breath before she spoke. She had the audible wheeze of the chronic bronchitic. 'Are you here about wee Troy? Any news yet? The other man couldn't tell me anything.'

'Most children turn up safe and sound,' Anderson tried reassuringly. 'He'll be well tucked in somewhere that his mother doesn't know about.'

'Not him; he's not like that.' Her voice was tremulous but sure. 'If he was anywhere he'd be here.'

'Miss Cotter.' Costello took a step forward. 'Would you mind if we came in? It's very cold out here. I think I saw you at the hospital this morning; you had the refreshment trolley?'

'Diet Coke? Ye're too thin, ma girl – Diet Coke indeed! Aye, I remember. Better come in then.' The door swung open, and the sweet smell of an overheated electric fire wafted into the hall as Miss Cotter led them into her front room. A cloth-covered dining table with four chairs took pride of place. On the table were some Christmas cards, a list of addresses, a cheap biro and some wrapping paper, a plastic car, a rolled-up wigwam, and a boxed game. Miss Cotter wearily took her seat at the table, lowering herself carefully as if her joints were sore. Costello nodded to Anderson, indicating the photographs of Troy McEwen on the mantelpiece.

'We are not disturbing your lunch, are we?' asked Costello, registering the smell of boiling cabbage.

'No, no.' She walked slowly into the small kitchen off the living room, her hands carefully repositioned from the back of one chair to another for support.

'So, Miss Cotter, could you tell us how often, roughly, Troy came in here? Once a week, twice a week?' Costello called through.

'Oh, more than that, young lady. Every night if he could. He was a nice wee boy. Oh, he could be a cheeky wee sod, but not like some of the kids I see,' Miss Cotter replied, opening the salon doors.

'And did you buy him Empire biscuits, and give him the little umbrellas we found in his bedroom?'

'I didn't *buy* him the Empire biscuits,' Miss Cotter

reproved her. 'I've always made them for the WRVS trolley to raise a bit of money, though that will come to an end, with the health and safety Nazis. Troy used to help me. Well, he made them by sticking two digestive biscuits together with jam and then putting the icing on. I make them properly, from scratch. Troy was always hungry, always had his fingers in the bowl, licking the icing. Wouldn't be the first time I'd made him toast and a wee bowl of porridge in the morning before he went to school. Alison wasn't much of a mother.' Miss Cotter coughed, covering her mouth with a hanky she pulled from her sleeve. 'But what can you do? He's not my boy.' Her voice cracked slightly.

Costello pulled out a photograph of Luca Scott. 'Have you ever seen this child?'

'Aye, that's that other boy.' Miss Cotter nodded, her lips pursing. 'I know *of* him, because he's been in the papers. And they're all talking about it down at the hospital café.'

'Did Troy ever mention Luca? It's not a name you could forget.'

Miss Cotter shook her head; she was quite definite. 'Do you have any idea what's happened to wee Troy? I mean, he can't just have disappeared into thin air, can he?'

'No, certainly not.' Costello asked, 'When did you last see Troy? How was he, was he well, was he happy? Excited about anything?'

'I last saw him about eight o'clock the night

before. He had mince and tatties, a good dinner . . . all kids like that, you know. Only so many burgers they can eat. At least he had something inside him to keep him going. He was excited about Santa, I suppose.'

'And he ate well, no sore throat, nothing like that?'

'He always had a sore throat, tonsil trouble or something. In ma day they wheeched your tonsils out and that was that. He was always on tablets for one thing or another. Alison probably got more money from the social for that.' Miss Cotter smiled a wry smile. She reached down into a plastic carrier bag and pulled out a teddy bear dressed in a Scotland football strip. 'This is what he's getting from Santa – I thought he would like it.' She handed it to Anderson. 'Would you like a wee cup of tea and an Empire biscuit yourself?' she asked.

Anderson signalled to Costello.

'That would be lovely,' said Costello.

They both watched as Miss Cotter walked into the darkness of the kitchen.

'*Come into my parlour, said the spider to the fly,*' Costello whispered to Anderson as the door closed behind her.

'Why not get in there, offer the old dear a hand with the cups and saucers?' he suggested.

Costello shot him a look that said she could make some caustic comment about 'women's work' but wasn't going to bother.

'Do you have much of a family yourself, Miss

Cotter?' she asked, once she was inside the cramped little kitchen.

'No, none.' Miss Cotter pulled the back of her hand across her thin lips.

'Yet you have so many photographs of children, in the living room,' said Costello. 'I thought they might be your grandchildren.'

Miss Cotter pulled two cups from their hooks, and placed them on two saucers on a tray. She didn't answer for a while, her thin fingers straining as they turned the dial on the geyser.

Costello waited.

'If I had a grandson, he'd probably be in his early twenties by now.' A plate and two Empire biscuits joined the tray. 'Mid-twenties maybe.'

'But you are fond of children?' asked Costello, picking up the tray.

The old woman leaned on the worktop and shook her head, suddenly weary. For a moment Costello thought she was going to collapse. 'Poor wee Troy . . . it just seems so much worse at Christmas.' She coughed again into her white handkerchief. 'Fifty-seven years in this flat, and I've always had a good reason for Christmas. It's not just for myself, see. There's always been someone for me to look after, nearly always wee boys, though there was one wee special girl; her granny lived across the landing there, in the same flat Troy does now. She was the bee's knees, that one, pretty as a picture, a sensitive wee soul . . .' Miss Cotter's eyes clouded over. 'Her mum was never around, and she got beaten up by her dad every two minutes, so she lived with her granny more often than not.' She wiped her nose. Costello put the tray down and waited. 'But you kept quiet about that kind of thing in those days. The wee lassie would come in here to escape. She still does sometimes, poor soul. There's a whole load of unhappiness in this world. But at Christmas, there's always presents under my tree for them, all my little friends over the years.'

'Yes, I noticed them as I came in. All labelled and everything. I haven't even bought mine yet.'

'You got a lot to buy for?'

'Not really.'

'You've no family at all, have you? You've that look about you.'

Costello smiled. 'You might be right about that.'

Miss Cotter steadied herself on the door jamb as Costello held the door open for her, and made her way back into the living room. 'I've friends at the WRVS who don't see their grandkids from one week to the next, but me, I've Troy in and out every two minutes, causing havoc. So, I think I'm quite lucky.' She looked from Costello to Anderson, and tears welled up in her eyes. 'Can you try to get him back for his Christmas dinner? I do miss him.'

IO

The smell of the close seemed to have invaded Anderson's head. He got up and opened the window a little in search of fresh air, glaring at DC Vik Mulholland whose lunchtime salad was stinking out the Incident Room with a heady mixture of Parmesan and basil. Combined with his aftershave, it could be tested as a chemical weapon. Vik slowly pulled himself from the window, totally unaware of being observed, and settled into his late lunch, leaning over his desk with a paper serviette tucked into the collar of his shirt. Anderson watched as DS Kate Lewis slid into the seat across from Mulholland, pulling it round so she was at right angles to him. She smiled as she stabbed at Mulholland's salad with a plastic fork, stealing a sundried tomato here, a piece of tuna there, then placed the forkful between her wide red lips and chewed slowly. Her legs were crossed, giving both Anderson and Littlewood another look at her long tanned thigh. She leaned close and started a quiet discussion into Vik's ear.

Costello tried to block out the inane conversation between them and concentrated on reading her briefing notes on Alison McEwen. It wouldn't be an easy interview. Troy McEwen's mother was an alcoholic and emotionally unbalanced, and she was not the brightest at the best of times. They would need to word their questions carefully. Costello was trying to make a list but Mulholland and Lewis were getting on her nerves. So far she'd heard what the boyfriend, Stuart, was buying Kate for Christmas, what Vik wanted to buy for beautiful Frances, and that Vik had invited Frances to Christmas dinner but Frances was ignoring Christmas altogether. Vik was worried 'Fran' wasn't taking him seriously. Good for Fran, thought Costello. Then Mulholland dropped his voice even more and Costello found herself straining to hear. Frances had phoned to say Mulholland had left his gloves at her flat. Vik was saying he would go round and get them. She had refused.

'So, she's playing hard to get. Women do that to keep you on your toes. What's she like in bed?' asked Kate, smiling provocatively, like a woman who knew everything.

Costello listened to their whispers and conspiratorial giggles, then heard her own first name followed by a stifled cackle of laughter from Lewis, which was hastily cut short with a single glare.

Costello leaned over to Anderson. 'If she dares call me by my name she'll wake up not knowing if it's New York or New Year. Cow,' she hissed.

'Do you believe if a man knows your name, he owns you?' muttered Anderson, holding drawing pins between his lips, adjusting the information sheet on the wall.

'I believe if that woman uses my name she'll be paying a visit to casualty. Just look at those two.' She nodded across at Mulholland, still deep in conversation with Lewis. 'If Vik is emotionally distraught, I would be the first to rejoice. But not here and not now. Why can't they just get on with their bloody jobs?'

'They're a couple of children,' said Anderson, pinning new instructions on the wall. He added quietly, 'Am I the only one who's noticed that Littlewood has stopped sharing his desk space? He never gets given anything to do by Quinn. They should be at each other's throats, but they aren't.'

Costello was quick. 'I've noticed his computer is password protected beyond normal, and his drawer is locked.'

'How do you know that?' asked Anderson.

'I was innocently looking for the magnifying glass,' she fibbed with extreme ease. 'Do you think he's had a sniff and he's been told not to tell us? I think he's definitely mulling something over. Something more than Lewis's arse, I mean.'

They watched Littlewood, deep in thought, pull a packet of chewing gum from his pocket and press through the bubble pack with his thumb. Costello's eyes were fixed on Littlewood's fat yellow fingers as he popped the chewing gum into his mouth. 'I think Quinn has pulled him off this part of the enquiry and got him started on something else. Nothing like fighting with one hand tied behind our backs,' said

Costello, her train of thought interrupted by the now-familiar 'Sex Bomb' ringtone of Lewis's mobile. 'Bloody answer that *now*!'

The response was a wide smile and a wink from Lewis.

'Do you know,' Anderson retrieved Costello's attention, 'after talking to Miss Cotter, something struck me. Both these boys – there's nobody. I've been looking at the phone log. In every other missing person case, especially young people – kids – there's a queue of folk phoning up, camped on the door-step, Family Liaison on twenty-four-hour call. But for these two, nothing. Except, of course, for Miss Cotter.'

Costello's mobile rang. She listened to a quick message and closed her phone with an annoyed snap. 'Nope,' she said. 'That was to say Troy's mum is downstairs now. She's sober and being fed coffee.' She handed Anderson a page of notes and questions from her yellow notebook. 'Me bad cop, you good cop?'

The reception area of Partickhill Station was bitterly cold, and a trail of water with clumps of melting snow led from the door to the enquiry desk. A bare Christmas tree leaned abandoned against the wall; maybe somebody would get round to it later. Anderson picked up the list Wyngate had been using: Troy McEwen's classmates, his teacher, the teaching assistants, a few neighbours who hadn't yet been contacted — all the people on the periphery of a seven-year-old's life.

'Can you not find somewhere a bit more appropriate to do that?' Anderson asked, halting Wyngate's finger in mid-dial. Wyngate opened his mouth to snap back and then remembered who was talking to him. 'You shouldn't be making those kinds of phone calls from the front desk. Anybody could be listening.'

'DCI Quinn told me to do it, sir,' Wyngate muttered. 'There's nobody about to man the desk, and she said I could be killing two birds with one stone.' He leaned forward and added in a whisper, 'And I'm keeping my eye on *her*.'

Anderson and Costello both turned round to see a skeletal woman sitting on the bench seat in leggings and jumper, her shoulders huddled into the warmth of an Afghan coat.

'Troy McEwen's mother?' asked Costello.

Wyngate nodded 'Keeping her off the ...' he mimed drinking from a bottle.

'Well, get her out of here,' Anderson growled. 'She should be in an interview room somewhere.'

'We're waiting for one to warm up. It's number ...'

Anderson glanced at his watch. He had wanted this to be over by now so he could look in on the re-enactment on his way past. He didn't trust Lewis to cope with Peter's extremely low boredom threshold.

The door opened and the reception area was hit

by an icy blast. A tall dark-haired woman came in, wearing a long dark coat with the collar up. She stamped on the mat, shaking the snow from her boots, then slid the black pashmina from her head. Her face was pale, with huge brown eyes, her perfect patrician features enhanced by the imperfection of a small scar on the arc of her cheekbone. She glanced a little uncertainly at Costello as Wyngate recovered enough to ask, 'Can I help you?'

She placed a small carrier bag on the counter, like the ones sandwiches came in from the deli. 'I'm leaving these gloves for Vik Mulholland – he's a DC...'

'Yeah, we know who he is,' said Costello, shifting the bag from the counter to behind the reception desk and simultaneously having a good look at the woman. Striking, but not as young as she had first thought.

The woman smiled, a beautiful but empty smile, both enchanting and vacant. Costello recognized a face that was used to keeping secrets – shameful secrets? She noticed faint white tramlines on the inch of pale skin between her gloves and her coat sleeve. Her mind shot back to Mulholland's secret whisperings with Lewis, to his concern and Lewis's trivial dismissal. She felt ashamed. 'I'll make sure he gets it,' she said quietly but the woman had turned away to sit beside Troy's mum on the bench seat.

'Alison, hello. How are you?' she asked softly, her hand touching the other woman on the shoulder.

Costello watched as Alison McEwen shrugged a little, biting back tears. Frances's long pale fingers closed over the woollen collar of the Afghan coat. A conversation ensued. It was too soft for Costello to hear, but the lovely Frances was definitely offering words of genuine comfort in her low husky voice. For a brief moment the haggard face of Alison McEwen flickered into a smile as Costello caught Frances's parting words, *He'll be all right, I promise.*

So far, the reconstruction was going well. DS Kate Lewis stood on the pavement outside the Joozy Jackpot amusement arcade, smiling. She was dressed in an oversized fluorescent jacket, rainproof clipboard in hand, doing what she did best – handing out orders and looking fantastic.

She had briefed Patsy McKinnon on the runthrough. The cashier had turned up early for her shift, wearing the same clothes she had been wearing on Monday 'for greater realism'. Indeed, it smelled as though she had never taken them off. Patsy was enthusiastic but not too bright, casually mentioning that one minute she had been filing her nails in the kiosk to 'I Have a Dream' by 'those nice Irish boys' and the next she had heard the commotion as Lorraine collapsed among the slot machines. No, she didn't get to hear the whole song, she said in reply to Lewis's question, but she knew the radio was tuned to Clyde Two. A brief whisper into the radio pinned to the collar of Lewis's jacket and, by the time

Irvine and Peter Anderson had turned up in an unmarked car, Lewis knew the song had been played from 4.08 to 4.11.

Lewis slipped up her huge yellow sleeve to glance at her watch; it was three minutes to four. Five photographers were present, hiding under the canopy of Kemper and Jones, twisting lenses on to camera bodies and looking up into the sleety rain, muttering.

They were right on time. Peter had already been dressed in a parka and jeans, and the two members of the security staff who had been working on Monday afternoon were already in position. A few regulars had turned up, eager to help, and had had their details surreptitiously taken by the two officers in the incident van. All would be checked and double-checked later. Already details were starting to filter through – the security officer remembered Luca sneaking in but couldn't remember him going out. They could remember rushing to Lorraine when they heard the crash of her head against the machine. One thought she had lost the plot after losing her last 10p and had wrestled her to the ground before noticing her body was writhing all by itself.

'Gail? Can you take Peter over to that machine – the Regatta, I think it's called – and on my cue, can you roll on the floor, please?'

'You want me to roll on this vomit and urine stained carpet?'

'Come on, everybody else is doing their bit,' said Lewis, brushing her objections aside.

'Why me?'

'You've got dark hair, so has Lorraine.'

'So have you.'

'I'm the DS, you're the DC, so you do as I say.'

'She's forty-two and I'm twenty-six. She's fourteen stone and I'm nine stone. I don't think the realism will suffer much if I decline.'

'You will do as you are told.'

'No, I won't.'

'I'll tell Quinn.'

'Why, do you think she'll volunteer?' With that Irvine walked to the back of the arcade with Peter. With her hair scraped back in a ponytail, and wearing her regulation black T-shirt and jumper, she looked much as Lorraine had looked, if younger and slighter. At the Regatta machine she turned, arms folded, and waited.

At ten past four Lewis instructed Peter to pull up the hood of his parka and keep his face tucked in. He walked out of the arcade, hands in pockets, and stood out in Byres Road as the photographers snapped away at him. Two uniformed cops circulated, ready to question anybody who was hanging around, staff in surrounding shops, and people standing at the bus stop. A sign on the central reservation asked drivers to pull over if they had passed that way on Monday.

Lewis whispered in Peter's ear, telling him to keep his face well hidden in the snorkel, as his dad had been so insistent. But as soon as she turned her back, Peter had his face out to see what was going on.

The photographs went on and on, while the sleet soaked them all through. A few buses passed, and faces peered through the steamed-up windows. Lewis was determined to keep everybody on site until the 'ambulance' arrived at 4.28. The police photographer was in an unmarked white Transit, taking panoramic views for later examination, giving the cops on the ground a chance to interview everyone. A small queue was forming outside the Incident Room. Irvine, annoyed, caught Lewis smiling to herself. There were two DSs on this case and Irvine would bet her bottom dollar Lewis planned to grind Costello into the ground. She saw DS Littlewood walking casually along the gutter, bumping his beer gut through the crowd, on his fourth or fifth pass of the arcade.

Lewis was rattling off the carefully worded press release prepared by Mulholland, as the cameras flashed. She was the new face of the Strathclyde Police Service – young, attractive, committed, intelligent. She finished off her spiel and turned to Irvine. 'I think that went well,' she said.

'Really? That photographer is asking Peter who he is, for God's sake!' Irvine hissed at Lewis. 'Stop him!'

'Do you mind? That's it – over! You have your photographs. Thank you so much for attending.' Lewis stepped back, giving the cameras another dazzling smile.

'So, is that Kate or Katherine Lewis?' asked a

young reporter, with fashionably spiky, peroxided hair.

'Kate.' She shook her hair free from her hood, so that her dark curls were garnished in a white gossamer of sleet.

'Dave Ripley,' said the reporter, holding out his hand and rattling off the name of a big tabloid.

Irvine felt her phone vibrate. A brief glance at it told her it was the Poison Unit. 'Well, while you two get acquainted I'm going back to the van to return this call.' She stomped off, her feet numb with cold, then half shouted over her shoulder. 'Remember to keep an eye on the wee guy.'

Silence has its uses. It can hang in the air, like water gathering at the tip of an icicle, hanging heavier and heavier till something has to give. Then words, like the water, will start to flow.

DS Costello wasn't talking. She was watching Alison McEwen. Troy's mother was staring at some distant point on the lino, which kept her focus away from the two police officers. She leaned on the fag-scarred table, looking older than her twenty-four years, thin folds of flesh hanging from the skeletal arms wrapped round herself. Her cracked lips were white, and the left side of her mouth had started to bleed. She wiped it with the back of her hand, leaving a smear of red, as though she had just eaten something that was still alive.

When Costello finally spoke, there was no

compassion in her voice. 'So, again – when did you last see your son?'

Alison shrugged, as though the question was too difficult to answer. Time, for her, was an elusive thing; it came, it went, it passed her by, it left her behind.

Anderson walked slowly behind the table, its top tattooed with cigarette burns, and glanced into Alison's bag, a hessian open-topped carrier left on the floor. He nudged it with his foot, hearing the clonk of a half-empty quarter bottle of vodka.

Alison scratched the sleeve of her coat with a spidery hand.

'Were you feeling unwell when you were in the park?'

'Ah sat down,' she said, her hand waving in mid-air, and her silver bracelets jangled on Costello's nerves. 'Ah sat down, an' he was playing on the swings. He likes to play on the swings.' Alison pulled her chin back, her head wobbling slightly as if to say: *And that's it.* 'Ah'm not thinking straight. Ah need ma meds.' She reached into her bag, digging about, careful not to reveal the bottle of vodka.

Costello watched as Alison emptied two blue capsules from a brown plastic bottle into the palm of her hand, and realized the pharmacist didn't trust her with the full prescription all at once. She would have sold it.

'When did you realize he was gone, Alison?' asked Anderson softly.

She shrugged. 'Ah think he fell off the roundabout,

or something. He was moaning about his foot, or his leg. Or something,' she repeated.

'Had he hurt himself?'

Alison shrugged again as if to say: *How should I know?*

'Did you see him hurt himself?' Anderson persisted. 'Please answer me.'

'Aye, he fell.'

Anderson caught Costello's eye. 'That might be an explanation for the small dot of blood we found. Did he hurt his leg, or his face or his arm? Did he cut himself?'

'I dunno.'

'How long were you there in the park for?'

Alison shook her head. She had no idea.

'Do you always take these capsules like that?' asked Costello, picking up the bottle.

'Aye,' Alison nodded.

'And they slide down easily?' She tipped one out on to her own hand.

'Ah get them on prescription.' Alison's eyes were suspicious.

Costello raised an eyebrow, looking at the capsule in her hand, at the two halves that fitted together so snugly.

Alison McEwen snatched the capsule back, repeating aggressively, 'They're prescription!'

'But what about Troy's prescription?'

'Wit?'

Costello took a deep breath. 'Look, the doc came

out, he looked at Troy and he told you to get him medicine. What was it for?'

'He was moaning he'd a cold or a sore throat. Or something . . .'

'But you didn't get the medicine for him?'

'Nae, he was fine.'

Anderson closed his eyes and prayed quietly, thinking of Claire, how quickly the infection had taken hold, how deadly it might have proved. He wondered if Alison had ever felt that mortal panic. Troy had been missing for as long as forty-eight hours. Time to play good cop. He offered her a fresh paper tissue and shot a look at Costello, warning her to behave, but she was ignoring him, looking out the window at the rain, deep in thought.

Lewis was standing talking to Dave Ripley, flirtatiously telling him that she couldn't possibly meet him for a drink later in a way that suggested she well might.

Irvine looked round, waiting for Lewis to notice her. The crowds were drifting back to work, and the press were disappearing into Bonham's pub. 'Lewis, I've got some important information. I need to get back to Partickhill asap. Can you take Peter . . .' She looked around. 'Lewis? Where is Peter?'

Lewis turned, annoyed at the interruption. 'I thought he was with you.'

'No, I left him here with you. It was the last thing I said – look after him.'

Dave Ripley was now interested. Lewis recovered herself and said to him, 'I know he went to the van, I saw him myself. Excuse me.' She turned away, and whispered to Irvine, 'Shit.'

'So, where is he? Where's Peter?' Irvine had her face two inches from Lewis's, her voice quiet but accusatory.

'He was here a minute ago.'

'Well, he isn't here now, is he? Excuse me, has anybody seen the ...' And that was as far as she got before being halted by a sharp elbow in the ribs from Lewis.

'Shut up. We don't want them to think we're completely stupid. He's a wee boy, he can't have gone anywhere far.'

'I bet that's what Lorraine thought.'

Lewis headed up Byres Road, gently pushing through the onlookers, and Irvine opened the door of the police Transit and stood on the footplate, looking up and down, gaining a good view over the heads of the dispersing crowd. But she could see nothing. She jumped down, and ploughed through the crowd, pulling her radio from her pocket. OK, so Anderson would kill her, but she didn't care how much trouble they got into. Her thumb hovered over the orange emergency button.

Anderson felt depressed as he wandered back to his desk, and guilty. Guilty that he didn't want to go home – anything was better than Brenda's ranting.

She had picked up his message and was none too chuffed. Maybe he wasn't so different from Alison; her distraction was the bottle, his was the job. He checked his mobile – three missed calls from his home phone. He turned it off.

He drummed his thumb and forefinger on the desk, agitated. 'Have you heard how the reconstruction is going?' he asked Costello.

'Peter's just standing in the street, having his photo taken, Colin; he'll be fine.'

'I thought they would be back by now.'

'Could be a sign it's going well.'

Anderson didn't look convinced.

'Phone them then, if you're worried.'

'Already tried. Littlewood was the only one who answered. Irvine was engaged and Lewis is on voice-mail. And Littlewood said all was well.'

'Well, what are you worried about?'

Anderson shrugged. 'It's all a bit close to home, that's all. They look so alike. What are you worried about?'

'Troy's medication. Just spoken to the family GP, he was worried about this Strep throat. I feel the clock is ticking for that wee boy.'

'You might be right.' He looked at the clock, thinking about Peter. 'Anyway, did you tell Vik about his delivery?'

'I will,' Costello answered. 'Eventually.'

*

Irvine got up on the footplate of the Transit again, and leaned on the top of the open door to gain more height. She hadn't pressed the orange button; she hadn't alerted the entire Strathclyde Police radio network to Lewis's incompetence. Or indeed her own, in trusting Lewis in the first place. She sighed, swallowing her panic. She had sent four cops up to either end of Byres Road, and the driver and Littlewood had gone east and west at a fair jog.

She couldn't think what to do. *Give it five more minutes, just five more minutes*, she told herself, and then she'd press the orange button. If the worst came to the worst – OK, she hadn't called the alarm, but neither had Lewis, and Lewis was the officer in charge. Irvine was aware, deep inside, of a snide pleasure that Lewis had fucked this up. She just hoped it wouldn't be wee Peter who paid for it. But at the end of the day, he was a cop's son and he wouldn't go without a struggle. He had to be somewhere.

The crowds were dispersing. She jumped down, pulled her padded jacket round her and set off.

She saw one boy, in a parka, but he had dark hair. Her heart jumped when she saw another, blonder, on the opposite side of the road, with the same airy way of walking that Peter had, face in the sky, arms swinging. He was immediately hidden by an Irn Bru truck pulling up to wait at the lights. Irvine skipped across the road through the traffic, caught sight of the boy again and a woman pulling him away, the boy not wanting to follow. Irvine touched the boy on the shoulder, knowing as she did so that this boy was too tall, a good couple of years older than Peter. His mother turned to look at her, an unspoken question on her face.

'Just in case you haven't got a child safety leaflet,' Irvine said, thrusting one into the woman's hand.

As she waited to cross back over the road, she looked at the French Café opposite, the seats outside clearly visible, those inside clouded by the condensation on the glass. A woman was sitting outside under the canopy, warming her hands on a mug of coffee, long coat drawn tightly round her, and in front of her a little boy was dancing. He was wearing a parka, and a dark hat with a red bobble. The woman's short cropped hair was in disarray, as if a hat had been pulled off. But the way the boy moved ... it was Peter. Irvine ran across the road, risking death from an overtaking black cab. She ran up to the table.

The woman lifted her head, taking her attention from the boy, and said, 'Hello, Peter here has been telling me all about it. How did it go?'

Irvine looked at the face, the close-cropped auburn hair; in her mind's eye she painted more flesh on those cheekbones, imagined the hair long and tumbling. 'Fine, just fine, thank you,' she said. 'How's Peter?' she asked, wishing she could strangle the wee sod.

'Oh, he followed me in there, saying he was cold,

but I thought he'd better be out here where you could see him. He said you had finished with him.'

'Not quite, Mrs McAlpine,' said Gail Irvine, the name coming to her at last. 'We have to take him home now.'

'I can do that, if you want.'

'Thank you, but we'd better do it.'

'I can go with Auntie Helena and do dragons,' Peter insisted.

'No, I don't think so, Peter.' Helena pulled her hat from his head. 'You go with this lady, and do as you're told for once.' Helena smiled up at Irvine. 'That'll be a first.'

Irvine took Peter firmly by the hand and led him away, texting Lewis to say all was well and to call the guys back. She glanced back over her shoulder. Helena, lifting her coffee to her lips, took a deep breath of its sweet aroma, watching them. Well, watching Peter at any rate, Irvine thought.

They exchanged a brief smile before Irvine turned away.

11

Somebody had closed all the windows in the toilet, the doors to the cubicles were shut, and the main door had also been closed before Costello opened it, yet the toilet was freezing. Irvine, trying to get her body temperature above zero, was huddled up against the radiator, with her arms drawn up inside the sleeves of her police uniform jumper, rolling them into mitts that enveloped her hands as she cradled her cheeks with the rough wool.

Costello had half expected a few handwritten notes to be left on her desk. It wasn't like Irvine to go in for subterfuge and clandestine meetings. But just the look on Irvine's face was enough to tell Costello that there was more to it. 'I take it you've something up your sleeve – apart from your hands, that is.'

'Before we get to the good stuff, can I just tell you first that Kate Lewis is a cow?' said Irvine. 'A complete cow.'

'OK, so I promise not to buy her a Christmas present. What do you have for me?'

Folded under Irvine's arm were a few pieces of A4 paper, some of them just taken off a fax machine. She shuffled along the radiator. 'I got a lot further than I thought I would, really quickly. We have a fair number of leads to follow up. Three unexplained, in inverted commas, deaths and one near miss.'

Costello stood still for a minute. She didn't know what to say. She and Anderson had made a deal in a quick conversation outside Interview Room Two: he was going to follow that lead, she was going after the cyanide, and he would present both to Quinn.

'I want to do the follow-up,' said Irvine, her voice hard with an undercurrent Costello could not place.

'Why shouldn't you?'

'The thing is, I'm fed up of getting shat on for the mistakes of my superiors.'

'Is that directed at me?' asked Costello.

'No.'

'So, we'll get this sorted first. Have you really come up with something?'

'Something big. But I won't get any thanks for it. You and DI Anderson get to bomb about while I get to roll on a shitty carpet and do your typing. And Lewis swans about like the Queen of the New Year. She is so up herself.'

It dropped on Costello with the subtlety of a mallet. 'Oh, for God's sake, Gail, I'll see you get credit for this, whatever it is. I'm taking it to DI Anderson; you know he's fair.'

Gail Irvine's face fell. When Anderson found out about Peter . . .

'So, come on, Gail. Out with it.'

'John Campbell was poisoned before he burned to

death. His daughter was poisoned as well, though not fatally.'

'She's still in the High Dependency unit, though,' Costello said. 'What else do you have?'

'Well, a woman called Nessie Faulkner, aged sixty-two, collapsed and died last Wednesday at the bowling club up by Hyndland Road. It was thought to be a heart attack but there was no evidence of it on PM. Cause of death was undetermined, but it's being reviewed on the advice of the Poison Unit. They think there might be a whole chain of ...'

They were interrupted by the sound of rushing water as a toilet flushed. Irvine looked horrified, and Costello tapped her ear, indicating that the person in the loo must have heard everything. It came as no surprise when the door opened accompanied by the sound of clippity heels and Kate Lewis came out, swinging her handbag over her shoulder, smiling broadly like a cat. 'Does the dishy DI know all that?' she asked in a conspiratorial whisper.

'Who?' asked Costello amicably, turning to wash her hands.

'DI Anderson – Colin, isn't it? He seems rather distracted; I think he and the Mrs are having a few problems. It's a shame, he's so nice. Does he know about all this cyanide stuff? Are you two on to something?'

So, she had been listening – and wasn't so stupid as to deny it.

'We have a few unexplained deaths to look into,'

said Irvine, holding out under the pressure of seniority.

'We know nothing for definite yet, and DI Anderson will know as soon as we do.' Costello tried to change the subject. 'And who wouldn't have problems at home? The hours we're putting in at the moment, his two wee kids will see more of Santa than him this Christmas.'

'I'm so lucky with Stuart. He understands what it's like.' Lewis looked unbearably smug as she checked her make-up in the mirror.

'Working five hundred miles away probably helps.'

'Well, I think DI Colin Anderson should be at home, nicely wrapped up in bed. Now there's a thought!' Lewis ran damp fingers through her hair, and her brown curls immediately revitalized and sorted themselves the way Costello's never did. She shook her head violently as if proving that the curls would stay there.

'Anderson? Colin? You don't have the hots for him, do you?' asked Costello.

Lewis pursed her lips. 'He's a good-looking man. Must be nice to have a man who knows where the towels are kept and who can put a load of washing on for you. Stuart has no idea about anything; the only thing in his fridge is beer ... and more beer. He sends all his clothes to the launderette. Have you never ... you know ... with Colin?'

Costello looked at Lewis in the mirror, wondering

how she managed to look like that after a twelve-hour shift. 'He's my boss,' she said simply.

'That's never stopped me in the past ... quite the reverse, in fact,' Lewis said, flicking the back of her hands on to her cheekbones to give her skin a healthy glow. 'Cheaper than blusher,' she explained.

'It'll burst the blood vessels in your face and you'll look like a Halloween cake by the time you're forty,' said Costello.

'Long way to go then. So, why was he answering your mobile?' Lewis asked coquettishly.

'I was being sick in his car at the time.'

Lewis shot her a gleeful look. 'Ah, the old sick-in-the-car routine.' She whisked a lipstick round her mouth then started pulling faces, pressing her lips against each other, before returning to her favourite subject. 'Stuart would go nuts if you threw up in his car; he drives a Lexus.'

'Obviously very well paid for his nine-to-five in the Met,' said Costello, shooting a look at Irvine.

'Not really.' Lewis looked at herself full length in the mirror and straightened her skirt. She sighed. 'He has other business interests.' She started spraying perfume over her long unlined neck. 'So, what are you two doing at Christmas?' she enquired.

'Oh, I always work over Christmas. I prefer it,' said Costello, finding Kate Lewis as sweetly irritating as a grain of sand to an oyster.

'Prefer it to being on your own?'

'Well, the TV's been rotten these last few years.'

'What about you, Gail?'

'Boyfriend's parents, deaf grannies, somebody having a punch-up, the usual happy family Christmas.'

Lewis shrugged with glee as her phone rang. That bloody 'Sex Bomb' ring tone was doing Costello's head in.

At first she tried to ignore Lewis's inane mutterings down the phone, then the words penetrated her brain, '. . . and Costello has a really good lead on this cyanide stuff. The Poison Unit has come up with a whole lot of new information.' She nodded at Costello. 'I'll be back the minute I've finished this call; you can give me the gossip then.' Still on the phone, she headed out of the door. 'I think . . .' What she thought was lost as the toilet door closed slowly on its retaining arm. She hoped Lewis was talking to her boyfriend; indiscreet as that was, it would be criminal if it had been anybody else.

Gail Irvine's face was ashen with realization. 'I can't believe she heard me call her a cow.'

'And you said she was up herself! But think of it this way – the truth will out.'

'I think DI Anderson is going to be very angry when he finds out we lost Peter at Joozy Jackpot.' Irvine looked at the floor. 'Lewis has told me to keep it quiet. *Ordered* me to keep quiet. But we couldn't find him for a good eight or nine minutes. It was DCI McAlpine's wife who found him.'

'Helena?' Costello smiled a tight smile. 'If it was

Helena Farrell who found him, then Lewis's goose will be cooked. Colin and she are good friends. She'll tell him, or Peter will, and then the shit will hit the fan. But if I were you, I'd get my version in first. If Brenda finds out, she'll disembowel him – slowly.'

'How well do they know each other? The DI and the DCI's widow? I mean, Kate's right, isn't she? Just because we think he's Mr B&Q doesn't mean he's not an attractive guy.'

Costello shrugged non-committally. Her mind was elsewhere. 'Whose fault was it Peter got lost?'

'Lewis. She was being chatted up by that reporter Dave Ripley.'

'He's a right sleaze.'

Irvine pulled her jumper down, smartening herself up. 'Right, I'll speak to DI Anderson but I'll need a coffee first.' Irvine thrust some papers into Costello's hand. 'I've scribbled on them. You might want to talk to this Dr Robert Garrett; he's a nice guy.' And she went off in search of caffeine to steady her nerves.

Costello perched her backside on the edge of the sink and glanced through the notes Irvine had made, her handwriting all over the place as she scribbled on her knee with her phone in the other hand. Four names, four doctors. She copied them on to a Post-it note and stuck it in her shoulder bag next to her yellow notebook. She looked at the four names again – three fatalities – Moira McCulloch, Barbara Cummings, Duncan Thompson. A Lars Lundeberg had survived, but only just. Underneath Irvine had scrawled *Costello – they'll fax details through to you.* She had very formally signed and dated it, making her point – she wanted credit where credit was due.

Did they have a serial poisoner on their hands? Was something leaking into some factory plant somewhere, silent but fatal? Costello felt her heart begin to race. Not this, not with two missing children – the squad couldn't cope with it. Not at Christmas. Costello looked again at the list of names, tried to focus on Lars Lundeberg. He didn't sound local. He couldn't have had much in common with the others. But he had survived. So, he was potentially a walking witness. She tried to focus on the letters as they blurred then separated.

She was shocked when the cold hard sink hit her on the back of the head.

I 2

After a frustrating half-hour of people promising to phone him back, Colin Anderson put the phone down, his throat raw from too much talking. No Miss Cotter was registered at Havelock Street but a Mrs Cotter was. It troubled him, a woman like Miss, or Mrs, Cotter living one floor up in a hilly area of Glasgow, with her wheezy chest. He tried her GP again; he wanted to know just how bad her chest was, what she might physically be capable of, but the GP was in the middle of a busy clinic. Even if Anderson got him, he would probably quote patient confidentiality and Anderson was in no mood to sweet-talk the situation with *Yes, but hypothetically speaking*...

He looked at his diary, flashing at him from the corner of the screen that there was a memo from Quinn. So, she couldn't be arsed walking all the ten yards from her office to his. The message was straight and to the point. There had been a suggestion from an officer on the house-to-house that the search was not thorough enough, that premises were being over-looked. Of the twenty uniformed officers who had been drafted in, Anderson knew about two. They were all meeting at eight the following morning in the dining room at Rowanhill Primary School where, later, in the gym hall, the car park and the street outside, there would be a special Christmas fair for the earthquake appeal. That would draw every kid in the surrounding area out of the woodwork.

He called up the database for the search. The last update had been from the night shift. He called up the list of premises where no access had been gained and cursed when he saw the length of it. He checked who had last updated it – a PC Smythe, probably some pen-pusher in an office somewhere. Anderson himself would have to go through it all again, get the grid map out and examine it inch by inch. There were too few ground troops, and they were too tired, too cold. Too sure in the knowledge there was nothing to find. Maybe they were not wrong. And as well as all this, the force had to babysit Rogan O'Neill for his public appearance tomorrow.

Anderson's phone sounded, a voicemail coming through from Peter. *When are you coming home? I need to do Puff.* He was about to reply when Wyngate thumped a buff file on top of the growing pile on his desk. 'I've been through every classmate Troy has, his teacher and classroom assistants; I've tracked down the few neighbours we still had to speak to, but nothing. Sorry, sir, nothing.'

'OK, Wyngate, nice try. Do me a favour and phone the delightful Miss Cotter's GP, see if you have any better luck than me. I'm trying to find out what's wrong with her chest. She wheezes as if she has

Chronic Obstructive Airways Disease and if she does, and it's bad, then we can strike her off the suspect list.' Anderson tapped his pen against the screen. 'It's going down to minus four tonight. That wee lad has only a thin fleece on, and he's in need of medication for his throat. We need to get it on the news that the boy is ill. Make sure Mulholland labours the point in the press release. Oh, get him to labour it even if the boy was fit enough to climb Everest backwards. Where is he anyway?'

'Nipped home. I think he had something or somebody on his mind. And, sir? If you want to go home for a bit and see Claire, sir ... We're all doing a double shift again tonight.'

'Oh,' said Anderson. 'Quinn missed that bit out of my memo.'

'I'll cover. No matter what Mulholland gets up to he will be in later, and Costello – Costello has disappeared.'

'Thanks, I'll take you up on your offer of a bit of home time. I think the wife is going out again. I'll take these with me and look over them. Can you get the addresses into some sort of geographical order?'

'No sweat.' Wyngate glanced down the list. 'Is this fair going ahead tomorrow? With two children gone, does the DCI think it's enough just to beef up security? Might be better to ...'

'Cancel the whole fair? Life goes on, Wyngate. But put the word out I want as many police in attendance as possible, informally. The dog squad are doing a display in the car park anyway. There's been muttering from Stewart Street HQ that Rogan O'Neill is going to pay for some kind of extra security. I suppose it's all grist to his publicity mill. But then again, with all those children around and unobtrusive security – who knows what it might pull out the woodwork?' Anderson swung round in his seat, and found John Littlewood staring at him.

'Risky,' said Littlewood, scratching his bald head, scattering dandruff on the shoulders of his leather jacket. 'Too risky. That re-enactment was risky.'

'But it went OK? Peter was OK?' Anderson asked.

Littlewood dropped his gaze, and blew a perfect sphere of bubblegum until it popped. '*Peter* was just fine.'

Anderson missed the nuance in the reply and looked back at the photographs of the two missing boys stuck on to the front of his monitor. He couldn't imagine never being there to touch his son on the cheek as he fell asleep, to read his bedtime story, to have the usual fight about bathtime and whose turn it was to spray the mousse and who was to scrub. The little bits of life that held a family together. But Luca Scott and Troy McEwen were both growing up without a father, and effectively without a mother either. What kind of family life was that?

Another memo popped up on his screen. Rogan

O'Neill's agent had been on the phone, offering a reward of a hundred grand for information leading to the safe return of the boys. Anderson let a slow whistle whisper through his teeth; Quinn, he noted, was waiting for agreement from HQ. He noticed Littlewood's head come up as the memo popped up on his own screen, and a slightly puzzled look cross his rugged face.

'Even if they say no, can they actually stop him putting up a reward if he wants to? I think we should just take Rogan up on his offer to do an appeal,' Anderson said. 'We need somebody like that to keep the boys in the headlines. He'd do better putting all that money into more security at the fair tomorrow, seeing as he's the big attraction. He's the one who's creating all the fuss anyway. Can you get a map of the school and review the security, the entry and exit points, check the security camera placements?'

'You think any kid is going to be safe – even one with careful parents – if someone in the crowd lures them with a Santa and Squidgy McMidge?' Littlewood said in disbelief, and walked away.

Anderson turned back to his own desk to think further. Posters, radio appeals and door-to-door searches had brought in nothing, but no bloody wonder if all someone had to do was not answer the door to avoid being questioned. Tomorrow, uni-formed personnel would be interviewing anybody in the Red Triangle, stopping them in the street, but again anybody who wanted to avoid that could.

And who was to say the kids were still in the area? Another memo appeared on the screen – the media liaison unit had asked Rogan O'Neill to firm up a time to film the appeal, and Vik Mulholland was going in front of the cameras in the meantime. Anderson took a sip of stone-cold coffee, and reread the statement Mulholland had prepared. Very easy on the eye was DC Mulholland, and he came over well. Although he was proving to be as much use as a chocolate fireguard today, away with the fairies dreaming about the new girlfriend. Anderson's phone rang again, and his home number flashed up on the digital display. He let it ring. It would be Brenda, wanting another night out and moaning about a lack of money. Couldn't she – just this once – stay at home and look after Claire?

'I'm OK, I'm OK . . .'

'No, you are not.' Lewis was kneeling beside her, trying to get her to sit up. But the more she helped, the more confused Costello's body seemed to become. She was on the floor of the toilet, with her legs crumpled beneath her, and could neither get up nor lie down. Her head pounded with every movement as Lewis tried to pull her to her feet, and she thought she was going to be sick again. She put her hand up, telling Lewis to leave her alone, and let her eyes focus on the contents of her handbag scattered all over the floor, knowing that they must be hers but not really recognizing the leather purse and the torn make-up bag with the black stain on the corner where her eyeliner had leaked.

She was seeing double – more than double – every time she moved left or right, and Lewis's face danced round her as though they were both in some strobe-lit disco.

'Costello, can you stand up?'

'I don't know, I just felt faint.' Costello tried to steady her breathing, fanning the collar of her shirt against her neck, letting the cold air cool the sweat. 'I'm fine now.'

'Yeah, you look fine. Could you walk across this room with your eyes closed?'

'Could I do that normally?'

Lewis helped Costello to her feet, placing her hands on the basin, and then took a paper towel, soaked it in cold water and held it against her forehead. 'I don't know why they do this on the telly but it always seems to work wonders. Do you want a paracetamol or an aspirin? Have you eaten anything?'

Costello smiled weakly, starting to feel better, starting to think Lewis might be a nice human being after all. 'I think I'm just hungry. I had a migraine yesterday, and I threw up everything. And I've had nothing to eat today, so it serves me right.'

'Well, you'd better get down to the canteen and get some food inside you, some sweet tea. I'll go and tell the boys what's happened; there's about to be another meeting.'

Before Costello could stop her, Lewis was gone. Costello didn't know whether she had said *tell the boys* or *tell the boss*. She decided she didn't care.

13

Mulholland had been swinging backwards and forwards on his chair, plaiting the fingers of his gloves and letting them spring loose. He wished Fran hadn't simply handed them back without asking to see him. He was even more miserable that his quick visit out to her house had been unsuccessful – she hadn't been in. He'd bought her a pink mobile phone, got it registered and charged up with a full card, just so he could tell her if he had to work on, but all he could do was leave it behind her storm door with a note. Was she really playing hard to get, as Lewis suggested? He didn't think that was like her.

He was supposed to be reading through his script for the press conference, but he couldn't stop thinking about her. He heard a phone ringing, checked it wasn't his, and went back to his script. But a glare from Colin Anderson, who was on his own phone, told him Costello's phone was ringing, and had been for a while. Anderson's pointed gesture implied strongly that Mulholland should answer it.

'Hello, Dr Robert Garrett from Gartnavel Hospital here.'

'Yeah?' Mulholland answered, only half listening.

'I was told to ask for DS Costello. I've been

speaking to a DC Irvine and Professor O'Hare,' said the voice on the telephone.

'DS Costello's not available at the moment.' Mulholland looked up. Costello was nowhere to be seen, and there were no notes on her desk, so he decided to play it by ear. 'This is her phone. I'm DC Mulholland, on the same team as DS Costello.'

'Oh, right. We were told to notify you if we hardened up any details of the fatalities I told DC Irvine about earlier.'

Mulholland was paying attention now; this was big. He listened, a smile slowly dawning on his face. Dr Garrett was innocently filling in the blanks; in fact, he was being very helpful indeed.

He pulled his own notebook from his pocket. 'Sodium cyanide. And it was in a capsule?' Mulholland narrowed his eyes in concentration, then turned away, aware of Anderson hanging up his phone and looking over, trying to listen in. Mulholland held tightly on to his pad and scribbled it all down, even to the description of the half-dissolved capsule one of the victims had vomited up in the ambulance.

Mulholland himself felt sick but thanked Dr Garrett, then sat and had a good look for Costello's notebook. He saw Wyngate chewing on his bottom lip like a cow looking over a wall, looking at the door for Costello then back at her desk where Mulholland now sat.

He didn't find much except a log of where

Costello had been and for how long, but not why. He noted Sarah McGuire's phone number, the same number for Karen and a different one for Thomas McGuire. He was itching to get to Quinn before he had to film his TV statement.

'You didn't see any of that,' he told Wyngate. 'I'm taking this to DCI Quinn.'

'Taking what to Quinn?'

'You'll be told as and when. Keep quiet about it.' And he walked away.

Wyngate was uneasy. His sense of unease increased when Mulholland met Lewis in the doorway and she pulled him to one side, stretching up on her toes to speak into his ear, excited, apparently desperate to tell him something, forcing a fold of yellow paper into his hand. Mulholland pulled out his notebook and they went into the corner to compare notes. Wyngate watched them together, two smart young people in designer clothes, both hungry for promotion. Costello's phone rang again, but nobody seemed inclined to answer it.

DS Costello was tucked up in a corner of the empty canteen with her jacket wrapped round her against the chill. The canteen had stopped doing hot food due to staff shortages but Agnes had said she'd fry her an egg and stick it in a soft roll. For now, she was drinking a cup of hot black tea and she had her mobile phone and a load of jumbled thoughts for company. She rummaged in her handbag for the original notes on their yellow paper, but she could only find her Post-it note. Puzzled, she started searching again, and then went through her pockets, just in case. But nothing. Maybe Gail had taken them with her. For the first time in days, her mind seemed to be clearing itself of its migrainous fog, and she wondered if the bang on the head had done her some good.

Logic was telling her that a leak at some factory somewhere would have had a bigger impact by now, and the Poison Unit would have identified it. This was something more local. All the victims came from within a two-mile radius of the two hospitals. Gail had said the painkillers at Sarah's house were Headeze, and she wondered if Sarah had regained consciousness yet. Where were those capsules bought? That was what Costello wanted to ask her. And what of Lars Lundeburg? She had phoned the hospital to find out that he actually lived in Gothenburg and had already returned home, after what he thought was the worst bout of food poisoning he had ever had. But the nurse she had spoken to had left a note for a nurse called Malin, who was Swedish herself, and had chatted away to him in more depth than the rest of them.

For the moment, Costello was stuck. She was staring at her street map of the West End when the doors of the canteen flew open, and Wyngate marched in, bouncing a Christmas tree and dropping pine needles everywhere. He slung it on the nearest table and gesticulated to Costello that maybe she should be upstairs. She shrugged. Nobody had invited her anywhere and she had some important phone calls to make.

'Can I ask you a question? Do you carry any painkillers with you?'

'Why? You not well?' asked Wyngate.

'I just want to know. What about you, Agnes?'

'I'll have a painkiller or two in my bag, got a bad back,' said Agnes.

'I just have my inhaler,' said Wyngate, trying to be helpful. He searched his pockets but found nothing. 'Did you know that Vik Mulholland . . . oh, hang on,' he said, wandering out the room and muttering that he'd be back in a minute.

'Can I see your painkillers, Agnes?'

Agnes shrugged and went off to get her handbag, as Costello pulled her jacket further round her, wishing that Kate Lewis had not soaked the fringe of her hair quite so enthusiastically. It was cold now, chilling her face, and her brain hurt as though she had eaten too much ice cream too quickly.

John Campbell had asked for some headache capsules the week before he died. There was that telltale blister pack, twisted but identifiable in the photograph. But had father and daughter taken two capsules from the same packet? Or was one a cover for the other? And where had bloody Wyngate gone?

Agnes came toddling out from the kitchen. 'This is what I have, hen.'

She proffered an old bubble pack of Transprofen. The tinfoil backing was marked and bent, and two of the capsules were poking their way through. If somebody she knew offered her that, Costello thought, she would probably take it, though she would have no idea whether it had been tampered with or not. And if somebody gave her the whole strip, she might walk about with it for months. She could see a plan there. She thought of Littlewood taking his blister pack of chewing gum from his pocket, popping out the pellets of gum and sticking them in his mouth without looking. But medication? Those packets were tamper-proof; after the baby food scare and the Tylenol case, they carried security labels and seals.

'Can I use these, Agnes?'

'That's what they're there for.'

'Thanks, Agnes; I'll buy you some more.'

Costello glanced at her watch. She was still waiting to hear back from a Dr Garrett at Gartnavel Hospital; she should really go upstairs and check if the good doctor had phoned. She started to gather her things together, pausing as she picked up Agnes's capsules, taking time to turn the bubble strip over and over, then frowning. She popped a capsule through its tinfoil backing, its plastic coating sticking to her sweating fingers, and pulled the two halves apart. A fine white powder spilled out on to the canteen table. She pulled another one apart, this time taking care to spill the contents on to a napkin, then she tried to refill the capsules with salt and slide the two halves together again. It didn't work; she couldn't even work out which went over which. Then she realized that the warmth of her hands was softening the walls of the capsule. So, she deduced, if she chilled one and warmed the other, it should be possible to fit them back together. The tinfoil backing was so battered, after weeks at the bottom of a typical female handbag, she couldn't tell if it had been tampered with or not. The tinfoil backing was fractured and split over the capsules, but secure round the edges. Costello looked at the blister pack sideways. No breach. She could see no way of getting at the capsules and replacing the foil. And anyway she couldn't even begin to think where an ordinary person would get their hands on sodium cyanide. Her mobile sounded, bouncing across the table in front of her. O'Hare was brusque to the point of rudeness. He was calling in; he'd be there in about ten minutes. And he rang off.

'Great,' she said, wondering how many bosses she could cope with at any one time. For some reason McAlpine came into her mind for the second time. *Follow the money.*

Anderson put the phone down and took a deep breath. He had never, ever heard his wife use language like that, but she had every right to be angry, and he himself was going to kill Lewis and Irvine when he got hold of them. They should have told him. Did they think a chatterbox like Peter *wasn't* going to tell his mum about his wee adventure – running away, and the nice policewoman ... he looked up at the sound of his name and his anger faded. Slightly.

He saw Helena across the office, walking with her usual elegant confidence, her long navy coat swinging from her shoulders as she made her way towards him. She looked as though she had been out in the rain; a wet knitted hat, with her short hair tucked inside it, emphasized the pallor of her face and the darkness of her eyes. Anderson could smell her as she approached. She always smelled faintly of turpentine and of Penhaligon's Bluebell. It was her trademark scent.

Helena smiled at him as she approached the desk, saying hello to John Littlewood and Gordon Wyngate on her way past. She was carrying a large carrier bag from John Lewis full of gift-wrapped parcels, swaying slightly as if it were too heavy for her, and a brown paper package on a string. He was glad the office was half empty. He felt his heart lift at the sight of her.

'Not interrupting, am I?' She looked apologetic, and her voice was low and soft, like an old charcoal drawing. 'I know you must have a lot on your plate but I just brought these in.' She rested the bag of gifts on the floor beside his desk.

'A welcome interruption, believe me. How did you get on at the hospital?'

'Well, I got the green light. I don't know whether

that makes me more or less nervous, but at least the end is in sight.'

He pulled a chair out for her. 'I took your tyre in this morning. They'll call when it's ready. I was late for work anyway. Claire had a bit of a bad turn last night.'

'Is she OK?' Helena sat down, her face concerned.

'Yes, it was just a throat infection that got out of control. She was unlucky to have a couple of parents who didn't get the prescription in time.' He shrugged. 'But they bounce back. This morning she was sitting up in bed, demanding food and talking back, so no change there. It's when my kids are quiet I worry about them.'

'Well, there's a present in there for her, but you have to give it to her now as I managed to get my hands on a dragon outfit for Peter. Two minutes on the internet and I found a supplier just half a mile away. I picked it up when I came out the hospital today. I had to hide it quick when I saw him in Byres Road.'

'Byres Road?' Anderson asked, slowly. 'So, you were there then? I've just had an earful from Brenda. What the hell happened?'

Helena pulled a slightly puzzled face. 'Well, he was just wandering about. Were you doing a reconstruction or something? I looked for you but you weren't there.'

'No, I wasn't there,' Anderson said, barely trusting himself to speak.

Helena was oblivious. 'And there's something in there for you, just a wee bottle, for helping me out last night. Colin, I was wondering about tomorrow night and the ...'

Helena was cut off by Costello popping her head round the door. 'Col, can I have a w–. Oh, hello, Mrs McAlpine.'

Costello's eyes flitted between them for a moment. Anderson was looking furious about something, something more than just being interrupted.

'I'll be on my way then,' Helena said, nodding a goodbye to Anderson.

'Bye then,' said Costello briskly.

Anderson watched her leave and then became aware of DCI Quinn leaning against the door of her office, watching the whole situation. She said nothing; she just re-buttoned her jacket and turned back to her office, closing the door with her stilettoed heel.

'You knew, didn't you?' he said accusingly to Costello. 'They lost Peter.'

'Irvine was told by Lewis to say nothing, but she told me in the loo. She was going to tell you herself.'

'She should have come to me immediately,' he said coldly.

'She's young. She knows how close Quinn and Lewis are. She was scared,' said Costello. 'I'd think twice about getting on the wrong side of those two.'

'No, you wouldn't, you liar.'

'I would if I was at Irvine's level. She's keen to get on.'

'Didn't help the wee man though, did it?' Anderson felt the colour rise in his face. 'I think I'm going to get Lewis and Irvine in here and disembowel them both with a stapler.'

'Go easy on Irvine.' Anderson tried to turn away from her, but Costello leaned over to speak quietly in his ear. 'Can I give you a piece of advice?'

'No,' he snapped.

'You need that kind of hassle like a hole in the head. She is your best friend's widow.'

'Don't know what you mean.'

'Well, you're fond of her, aren't you? You both lost Alan, and it would just be too easy to misconstrue the emotions that got stirred up as something else. And . . .' Costello's pinched face was earnest. 'She has no family. It's Christmas and she has nobody. I know from experience what that's like. I'm used to it. She isn't. So, don't . . .'

'Take advantage of her? What kind of guy do you think I am?'

'That's not what I meant . . .'

'Thanks, but Helena and I have always got on well. She's simply the wife – widow – of a good friend. End of story.'

'As long as that's all it is.' She handed over a file.

'Costello!' A not-so-discreet cough made them both turn, and DCI Rebecca Quinn summoned Anderson with a gesture that made the hair on the back of his neck stand on end. 'My office, now, please, both of you.' She left, clearly expecting them to follow.

'Well, better get this over with quick then,' Anderson muttered.

'They said that about the First World War,' Costello muttered behind him.

Quinn sat down on her chair, ramming it backwards with a foot on the leg of the desk. Costello and Anderson had followed her in before they saw O'Hare was standing, leaning on the filing cabinet. He seemed to have the weight of the world on his shoulders.

'Three more deaths, Costello. Three deaths, and you told me nothing. Do I need to remind you – Duncan Thompson, Barbara Cummings, Moira McCulloch?'

Costello glanced at Quinn's desk and recognized her own yellow notepaper. She then looked at O'Hare but he looked straight back, his face unreadable. She turned her glare to Quinn. 'Those are my notes.'

'Really? Lewis and Mulholland gave them to me.' Quinn picked them up between her thumb and forefinger and waved them in the air.

'That was my investigation,' Costello's voice was quiet and angry.

'I can second that. I witnessed that call coming through on her phone.'

'Yes, I know that. But you didn't tell the rest of the squad, so how was DC Mulholland supposed to act on this in your absence?'

'I wasn't well. I . . .'

'You are either at your work or you are not. And if you are not, DS Costello, this station will try and do its best to carry on without you,' said Quinn with consummate sarcasm.

Costello snapped back. 'All I had was three names. I had been told to wait for a call back from the Poison Unit. If I'd come to you with that, you'd have accused me of wasting your time and told me to wait until they rang back, wouldn't you? I am a detective, you know.'

'Debatable,' said Quinn. 'So why were you in the canteen, stuffing your face?'

'I passed out because I hadn't eaten for forty-eight hours, ma'am. I've been doing just a tad overtime lately. And I was thinking . . .'

'New experience for you.'

'. . . about the case.' Costello put the map in front of Quinn, forcing her to look at it. 'Look! The Western is here, Gartnavel's there. Headeze is only sold by the Waldo chain.'

'What?' Quinn interrupted.

'The painkiller I suspect carried the cyanide. Waldo is here in Byres Road. There are a few in town, and there's one out in Anniesland, but I think we need to look at this one first. John Campbell lived here,' Costello stabbed with her forefinger, 'up on

Partickhill Road. His daughter was going from the tennis club – here – to where she lives down here in the Mearns.' Costello's finger darted from one side of the map to the other. 'She would drive down Byres Road, past this branch of Waldo.'

By now O'Hare was leaning in, looking. 'Lars Lundeberg, the one who survived, is at Glasgow Uni and lives in student accommodation in ...' He spun his finger, locating a street. 'There, Peel Street. He walks past Waldo to get to Uni.'

'But it's Christmas and he's gone home – to Gothenburg not Peel Street. Somebody is supposed to be phoning me about him, or maybe they already have and nobody's told me,' said Costello, sulkily.

'And Barbara Cummings worked in Rowanhill Library,' O'Hare continued as if she had not spoken.

'But lived on the south side,' said Quinn, reading Mulholland's notes. 'Did she drive?'

'Eyesight too bad, I would have thought. So, if she used public transport, that could put her on Byres Road as well.'

'DI Anderson, go out and get somebody to check up on this. Find the next of kin and ask if the deceased ever took Headeze and where they did their shopping. Same with Duncan Thompson. He lived on Novar Drive. And Moira McCulloch, she's out in Bearsden. Now, Anderson,' prompted Quinn. 'Do it now.'

Anderson got up and threw Costello a quick look

as he reached the door, *not the time or the place*, as Quinn and O'Hare looked at the street map.

Costello broke the silence. 'I've been trying to work out – is this product-tampering meant to hit Waldo supermarkets? If so, what's the point? It can't be blackmail, as we've had no demands.'

'But the Poison Unit would have noticed a pattern if it was more widespread. We've put out a nation-wide alert. No response. This seems local,' said O'Hare. 'Doesn't make any sense.'

'So, what *is* the point?' said DCI Quinn.

'I think somebody is going to commit murder and get it put down to the tamperer while everyone is dropping like flies,' Costello said urgently. 'I mean, look at Sarah McGuire. Say she gave it to her dad meaning to kill him – mightn't she take a little herself by way of a wee contingency plan in case we got too close? She would know to eat something to retard absorption. I remember you said it yourself, Prof – John Campbell had a thin stomach wall and he hadn't eaten anything, so he died quickly. But on a full stomach, with a healthy stomach wall, absorption is slowed so you're more likely to survive.'

'Indeed,' said O'Hare, with faint amusement.

'Sarah was dead keen to find out how much of her inheritance is left undamaged. She inherits all three flats above her dad's as well, you know . . .'

'How hard was that smack on the head, Costello?' asked Quinn, slowly.

'I'm serious.'

'I was worried you might be. Forget it. One step at a time. Check the availability of cyanide, check out all possible motives, the shop, the staff, the family, the friends, who knew who, whether there's any interconnection between the families. All credit to the good professor for picking it up. Get the store to withdraw stock and put a warning in the press – something general; I don't want a panic. Though with our track record, I hope we bloody nail it before anybody else dies. We'll keep the countrywide alert on red, just in case this is only the first tampering that has been picked up. It could be happening all over the place.' She turned her gaze to Costello. 'Please, Costello, just do what you are told, and report back to me. And don't go off at any tangents. Do you understand?'

Costello stood her ground. 'At the risk of labouring the point, Sarah knew her Dad was getting headaches from being kept awake by the noisy tenants upstairs. Sooner or later he would take a Headeze. All Sarah had to do was tamper with a few boxes and give her dad one. If nobody notices the deaths are due to poison, so nobody asks for a toxicology report, well and good, she gets away with it. If somebody else is found to have died from the poison, there is absolutely no connection, and she still gets away with it. Her dad setting his house on fire is a fantastic stroke of luck, until I notice the smell. And even when we have a whole cluster of them, Sarah just has to point out she's a victim as well, and guess what – she gets away with all of it. It's ingenious. I could quite admire her if she wasn't such a stuck-up cow.'

O'Hare was gazing out the window at neutral ground, having no desire to get caught between these two. He was saved by Anderson knocking at the door.

'We've got Wyngate on to it, ma'am; he's good at this kind of thing,' he said, taking the spare seat.

'Glad somebody is.' Quinn marked something in her diary, apparently ignoring Costello, who was breathing heavily after her outburst. 'Oh, and DI Anderson – while you're here – please don't let members of the public wander round our investigation room unaccompanied.'

'Who?' he asked, confused at the sudden change of subject.

'Tall woman, long dark coat. Ten minutes ago?'

His lips tightened. 'That was the Boss's – DCI McAlpine's – widow, ma'am.'

'Yes, I know. She's an artist, isn't she?'

'Yes.'

'Not a member of Strathclyde police.'

Anderson did not respond; he just looked Quinn straight in the face. It was her gaze which dropped first. 'No, ma'am, but her husband was.'

'Rebecca?' said O'Hare. He reached out to put his hand on her shoulder but she pulled away.

Costello took advantage of Quinn's fire being drawn elsewhere. 'DCI Quinn? You told me Lewis gave you those notes. Did you ask her how she got them?'

'It doesn't matter. The information should have been given to me straight away.' Quinn opened a drawer, attempting to end the conversation.

Anderson stood up, ready to go; Costello did likewise but leaned lightly on Quinn's desk, pulling herself up to her full five feet five. 'But just for the record, those notes were actually on my person and were removed from my person when I was unconscious. In fact, they were removed from my handbag while I was waiting for confirmation of the *facts*,' she emphasized. 'So, a theft occurred while I was on an active enquiry, a theft of important information pertinent to that enquiry.' Costello pulled her jacket round her. 'You might like to think about that before I make a very public complaint.'

'Are you threatening me, DS Costello?' asked Quinn.

'Yes, DCI Quinn. Goodbye,' she said airily, and walked out the room. Anderson, following her, added a cheery goodbye of his own.

Costello slammed the door of the locker room. A uniform, following her in, sensed trouble and did a prompt U-turn.

'I'm sorry?' said Mulholland who was examining his eyebrows in the mirror.

'Do I look like I enjoy getting my arse ripped off by Quinn? You should have come to me with what

Garrett told you, instead of leaving me standing there like a right fucking idiot.'

'If those papers were important, you should have kept them safe.'

'They were in my handbag.'

'They were on the floor of the loo.' Mulholland didn't stop his preening. 'Make your point, Costello, or leave me alone. Your big mistake was that you were sitting on information, and you got caught out.'

'I fainted in the toilet.'

'So, faint in the Incident Room in future.'

'I was still on an active line of enquiry.'

'Good for you.' Mulholland flicked his fringe a few times with his fingers. 'Maybe you could get away with that crap when you were McAlpine's blue-eyed girl, but not now.'

It was half past five and pitch dark when PC Smythe pulled up beside the railings outside number 3 Crown Avenue. He wasn't due back on duty at Partick Central until much later but he'd found he couldn't sleep. He'd read all the reports as they came in, and he'd heard a rumour that the Partickhill team was about to get bogged down in another investigation, something to do with product tampering. It was OK to say airports and ferries were being watched, but the truth was you didn't have to smuggle a kid out of Scotland, most of the country was empty. But nothing justified the laid-back behaviour of some of the search team, thought Smythe. Searching was a boring, cold, relentless, unrewarding job. But it had to be done. He'd been told often enough that he was young and idealistic. But if two missing kids wasn't something to get idealistic about, what was the point of the bloody job? One sloppy short cut could make the difference between life and death.

He got out of his car and walked along the front of the terrace, then under a beautiful blond sandstone archway into the lane. He looked up, catching the gargoyles and angels in the beam of his torch. The lane was little used by cars. It had been grassy, with two indistinct tyre tracks that somebody had once tried to cover with stone chips. Now it was a patchwork of snow, ice, stone and moss. Smythe's steps sounded hollow as he went into the darkness beyond, and he held his torch a little higher.

Thirty yards or so in, the lane divided into three. He tried to orientate himself, swinging his torch from left to right in a wide sweep. The track to the left went along the back of Crown Drive; the other, to his right, would go up Crown Avenue. The third, nothing but a short-cut footpath worn by habitual but unofficial usage, disappeared into the darkness. His heart sank – how many more such little ways existed, gifts to any child abductor? Were any of these even on the search grid?

He shone his torch along the side of the terrace, where the wall dropped to a height of ten feet or so. He couldn't see any of the back courts from here so he continued on a good fifty yards, past an island of broken-down garages, their front doors hanging off, their roofs caved in. He shone his torch inside, over broken lawnmowers, old bedsteads, junk of every kind; an Aladdin's cave to any kid.

He was getting cold, the chill was eating into his bones, and he was unnerved by the sheer isolation of the place. He'd bet his bottom dollar this place wasn't even on the search grid. He pulled out his mobile and photographed the garages; not a good image, but it was something to show, some proof.

He turned his torch off and went back to his car, immediately turning the engine on and putting the heating up full blast, blowing on his hands to get his fingers working again. He looked up at the houses. Four storeys? Five, if they had a converted basement. Multiply that for the entire West End ... And the evening search team were content to sit on their fat arses!

He wished there was somebody on the case with a conscience, a detective with kids. He had heard about a Detective Inspector Colin Anderson.

Smythe put the car in gear and drove up the hill towards Hyndland Road, and Partickhill Station.

14

Lynne had a quiet meal planned at Mother India, just her and Douglas. Douglas would come by taxi, carrying a big brown envelope so that even if Stella McCorkindale, his secretary, glanced out of her window at the wrong moment, it would look as if he were dropping off something important after their meeting.

On her way home she ran through her routine. Eve was at her neurologist's and his clinic always ran late. So, first Lynne would have a nice twenty minutes with her feet up and a cup of Earl Grey. Then she'd have a leisurely bath, shave her legs, tidy up her eyebrows and slather on the new luxury moisturizer from M&S. And her Clinique Aromatics that Eve hated.

She stood on the front doorstep for a few minutes, fantasizing about moments of stolen passion with Douglas. She slid the key into the lock. Her dreams evaporated.

Eve was in. The smell of chips and curry welcomed her in the hall. Her bloody sister had got the taxi driver to pick up a takeaway on the way home. Lynne lowered the shopping bags gently to the floor, closing the door very slowly behind her, and tiptoed along the hall to find the door of her bedroom open. She always left it shut. Always. She looked at the pile of the carpet. It was perfectly regular, perfectly even, showing no wheelchair track marks.

'Hello?' a voice shouted, not from the study. Wherever she was, Eve sounded happy at least.

'Yes. It's me,' Lynne said. 'I'll be through in a minute.'

'You alone?' The voice came from the back of the house.

'Wish I was,' she muttered. She picked up the shopping, and walked through to the kitchen, to find an empty tube of Pringles crunched up and tossed on the floor.

She put the shopping on the worktop and walked round the corner to the dining room. Eve had covered the whole of the dining table with drawings and illustrations – pastels, watercolours, pen and inks – and, from the look of the mess on the carpet and on the table, she had been busy. She did not lift her head as Lynne entered, engrossed in examining picture after picture, each covered with a fine leaf of tissue paper, most of them going on a pile to her left, a few going on a pile to her right. The room was stiflingly hot. Lynne tutted quietly and walked over to the window, to put her hand on the radiator. It was up full blast.

'Don't open the window; it makes the paper flutter about.'

'We need fresh air,' said Lynne, noticing that her

sister had on different trousers. So she had got changed on her own.

'What are you doing?' Lynne asked, keeping her voice calm.

'Looking for somebody I can resurrect. Expand my portfolio a bit. I'm not spending my whole career being famous for a bloody midge – sorry, Squidgy.'

Squidgy, squatting at the top of the table, ignored her.

'Why? You're always late with deadlines as it is; you'll be even worse if you take on more work. You have obligations now, Eve. You have to stop messing people about.' Lynne could hear the panic in her own voice.

'I'll leave that type of thing to the anoraks of the world. Like yourself. I have bigger ideas.'

Lynne didn't answer; she looked past her sister, out to the garden, *her* garden. The trees were bare, and the grass was gently spiked in white. Her bird table looked dirty and deserted. She remembered buying it the week Eve had gone to art school. It had also been the week Eve had discovered men. For the next few years she hadn't spent a single night in the family home until she was wheeled in after the accident and a lengthy stay in hospital; she had hardly gone out since. Yet during the years Eve had been away, while Lynne had nursed their mother through unimaginable pain, the garden had been her salvation, her respite – from the ever-permeating smell of disinfectant, from the debt collectors looking for Eve, from the world. Many an hour she had spent out here, sitting on the steps in the middle of winter – she loved the cold – in her big coat, sipping her Earl Grey. When had she stopped doing that? When their mother died? When Eve moved back? Or when she found out her mother had left the house to Eve? She shuddered as she recalled the shock of betrayal, of being dispossessed. Well, it wasn't going to happen twice.

Lynne picked up the proof of a single cover Eve had designed years ago for Rogan O'Neill. It would be worth a fortune now to a collector of Rogue memorabilia. It was a fine line-and-wash ink drawing of Rogan leaning against a tree, dressed in something long and black, his posture brooding. The tree-lined lane swept backwards, and each tree had a Rogan leaning against it, slowly losing his form, evolving himself into the musical notes that lay entwined against the final tree – all beautifully executed.

So talented, her sister, but so discontented.

She was the one who had the right to be discontented, Lynne thought; *she* was the one who'd had to abandon her own adult education halfway through, with no chance of going back to it, to nurse their mother. But all the excitement had been about Eve and her talent, never about Lynne and her eternal patience and sacrifice. It was always all about Eve. Lynne bit her lip, repressing the feeling of dread that churned in her stomach. Her life had been set on a single-track road to nowhere. And she didn't know how to get off.

Lynne noticed that her chessboard had been moved; the queen had fallen to the floor, undignified, face down. It had been her mother's chess set, and her mother's before her, made of pure ivory, dulled with age. Lynne sat down on a dining-room chair and tried to reach the queen, but she couldn't. Even pulling the chair right over to the sideboard, she couldn't reach it. She turned round to see if Eve had been watching, but her sister was engrossed in a drawing, head down, eyes screwed up. She knelt down and picked up the chess piece, caressing its familiar shape with her fingertips.

'Have you had any visitors today, Eve?' asked Lynne.

'No, who would visit me?' Eve sat up, wincing at a pain in her back. 'Oh, you know you're going out to Mother India tonight? You'll have to make your own way there, he says. Oh, try not to look so bloody miserable. You'd think somebody'd run over your favourite teddy bear.'

'Did he phone then?'

'Yes, didn't I say?'

Lynne said nothing but knocked the king over with the foot of the queen, and returned her to her rightful place.

Everything was just as it had always been; the plush white settee, the cream carpet, the Persian rug hanging on the wall. At the window an opulent swathe of white muslin coiled round its brass pole, the material cascading down and piling elegantly on the floor. The Japanese plant stand was still here with its four little bonsai trees. Anderson fingered the delicate branches, feeling them tough but supple. He remembered being here on a cold and rainy night, just like this, the last time he had seen his boss alive. If he closed his eyes he could imagine turning and seeing the ghost of Alan on the settee, in a suit he had slept in.

He moved over to the fire and stood with his back to it, letting its gentle heat caress the back of his legs. He felt his feet sink into the thick wool pile of the carpet. The bare lino floors of Partickhill Station were less than five minutes away but he could have been on another planet.

This was a house of consummate taste, luxurious but homely. The baby grand piano still stood in the corner, and there seemed to be more photographs on it than there used to be, more photographs of Alan and Helena together. He was touched to see, in a montage of colour, the faces of his own two children peering back at him, Peter wearing a policeman's helmet, his broad grin showing a loose front tooth at a precarious angle, and Claire posing like a twenties flapper, her chin on the point of her finger. It looked like the station Halloween party last year, but he could not remember the pictures being taken. This room, with the big settees and piles of foreign art books, would never see kids growing up. Not for the first time he wondered how Helena actually felt about being childless. How much more might she be feeling it now, with her husband gone, and her own life in limbo?

He turned to face the fire, and the Pre-Raphaelite-style self-portrait that hung over the fireplace. It had been Alan's favourite; he joked that he liked it because it didn't talk back. Helena was wearing a dress of deep-green pleated velvet, a sumptuous colour next to a sumptuous cleavage, and always that long tumbling auburn hair. The day after Alan was buried, she had cut it off.

Helena came in carrying a tray, kicking the door closed behind her. 'I've got no cream,' she said apologetically. 'Just milk, I'm afraid.'

'Fine,' he said. 'At home I'm lucky to get milk that's still in liquid form these days.' Anderson's mobile phone beeped.

'Are you in a hurry?' she paused, cafetière in mid-pour.

'No, no, I'm just getting text messages from people I don't know. A PC Smythe.' He read the message, raising an eyebrow before snapping the phone shut, then moved across to the settee and sat down, feeling it an imposition to stand in front of a fire that wasn't his. 'Still no word from the garage. You OK on the spare for now?'

She didn't ask: *So, why did you not just phone then?* Brenda would have, and more than once. She said,

'Yeah, I'll be fine. I'm not doing anything much, just going to the hospital, and I wasn't taking the car there anyway.' Helena handed him his coffee and for an instant Colin's fingers closed over hers.

Helena smiled tightly and pulled away. 'Did Peter like his outfit?'

'I've not been home yet, but I wanted to say thank you. I hope he gets a chance to wear it.'

'They're not thinking of cancelling the fair, are they?'

'No, nothing like that. I just can't see how to get him there. He'll be at his granny's cos Brenda is busy ...'

'Doing what?'

'Stuff?' Colin shrugged. 'That type of Christmas running around that blokes don't see the point of. And I can't commit to go out and get him as the case we're working on is opening up and ...'

'If you want him picked up, I'll get him in a taxi. We'll enjoy ourselves, maybe go for a Monkey Meal and more Cheeky Chips.' She smiled mischievously. 'Seriously, it would be fun, fill up my day a bit. I must say, I'm intrigued as to what Puff the Magic Dragon has to do with the Nativity.'

Colin sank back into the settee, warming his fingers round the coffee mug. 'They were all told to come up with an idea – and that was his.'

'You have to admire him, really,' said Helena. 'Improving on the greatest story ever told takes some doing. Puff has to beat Tiny Tears wrapped up in swaddling clothes and Matron's whippet dressed as a donkey.'

She crossed her legs, dangling a black moccasin from her toe, and asked, far too casually, 'How's the new DCI – Rebecca Quinn, isn't it? – settling in?'

'As any praying mantis settles in.'

Helena smiled, and sipped her coffee.

It would have been far too easy just to stay there, Anderson felt, talking about Alan with somebody who knew him, relaxing in a warm sea of shared memories. He would never have moved again. He stood up, before temptation got the better of him. 'Helena, if you want anything, just phone me,' he said. 'You have my mobile number.'

'Thanks, Colin.' She stood up, and walked to the door, then stopped. Placing her hand on his jacket she said, 'Really, let me know if you want me to look after Peter tomorrow. You looked after my husband often enough.' She did not move her hand; she stared at it, and her eyes filled with tears. She was looking at her wedding ring.

Luca Scott opened his eyes. He was lying in a warm bed, comfortable and content, but slightly confused. He was still here, in the happy place. Above him he could see, not the blue cracked ceiling of his own bedroom; this one was mottled grey and black. He could see patterns in it, of horses and Power Rangers, palm trees and dinosaurs. If he looked away, they moved. But he wasn't scared. He felt safer than he had ever felt in his life ... without his mum. He hoped she was OK. He had known what to do when his mum had a funny turn – leave her alone until she stopped wriggling then make her comfy. But back in the arcade she hadn't stopped and then she'd hit her head and blood came out and somebody started screaming at her. He'd found himself being pushed away, lost in a maze of legs. Then he was out in the street. He'd got very cold, standing in the gutter, getting his feet wet, not able to see anything and trying not to cry. And his nose started running and he couldn't find his hanky. His mum went mad when he wiped his nose on his sleeve.

But he was warm now, snug as a bug in a rug. He rumpled his duvet tight up round his neck and wondered what would happen today. Maybe another shot on the Game Boy, another go at running across the floor and bouncing off the mattresses that leaned against the walls, or maybe they could even make another slide. He was never allowed to do anything like that at home. Here he was even allowed to eat chips and drink Coke out the can, and yesterday he'd rubbed his salty, chippy fingers into the arms of the settee and nobody'd said a word. He'd been told to go to sleep when he liked as he was a big boy now. So, he'd stayed up really late and watched *Garfield* and eaten chocolate. He'd sat on the settee, wrapped in the special blanket that was his, and only his. Troy had been on the other side of the settee and they'd played Kerplunk and eaten Empire biscuits. Troy was a good laugh; he said words that Luca's mother would never allow him to say, but it was funny when Troy said them. And Troy was a tough boy. He refused the hugs so Luca thought it was best if he did as well so he could be tough too. But he'd beaten Troy on the computer game, squishing twice as many frogs as Troy had squished. That had made the day perfect.

He thought about getting up, but he was too snug and warm, though his nose was getting cold. He stuck hands and feet out from under the duvet in different combinations, to see how long he could keep them out before they froze off and then pulled them in to get warm and toasty again.

He thought about his mum. He'd been told she was better and being looked after in the hospital and that she wouldn't want him to worry. The duvet smelled like her, kind of soft and lemony. He pulled it over his head, wondering if they were putting enough milk in her tea in the hospital. She hated it too hot.

Maybe he could ask to go and visit her; she would like that. He thought about asking Santa for the game where he could play footie with the telly. He drifted off to sleep again, not hearing the gentle squeak as the door opened.

Anderson left Kirklee Terrace, crossed Great Western Road and turned immediately up Hyndland Road, slowly meandering the Astra through twists and turns up to Crown Avenue. At the far end, underneath the trees at number 3, he saw a dark-coloured Corsa, its interior light on, the sole occupant sipping from a steaming cup of takeaway coffee, head down, reading something.

Anderson cut his engine, killing the lights of the Astra. The occupant of the Corsa got out. PC Robert Smythe, Anderson presumed. His uniform was neat, hat on, ID visible, and he carried a weatherproof clipboard, not standard issue. This was somebody who cared. As he approached, Smythe stopped directly under the glare of the old-fashioned neon lamp. He looked about twelve.

'DI Anderson?'

Colin nodded.

'Can we have a chat, off the record? I want to show you something.' Smythe pulled his torch from his pocket, flicking it on and off, checking the batteries.

'It's getting late.'

'It's ten past eight; you'll be on your way by twenty past.'

'Fair enough. Do we have a problem?' asked Anderson.

'We have a huge problem,' said Smythe. 'Follow me.' He shone the beam under the sandstone archway, illuminating the lane.

Anderson followed, listening to Smythe relate the story of the search, his own experience and difficulties, hinting at the lack of commitment from some of his colleagues. He was careful not to accuse, but his meaning was clear: too much was being left to chance. Anderson followed the beam of the torch as it panned the whole row of back gates, then as it shone on the search report sheet. Less than thirty per cent completed. Smythe swept the torch up and down the line of derelict garages, then back to the clipboard – they weren't even on the list.

'I wouldn't be happy with that if my son was missing on a night like this.'

'Me neither,' Anderson agreed. 'I'll get on to it asap. You were right to bring it to my attention.'

Smythe turned the torch off, and they fell into an easy stride along the lane going back to the cars. 'I noticed the name Cotter was up on the board,' Smythe said. 'Is that the old dear who lives in the same building as Troy McEwen?'

Anderson nodded, careful not to show too much interest.

'Thought it rang a bell. Two weeks ago, maybe a bit more, a Miss Cotter, lives just over there, picked up a child on Byres Road,' he told Anderson. 'The kid was lost, and greetin' in the street, and Miss Cotter was just coming out the hospital. She got a passer-by to phone 999 on his mobile. By the time we got there, some man had tried to take the kid away, said he was his uncle. The old biddy caused a bit of a scene, saying she'd only hand him over to his mother. So, the uncle phoned the mother, who was searching the wrong end of Byres Road. Turned up frantic. She was a real dragon, not prepared to let the kid go. But once it was all sorted, she was just another little old lady with a bad chest. Is it the same one? Not a common name.'

'Certainly isn't,' said Anderson non-committally, glancing at the big houses on Crown Avenue. The lane between them lay hidden in darkness and shadows. These were houses used to keeping their secrets.

'She didn't sign, you know.' Lynne grabbed Douglas's hand. 'She simply left without signing the contract.'

Douglas discreetly pulled his hand free. 'Just Eve exerting her wee bit of power.' He popped another piece of poppadom into his mouth. 'Nobody round that table was in any doubt – she'll sign when the mood takes her. *Evelynne* Calloway has to be a single legal entity and she has to accept that you are the public face of it. One newspaper story about all her drug use and her abortions, and her career as a children's writer is over – she knows that perfectly well. Look at yesterday – you were so good on the radio; she'd never get through that without using the F-word or the C-word. The thing is with Eve, if you say yes, she'll say no for the hell of it. The docs say she needs to diet, so she eats more. She's not allowed to drink alcohol with her tablets, so she downs a whole bottle of red every night. It's her way of keeping control, her way of coping with being in the chair, I suppose.'

'And she blames you for being in that chair, Douglas. She's obsessed with it. And you.'

'She has a right to be bitter. She nearly died, Lynne.' He sipped his Kingfisher. 'You have to remember that. But at the end of the day, she knows I was only doing my job.'

'But does it not scare you, that she knows? The way she talks about you, calling you a ...' Lynne's mobile phone sounded. She looked at the caller ID; it was Eve. Typical – thirty minutes and she was already being recalled. *I need the toilet. I need a drink.* But this time with Douglas was too important.

His hand reached across the table to snap the phone shut. 'Leave her, Lynne; she has to learn to get on without you.' Their eyes met. Lynne nodded and slipped the phone back into her handbag. 'You know, I've been thinking more about your situation. You might be more comfortable being financially independent. You *could* make a mint out of Squidgy, but if you feel you can't rely on Eve, then you should utilize your only asset. You should do what Stella did – sell your house to me to divide into two, and buy back one flat for a good price. You'd get a nice flat and money in the bank. Then I'd sell the other one for an obscene profit.' He grinned.

Lynne nodded. 'It's certainly something to think about. Maybe we could do it as a joint venture. Our first joint venture?'

'Indeed.'

'Our little secret.' Lynne ran the pad of her finger

contemplatively round the rim of her glass. 'Eve has her little secrets, you know. She has visitors when I'm not there. She denies it, but I know. She's up to something.'

Douglas said, in a quiet voice, 'All the more reason why you should think about selling the house. Take control, Lynne.' Douglas put his onion-laden poppadom back on his plate. 'You've bailed her out at every stage of her life. I know you gave up your career to look after your mother, when Eve couldn't be trusted even to stay sober. Then just as you'd got your life back on track you had to give it all up again because Eve got smashed up. You've lost as much as she has. You can't even get out of the house without her wanting this and demanding that. But if you keep doing things for her, she'll never do them for herself. She's not a child, Lynne. It's time for both of you to move on.'

Lynne heard her mobile sound again. 'Difficult to move on when she weighs me down like an anchor.' She ignored its insistent tinny ring. Douglas didn't know that Eve owned the house. Eve held all the cards. 'She doesn't need me. She knows she can just walk away at any time.' She realized she had spoken out loud, but Douglas just put his forefinger to her lips.

'My dear Lynne, the one thing your sister cannot and will never be able to do, is *walk* away.'

15

Vik Mulholland slipped his arm from underneath Fran's neck, slowly and carefully so as not to disturb her. She shivered slightly in her sleep, murmured something he could not make out, then turned over, long dark hair spilling on to her bare shoulder. He pulled the duvet up to cover her, wondering how the hell she kept warm in this ice house. Easing himself up the bed, he rested his head on the wall behind him, missing the big leather headboard of his bed at home. He pulled the pillow from underneath him and placed it behind his head – he wasn't convinced this wall wasn't damp – and let his eyes adjust to the intermittent light that filtered through the thread-bare curtains, from the security lights in the back court he presumed; they would be flicking on and off with the movements of foxes, rats and God knew what else that lived out there.

Vik yawned, a yawn of tiredness and contentment. Sleep seemed to be an elusive friend these days. But to sleep was to lose some of the enchantment of the witching hours.

It was pain that kept Fran awake. He had noticed the little segmented box of capsules and tablets beside her bed – one to sleep, and four to control the pain that attacked her face with such ferocity that she would cry out with no warning, abruptly flinching as though she had been slapped. Tonight, he had held her as her face contorted and silent tears poured down her cheeks. Later, in answer to his questions, she had said it was like a red hot poker being thrust into your eye. And twisting. He imagined he understood. But for now she was asleep and at peace. And he was at peace, if not asleep. He had a big day tomorrow; he knew he had broken the back of the tampering case, and he was going to revel in his moment. DCI Quinn would be impressed, then a quiet word about his application for promotion would follow. He smiled to himself, imagining he heard a baby cry, a quiet mewling. The door opened slightly and Yoko the cat walked in, regarding him haughtily, and meowed before walking out again in distaste. Mulholland stuck two fingers up at it. Yes, he had the bed, he had the warm spot beside Fran, and the cat could bugger off.

Mulholland stretched. Looking round the room, he had a sense of impermanence, as if she were just passing through. Her bedroom looked like a room in one of the cheap hotels in the West End where they rent by the hour, just a bed, a carpet, a chest of drawers and small wardrobe. He thought about other girlfriends he had known, and all that female stuff they had lying about. Fran had none of that. He made a mental list of things to buy her for Christmas.

They were going to spend their first Christmas together, he was determined.

Eve was listening to the birds singing. It was a clear sunny evening, not warm, but the early spring light was spectacular. She heard the call of a collared dove in the tree above her and looked round for its mate — it would not be far away. She opened the car door and put her camera on the roof, thinking about the light and the fall of the shadow, looking at the silhouette of branches on the pale sky, wondering if she could line up a good picture. She lifted her camera, standing between the door and the body of the car, one foot on the running board, steadying her elbows on the roof, as she adjusted the focus. She waited until the collared dove turned its head and . . .

Eve woke in a sweat. She always woke up just before the impact, yet somehow the memory ran on. She could see herself turning at the noise of the car engine, too close. A shattered windscreen beyond it, and behind that — the face. The bit in between — the impact itself — was mercifully blank, but she would always remember that face, the mouth open in horror like a gaping fish, before the car was slammed into reverse and roared away, leaving her for dead. Yeah, she would remember that drunken bastard's face for ever.

Eve Calloway stared into the darkness. Being powerless was not for her; she had tried it once and it had left a bitter taste. Being the fat kid at school, having the shit kicked out of her, her lunch money stolen. And Lynne never ever standing up for her. So she'd learned to stand on her own two feet – she smiled at the irony.

Of course, the experts on spinal paralysis could all walk perfectly well. They were very good at telling her how to look after her skin, her feet and her bladder. At telling her to test bath water with her hand, not her feet. Never to sit close to the fire, as she'd smell her flesh burning before she would feel it. *And this is what gangrene smells like ... if you smell that, phone.* But the worst thing for Eve was being ignored. She could just about put up with spending her life staring into people's groins. In fact, when talking to Douglas Munro she liked to remind him that that was exactly what she was doing. If you considered the domino effect of causality, it was his bloody fault she was in the chair. That was good enough for her. And it wound up her bloody sister.

She decided to lie on the floor of the bedroom. The red figures on the clock glowed 11.55 p.m.

She was quite content, lying in the dark, watching the minutes flash past, listening to somebody park badly, kerbing the wheel, and to the hypnotic click of the central heating. She sighed in the silence, enjoying the wait. At least she wasn't lying under a pile of rubble in Pakistan for the third freezing night running, and she wasn't some wee kid who had been abducted. She was warm and comfortable, and the bits that weren't comfortable were numb.

She opened her eyes, allowing herself a little shuffle for comfort. Lynne had ignored her phone calls. So, she must be made to feel guilty. Which meant Eve had to stay awake and be shouting for help when Lynne came in. Lynne would call on the gold-digger for help, as Eve was way too heavy for Lynne to lift on her own. A whole tin of Jaffa cakes … Eve sniggered to herself. She couldn't feel her left buttock but sensed that the floor was pressing into it, right where her ulcer had been. It had taken seven months of some graduate from the Eva Braun School of Nursing poking at her arse to get that healed, the skin coming off in layers with the plasters. It was still as thin as parchment, and puckered at the healthy edges as if pulled far too tight in the middle. She could imagine it opening up again like the San Andreas Fault. She began to sing 'These Boots Are Made For Walkin''. Or not, as the case may be. The clock had just flashed 12.15 when she heard the Audi pull up, bloody Céline Dion on the car stereo. The engine was turned off. It was 12.27 when she heard the snick of the gate, then the click of Lynne's kitten heels on the pavement, a little conversation, then the rattle of the door, open, shut, the bolt ramming home. Eve started to roll around, contorting her body into the most uncomfortable-looking position she could manage, and then, only then, did she start shouting for help.

Friday, 22 December

16

It was eight thirty in the morning, still dark and the day looked as though it wasn't going to make much of an effort to get any lighter. Fine flakes of snow danced in the air and whipped the faces of the unwary, stinging warm flesh and bringing tears to unprotected eyes. The temperature outside was minus two, and it wasn't much warmer in the station. The non-accidental meeting in the corridor between DCI Rebecca Quinn and DI Colin Anderson only served to drop the temperature even further.

Anderson was polite, but firm. He blocked her way, forcing her to a halt. 'I want a word with you.'

'I'm busy, DI Anderson, and we have a meeting, now. There is a time and a place ...'

'Yes, and it's here and now. This meeting is about the cyanide, isn't it? Not about the boys?'

DCI Quinn bit her lip but didn't answer.

'The search teams are in disarray and nobody cares, nobody is checking, least of all you, which makes me think that you are, to put it politely, merely going through the motions on one case. All the intelligent resources are going to the other. So, what's going on?'

'DI Anderson, I can appreciate your point. But five

people have died from cyanide poisoning, the source of which has not yet been confirmed. Five people. If that was a series of murders, with visible blood and guts, we would not be standing here having this conversation, would we? Just because the method is subtle does not mean they are any less dead; it does not mean the victims or their families suffered any less.' She hissed the last words under her breath as a cleaner walked by. 'As for the children, we are following leads, you know that.'

'What leads?'

'Leads. The biggest lead we have is being followed up, I assure you. We are doing everything we can. But *you* are not doing it.'

'So, who is?'

Quinn betrayed herself by a little sideways glance through the glass wall of her office. 'I need to go.' She walked away, sidestepping him, her heels clicking efficiently on the lino.

'It's difficult to run two parallel enquiries. It could be dangerous. If your big lead is wrong, if you get found out ...' Quinn stopped in her tracks and turned. 'We need to be squeaky clean on this – you said so yourself.'

'And if my hands are tied?'

'Untie them. Give me PC Smythe.'

'PC Smythe? Don't know him.'

'So, you won't miss him. And give me Wyngate for the IT. Give me the original search team back. A vehicle on site. A civilian who knows their way around a Home Office database. Let me do it properly.'

Quinn looked thoughtful.

Anderson pressed the point. 'Then if the shit hits the fan, it won't land on us. Not on our shift.'

Quinn nodded slowly. 'OK.' And turned away.

Anderson followed the line of her earlier glance. DS Littlewood was on the phone, eyes closed, his thumb and forefinger pinching the bridge of his nose. He looked as though he had been there all night and Anderson had no reason to believe otherwise. Littlewood's computer was locked; he was working on his own . . . Then Anderson remembered Littlewood's years on Vice.

The dirty squad.

Paedophiles.

Anderson leaned back against the wall and cursed.

'Right, you lot, important developments.' DCI Quinn tapped the edge of a file against the edge of the desk, waiting for silence. 'Can we have some more lights please?' She waited until the fluorescent strips flickered into life with their low, steady hum. 'Right, Lewis, do you want to take them through this? The tampering?'

Almost as one, the squad shifted a little in their seats. Costello looked at Anderson who was staring out of the window, looking at the dark clouds gathering, his thoughts miles away. He wasn't paying one bit of attention. He wasn't pointing out this was hers ... *her* investigation ...

Lewis handed a set of photographs to Mulholland, and gestured to a gap that had been cleared on the wall.

'The first victim that we found was Barbara Cummings. She worked up at Rowanhill Library. She was forty-six, divorced, with three kids who all stayed at home. She worked full-time and travelled every day by public transport, which took her up Byres Road. She collapsed at home on Saturday, 9th December, sometime in the afternoon. There was nobody in the house at the time. She was found dead in her armchair. The PM report was unremarkable, the slight red flush was noted but ascribed to her previous alcohol dependency. No Toxicology report was requested, so she was cremated exactly one week later. She was in the habit of using over-the-counter medication for the headaches she put down to eye strain, and in the past she had used a tablet called Headeze. She shopped at Waldo for odds and ends that she could carry on the bus.'

Mulholland hung up a photograph of a woman, dark-haired, with a wide smile showing very uneven teeth.

Costello thought she looked familiar. Rowanhill Library? She thought she had spoken to her, maybe earlier in the year. There'd been a vandalism problem up at the library, and she remembered a small, broad woman with thick glasses and quiet, librarian shoes. Yes, it was definitely her. The photograph had a new hairdo but it was definitely the same woman.

'Chronologically, however, the first was Duncan Thompson, who lived up in Novar Drive.' Another photo went up – a young man with a wide smile, number one haircut, and a small stud in his nose. 'He was twenty-eight, worked at the Department of Work and Pensions or whatever it's called these days. He was found dead in his bed on the evening of Monday, 4th December. He had been last seen at his office Christmas night out at the Marriott on the Saturday night, where he had got very drunk. He didn't make it to work on the Monday. So, a colleague tracked down his sister, who called round and found him dead. He had choked on his own vomit sometime on the Sunday morning. That seemed like a pretty clear cause of death, so – again – no Tox report was done. The sister said that he'd had a packet of Headeze on the worktop beside his kettle and a glass of water beside the bed, as you would if you were expecting a monumental hangover, but neither item is still around to be examined. He was buried on Friday, 8th December.'

Lewis turned to another photograph. 'Moira McCulloch collapsed at her mother's flat, and died in the ambulance on the way to the Western. There was some cause of doubt re the death certificate – it was noted she was red-faced with blue fingertips and extremities, and her brain was very swollen. All that might point to cyanide. However, because of the impossibility of establishing cause of death, her body is still available for testing. We've asked for a Tox report to be done as a matter of some urgency, and we're awaiting results.

'John Campbell and Sarah McGuire, we are familiar with. And lastly, Nessie Faulkner.' Mulholland pinned up his last picture; a small grey-haired lady, with small round glasses under a white bowling hat, smiling for the camera in triumph. She looked like everybody's favourite granny. 'We know from her son that she definitely did purchase Headeze capsules, probably on Wednesday, 13th December, from Waldo in Byres Road.'

Costello noticed that Lewis hadn't acknowledged Wyngate or Anderson for their hard work. The hyena was reverting to type. She decided to step in.

'I've had an e-mail from Malin Andersson, two s's. She was the nurse who was on duty while Lars Lundeberg was in hospital. Being Swedish herself she got to know quite a few of his visitors during his five-day hospital stay. She did a bit of asking around for me. Well, Lars's flatmate Shona remembers giving him a Headeze for a hangover. He was always on the scrounge for them, apparently. As you know, the flat is at Peel Street, and Shona shops at Waldo. Over and out.'

'Thank you for that, Costello,' Lewis said, the words almost choking her.

'Well, we are a team,' Costello smiled sweetly.

'There's no widespread pattern, no other cases reported by the Poison Unit,' Lewis resumed, almost as though she regarded Costello's information as an unwelcome interruption. 'All products have been removed from shelves nationwide and a recall put out: *Do not use under any circumstances.* As yet, we can't find anybody who is *that* pissed off with that branch of Waldo. Or indeed, any branch of Waldo. In the meantime anybody admitted to A&E with symptoms of high colour and difficulty in breathing will get red-flagged on arrival – oxygen, clothes off, skin washed, stomach pumped, all to slow absorption, because the test can take longer than the cyanide takes to kill you.' She turned to Mulholland. 'Vik? Any news?'

Mulholland smiled, like the cat that got the cream. 'Well, listen to this. The obvious place is the Uni, but as there are no students in at the moment the labs were quick to tell me no cyanide has gone missing. They assured me their systems are foolproof. Even so, they're sending us a list of students and staff who have access, just in case somebody has approached them, in the pub – you know the kind of thing.'

Quinn pressed her hands to pursed lips as though praying. 'So far, so good. What else?'

'There are three chemical plants within a thirty-mile radius that use sodium and potassium cyanide,' Mulholland resumed. 'But again, it's carefully regulated. They have to record any loss, and there's been no spillage to account for the amount our tamperer would have required. I've thought about printers' labs, et cetera, but the guy at the Poison Unit says that's not the right stuff.'

'Schools don't use it?'

'No, ma'am; too risky, apparently.' He flipped over a page in his notebook, checking he had missed nothing, then smiled again, this time like the cat that got the cream of the cat next door as well. 'Then I tried the internet, and within four minutes I could have bought any amount from the States, and it would have been here within the week. And as this type of criminal is organized and patient, the psychology of waiting wouldn't be an issue.'

Quinn looked at him. 'And?'

'Texas. The fourth one down was St Andrew's Pharmaceuticals, so I thought I'd try them first – the name, you know ...'

'And?'

'And they acknowledged an order from Scotland – a recent order – but refused to go any further without authorization.'

'I'll get clearance. Christ – Texas! *Texas!* Do they really have such lax drug laws? Wyngate, you get a list of all companies that sell on the net, and start asking if any of them have had a recent enquiry from Scotland. If there was a purchase made, it would be by credit card and therefore traceable. Get on to it. And get back to me within twenty-four hours.'

'There's a time difference,' said Wyngate cautiously.

'Twenty-four hours is twenty-four hours; it doesn't matter which side of the bloody Atlantic you're on. Tomorrow, nine thirty, get to it. I'll give you both the clearance you need to obtain the bank card details.'

The laser eyes of DCI Rebecca Quinn fired round the room. 'I don't need to tell you how carefully we are going to have to play this.' She glanced at her watch. 'I have a meeting with Peter Moss of Waldo at ten and I'm requesting advice from the Serious Crime Squad – the next logical step is a blackmail demand, and we're not equipped to deal with that. Forensics are awaiting the recovered boxes of tampered capsules from Sarah McGuire's place, so if they can be brought to my desk asap, Irvine . . .?'

Everybody turned to Irvine, who went very red.

'But these things are tamper-proof, surely,' said Anderson, turning away from the window. 'This isn't the first scare like this. Tylenol? The baby food tampering?'

'One thing this is *not* is a scare, DI Anderson.' DCI Quinn snapped. 'Malicious product tampering is terrorism. It involves lots of innocent victims. And it only takes one bozo to get lucky once, don't forget that. Costello and Lewis, I want you to follow the cyanide once Mulholland gets his information clarified.' The team looked at each other, immediately wrong-footed. 'Problems? No? Good! Costello, you've been quiet for too long. Have you anything else to add?'

Undeterred by the note of sarcasm in Quinn's voice, Costello seized the moment. 'DI Anderson is right – these should be tamper-proof,' she said. 'But I spent some time yesterday figuring out what I would do if I were a tamperer. Shall I show you?' Everyone crowded round, happy to witness something concrete. She pulled out the pack of painkillers Agnes had given her. 'So, the tamperer buys two boxes, takes them home, peels off the safety tab with a razor blade, and removes the bubble pack.'

She then, to an engrossed audience, demonstrated how to lift the foil from the plastic strip. She tipped the red and white capsule into her hand, where she pulled it apart, spilling the white powder into the cup of her palm. 'I had a go at re-filling a capsule with salt in the canteen, and it was almost impossible to get the two halves back together without creating a dent or squashing the edge. But if you warm one in the palm of your hand, and put the other half in the fridge, it's a lot easier. After that, all you do is reverse the process to package it up again. And do some inverse shoplifting. *And* ...' Costello hurried on as though afraid someone would interrupt her, '... Karen McGuire was doing a history project on the fall of the Third Reich. The Nazis used cyanide as a method of suicide, and there were books about the war in the house. That makes me very suspicious of that family.'

'So, is the mother on the suspect list for definite?'

asked Anderson, looking at his notes. 'Bloody stupid of her to take it herself.'

'If you crunch a whole capsule between your teeth, death is quite quick,' Costello repeated patiently. 'But if you take a smaller dose on a full stomach, absorption is slower. She knew her daughter was in the house, she knew she was safe.'

'So,' said Quinn, taking the floor again, 'if you are right, do we think the others were killed at random to sidetrack us?'

'Could be. But I'd say the money motive is too compelling to pass over,' said Costello with conviction. 'Sarah is dead keen to find out how much of her inheritance is left undamaged. She inherits all four flats, you know . . .'

'Costello,' Quinn cut in. 'Just watch your attitude. Not every lady who lunches is a patricidal sociopath.'

'I'm serious!'

'That's what worries me.'

A nervous-looking Gail Irvine crept over with the bagged and tagged Headeze from Sarah McGuire's house. Quinn gave the package a cursory glance and passed it back to be sent to Forensics. She looked tired, almost defeated, then she took a deep breath and tapped her pen in the palm of her hand. 'But if money really is the motive here, don't let us forget Waldo's management team; who is in financial difficulty, whose ex-wife is in debt . . .? We'll put Irvine on that. Whatever dirt you can find, Irvine, dig it out.' Quinn straightened, and her voice became brisk once more. 'Right, we'll run with both these: the targeting of Waldo by those unknown, and the possibility that someone – possibly Sarah McGuire …' she nodded some kind of *well done* at Costello, '… but possibly someone else, is attempting to hide one murder among several.'

'What about video footage?' asked Anderson. 'Any from the store?'

'Only folk buying their groceries,' said Quinn. She dusted one hand against the other. 'Might be worth another look once we have a suspect we can recognize.'

Lewis had been fiddling with some tablets of her own. 'Look at my Piriton; it's impossible to tamper with this.'

'Well, you'll be all right then, won't you?' Costello muttered. 'Pity.'

'Fuckin' child molesters, should be strung up by the balls,' Littlewood grunted as he bumped into Anderson's desk for the third time.

He was not a quick-witted man. He was an old-school detective, big and brusque, and being kept at the station made him feel caged. He was pacing up and down, muttering obscenities and scratching every part of his anatomy.

Anderson got the feeling Littlewood was hanging around for a reason, but he could wait. His phone rang, showing his home number; he ignored it. 'If you have to keep fiddling with yourself, could you go and do it somewhere else? I can do without the distraction. Can you believe this – Quinn has just detailed me to find some staff to go through the hundreds of crank calls we are about to receive because word has got out about that bastard O'Neill putting up £100,000 reward money for information leading to the safe return of these boys. £50,000 each! And now – can you believe *this* – I am supposed to go up there and say thanks to the nice man.'

Littlewood stopped pacing. 'It's not been confirmed, so who put the word out? I thought we'd put the brakes on that.'

'Wouldn't put it past his PR people to leak it. It'll look really bad if HQ doesn't allow it. Rumour of a fiver is enough to get some folk selling their granny.'

Littlewood leaned over Anderson's desk, gnarled nicotine-stained fingers splayed wide. 'So, you're going out to see Rogan O'Neill today,' he said quietly.

'I just said so, didn't I?'

'You and Costello are going to keep him sweet so he'll stay in line about the reward.' Littlewood leaned over, talking right in Anderson's ear. 'And you've to give him a big thank you for the security for this afternoon.'

'How do you know all this?'

'It's my business to know.'

Anderson could smell the stale tobacco on his skin, see the nicotine-stained hairs in his nose. 'And? Spill, Littlewood, I'm not daft.'

'Officially, he's just doing an appeal, and donating money to the cause. Unofficially, I have a plan of my own.' Littlewood shrugged. 'Costello, come here, will you? I want you to ask O'Neill when he got here – and find out when his crew arrived.'

She came over, and folded her arms sulkily when he told her where she and Anderson were going.

'If you meet *her*, the blonde twiglet, make friends and be nice,' said Littlewood.

'Why?'

'Just do it. Do the casual chit chat. Find out who's with them and why, find out whether Rogan carries the same crew – sound engineers, roadies – with him all the time, especially Dec Slater and Jinky Jones. Be nice to him too – good cop, inquisitive cop, act infatuated, flatter him – you know how to do that.'

'I'll tell him I was his tambourine girl once.' She ignored Anderson's wry smirk. 'More than once, actually. Oh, yes! I was plucked from the audience and sat on his chair and serenaded.'

'By a bald aging sex machine? I thought that whole tambourine thing was a ploy to get into the knickers of the best-looking chick in the audience,' growled Littlewood. 'And you were the best he could do?'

Costello smiled a saccharine smile.

Anderson raised his eyebrows. 'So, what does it mean, that bloody song? The best bit is that husky "Goodnight". I've heard it twice at funerals ... puts a tingle down my spine every time.'

'What I want to know, Costello,' said Littlewood, leaning across the desk, 'is – did you shag him as well?'

'Well, you'll never know the answer to that, will you?' said Costello. And she turned away, humming: *Say hello to the tambourine girl.*

Walking into the Glasgow Hilton, Colin Anderson realized he was angry – angry at Lewis and Irvine, angry at Quinn, at the job, at Brenda. Angry at Santa and the season of goodwill. He and Costello had walked round to Rogan's hotel from the station, the roads being closed due to the fair and Rogan's personal appearance. He was relieved he had Costello with him. She was happy to walk in silence; she didn't need to yabber on all the time. Anderson thanked God he hadn't been sent out with Kate Lewis; he would have strangled her by now.

Just before they walked into the hotel foyer he said, 'Do something for me, Costello? Brenda's busy, and Helena offered to pick up Peter and take him to the fair. Could you ring her and say I'm taking her up on it? Voice an opinion and you're dead.'

'Fine, boss,' said Costello, barely concealing an impish smirk.

In the lift, they stood in silence, watching the green light climb up the floors. Costello waited until the lift door slid open. 'Colin? Is that a CD in your pocket or are you just pleased to see Rogan?'

'Leave it,' said Anderson out of the side of his

mouth as they both showed their warrant cards to the beautifully groomed receptionist.

Anderson straightened his tie, and patted the jacket pocket that held the Rogan O'Neill's *Greatest Hits* CD set Vik Mulholland had given him for Rogan to sign. Vik had been seriously annoyed when he heard about the interview, and that he wasn't going.

Costello had imagined Rogan O'Neill dark and tanned, greying a little at the temples, walking around his luxury suite in the Hilton wearing a thick white towelling robe, with hot and cold running champagne on tap. Instead, he was sitting in an armchair wearing a blue crumpled tracksuit and eating an orange, his white stubby thumbs waggling the segments apart. His single earring, the star-shaped pinkie ring, the gold chain round his neck, were the same as always, and although he was starting to look his age, whatever age he was, he was still desperately handsome.

'Oh heck, it's the polis,' he said in broad Glaswegian, genuinely pleased to see them because he was so bored. And he seemed to be having trouble with his podiatrist, who was balancing his foot on a small surgical plinth.

'If it's a bad time, we'll wait outside,' said Costello, somehow uncomfortable with the idea of interviewing her hero while he got his toenails cut.

The podiatrist, kneeling at Rogan's feet, held up a scalpel and steadied the sole of his foot in a latex-gloved hand. She glared at him. 'Stay still!'

'You two have a wee seat and watch. This silly bint is trying to slice my toes off and if she's going to commit grievous bodily, I want witnesses.'

The podiatrist rolled her eyes in Costello's direction. 'If I was at all humanitarian, it would be your vocal cords I'd slice.'

Rogan pointed at her. 'You keep your eyes on the job, hen. I have to use my toes to count, you know.'

'I remember,' said the podiatrist. 'I was at school with you.'

Rogan shoved a segment of orange in his mouth sideways and pulled his lips back in an orange smile. 'Bloody ages since anybody even half interesting came to talk to me.'

'Cheers,' replied the podiatrist, with the gentle sarcasm of an old friend.

Costello had never been in the main suite in the Hilton, with its leather settees and huge white curtains that cascaded to the floor. Matching Osprey luggage was strewn everywhere, trunks and cases and bags, most of them open and rummaged through. In the corner stood a computer, the only thing in the room that was set up with any degree of permanence.

'Two things I wanted to say,' Rogan announced, getting straight down to business. 'One: I'm putting up a reward about these two missing kids – a reward for each, for their safe return.'

'While we are grateful,' said Anderson carefully, 'it's not always a help. It can bring a lot of pranksters and timewasters out the woodwork. And there are rules, regulations . . .'

'Fuck 'em. It'll help, and it's a done deal officially now. You're the first to know. My secretary got a fax from Stewart Street.'

Anderson looked nonplussed. 'So, excuse me for asking, did your publicity machine leak it before that? Just to get the jump on it?'

Rogan shook his head. 'No, but if it hadn't been agreed, I would have gone public with it anyway. Looks like one of your lot blabbed,' he added in mock innocence.

'Seems so, since the press are aware of it.'

'Well they're not aware of the fact I'll double it if another kid goes missing. Money is the only language some folk speak.' Rogan looked at him, carefully. 'Sorry, son, didn't catch your name.'

'DI Anderson.'

'We didn't have coppers like you when I was a wee lad. They were big blokes, took you up a close and kicked yer arse, told yer dad, and if you were really unlucky they told yer mam and ye got yer arse kicked again. Anyway, you can put up with a few timewasters if it gets the kids back a bit quicker. Somebody knows where these wee guys are, and the amount I'll put up will entice them out, believe me, pal. And two: I'm opening this thing at the school later. See that bit of paper over there?' Costello got up and picked up from the walnut sideboard some sheets of A4, headed *Arm-Strong Security*. 'Just thought

I'd let the police know what security I was bringing with me.'

'Surely all this was cleared with the community police when you agreed to open the fair?' asked Costello.

'That was then, this is now. I'm offering to foot the bill for a whole load of extras. That wee midgie guy is coming along, isn't he?'

'I believe so.'

'That'll draw the kids. And I'm not having any more taken. Do you know, they've a three-foot midge on the front of the first relief truck, so instead of switching on the Christmas lights, I'm turning on a midge ... not a sexual experience I've had in the past.' He paused, looking at Costello as if he'd just noticed her. 'Do I know you from somewhere, pet?' he asked.

'I was a fan in the old days,' said Costello, sneaking a look at the floor plan. 'This is very generous of you, Mr O'Neill. Security like this is not cheap.' She didn't know a lot about it but it looked comprehensive.

'Ma pals call me Rogue. No probs; I know how short-staffed you guys are with this illness and it being Christmas an' all. Where you from, hen?' he asked Costello.

'Cardonald,' said Costello.

'And you were a fan, you say?'

'I've still got the video of the Blackfriars concert.'

'Remind me?' said Rogan, circling his forefinger in the air.

'It was filmed by one of your fans. You might remember him – he was a crazy guy who turned from heroin to being a Jehovah's Witness in a week. He asked you not to swear during your set.'

'And then went on to sell double glazing?'

'That's him,' agreed Costello.

'Aye, ah know who you mean, hen. He used to copy the videos and flog them for a couple of quid. He gave us the dosh – we needed it in those days.'

'I know, I had to buy it, four times over. Lucky me,' said the podiatrist dryly.

Rogan looked at Costello, as if seeing her in a new light. 'Were you one of my tambourine girls?' he asked her, smiling flirtatiously.

Anderson smirked.

'Yes, I was.' She coloured slightly.

'One of the onstage ones, or one of the ones in the back of the van?' Rogan laughed. 'Don't answer that – we only chose the lookers,' he informed Anderson. 'You know, I never think of them as having grown up.'

'I was only sixteen at the time, if that.'

'Wouldn't have bothered him,' said the podiatrist. 'He only takes women from the audience who are half his age – well, a third his age these days, even a quarter if he's in some American states.' The podiatrist had a wee smile to herself.

Rogan winked at Costello. 'Well, you must have been a stunner in your day, hen.' He turned to Anderson. 'And that's the problem; they come out the woodwork twenty years later and spill to the tabloids.' He brandished a newspaper with a blaring headline: *My three-in-a-bed romp with Rogue*. Rogan glanced at it again and looked pleased.

Costello dived in, scenting revenge. 'Oh, DI Anderson has a CD for you to sign. For a *friend*.'

Rogan reached into his pocket for a pen. 'Which one is it you have, son?'

DI Colin Anderson blushed at being called son again. 'Your gift-boxed CD collection. And it's not for a friend, it's for a colleague's girlfriend. Could you sign it "To Fran"?'

'Aye, nae probs. Is she good-looking?'

'Just remember, Rogue, you're supposed to be a sensible father now. You're saving kids these days, not shagging them,' said the podiatrist. 'Despite what it says in the papers.'

'Wish I had the bloody energy. Have you taken a trip down to Cardonald recently ...? Sorry, pet, what was your name?'

'Costello.'

'You have a first name?' Rogan winked winningly.

'Detective Sergeant.' She winked back, and refused to look at Anderson. She was glad when the door from the adjoining room opened.

Even with her face devoid of make-up and her hair pulled back into a scrunchie, spiking like a blonde cactus, Lauren McCrae was stunning.

'Hi,' she said, her broad smile showing incredibly white and even teeth. Anderson nearly fell off his seat, and even Costello found it difficult to keep her eyes off her.

'Get some drinks out the cabinet there, sweetheart,' Rogan ordered. 'I'll have a lager.'

'Honey, you're doing an appearance later. You can have a Coke.'

Rogan ignored that. 'Oh, and put it in a glass for me.'

'What did your last slave die of?' asked the podiatrist.

'Blood poisoning, and you watch what you're doing with that scalpel.'

'Oh, honey, you just be quiet now.' The honey-dripped Canadian voice was gentle.

'So how do you find Scotland, Miss McCrae?' asked Anderson.

'She got off the fucking plane and there it was! Jesus, you polis can be thick.'

'I'm finding Scot Land just fine,' Lauren put in smoothly. 'It's maybe a little rainy, but I guess it's fine.' She shot a look at Costello, smiled shyly and looked away.

'She's from Toronto,' Rogan said through a mouthful of orange. 'They get cold, they get wet, but they don't do cold and wet together.'

'So, when did you fly in?' asked Costello. *Make friends, be nice . . .*

Lauren smiled at her. 'God, did you see the state my skin was in? You rehydrate and rehydrate, but it still shows.'

Costello nodded in wry sympathy, noting her question hadn't actually been answered.

Lauren handed Rogan his Coke, and her hand shook slightly. She even moved, sinuous and silent, like a nervous racehorse.

Nervous? Scared? Wary ... Costello searched for the right word.

The podiatrist picked up something that looked like an iron file.

'In my day I'd have used that tae break out of Barlinnie Prison.' Then Rogan remembered who he was talking to. 'Not that I've ever been there – much.'

Costello tried again.

'Do you still carry the same road crew with you as you did back then?' she enquired. 'Or did you leave them somewhere along the way?' Costello was aware of Anderson looking at her.

Maybe it was her imagination, but Rogan paused before answering, as if thinking about what he was going to say. 'No, the boys are still with me. We met when we were eight, and we're still together ... and that's not PR, that's the truth. See, I don't like being surrounded by yes men, and those two will always tell me where to go. Jinky Jones and Dec Slater. We stick together.'

'Ain't that the truth!' Lauren sighed, with a degree of bitterness that Costello didn't miss. And there was something else – a small prickle in her posture, a little lie somewhere. 'He even sent them over here last week, so they could see the castle before us. They'll end up *living* with us. Again.' She didn't sound over-joyed.

'And they're here with you now?' Costello probed.

'Yeah, we move, they move. Same as for ever,' said Lauren, spanning her fingers and examining her perfect nails.

Rogan O'Neill turned his head quickly, his jovial manner gone. The podiatrist halted the scalpel in mid-scrape.

'Lauren is pregnant. I want my son born on Scottish soil, so we're buying a castle. Look, you get back to your bosses, and tell them I'll pay for *all* the security at the fair, and the sky's the limit. You just send me the bill. I'm not having any more wee kids nicked while they're waiting for Santa.' Their dismissal couldn't have been more obvious.

'We'll pass that on to our superiors. And we thank you for all your help.' Costello walked towards the door, and Anderson followed.

'Ouch!' Rogan pulled his foot back quickly; a small bubble of red was growing on his big toe.

'Oh, Rogan, I *am* sorry.'

17

Peter Anderson was excited. He had waited in the queue that snaked round the railings of Rowanhill Primary School for a full twenty minutes. Then he had carefully handed over a pound coin from his own cold hand into Santa's, whispering, 'A computer game, and a dragon jigsaw. And a dog. And if I can't have a dog, then can I have a goldfish?' Then he thought for a moment and added, 'Thank you, Santa.'

Santa, who bore a striking semblance to Alan Arnett, chairman of Partickhill tenants' association, nodded and said hello to Helena McAlpine. He ruffled Peter's hair, extracting a promise of good behaviour till Christmas Day at least.

The Rowanhill School Christmas Fair in aid of Andy's Appeal was going well. Braziers were burning brightly round the playground gates, and four uniformed coppers, tinsel round their necks and Squidgys on their helmets, danced from one foot to the other to keep warm, toasting gloved fingers over the flames. Parents stood about in the semi-darkness drinking mulled wine out of polystyrene cups. Arm-Strong Security was displaying a not-so-discreet presence. Rogan O'Neill was in the school building and, even though it was starting to snow, the queue for him to sign his new CD was snaking out of the gym hall and into the playground. Every time another hundred pounds was raised for the appeal, another helium balloon was added to a tree of helium balloons, each addition punctuated by a whoop from the crowd. Among the Santas and the snow-men, huge black and white photographs of freezing orphaned Pakistani children reminded everybody exactly why they were there.

Both Evelynne Calloway and Rogan O'Neill were making personal appearances. Evelynne, a charmless thin blonde stick of a woman, dressed in a long black coat three sizes too big for her, had arrived to open the fair in an open-topped bus bedecked with an inflatable Squidgy McMidge, and had given away a thousand Squidgys to adorn the tops of Christmas trees, as well as donating an original signed drawing of him for the auction. The auction was to start at four o'clock, with Rogan O'Neill at the micro-phone, and – as the top prize – a VIP box for his fund-raising Hogmanay concert at Hampden Park. The original concert dates had been sold out for a whole year, and rumour said the bidding was already standing at over six grand. Out in the street stood a huge relief truck donated by a local firm of haulage contractors keen to get their name in the papers. The plastic midge on the windscreen, legs akimbo as if it had been splattered in a high-impact collision, flashed bright red and blue as the volunteers on board accepted shoebox after shoebox for the relief effort. Somebody had threaded some tinsel through the handles at the back of the truck, and, like autumn leaves gathering in a sheltered corner, the van had acquired a festive adornment of tinsel, baubles and glitter.

There was the usual array of Christmas lucky dips and face painting, bring and buys, tombolas and raffles, and everywhere the smell of frying onions from the hotdog stand. It was busy, and that was the main thing.

But in the air hung the ever-present feeling of menace from an unseen enemy. Parents held their children a little closer, watchful for any strangers who came too near, and lots of children were wearing light-blue rubber armbands with a fluorescent strip, so they would not forget Luca and Troy. And everywhere, on every wall, on every door, were posters with photographs and a grim caption: *Have you seen these boys?*

Inside the hall, Evelynne Calloway sat signing Squidgy postcards and flick books, smiling for the cameras, while an assistant handed her copies and presented children to her as if she were the Queen.

In the corner behind her sat a grossly fat, squat woman in a wheelchair, her auburn hair curled under a woollen hat, tree-trunk legs wrapped in a red tartan rug. She was eating her way through a cheeseburger – the torn papers on her lap showed that it wasn't her first – and she looked as miserable as sin. She finished her cheeseburger and picked up a Squidgy McMidge balloon from her lap. She blew into it and then let the air out slowly, doing a very good impersonation of a flatulent elephant. She drew a few dark looks from the parents in the baked potato queue, but some of the children round her giggled, and she laughed, pulling her woolly hat down over her face.

Wandering round with Peter's hand held tight in hers, Helena was glad of the comfort. She had been pathetically grateful when DS Costello had phoned, short and to the point as usual. Anderson was the most senior officer at the station, so he couldn't leave. Brenda was already up in Glasgow with the car, finally getting away from the kids to do the Christmas shopping. Could Mrs McAlpine pick Peter up from his granny? Now Helena was being pulled around by a bundle of boundless fun and nonsense dressed in a dragon suit.

Out in the playground, it was getting dark, and the flames from the braziers cast dark shadows into the corners. The spotlights were starting to flicker into life.

Peter started stomping impatiently, wanting to know where his dad was. But Helena had no idea. Colin could be anywhere – walking round the perimeter fence, seeing how the troops on the ground were doing, checking that the makeshift communication system was up to the job. That's what Alan would have been doing. Her eyes rested on a boy on his own, eating a baked potato from a polystyrene bowl. *On his own.* The boy was transfixed by the coloured lights on the illuminated snowman and the sequence of on-off, on-off flashes.

Helena glanced quickly round. She didn't want to speak to the grotesquely fat woman in the wheel-chair, who already had a little audience for her theatre of rude noises. She pulled out her phone and called Colin's mobile, watching the boy all the time until Colin answered and barked instructions to a third party. A uniform in a Santa hat appeared from nowhere and took the boy by the hand. The uniform gave Helena a slight wave. *Situation under control.*

'Where are you?' Colin asked. 'I'll come down in a minute.'

'I'm about to be attacked by a six-foot penguin,' Helena answered.

'Be there in a mo.'

'Pat the Penguin's here!' shouted Peter. 'Auntie Helena! It's Pat the Penguin!'

'Oh, lovely,' said Helena, with little enthusiasm.

'Can I have my photo taken with him?' Peter slipped from her grasp and ran through the crowd to the six-foot penguin. The community police, and Willie McCaffrey who was annually incarcerated in the mouldy penguin suit, were known for their intolerance of anyone under four feet tall, but now the penguin was looking nervous, and it moved quickly – followed by the police display team's Alsatian, Bruno, which was licking its lips. The dog was in a foul mood, having suffered the indignity of doing a magnificent display of canine police work with a garland of red tinsel round its neck.

'Those bastards have rubbed Pedigree Chum all over the suit,' Willie hissed through his beak, 'and that dog's after ma arse.'

'Could be worse, Willie,' Anderson laughed, joining them. 'Could be Rogan O'Neill after yer arse. Hello, wee man, how's my Puff?'

'Picture! Picture!' said Peter, pointing at the camera.

The penguin bent over, his wing round Peter's shoulders, and a flash went off. 'Right,' the penguin announced, 'I'm going for the Glühwein. Merry Christmas.' And off he stomped with all the subtlety of a combine harvester, leaving Peter to make friends with Bruno instead.

Anderson smiled at Helena. 'Thanks for picking Peter up; it was a great help. Brenda will get off my back now.' His voice mellowed a little. 'She has a lot on her plate right now.'

'Well, there's your daughter over there. About two o'clock as you cops would say. She's with a boy, so don't make it obvious.'

Claire was indeed talking to a boy. She went very red and waved a little when she saw her father, before weaving through the crowd to join them.

'Can I go to the disco tonight with Graham?'

'Disco?' It was the first Anderson had heard of it. 'Graham?'

'Mum said I could. She's going to the German Market and I don't want to go.'

It dawned on Anderson that his daughter was being asked out on a date. 'What disco? And who's ...'

'Tonight at six. It's for the twelve and unders. You said you'd think about it. Well, Mum said you'd think about it.'

At that moment, Miss Saunders, the primary teacher, displaying a worried smile and three forms of ID, collected a very excited Peter for the nativity play and joined him to the end of a chain of equally excited five-year-olds. They were led away, Peter shouting over his shoulder, *'Watch me, Daddy! Watch me!'* Anderson waved his son off, thinking about Claire's party. Brenda was out doing her Christmas shopping and her mobile was off. Disappointment hit him in the stomach. He really wanted to go to the carol concert with Helena but he was going to spend the evening sitting alone in the car park, waiting for his daughter to finish partying. 'How do you know this boy?' he whispered, his father's instinct telling him that anybody after his daughter was a child molester in the making.

'Dad, he's in my class. It was his mum who picked me up today. Dad, everybody else is going,' Claire whined.

'My mum works here at the school, and she said I was to give you this.' The boy handed over a piece of paper with a woman's name on it and a mobile number. Anderson couldn't help noticing the boy had clean hands and unbitten nails.

'How old are you?'

'Ten. My name's Graham, Mr Anderson. Graham Smeaton.' Clean hands *and* polite. Helena had to hide a smirk behind her scarf.

'And where is your mother?' Anderson asked.

'She's on the tea bar. I've to stay with people I know,' Graham recited, 'not leave the school under any cir-circumstances. And I've to check in every thirty minutes. Otherwise she'll go mad,' he finished.

'Rightly so.'

'She says you can phone her if you want. She's going to be there tonight, supervising,' the wee lad said carefully. 'She's taking six of us. We're going back to the house for pizza until the other parents come.'

Anderson knew he was being outmanoeuvred by an expert. Equally, he saw his evening with Helena coming back into focus. He phoned Graham's mother. Yes, she said above the rattle of teacups and the intermittent rush of tap water, she would take Claire and the other kids to the disco, then back to Clarence Drive for pizza and juice. He could come over later and pick Claire up. He said he might be late. She said not to worry, lots of the mothers were taking the opportunity to wrap presents and do last-minute shopping; there was an open invite for the dads to go to the German Market to sample the wine, the beer, the cheese, more beer and maybe a spot of Bavarian dancing. They weren't expected to stagger back until gone midnight. Colin could be as late as he liked.

Claire was now smiling up at her young man.

'My daughter has grown up,' Anderson said to Helena, bemused. 'She has a boyfriend!'

'Yes, but it'll be a "Can I borrow your pencil?" type of boyfriend, not a ...' she thought carefully, '... not a behind-the-bike-shed type of boyfriend.' She caught him smirking. 'Well, I wouldn't know! I went to a girls' boarding school.'

'And I always thought they were supposed to be the worst.' Anderson shook his head. 'But down here in the real world, in Greenock, there's a boy of twelve who's a father – and I kid you not.'

'I don't think you need to worry.'

'I'm a parent. I always worry.'

'Colin, Claire's a sensible kid. And so is Peter, though you might not think it. Look, he drew a special little Squidgy for me.' She showed him a drawing of a dragon-like midge, with short spiky hair that almost matched her own. 'But now, I have some judging to do. Four hundred pictures of demented midges. I'll speak to you later.' And she was off through the crowd.

Colin Anderson turned, and walked right into Miss Cotter carrying a tray of her Empire biscuits to the tearoom. She said hello, distractedly, as though trying to place his face, and he stole a biscuit and winked at her, catching – out of the corner of his eye

– Helena trying to look dignified as she was introduced to the wall of midges. Anderson felt sick suddenly. Here he was, on the brink of something he had never thought possible – and he was terrified.

'Hello, I couldn't get parked.' Brenda Anderson tapped him on his shoulder, wrenching him from his dream. 'Where's the wee man – you managing to keep tabs on him this time?'

'Not now, Brenda.'

'Did you have to send that McAlpine woman round to my mum's to pick him up, queening it in a taxi? She's no better than she should be, that one.'

'Well, you wouldn't drop him off, would you?' Colin hissed under his breath. 'And what's this about Claire at this disco? You should tell me these things, you know.'

'If you were at home I would have told you, but you're always at your bloody work. And when you are at home you never bloody listen. I mean, you're not listening now, are you?'

Indeed, Anderson was not listening. He was looking past his wife to Helena, who was patting the head of a toddler and pointing at a green blob of a cartoon.

He looked at his wife, standing with her hands on her hips, her face drawn into a scowl. And something inside him died.

'So?' Littlewood was insistent. 'How was our resident superstar?'

'Exactly as I thought he would be.' Costello frowned at the two desks that now looked like a computer repair shop. A large multicore cable ran across the floor of the Incident Room. 'What is all this?'

'It's the cameras for the school, so I can see everything that's going on.'

'You can't see anything; it's as black as the Mariana Trench at midnight.'

'Where's Anderson?'

'Away with his kids to the fair.' Costello tried to twiddle a knob, which earned her a slap on the wrist.

'Leave it. Was there anybody there with Rogan? Declan Slater? What about Jinky Jones?'

'He still has the same crew, from way back, apparently. They're here in Scotland, and they flew in a week ago. Why?'

'Rogan's just bought Muirmakin Estate: twelve bedrooms, turrets, dungeons, and the right to murder the local wildlife and eat it.'

'You didn't answer my question. Why do you want to know?'

Littlewood dodged the question a second time. 'Lauren McCrae – how was she?'

'Stunning. Look, John, we know you're on to something – what else are you thinking of?' Costello caught sight of a pile of pictures and snatched them before Littlewood could stop her. 'These are from a newspaper archive. How did you get them?' She flicked through them. All were of Rogan through the years, but never just of Rogan. In each shot either Jinky Jones or Dec Slater was hanging around, like the proverbial bad smell. On the desk another pile, all those that showed only Rogan, had been stacked separately. 'What did you promise the paper?' she asked quietly.

'First bite. It was that journalist who was chatting up Lewis – Dave Ripley.'

'Dangerous.'

'Who gives a fuck?' Littlewood shook his head. 'Did you pick up on anything? About Lauren?'

Costello shrugged. 'She was definitely uncomfortable. She struck me as nervous more than anything else,' she said. 'Well, maybe not nervous ... out of her depth.' She leaned against the wall.

'Did he remember you?'

'Apparently I am instantly forgettable,' said Costello.

'DS Costello, you are far from being instantly forgettable,' said Littlewood, noisily moving his chewing gum from one side of his mouth to the other, and snatching the photographs back. 'For one thing, you're too bloody irritating.'

'I was going to leave the car here and walk round. Believe me, it'll be quicker.' Vik Mulholland unclipped his seat belt. 'That OK with you? It'll be fun. Have you got your mobile with you? I put "Jingle Bells" on it as your ring tone, did you notice?'

Frances nodded. 'Christmas and fun. Fun and

Christmas. Not two words I automatically put together.' She slid out the car. 'Do we need to go, really?'

'Yes. Come on, I'll get you singing along to "Wombling Merry Christmas" if it kills me.' Vik folded his hands on the roof of the car and leaned his chin on them. He smiled. 'I might even seduce you into thinking about Christmas Day and what you might want for ...'

Frances's face grew dark. 'Maybe,' she said, mimicking his posture on the roof of the car, dark hair framing her face, the snow speckling her coat. But she was gazing over his shoulder, her eyes lost somewhere. 'Maybe.' Then she smiled at him, and his heart lurched.

'We don't *really* need to go,' he said, in a voice he hoped was mildly suggestive and sexy.

'You just said that we *do* need to.' She wiped a comet of snow from the roof of the car and stretched her gloved hand out to his. He tipped a snowflake from her nose and kissed where it had been.

They walked slowly up Beaumont Place, Vik on the pavement, Frances in the gutter, her boots kicking up the sodden leaves.

'There's a fair crowd gathering. I hope the security boys are on the ball,' Vik said, aware that Frances was deep in thought about something that didn't involve him. 'Rogan O'Neill is paying for it all.'

'It's him that's caused it all, so why not?' she muttered, almost as if she had not heard him.

Suddenly three kids came running round the corner. The two boys had the St Andrew's flag painted on their faces – wee Bravehearts – and the girl held a Squidgy balloon on a stick, one in each hand, and little lights flickered up the sides of her red wellington boots. Frances watched as they went dancing across the end of her road.

'Stay together, you lot!' Mulholland shouted after them, but they had gone. 'I hope they look out for each other. Where are their bloody parents?'

'Some folk just don't deserve kids. Vik? Could we just go for a coffee at the French Café, then you could go along on your own,' said Frances. 'Please.'

He stopped and pulled her face towards his by grasping the collar of her long woollen coat. 'Look, it's leaving three o'clock, I have to be there asap, and you are coming with me.' He kissed her on the forehead, a quick stab of the lips. 'And you are going to meet Squidgy McMidge, Santa, Rogan O'Neill and my work colleagues.' For a moment Frances looked disconcerted. 'That was in descending order of intelligence.'

She had to smile at that, but only just. Then she turned away quickly, but not before Vik caught the look of fear on her face.

'You don't have to if you don't want to – meet them, I mean,' Vik said as they joined the crowds on Rowanhill Road. 'I just have to let them know that I'm on the premises, that's all.' He took her by the arm. 'You OK?'

'I'm fine,' she said, but in a tone that suggested she wasn't. She pulled her scarf and collar up round her face, as if she were hiding. 'I'm just not that good with people. That's all.'

'I'm not asking you to be good with *people*; I'm just asking you to be good to me.' Vik was careful to keep the humour in his voice but he knew Frances was already upset about something and had walked on ahead so he wouldn't see her tears.

18

'He did well, didn't he? Are you two not really proud?' Helena smiled at *Mr and Mrs Anderson*, as she tried to think of them, but failed.

Colin and Brenda exchanged glances. 'Who?' asked Brenda.

'Peter? Doing his Puff on the stage over there,' she gestured vaguely. Her eyes flicked towards Colin. *Don't tell me you missed it!*

They had been arguing non-stop, Brenda's voice rising until Colin had pulled her to one side of the hall where the argument had continued in low heated whispers, and they had got so embroiled ... 'We got caught up in something.'

Helena shrugged uncomfortably. 'Well, he did really well. The girl behind him stood on his tail during his wee dance and he told her, in no uncertain terms, to remove her foot. You must have heard the laughter ...'

Colin had indeed been aware of a sudden burst of adult laughter, and he had recognized the tune, badly played on the gym hall piano. God knew, he had heard it enough recently.

'If he used bad language, it's you he gets it from,'

said Brenda. 'I'll go and see what he's up to.' And she went off without another word.

'Sorry about that,' said Colin.

'Stressed out, Christmas, the kids, being married to a cop when his mind is elsewhere – I can sympathize.' Helena rubbed her hands together. 'Well, I've done my bit. God, that Calloway woman is a right prima donna. From what she writes and draws I thought she'd be warm and wickedly witty, but she's horrible. She hates kids.'

'I guess you can never tell,' said Anderson. Helena took a step towards him to avoid the obese woman in her wheelchair, making for the exit with the speed of Michael Schumacher but none of his skill. Helena was now standing so close to Colin Anderson he could smell her perfume, the clean scent of Penhaligon's Bluebell, but with an undertone of something antiseptic. He took a deep breath and said, as casually as he could, 'Claire seems much better. So, the disco is a done deal. Which means I'm free.'

'Oh. So, you can make it tonight?' Colin was flattered to hear genuine pleasure in her voice.

There was a sudden bark from the corner of the room and a ripple of movement as people turned to look. Pat the Penguin was struggling to get free of the huge growling Alsatian, which was hanging off his tail with bared teeth.

'I'll see you outside the Theatre Royal. About twenty past seven?' She smiled, and he wished he hadn't changed into his old jeans. 'I think you'll need to go home, Colin – to drop off the new family pet.'

Coming the other way was Vik Mulholland, carrying a plastic bag with a goldfish in it. Peter, dressed in his dragon suit, was carefully poking the bag with his finger, and chatting to the fish. Two steps behind, Brenda was berating him for not looking where he was going.

'Dad, look! A goldfish!'

'So I see,' Anderson nodded at Vik.

'This is my girlfriend, Frances,' said Vik, and the tall dark-haired woman with him smiled shyly, holding her hand up to the side of her face as though she had toothache.

'I've just won it in the lucky dip. Would you like it?' she asked. Peter's face lit up like a light bulb, and Mulholland, ignoring the filthy looks from his boss, handed the goldfish over.

Peter took it with both hands. 'And did you see me sing my song? I was best.'

'I'm sure you were,' said Frances, in a low husky voice.

'Mum and Dad missed it,' hissed Peter.

'Tell everybody, why don't you?'

'Well, I'm going away with my goldfish,' he said petulantly.

'Your mother . . .'

'Let's go and buy him some food,' Helena suggested tactfully. 'You hold tight to my hand now.

Maybe I can take the goldfish home and look after it and you can come and visit it when you want.'

'Auntie Helena? It's not a *it*, it's a *him*,' squealed Peter, swinging on Helena's arm, making her wince.

'Don't pull on Auntie Helena's arm like that,' Anderson hurriedly reproved him.

'But he wants a hamburger,' said Peter, as they walked off. 'Doesn't he, Auntie Helena? I'll help him eat it.'

Wyngate came rumbling across the empty room on his wheeled chair, and pulled a piece of paper from the fax machine. 'I have a result. Well, Mulholland has a result – he did the donkey work – but I have the fax.' He read it, eyes skimming for the pertinent points. 'We've moved on the cyanide order from Glasgow and we don't know exactly who, but we do know where. I've traced it to an internet café in Sauchiehall Street. The order was for sodium cyanide, chemical symbol NaCN, very specific; the person knew what they were after.'

'Sodium cyanide?' Costello pulled O'Hare's report and the printout from Toxicology from the huge pile of papers on her desk. 'Is that what O'Hare was expecting?'

'Yip,' said Wyngate, waving the piece of paper back and forth. 'The café is called Bijou Bytes.'

Lewis slid from her desk and sauntered over. 'I know that place. They do a great chocolate croissant.'

Costello noted it down. 'And how did they pay?'

'Credit card, and I have a trace on that as well.'

'A break and a chocolate croissant?' Lewis grinned. 'What do you say, Costello? You could do with some fresh air. And I'd get a chance to do some Christmas shopping.'

'It's the back of three now. Time is a bit tight; we have to appear down at the fair, remember?'

'Another date with Rogan?'

Costello ignored Lewis to answer the phone. 'Yes? Oh, hello.' She paused, her eyes slanting sidelong at Lewis. 'If it has any bearing on the case – no, I'm afraid we can't talk in confidence.'

Costello gestured for DS Littlewood to lean over her desk and listen in. *Lauren*, she mouthed. Littlewood nodded, urging her to keep talking. 'But we can have a chat now, if you like, and you can let me know what's on your mind ... I'm more than a little busy here. Well, if you really don't want to talk about it over the phone ...' Costello raised her eyebrows at Littlewood, who scribbled *Botanics tomorrow* on the back of his hand. 'What about meeting in the Botanic Gardens? It's warm in there and we can have a coffee and a chat and look at the plants. Tomorrow? About eleven – yes, me too – see you then ...'

Costello tapped the phone against her chin, thinking. 'Cheers for that, Littlewood; I really need to babysit a supermodel.'

'Good. Can you spare me ten minutes before you go out?' asked Littlewood. 'I want to bring you up to speed on a few things.'

'I haven't got ten minutes right now. We need to get over to the fair. Quinn has triple underlined it,' she said. 'But . . .'

'You go,' Littlewood grunted. 'The *Mary Celeste* had more crew than us.'

'OK, tomorrow we can do the internet café and the credit card at the same time.' She marked it on the wall and signed it.

'Why did she phone you?' asked Lewis. 'She's an international supermodel. Why you?'

Costello sighed. 'Probably because we have so much in common.'

Up to now Eve had been merely acting miserable. Now she actually was miserable. She was being ignored by her bloody sister, and she had an unpleasant feeling that her bladder wasn't going to hold out much longer. She had been texting and phoning Lynne to tell her she needed to go to the loo but her sister was too busy posturing and being photographed with Helena Farrell, no doubt boring the knickers off the poor woman.

She had been people-watching long enough to know that the Farrell woman, who was holding a goldfish, had a thing for the tall blond bloke who had been hanging around her with two kids. Where the smaller, dumpy woman with the red hair fitted into the picture, she had no idea but she was arguing with the blond bloke as if they were married. He looked like a cop. So did the Johnny Depp bloke who was forever kissing the long-haired hippie chick. Eve leaned forward in her seat, trying to get a better look at the girl. Now, there was a face to paint, with those long bones and cavernous brown eyes. The expression never seemed to change much, although Eve noticed it softened a little when she looked at the Johnny Depp guy. But when she started a pat-a-cake clapping game with the little fair-haired boy with the goldfish – Eve hadn't seen that since she and Lynne were kids – the patrician mask melted. That would make a good painting. The hippie chick turned, her eyes fixed about two feet above Eve's head. Eve had a feeling she knew her, but couldn't quite place when or where.

She sat for some time watching as her sister and Helena Farrell lined up for more photographs. She eased her chair out a little way, to see if she could spot anybody she knew, anybody she could ask for help to find the toilets. She knew she had to go now. She decided to trundle over and ask the blond policeman with the children for some assistance. She had to slow down as a crowd jostled past, bumping into her, ignoring her. She parked her chair at a window and looked out. Lights were starting to come on in the car park. She smiled to herself, and looked at her watch. The fair was running late. It was ten past four.

The children's faces shone in the light of a hundred candles as they finished a final chorus of 'Oh Come, All Ye Faithful' and the last shoebox was loaded on to the truck. In a whirr of cameras and flashlights Rogan climbed into the cab, a lone piper taking up the refrain of 'Auld Lang Syne'. The candles wavered in the air, then the piping stopped, and a countdown started. There wasn't a dry eye in the street when, on cue, Rogan O'Neill finally fired up the engine of the sixteen-wheel truck. Slowly, almost imperceptibly, the huge vehicle inched forward, and Rogan drove it all of five yards in the direction of Pakistan.

Helena held her handkerchief to her face, the tears pouring from her eyes. She looked at Peter's goldfish, motionless in its plastic bag, the slow opening and closing of its mouth the only sign of life. She wrapped her scarf round it – the poor wee sod could freeze out here – and held the bundle carefully to her chest. She would make sure it got home safely. There was so much goodwill in the street, with everyone so genuinely happy and generous, that her heart was touched. This was the true meaning of Christmas. She looked at her watch. She had to phone the hospital before she went out tonight, just to make sure it was all going ahead. But for the moment she wanted to be among people, and who better than children at Christmas time? She stood back from the crowd, easing herself to lean on the wall of the playground, apart from the scene but able to see it all. Every child was waving – candles, tinsel, scarves and Squidgys swayed in the air as the truck pulled away, now with its driver on board, and everyone cheered it on its way.

Helena saw Vik Mulholland chatting to Costello; the body language looked argumentative. Little Peter Anderson was running in and out between them, battering his Winnie-the-Pooh rucksack with his knees, his breath condensing in the air. As he ran, she caught his voice singing his 'Puff the Magic Dragon' song, the song that had been the highlight of the nativity play. Peter knew perfectly well his parents hadn't even bothered to listen to him and he was playing up now, wanting attention. Then she saw Colin go up to talk to Mulholland, a serious talk. Colin pointed to his watch, then Mulholland looked at his.

Helena started to make her way through the crowd. Peter was no longer in sight but then she saw Brenda Anderson talking on her mobile and poking at Colin, who turned to say something. It was clearly acrimonious. Helena stopped in her tracks, her little moment of Christmas cheer shattered. Suddenly she found she was in tears again. She watched as Brenda kept jabbing at her husband with her forefinger, punctuating her argument. She had it all, Brenda: the love of a good husband, a wee live wire of a son, and the companionship of a daughter. God, she would regret it if she ever lost Colin. Helena wiped her tears on the end of her scarf. She heard Costello ask Mulholland where Frances had got to. So, was that her name – the dramatic-looking woman with the face of a Byzantine icon who had taken Peter by the hand for a moment and joined in his strange little dance? But now Peter was dancing alone, his dragon hooves tapping on his shoes, ignored by the adults again. She sighed, checked on the goldfish, and turned to walk back up to her house, high up on the terrace.

Costello pulled her quilted jacket tight and tipped the collar up round her ears. She was cold, bloody freezing. She'd just about kept warm while walking up to the school but standing around waiting for the charade with the truck had chilled her to the bone. And she needed the toilet. She turned round and started slowly up Rowanhill, back to the station. She wanted to be back there before six.

'Excuse me,' she said as she walked into Vik Mulholland, standing in the middle of the pavement, staring into space. 'I can go through you or round you. Your choice. But don't you think for a moment that I'll hesitate to walk all over you, you arse. It's been a long day and I'm not taking one step further than I actually have to.'

'Sorry.' Mulholland immediately acquiesced and stood aside.

Costello paused, then turned round. 'You OK?'

He shrugged.

'Oh, Vik, don't be so bloody miserable. She only left because she wasn't feeling well. It's not the end of the world.'

'She just didn't say goodbye.'

'Oh, you poor diddums.' Costello stood, slapping

her hands into each other in an attempt to keep warm. 'What's up with her, I noticed her clutching her face? Does she have the toothache or something?'

'No, she has a trigeminal neuralgia.'

'A what?'

'Like migraine in your face.'

'Well, I can sympathize with that.' She walked away through the crowd, Mulholland following like a lost lamb.

'I just don't understand her,' he complained.

'She's a woman; you're not supposed to understand her,' quipped Costello.

'I'm serious,' he snapped.

'God, you *are* serious. Congratulations, Vik, you've joined the human race. You care more for a human being than you do for your BMW. That's something.'

'One minute she blows hot, one minute cold. One minute all over me like a rash, next minute ignoring me. I bought her a mobile, but she says she won't use it. She can't even be arsed to spend Christmas with me. And all I want is to . . .'

Costello stopped mid-stride. 'Bloody hell, Vik. You've got it bad.'

'Yeah,' he admitted miserably. 'Lewis says she's playing hard to get, just to see how far she can push me.'

'Lewis is talking shite. Frances wouldn't play games like that, she's not the type. Vik, just how well do you know her?'

'What do you mean?'

'I thought you were a detective. Look, she's – what? – a good ten years older than you? She lives in a huge rambling flat in Beaumont Place, on her own. She's intelligent, but she doesn't work. She's skint.'

'She's not well, she's on disability . . .'

'Yeah, but any other woman would flog the place. What's it worth – three hundred thousand? A bit more?' It hadn't dawned on Vik but Costello was right. 'So, what's holding her there? I'd say she's not had an easy life. I bet nobody ever gave her a goldfish to keep her company when she was a kid. Then you come along. I mean, I think you're a pain in the arse but you're solvent, you're nice to your mother, you drive a nice car . . .'

'A very nice car,' smiled Vik, warming to Costello's train of thought.

'And underneath all the pretentious crap, you're quite a nice bloke, I suppose. I bet Frances is scared shitless.'

'Of what?'

Costello shrugged. 'Getting close to you? Losing you? We all judge things on our past experiences, and how do you know what she's been through?'

'I don't. I just want to look after her, give her things, make her happy . . .'

'But, Vik – how long for? Maybe she can see a time when you won't want to be with a woman ten years older than you, who's on disability. Then what'll happen to her?'

'So, what do I do? I really am — well — serious about her.'

'Like I'm an expert? Oh, Vik, how the fuck should I know? Just don't get pissed and shag Kate Lewis at the Christmas night out.'

At six o'clock Costello was drying the hems of her trousers on the radiator, fending off the questions from Lewis about Colin Anderson and Helena Farrell which were interspersed with a discourse on how totally perfect her bloody boyfriend, Stuart, was.

Costello had never met the bloke but she disliked him anyway. 'So, why are you not going out with him tonight?' Costello asked sourly. 'I thought he drove up yesterday.'

'He's busy,' said Lewis with a sly wink. 'After Christmas, we're going to book a holiday in the Seychelles,' she added, wistfully.

'What makes you think you'll get any time off? We're too short-staffed,' said Costello, shifting to sit on the radiator, trying to dry the seat of her trousers.

Lewis ignored her. 'I hope I don't have to make do with Tenerife again. I just need some quality sun.'

Costello thought she was starting to get the hang of DS Lewis now: she talked the talk, walked the walk, but cheap charm wears off quickly. Or did her self-confidence know no bounds?

'You having a holiday this year, Winifred?'

'Fuck off,' said Costello, quietly.

19

Luca thought this had been his best day ever. He'd had a strawberry milkshake and a whole Monkey Meal with Cheeky Chips to himself. He'd wanted to go to the fair to see Squidgy, but in the end he'd spent all afternoon lazing on the big settee watching DVDs. He'd sent a letter to Santa saying what he wanted for Christmas; and he'd helped Troy write his, because he could write better than Troy, who said he hardly ever got to school.

He was all warm and snug now, so he wasn't going to get out of his bed. He could hear music – Christmas music – the sort of thing he was supposed to sing along to at school, 'Hark, the Herald' and that stuff.

He wanted to see his mum. He knew she was ill again because of the way she'd rolled around making such an awful noise at the amusements. But he'd been promised he'd be home in time for Christmas, which meant his mum would be better soon, so it was all going to be OK. He wondered what day of the week it was. And if Santa was coming soon.

He put his arms outside the duvet, into the cold air, stretching out his hands as far as he could reach on both sides. *Glory to the new born king* . . . he saw a movement from the corner of his eye, just catching sight of the rat before it scurried off.

He pulled himself back under the duvet and drew the cover over his head. The rats worried him. He didn't really know why he'd been put down here. And he didn't know why he wasn't allowed to see his mum. He liked his mum and he always cheered her up when he went to see her in hospital. So, why was the door locked?

He looked across at the big wooden door. It was old and the wood was all dry and splintered, and it hurt his hands if he leaned on it. But the lock – that was bright and shiny.

He looked up at the sound of footsteps overhead, a door closing, then another. The footsteps stopped.

'Goodnight, Troy,' Luca whispered. But there was no answer.

Miss Stella McCorkindale was sitting in the deserted canteen, still wearing her dark-blue coat and a Squidgy McMidge on her lapel. She appeared slightly agitated as she followed them to the interview room, and kept pushing her glasses further up the bridge of her nose, as if she had difficulty focusing on close objects with her slightly protruding eyes.

Stella had given her age as fifty-six, and stated her occupation as legal secretary in a company that now specialized in property work. She lived in Horselethill Circus. Troy had gone missing from the park outside her flat. Littlewood had underlined that bit. He had said she was a good clean witness, not over helpful, but thoughtful and measured.

Quinn and the witness sat opposite each other; Costello sat a little further back, following her instructions to act as a casual observer, and form a clear picture of Miss Stella McCorkindale.

Her story was precise, and she never wavered from it.

'I was coming home from work on Tuesday, I was a bit earlier than usual . . .'

'Do you know what time, specifically?' asked Quinn.

Stella shook her head slowly. 'The back of four, maybe a bit later . . . sorry I can't be more precise. You see, I came out of the subway at Hillhead, then I popped into M&S and started walking up Observatory Road. It was there I saw him.'

'Why did you wait so long to come forward?'

'I didn't realize who he was.' She shook her head, the palm of her hand out in front. 'What I mean is, I saw him but didn't know it was the boy who was missing. I went home today and there was a card behind my door; you missed me on your initial enquiry. I came here to save you coming to me.'

'Do you know Troy?' asked Quinn lightly.

'One thin boy in a hoodie is exactly that. But when I saw the description of his mother . . . well, I've had to phone the police to get her moved from the gardens in front of my house. She wears that silly coat, I would always notice the coat.'

Quinn nodded. 'And the boy? When you saw the boy on Tuesday?'

'Well, if it's the boy I saw, he was limping a little. He has a cheeky way with him.' She shook her head as if clearing her mind. 'I'm sure it was him.'

'What was he wearing?'

'I read in the paper, sweatshirt.' She nodded. 'He had thin legs, wee skinny legs. Definitely him.'

Quinn's face was quizzical, pretending she was trying to work it out. She was good, Costello thought. 'Was he on his own?'

The specs got pushed up the bridge of Stella's nose. 'There was a few folk walking up Observatory Road at that time. It was dark, I can't say if he was on his own or not.' Stella was talking again. 'It was dark, it was sleeting but not heavily. The pavement on Observatory Road is all bumpy with tree roots, so I'd been watching my feet. I've come a cropper there before now.'

'But he wasn't struggling? He didn't appear restrained in any way?'

Stella shook her head. 'No, quite the opposite. He was limping, but he was ... skipping, I suppose.'

Quinn said thank you and gestured to Costello that they should leave. In the corridor she said, 'Not a lot of use that, is it? Do you think that was Troy? It's all been suggested by something else. It was the mother she recognized really, not the boy.'

'I'll get Gail to sit with her and show her a few photos. But it kind of makes sense, taking him down there, where all those wee lanes and paths are. If it was him, he could be anywhere by now.'

Quinn swore under her breath, 'OK, get Gail and get her a cup of tea. Maybe she'll remember something she didn't read in the paper.'

Carols by Candlelight was living up to its reputation as one of the events of the year. Colin Anderson was enthralled by it all: the costumes, the candles, the spectacle, the glorious music, the exuberance of the singers, and the sheer pleasure of watching something very difficult being made to look easy.

Most of all, he was enjoying just being there, with the woman sitting next to him. Helena was wearing her favourite deep-green velvet dress, which folded around her in a coil from one shoulder to the other. Her pale thin neck was circled by a single string of creamy pearls, small, expensive, real. If he looked carefully, he could see the finest wrinkling of her skin, tiny creases that deepened and flattened as she moved her head. Green eye shadow emphasized the catlike slant of her eyes, and the first signs of crow's feet that deepened as she laughed, which she did a lot.

He was touched by how apologetic she had been for arriving late; he didn't mention that he had stood outside in the cold, thinking that her standing him up would put the tin lid on a bloody awful day. He had been surprised at how much relief he felt as she came running round the corner, breathless and beautiful, her long coat swirling behind her. He had been surprised how guilt-free he felt as he waved Claire off to the disco and Brenda took Peter away to go to the German Market. And surprised at how little he was thinking about work. But he had phoned Brenda at the German Market, shouting over the Bavarian music and the sound of lederhosen being slapped in the background, and warned her to take care of Peter. She said she was on her way back to the car, then told him in no uncertain terms that she was quite capable of looking after her own son. Colin asked to speak to him but Brenda had already hung up.

After a while Colin realized that he was watching Helena more than he was watching the performers. Then she would turn to look at him, aware that he was watching her. *Enjoying it?* she mouthed to him.

He nodded. Mozart, in full costume and holding a candelabrum, was making his way on to the stage.

He felt a lump in his throat and closed his eyes, allowing the beautiful sound to wash over him. He really was enjoying it. And he found himself relaxing. Dangerously close to sleeping.

He felt a dig in his ribs. Helena was gazing intently at Mozart, a faint smile playing at the side of her mouth.

Then, totally unexpectedly, a massed pipe band entered from the back of the hall, and marched down every aisle abreast playing 'The Flower of Scotland', causing a flutter of laughter on the way as the audience noticed every piper was wearing a Squidgy instead of a sporran. They filed up on to the stage, and stood in ranks, playing a medley of Christmas tunes. Then, to thunderous applause, they all marched out again. The first half was over.

Out in the foyer, Colin was amazed at Helena's social grace. She knew everybody. 'This is Colin Anderson,' she said to everyone they met. 'He was a great friend of Alan's.' Then a small whisper – 'His wife's let me borrow him for the evening.' For once he was glad he looked like a copper.

Helena dished out *hellos* and air kisses, flutters of the fingers and *I must catch you later*s. Then suddenly she seemed to have had enough.

'Would you mind if we didn't stay for the second half? I think I've had enough. Oh, Christ,' she said suddenly, and retreated behind a pillar. 'See that guy over there?' Colin surreptitiously turned to look. 'Tall, slightly greying? With a woman who'll have a dead rabbit or something round her neck?'

'I can see the guy with the old dear – yes, covered in a dead animal.'

Helena ducked further out of the way, pulling gently on Colin's jacket. 'God spare us, every time he sees me he tries to buy my house.'

'Why?'

'Because his mother owns the one three doors down. But he never misses a trick. He'd love to buy up the entire terrace to convert them into flats.' Her voice suddenly went quiet. 'He came to my door three days after Alan's funeral. *Three days.*'

Colin looked carefully round the pillar. 'Tell me what his car number plate is and I'll get him clamped.'

'No need. The word is he's in the financial pooh; at least his company is – Munro Property – you must know them.' Helena put a slender finger theatrically to her lips. 'But Mummy mustn't know the company is on borrowed time.'

'Is that his mother he's with?'

'Yes, Mrs Eleanor Munro, Doctor of Law, with the social conscience of Attila the Hun. And he has A Levels in smarm.'

'Remind me to ask you next time we need intelligence; you've a better network of gossip than we have.'

'Not difficult,' Helena chided him. 'Anyway, he never goes anywhere without his bloody mother. They still live together, can you imagine that? I've heard him pretend he's married. I mean, don't normal men pretend that they are single! I think he might be a perv ... Oh, hello, Douglas, how are you?'

'I'm fine, Helena. How are you?' The man caught Helena's fine-boned hand in a limp handshake, and his gold bracelet rattled loudly. He looked nervous.

'I'm fine, thank you. And you, Mrs Munro?'

Helena turned to Anderson, and pulled a face of apology. Douglas Munro, smiling nervously, steered his mother away. 'See you ... later.'

'So, you owe me some info, Mrs McAlpine. Shall we go?'

'I'll tell you in the car,' said Helena, giving a fifty-pound note to the collection bucket for Andy's Appeal as they left the Theatre Royal.

Anderson drove Helena home in her Beamer, and she sat in the passenger seat looking at a snippet of Peter's dragon cartoon she had found in her coat pocket. 'I can't imagine it, can you?'

'Imagine what?' asked Anderson, keeping his eye on the road, the lightness of the Beamer's steering unfamiliar to him, as he headed down to Charing Cross.

She didn't answer; she seemed to relax in the warm silence of the car, then started quietly chatting. She talked about the fair, about Christmas, about the school – talking, but saying nothing. Anderson was content to let her, knowing she was warming to something.

They were leaving Charing Cross when she said conversationally, 'Your children are something special, Colin.'

'I think so, but I'm biased,' he laughed, making light of it.

'They are your legacy,' Helena said flatly, looking out the window. He could hardly hear her over the hum of the engine. 'They are a testament to your existence.' She put her fingertip up to her lips, for a moment, as her face lit up in the headlights of an oncoming car; she looked little more than a child herself. 'But when I am gone, Alan and I are both gone. Somewhere along the line we should have stopped to think about a family but I always had a deadline, he had a big case, I was travelling, he was drunk. Time goes past and you can't get it back, then it's too late.' She fell silent, and the silence still hung in the air as Anderson parked the Beamer outside her house.

He had rarely seen her this vulnerable. He got out the car to walk Helena to her door, flicking his mobile phone on, giving himself time to think. He could hear Alan's voice asking him not to leave her like this and Anderson felt guilty, relishing the fact he was needed.

Helena turned to face him as she reached her front step. 'Sorry, I've not been much fun to be with but I really needed a night out.' She placed the palm of her hand on the front of his coat, a light touch.

He covered her hand with his, slipped his fingers between hers, squeezing gently.

'I'll say goodnight,' Helena said, letting her gaze fall on to their entwined hands. Then she reached forward, pulling Colin into the deeper shadow, and kissed him on the cheek. She pulled back slightly, not far enough to be a rejection, still close enough for him to feel her eyelashes on his cheek, her breath on his neck. He put his finger under her chin, tilted her head and kissed her forehead, delicately but with purpose, feeling his heart pounding.

Then he pulled her close and hugged her, and felt her body leaning into his. Nothing he could remember had felt so good. He rested his lips on her cheekbone, breathing in the scent of tea tree oil and bluebells.

She was smiling now, that slightly flirtatious smile he loved. It was years since he had been smiled at like that. Then she leaned her head against the wall behind her; her green eyes – the greenest eyes he had ever seen – were suddenly tearful. 'I'm sorry, I shouldn't have asked you along to that. But I just wanted to go.'

'That's what friends are for.'

'I'm not sure I invited you as a friend.' She sighed. 'I invited you to fill a great vacuum.'

'And that's what friends are for,' repeated Colin. 'If me planking my arse on Alan's seat gets you through a difficult hour, I'm happy to do it. Honoured, in fact.'

He ran one hand through her hair, ending with tipping the end of her nose with his finger. She didn't pull away. They looked at each other.

He saw her lips move.

She said something. He felt it rather than heard it. A murmur. His brain was trying to translate it into something low and seductive.

'Your phone's vibrating.'

'Ignore it. I've just turned it on.'

'Answer it,' she said with a wry smile, letting her fingertips linger on his wrist, as if telling him to follow her into her house. But then he pulled away as though the phone had electrocuted him, his face drained of colour. 'When?' he said, his voice harsh with anger, close to panic.

Both hands were on the phone as he pressed the End Call button.

Helena turned round. 'Something bad?'

'Peter's gone.'

20

'OK, Costello,' Anderson snapped. 'What's happening?'

Costello had been waiting in the street for him, dressed in somebody else's anorak, and she was chilled to the bone. She ran to keep up with him, as he crossed Hyndland Road to the police station where she jumped up the steps in front of him, stopping him from going any further. 'You know Peter was out with Brenda, at the German Market?' she panted. 'They were in the car park at Byres Road. Brenda just turned round and he wasn't there. We're examining the CCTV footage right now. But nobody could find you and I didn't want you walking in ...'

'Yes?' Anderson snarled.

'Colin, Brenda's here. I'm not letting you walk in there with lipstick on your face. At least make it look as though you've been interviewing Helena.'

Anderson took the steps two at a time. He paused at the top. 'Thanks, Costello.'

'You owe me,' she said.

DCI Quinn made it through the door of the Incident Room one second before Anderson. She had changed from her usual navy-blue suit to a black cashmere jumper over tight blue jeans, and the untied laces of her trainers were dirty and soaked. Her face was devoid of make-up, her hair pulled back in a scrunchie.

Gail Irvine was sitting in the corner with her arm round a shocked Brenda who was cradling, but not drinking, a cup of tea. Gail was talking to her, a constant stream of delicate questions. Brenda shook her head. Anderson glanced at his wife, bit his lip, then walked on without exchanging a word. Brenda saw him pass, and reached towards him, the fingers of her outstretched hand trembling. He ignored her. Shocked, she put her hand to her mouth and the tears started to flow in earnest. Word had got around, and more than one officer had come in from sick leave. The room stank of strong coffee and VapoRub. The radio chattered constantly, different voices answering, and Anderson recognized the Partick Central code. The situation was personal now – one of their own was missing.

DS Lewis was on the phone to Partick. 'Yes, *all* your CCTV tapes,' she was saying for the third time, with exaggerated patience. 'Because we need to check every single one, that's why.' A voice garbled down the phone. 'Yes, I appreciate you're short-staffed. So are we. So, if you could . . . look! Three children in five days! Every minute you spend making excuses is a minute wasted. *You moron!*' she hissed so the idiot on the other end of the phone couldn't hear. She clammed up the moment she saw Anderson.

Anderson was looking at the wall. And now Peter had gone, from right under their noses.

Quinn came up to him, placing a hand momentarily on his shoulder. 'Sorry, Colin, but we can't have you in here. You need to go and speak to Brenda.'

'No, thanks.'

'She's upset. She was the last person to see Peter. Irvine's getting nothing concrete out of her. She says she was walking down Byres Road, she turned round and Peter wasn't there. We need more than that, Colin. We need you to try. We'll take her to the interview room, and you can speak to her in there. We'll keep you informed of our progress.'

He realized she had been walking him, slowly, out of the Incident Room and along the short corridor to the nearest interview room. Irvine withdrew as they appeared at the door and, before Colin could say anything, he was alone with his wife. Brenda was wearing the same coat she had had on at the fair, but apart from that he hardly recognized her. She was red-eyed, blotchy-faced and totally distraught. She moved towards him, her arms open. He took a step back, then stood behind the table, physically emphasizing the barrier between them.

Brenda held her hands to her face, the tears pouring down again. 'I'm so sorry.'

'Did you have to let him go? Could you not have held his hand?' He stabbed his finger in front of her face. 'Was it too much bloody effort to look after your own kid?'

Brenda bit at the corner of her mouth, the tears still streaming. 'And where were you? We both let him down.'

'Speak for yourself. I'm not a bad parent.'

'But you're a crap husband, and sometimes that's the same thing.'

'Don't dump the blame on me,' Anderson hissed, angry at Peter, angry at himself. Angry at Brenda for speaking the truth.

'Well, you should be out there looking for him.'

'At least we agree about something. I'm going, but first we need a statement from you.'

'Nothing happened, Colin, honestly. One minute he was there, the next minute he was gone. I've told that girl all I can think of.'

Colin looked at the pad, with the few scribbled notes Irvine had taken. He scanned through them. 'Not good enough. Think a bit harder.'

He looked at her. The whites of her eyes were red-veined lilies, her face puffy and swollen, and she was shaking. Her fingers constantly writhed, squeezing the blood from the tips, leaving them blue and cold.

'Sorry, love, I'm just ... I'll get us a coffee. You sit down and take a deep breath, calm down. Panic will get us nowhere. Just relax.' He stilled her hands with his own, pushing all thoughts of Helena from his mind. 'Brenda, try to relax and think. Just set your mind free and think about him walking beside you –

what happened then? Tell us everything you see and hear . . . you are the best chance he has.'

Once Lynne was sure Eve had fallen asleep again, with a sleeping pill and three glasses of red wine inside her, she pulled the raffia folder from under the blanket on the settee. It didn't feel like an art folder full of A4 paper; it felt more like a scrapbook. Lynne even felt slightly amused as she sat back in her armchair and curled her feet under her, looking at Eve asleep and snoring. She had caught her sister out at another of her little games. And this one might be more dangerous. She opened up the folder and stared, her amusement turning to nausea.

It was full, not just of printouts from the internet, but of cuttings from the newspapers about Eve's accident, and about Neil Thompson's previous acquittal for dangerous driving. And about the defence counsel who had achieved that acquittal, Mr Douglas Munro. Eve had then traced his every move, noting every court case, and then every planning application as he changed career. She'd even delved back far enough to download from the internet a page from his yearbook at his private school, and an old newspaper report about how an outward bound school trip up to Lord Berkeley's Seat had gone wrong. There was a photograph in the paper of a jaggy outcrop in the middle of nowhere; Douglas had been hospitalized after the trip with hypothermia, among other things. There was a covert shot of Douglas and his mother outside the house at Kirklee Terrace; his graduation picture, his mother proudly on his arm; and the business card of Munro Properties. Lynne's self-interest took over; she flicked the pages back and forth but there were no pictures of Mrs Douglas Munro or the wedding. And, Lynne noticed, there was nothing at all about the accident that had crippled Eve and earned Thompson a custodial sentence. Douglas had not been involved in that at all.

For someone who couldn't even get dressed without help, Eve had got a long way – or was someone else doing this for her? Someone tall enough to nudge a painting with a passing shoulder, somebody who knocked over a chess piece sitting on a sideboard without noticing? Lynne paused at a well-fingered photocopy of a photograph, taken outside the court, of Neil Thompson walking away from a dangerous driving charge with his driving licence intact, followed by Douglas Munro. A few months later, Thompson had downed half a bottle of vodka and smashed his car into Eve's. And into Eve.

Lynne breathed out slowly. OK, so Eve knew. Anybody could have found it out from the Sheriff Court. But this – this obsession – was something else. Thompson was in jail, way beyond her reach. But Douglas, he was close to home, too close for his own good. Lynne folded the photocopy back along its original crease. What would she do about it? The first thing was to find out who was helping Eve. And she knew just who to ask.

Over the road, Stella's lights were still on. Lynne glanced at her watch, put her coat and boots on, opened the door and slipped out. If anybody came and went from this house, Stella McCorkindale would know.

On the settee, Eve opened her eyes, stretched and smiled wickedly.

'Are you sure you want to watch this?' asked Quinn. 'You don't have to, you know.'

Colin Anderson nodded, biting his lip hard, eyes not moving from the screen.

'He's my son,' he said quietly. 'Just play the tapes.'

'Colin,' Quinn persisted. 'We have to move quickly. We knew about Peter within an hour, so we have to strike now. It might be more useful if you helped Brenda with the appeal. You know we can't let you do it; you're a cop, you're too well known. Brenda is your wife; you can get the best out of her.' Quinn's voice was almost pleading. She looked across to Costello for support.

'Might be worth a try, Col? We're ahead of the game here. Go and do something that will help.'

'She's doing her best. Just play the tape,' he said, his voice unnaturally steady.

Costello shrugged in defeat. They had watched the footage again and again, and they knew what it showed. It echoed exactly what Brenda had said, but hearing it was one thing, seeing it was something else entirely. The image of your own son, there one minute, gone the next. No idea when or if he would ever be seen again.

The monitor flickered into life, and black and white images began ghosting from the left of the screen to the right. The two cameras looked out from the west side of Byres Road on to the small triangular car park at University Avenue which was playing host to the German Market, and an overspill of cheery Christmas shoppers treading through dirty slush and puddles.

The time stamp showed 19.20.

When life had been normal.

'How quickly was the alarm raised?' asked Costello.

'As soon as she got to the car,' answered Quinn equally quietly.

'Don't act as if I'm not here,' said Anderson, his voice sharp with anger. 'So, she'd walked a fair way down Byres Road before she noticed he wasn't behind her? The car was down at Dumbarton Road, for God's sake!'

'It was busy, Colin, she . . . oh, never mind. On you go, Gordon.'

Wyngate sat back, including Anderson in their circle. 'We've watched this fifteen times or so,' he sighed. 'See this man here, with the hat? Keep your eye on him. She's just behind him, and coming this way.'

People walked back and forth, carrying bags, pushing prams with rolls of Christmas paper poking out like jousting lances. The images were grainy, and with the elevated position of the camera giving a fish-eye distortion to the screen it would be all too easy to miss something.

'That clock is correct, I take it?' Mulholland pointed at the time stamp.

'It's spot on. I've checked.'

Brenda appeared behind the man in the hat, turned a little as if saying something over her shoulder, then shifted her shopping from one hand to the other. 'I thought she was waiting for him at this point,' said Wyngate. But Brenda kept walking. Nobody said anything. Costello touched Anderson lightly on the forearm, but he quickly pulled away.

The grainy figure of a man in a long dark coat, leaning against an estate agent's window, appeared in the middle of the screen.

'Is he waiting?' Costello asked. 'If so, what for?'

Figures continued to drift across the left monitor to be picked up on the right. Silent, ethereal, their motion slowed by the camera, they looked like the living dead.

'This guy ...' Wyngate pointed with his pen to a single man in an anorak and jeans, '... is just behind them. We're trying to get a still of him, trace him, find out if he saw anything.'

Anderson was peering at the screen with ferocious intensity. At twenty past seven he'd been outside the auditorium, waiting for Helena McAlpine. He had been thinking about enjoying himself ...

Wyngate butted in. 'And he's carrying a small bag from one of the stalls. We have a list of the stallholders.' He tapped his pen on the monitor. 'It looks like one of those long German sausage things.'

Costello felt herself tense, waiting for Anderson's reaction, as Brenda walked into view, buttoning up her coat and yanking her shoulder-bag strap up on to her shoulder.

'Where is Peter?' said Anderson, whispering under his breath.

Now Brenda was walking away from the market, on the pavement, perfectly framed by the camera. A wee boy carrying a Winnie-the-Pooh rucksack with a dragon dangling from it followed, trotting fast to try and keep up. Peter still had his dragon trousers on; they could see the hooves swinging loose above his shoes.

'Christ!' said Anderson. 'How far behind is he?'

'Not as far as it looks on this – ten, fifteen feet maybe?'

'It doesn't matter – it was enough.'

Wyngate put the film on to slow motion. Brenda, shuddering slightly on the film, stopped and turned as if Peter had called her. She was angry; it was obvious from her body language. Peter ran towards her, and was briefly lost in the crowd of Christmas revellers, then he appeared again. But, turning her back on him, his mother continued to walk away, her stride quickening. Leaving him behind.

Peter didn't follow. He stood his ground.

How easily it happens, thought Costello, her heart going out to Brenda. That moment would be forever in her memory. A whole lifetime of: *If only I'd held on to him, if only I hadn't turned my back*. And Costello knew Colin well enough to know that he would not forgive. Who would?

'So far,' Wyngate said, leaning forward again, 'this is the only tape where we can actually see Peter and Brenda. It's not much. '

When they looked at Brenda on the other screen, Peter wasn't following.

There was complete silence in the room now, the passing time marked by the slow click of the tape in the machine. Nobody said anything. Nobody said: *But it's all we have.*

Wyngate broke the silence. 'Watch this.' Two people walked left to right; one, a lone female, stopped under the camera, checking a shopping list, then turned and walked back the way she'd come. '*This* guy ...' said Wyngate. 'Him in the long coat. We saw him earlier, and here he is again. And these two, hanging around up here ... you can see better from this one.' Wyngate moved his chair out of the way of the second monitor. 'Two men, here, leaning against the glass, one also in a long coat. He puts a baseball cap on, kicks himself upright off the glass and goes; the other follows.'

'Is that a logo on the cap, a name?' Mulholland pressed his face against the screen. 'If it is, can we get it blown up?'

'I'm on it.' Wyngate made a note. 'Now one of them goes to the door ... and see this ...' Wyngate tapped the glass of the first monitor. The other figure pulled a mobile phone from his pocket and started dialling, pacing back and forth, moving in and out of the view of the lens.

'What's he doing?'

Littlewood shrugged. 'Worst-case scenario, he was watching the lad, saw him separated from his mum, so he phones a colleague waiting further up the road ...'

'Oh, Christ!' Anderson swore. 'I can't believe this. What does *she* say?'

'She thought he was behind her,' Wyngate recited. 'She was digging in her handbag for her car keys, looking for her car. Well, she got to the car, opened the door, and when she turned round the wee lad wasn't following. Nobody saw anything.'

'How could they not see anything?' Anderson's voice was harsh.

The room was silent. 'A small boy in a busy market place, crying, is just a kid having a Christmas tantrum,' said Costello. 'I'm sorry, Colin, that's what people would see. Even with Luca, Troy and now Peter being taken, that's still what they would see.'

'Did Gail get anywhere with Stella?' asked Quinn. 'Was it Troy she saw?'

'We got nothing useful, ma'am. She could only remember what she had already told us and that memory was prompted by the newspaper description. Not reliable – sorry, Col.' Costello offered a tentative smile.

Anderson raised his hand to stop her; he didn't even want to think about this. 'Look, Luca must have gone up Highburgh Road, towards here. If that boy was Troy, he went the same way. Might Peter have been taken that way too? Have you got somebody down there?' He looked at the map, the junction where Byres Road intersected with University Avenue, Highburgh Road, the car park and a crow's foot of minor roads and pathways within fifty yards.

'It was the first thing we did,' said Quinn following his gaze. 'The Search Unit was in Crown Avenue, Colin; you put them there yourself. They were on site within three minutes.'

'What about those two guys in the long coats?' asked Costello.

'We think we have a lead on them. They were seen getting into a big car ... We have twelve uniforms down there, and they're working on it now from their end. We're trying to get a lead on that logo. We'll get it traced, don't worry.'

Wyngate shrugged and stopped the tape. It paused as the man with the mobile momentarily faced the camera. They all stared at the image, committing it to memory.

'Hang on a minute,' said Mulholland, pointing at

someone else, further away. They all looked at the tall figure, wearing a long woollen coat, frozen in mid-stride. 'Run that on a bit.' The figure jolted into action, as Wyngate edged the film onward.

'That's Frances,' said Mulholland in a hurt voice. 'She said she was going home – she said her face was sore.'

'So, she changed her mind,' said Costello.

'That girl is messing you about,' said Lewis.

'I'll see if she remembers seeing anything.' Mulholland left the room, pulling his mobile from his pocket.

'But if Brenda and Frances bumped into each other – then if Peter had lost sight of his mother, could he have tried to follow Frances?' asked Costello.

'I think we need to get her down here. Not that I don't trust Vik, but we have to do things by the book.' Costello looked at Quinn for tacit consent before going to the door. 'Vik, ask Frances to come down here. She must have walked along the street within a minute of the abduction. We need to talk her through it.'

'Well, I'll ask her, but she wasn't feeling too well . . .'

'If she was well enough to go to the German Market, she's well enough to come down here,' said Costello. 'Or I'll go and get her myself, understand?' She turned to see another picture being pinned up alongside Luca and Troy . . . a little blond boy with a gap-toothed smile and both arms round Pat the Penguin. To Costello it seemed a lifetime ago.

'There's no answer on her moby,' said Mulholland, coming back in a moment later.

'Did you leave a message? Is she calling in?' Costello's voice punched the air.

'Her phone was off. She might be in bed – it's late, you know.'

'Well, get yer arse round there then!'

'Yes, go, Mulholland. Now!' Quinn said, coming out from her office, sipping strong black coffee. 'We need to know what she saw. And we need to ask Brenda if she was aware of Frances. If neither saw anything, then it was very smooth, very quick, the way . . .'

'A paedophile would do it?' Anderson finished the sentence for her. 'You're thinking this is an organized thing, aren't you? With a car and a driver?' The question was directed at Littlewood.

Quinn shrugged.

'But there's no other reason to think that.' Costello now turned to Littlewood. 'Unless you know something we don't.' Littlewood passed a look to Quinn, who kept her face down, swirling her coffee in her cup.

'Well, it's still just a possibility we have to consider – the boys are all of a type; pretty-looking, blond, thin,' said Littlewood. 'Peter might just fit the bill. Sorry, Colin.'

Costello felt close to tears, remembering the photo

of Peter that Anderson kept in his wallet. Absurdly, she thought of her own father, wondering if he had ever kept a photograph of her. She doubted it. She looked from Anderson to Littlewood. They had locked eyes; something was going on that she didn't know about. Anderson looked more angry than she had ever seen him.

'Right,' Quinn said. 'Get Irvine to talk to Brenda, take her through it again. Wyngate, start ringing round, see if any bus drivers or taxi drivers saw anything. Get them to think, what was parked in front of them, what was parked behind. Anything unusual, no matter how small. We have somebody on every corner; it's all roped off, nobody's going in or out.'

'I'm going down there,' said Anderson with quiet anger.

'Not a good idea, Colin. You'd probably hit somebody. Leave it to us. Shouldn't you be with your wife?'

Anderson didn't reply. He covered his mouth with the palm of his hand, and shook his head, not trusting himself to speak

'Go home with Brenda when Irvine's finished,' Quinn said gently. 'Try and get some rest.'

'For Claire's sake,' Costello contributed.

'Claire's staying with Graham's mother, and I'm not going home without Peter.'

How often had Costello heard parents say that? But hours turned into days and days into months.

The dead did not come back. Costello stepped into the corridor, checked there was no one there, pulled out her mobile phone and started scrolling for a stored number.

The effing bloody profiler, the Boss had called Mick Batten. But then the Boss had always said: *Get the help you need where you can.*

21

Eve lay looking at the ceiling, waiting for the distinctive clunk of the gate as Lynne sneaked out. She had lain quiet and listened as her sister searched her desk, God knows what for – she wouldn't find it. She had probably only found the file on Douglas – well, the bits Eve had wanted her to find. They really were stupid, those two. It was a shame, what was going to happen to Douglas. She had enjoyed tracking down every little aspect of his tawdry but charmed life. She felt like a stalker after a prize stag. She could admire its beauty, salute its majesty, but she would enjoy putting a bullet through its brain even more.

She stretched her legs out, slowly and carefully at first. The pins in the right one made it very stiff, and she still had to be careful about initial weight bearing. But, even though she had practised for long enough, she often surprised herself by how easily she could get to her feet.

Poor Lynne, silly frustrated old cow – if the house had been left to her rather than Eve, that bastard Douglas would have had it sold ages ago. The fact he was still sniffing round Lynne proved she had never put him right about the house not being hers at all. If it were, he would have taken her for everything she had, and Lynne would have found herself stuck in a dismal wee flat blighted by cheap conversion work, waiting for him to leave his 'wife'. Which he would never do.

Eve limped to the window, and watched her sister hurry across the road and up the path to Stella's flat. Stella would think Lynne was mad, going across to see her at this time of night on some strange whim.

Eve lumbered through to her own room, holding on to the wall for support. In her bedroom she got down on the floor, lying flat on her stomach. Kneeling was something she hadn't quite mastered yet. She reached under her bed, pulled out the under-bed storage bag and groped around for a green shoebox secured by an elastic band. She opened it, checked the contents, and smiled at the little bag of white powder, its sticky yellow label marked with the letters NaCN, bordered by a black skull and cross-bones. The bag was wrapped up in the grey wig, accompanied by her mother's glasses, a scarf and an 'old lady' brooch from the Oxfam shop in Byres Road. Lynne had already gone through the desk, so that would be the place to hide this now. She knew her sister, knew she wouldn't give up; and if she got anything out of Stella McCorkindale, then she'd be even keener. Eve put the box on top of the bed and shoved the plastic storage bag back, making sure it was exactly where Lynne liked it to be. She took her time getting to her feet, her right leg sticking grotesquely out behind her. Upright, she waited for the dizziness to pass, then picked up the shoebox and went into the drawing room. Five minutes later, the contents of the box had been distributed throughout her desk, bits hidden here, other bits there. Most of it fitted under the removable shelf of her pastel box. Lynne would never look in there; it was far too messy. Eve then ripped the shoebox into tiny pieces and pushed them to the bottom of the bin in the kitchen.

By the time Lynne came back, Eve was back on the settee, complaining. 'I'd just dropped off to sleep, and you woke me up, banging the bathroom door. It's gone eleven! You know how hard I find it to get to sleep. Could you not be a bit more considerate?'

Peter Anderson was cold, colder than he had ever been in his life. It was quiet; there wasn't even the sound of traffic up here. There was a door – it was slightly open – he had tried to push it closed but the concrete underneath was bumpy, the door got stuck. He had tried to pull it. The door had juddered and sprung back. The stab of the skelf into his thumb made him cry out; his hand started to bleed.

He put his hand against the door again; it didn't move at all. Now he couldn't get out, the gap left was too small.

He pulled his jumper tightly round him and put his anorak on back to front, the way he'd learned in the Cubs. He could snuggle into it now, and he sat on the floor with his back against the wall, hugging his knees, his head nodding backwards and forwards, muttering his Puff song to himself. Every so often he would hear a door open and close, hurried footsteps over his head. Once he had gone up to the smaller door and tried to open it, but it was locked.

He decided to call out the next time he heard footsteps come, but they never did. He must have curled into a ball and fallen asleep, then he was awoken by a noise. He put his hand out for his dinosaur. Instead of the warmth of his duvet, his fingers touched cold, hard concrete. Then he remembered.

He heard a car drive away. Then there was only dark and silence.

And it was very dark. He was trying hard not to be scared. He could hear music from somewhere, like a brass band doing Christmas songs, but nobody was singing and it all sounded very far away. He joined in with the words he knew, and those he didn't know he made up, singing quietly to himself. And waited for his Dad to come and get him. His hand began to hurt again so, for the first time in two years, he sat down and sucked his thumb.

Vik Mulholland pulled on his gloves as he left the station, glad to leave the chaos behind. It was a bitter cold, clear night; snow was falling, and he had to take care to avoid stepping in the piles of slush at the side of the pavement and in the gutter. He could hear them still having a right knees-up down on Byres

Road. The West End in particular was treating it like some kind of winter carnival and nature had obliged by producing this, the most beautiful fall of calm snow. As he headed down Hyndland Road, he could hear the Salvation Army brass band in the distance having a go at 'Rudolf the Red-Nosed Reindeer' – everybody in the West End could probably hear it.

Vik quickened his pace as he turned into Beaumont Place. Outside number 42 Frances was standing in the street, her collar up round her neck, shoulders hunched – a slender black witch delicately outlined against the snow.

'Fran?' Vik called, loudly. Then, more quietly when she did not answer, 'Fran, are you OK? It's nearly midnight, for God's sake. You'll freeze out here.'

'They look like ghosts, don't they?' she muttered in her husky voice, the words clouding with her breath and melting into the air.

Vik turned to look at the Sally Army band, just visible on the corner of the street. What little light there was played around their feet, their silhouettes anchorless, adrift.

Frances had been crying; slow, silent tears had marked her face. Vik lifted her chin with the knuckle of his forefinger and wiped them away.

'I was trying to be festive. I thought if I stood out here in the snow listening to that music,' she sniffed, 'I might come over all Dickensian and romantic.'

'And cold,' added Vik, his feet thumping the ground.

'But I just get so depressed.' The tears started again. 'It's all so bloody depressing.'

'Well, maybe this time . . .' Vik took both her hands in his. 'Maybe this time it will be different. This time you stand a chance of being happy. What about that for a present?'

'Yeah, what about it?' But she was smiling. She leaned forward and kissed him. 'I've been thinking about . . .'

No, not now. He pulled away. 'Look, I need to speak to you about something. Work.'

'Oh . . .' Frances sounded hurt. She turned away from him slightly, as the band switched to 'Santa Claus is Coming to Town'. 'I thought you were here to see me.'

Littlewood was the only one who still had his own desk nowadays, the only one whose computer the others couldn't access. Costello had spent ten minutes furtively tapping away at his computer, but all her guesses at his passwords had failed. At the same time, she was dialling the eternally engaged Mick Batten. She glanced into Quinn's office. Something was happening. The most experienced guy in the field was working on his own, on a need-to-know basis, and the rest were not privy to whatever was going on. If she hadn't found out what Quinn and Littlewood were up to by midnight, she was going to go in there and lose the plot with both of them. Quinn and Littlewood looked as though their meeting was breaking up. Costello went back to her own desk, and dialled Mick's number yet again.

'Costello! So, what gives?' The Liverpudlian voice of Dr Mick Batten sounded weary at the other end of the phone.

'Sorry for disturbing you so late, Mick.' She glanced at the clock, the hour hand almost at the witching hour.

'You're not the first.'

'I'm worried. Colin wouldn't speak to you. So, I feel I have to . . .' Costello's voice trailed off.

'About what?' Batten sounded quite unperturbed.

'These missing boys, Mick. We need your help.'

'While I'm flattered, Costello, you know what I'm going to say.' She heard him sip something, and a gentle clink as if a teaspoon had rattled in the mug. Or ice in whisky. 'I've not been instructed to act for you. And I told you when you were working on the Crucifixion Killer case, it's all educated guesswork. Your force will appoint somebody who is good.'

'Yes, I know that. But it's Christmas, Mick. The bloody request form won't be filled in until the admin staff come back.'

'And?' A slow, appreciative swallow. Whisky.

'They won't be as good as you.'

'You are not one to flatter.'

'No, I'm not. It's a fact.' Costello snapped back, her voice quiet and crisp. 'Mick, they've taken Peter

Anderson. It's been four hours. We need some help here. Please.'

There was a slightly confused silence on the other end of the phone. 'Peter Anderson? I know that name . . .'

'Colin Anderson's son. You know how important the first few hours are, and the clock is ticking.'

The silence on the phone intensified; she knew Batten was gathering his thoughts and putting his analytical brain into gear. She pushed on. 'We think we're under pressure from upstairs to follow certain lines of enquiry.'

'Is that not the point?' asked Batten.

'Not when the ground troops are thinking otherwise. We think any profiler will only be asked to look at the profiles of paedophiles. The investigation is getting narrower when it should be getting wider . . . Things are being leaked to the press.' She sat down, her legs suddenly too weak to hold her up. 'I'm not sure what's going on, but the new DCI and John Littlewood seem to be going off at a tangent that nobody else knows about and I – well, I don't think it's healthy. If you were here, you'd agree. Can I send you some stuff to look at?'

'Like you said, it's nearly Christmas. It would take ages to get permission.'

'Without permission?'

'Costello, how well do you know Peter Anderson?'

'He's Colin's son. How well do you think I know him?'

'Then you should distance yourself from it, you know that. Knowing them means you cease to function effectively. Look, I spent yesterday talking to a man ...' the voice faltered a bit, '... talking to a man who'd picked out his daughter's eyes with a knife because he thought she had the eyes of Satan. The child was four years old ...' A sip of whisky, quickly swallowed.

'Jesus Christ!' Costello felt a cold wave of nausea.

'... and my daughter is four years old. So, how long would I survive in this job if I let it get into my head?'

'But how would you feel if your daughter was taken and I quoted the rulebook?'

Silence. Ice chinking on to crystal. 'We didn't have this conversation. You have my fax number?'

Costello bit back her tears, said a quiet thank you, and hung up. She looked round; nobody was watching, and the fax machine was blinking idle in the corner. She took a deep breath, picked up the briefing summary sheet, and prayed to a God she didn't believe in.

As Mulholland trudged slowly back up the hill to the station, the night was eerily light with undisturbed snow, and no wind stirred. The sounds of drunken happiness were muffled. *All is calm, all is bright.* Everything seemed to be waiting.

Frances's eyes had filled up the minute he had mentioned work. '*I thought you were here to see me,*' she said. She had sounded hurt, angry even. When he explained about Peter, she had become distressed and in the end she had fled back into her house, wounded, hurting.

No, she hadn't seen Peter or Brenda at the German Market. She just hadn't wanted to go home on her own after the fair. She was depressed and she wanted to be among people. Yes, she had noticed the men in the long coats, and yes, she had recognized the logo. And she thought she had recognized the two men. Mulholland quickened his step, breaking into a run – they needed to know about that at the station. Frances was sure they were Dec Slater and maybe Jinky Jones. She was sure about Dec, not so sure about Jinky.

The logo was that of Rogan O'Neill's homecoming tour – anybody would know that.

'Right, guys.' Quinn rapped on the table for silence. Behind her on the wall someone had pinned up a map of the United States, but no one was brave enough to ask why. 'I know we're all tired, but we've got Colin out the building for half an hour – he's in good hands, Burns will keep him calm, he's taken him for a walk and to get some food into him. We can only imagine what he's going through.' Quinn stopped and adjusted the elastic that held her ponytail. 'Of course, he's not going anywhere until we get the wee guy back, but each and every one of us would be the same.' There was a murmur of empathy. 'So, thanks to you all for coming in. Now, first, let's check out what we have. Brenda Anderson has given us a minute-by-minute account of her shopping trip, and Irvine has the list of all the stalls she visited prior to Peter's abduction.

'We've caught the first edition of tomorrow's paper – we're banking on the front page, and a photograph. However, we're keeping Peter's father's ID to ourselves for now. The media are honouring that. Somebody from Stewart Street is coming down to interview Colin, to go over old cases, dig up old enemies, just in case this abduction has nothing to do with the other two and some bastard's been given ideas. Burns will stay with him. Meanwhile we are reviewing the film of the reconstruction of Luca's abduction, which featured Peter Anderson of course.' Quinn noticed Costello's eyes narrowing; she paused, as if inviting her to say something, but Costello shook her head.

'I want a team to go up to Miss Cotter's flat and take the place apart. I know we've already searched that area, but just in case she really is a raving nutter we need to go through any outbuildings in the back court. Has she a plot or an allotment? Or a garage somewhere? Is this the only property she owns? If she has these children, she must be hiding them somewhere. Over the next twenty-four hours the temperature is going to plummet and the snow will freeze. Tell her it's best for her to stay in and keep warm – well, we don't want her falling over and breaking a hip, do we? And if she does leave the house, we'll follow her. I'll get the team organized for first light. We are leaving nothing to chance. I'll get PC Smythe on to it.'

The door of the Incident Room opened, and Mulholland walked in, snow still clinging to his hair. 'Those two guys on the CCTV tape? The logo was of Rogan's tour, and Frances recognized them as Dec Slater and Jinky Jones. Dec hasn't changed much over the years, but Jinky has. She got really upset, and I didn't have the heart to bring her down here.'

Lewis swore under her breath, loud enough for everybody to hear.

Quinn nodded slowly. 'Littlewood, take over here, will you? And I'll remind you lot that anything said in this room is highly confidential. It goes no further, not to your wife, husband, kids – nobody. And particularly not to Colin Anderson, in view of what you're about to hear.' And she busied herself putting papers into a folder, then went into her own office and closed the door as if with a sense of relief.

Littlewood took an armful of transparencies, folders and envelopes from his drawer and placed them on his desk. He got straight to the point. 'Here is a map of the USA,' he began.

'Yeah, we got that,' said Lewis.

Littlewood ignored her. 'And marked in blue are the locations of the disappearances of eight young boys over the last ten years, plus dates. Not much, you might reckon, for a country that size and given the movement of the population, but these disappearances correlate directly with – this.' He pinned up over the map a transparency showing a second annotated map. 'This shows the tours made by a certain rock star over the last ten years. Rogan O'Neill. When you superimpose it like this, you get an exact match of times, dates, states.'

'Jesus! Is this what you've been working on?' Costello leapt to her feet. 'Why did you not say sooner? Why did you let it get this far?'

'Go on, call me an arse; I know you want to,' said Littlewood, unperturbed. 'It was all very gradual at first. I was asked by upstairs to keep an eye out for any unusual activities of Rogan's, then all this started happening. First Luca – well, we didn't even think that was an abduction at first – then it all moved too fast. We've now decided that you do need to know.'

'About time.'

'Now obviously we can't exactly walk up to O'Neill and search him, but we have a way in, don't we, Costello?'

'Lauren the bimbo? Yes, indeed,' she said harshly. 'And I'll get something out of her, if she ...'

'She might not know,' said Wyngate.

'Oh, she knows. Or suspects,' Costello's voice was cold with ill-disguised disgust, remembering that one flicker of fear in Lauren when Rogan had spoken to her.

'I am going to leave this envelope of photographs lying here. They don't leave this room, they do not even leave this table. Anybody who looks at them needs a strong stomach. 'Nuff said.'

Mulholland slowly flicked through the pile of photographs, looking at each one before putting it to the back. The expression on his face did not change one iota but his skin paled. Occasionally he would pause, turn a photograph ninety degrees and then proceed with the next.

He handed one photograph to Wyngate, and Wyngate, already red-eyed with fatigue, swallowed hard and handed it back. 'You don't need to see these, Costello,' said Mulholland.

'You're right, I don't.'

'Neither do I,' said Lewis, sounding bored. She stood at the window, looking out, beautiful in profile, her make-up perfect, her curls still shiny in precise twirls. 'I have a phone call to make.' She strode past Costello, as if she had somewhere more important to go. Costello resisted the urge to trip her up.

'I don't believe some of these pictures,' Mulholland said. 'Every boy used, abused, brutalized, killed – who in the world . . .?'

'Yeah, who?' Anderson was leaning on the wall at the door.

'Sorry, mate, didn't see you there.'

'Obviously.' Anderson put his hands deep in his pockets, and looked directly at Littlewood. 'What's going on?'

DCI Quinn was out of her office like a bat out of hell. 'OK, Anderson – you are now a witness, not a detective. Littlewood, take Colin down to the canteen, and go through the conversation he and Costello had with O'Neill, right now. What you said to Rogan, what he said to you, Colin, and what Costello said to him. Then show him the photos of the crowd that turned up outside Joozy Jackpots, or whatever the bloody place is called; he might recognize somebody.'

Littlewood put a hand on to Anderson's arm and led him out, following Burns who had already started down the stairs.

'Will somebody keep an eye on him? For a big man he's a right creeping Jesus. Wyngate, get out the CCTV from the fair again and home in on the time frame. Then do the same with the films of the German Market. See if you see any hats with logos of Rogan's homecoming tour at the fair. Phone the hotels where Rogan's crew are staying; they'll have a record of door entry activity for each room. Another thing – try and get the ID photos for everybody involved in that US tour. I want to know if those two guys we see hanging around are Jinky Jones and Dec Slater. Those two and Rogan himself are the only three who link every incident in the States, but for God's sake be careful who you ask. Just try to marry something up. I'll get Irvine to help you once she's free.'

DS Lewis shimmied back into the room. 'What are you giving Costello to do, or is she off on one of her tangents?'

'What do you mean – Lauren McCrae?' asked Quinn.

Lewis shrugged, her lips tauntingly drifting into a smile.

Rebecca Quinn settled herself behind her desk, indulging in her usual disconcerting habit of looking at her paperwork while relishing the disquiet of her victim.

'So, what are you up to?' She put her index finger to her lips and licked it, spikily turning over a page of some update she was reading.

'Working,' Costello said petulantly.

'It's wearing a bit thin,' said Quinn. She sighed and twisted her seat from the desk, bending over and tightening the laces on her trainers. 'Are you doing something without my permission? And I don't mean the Lauren McCrae thing.'

'I'm talking to Dr Mick Batten. Without your permission.'

'About what?'

'Peter's disappearance.' Costello stopped. Quinn looked up. 'He says I shouldn't get involved.'

'But do you ever do as you are told? You are off the case.'

'What!'

'You heard – you're off the case. Now be quiet, Costello,' said Quinn, not unkindly. 'Sit down and listen. Are you and Colin Anderson having an affair?'

'No.'

'Have you ever?'

'No!'

'OK, just wanted to make sure.'

'That's Lewis, gossiping . . .'

'A bad habit of hers. But you two are close, so you are very involved and I don't like it. It's not healthy on a case like this. And you have no idea how hard it is to take over a team that's as close as you lot. You seem to hate each other but you slip and slide together like a well-oiled machine; so well oiled I can't seem to get a grip on any of you. You don't trust me.' Their eyes met. Quinn dropped hers first. 'And that affects how well the team works.'

Costello didn't know what she was supposed to say. 'It's just the way we are, ma'am, nothing personal.'

'But it is too personal, and you're too close. I can't have you and Colin going off at your own tangents. And for that reason you are both off the case. Burns is babysitting Colin, and he's big enough to hit him if he has to. I've no doubt that everyone out there would speak to him before they'd speak to me, regardless of procedure.'

'True.'

'And you have to *stay* off the case. I know you're seeing Lauren McCrae,' Quinn glanced at her watch, and sighed when she realized the minutes and hours had crawled into Saturday, 'today – Littlewood will brief you – but once that's over, you're on the cyanide stuff; you can make your own case, do your own thing. God knows you do that anyway.' Quinn pursed her lips. 'But if you feel like obeying orders for once, you can get out and get on with your own work. If you don't, and all this documentation disappears and gets faxed to Mick Batten behind my back, I'll be very upset . . .'

Costello's hand paused on the door handle, and she held her breath.

'. . . But not as upset as I would be if it didn't.' Quinn slowly pushed a narrow beige file across her desk, close enough for Costello to reach easily, then she stood up and turned away to look out of the window. 'Shut the door behind you.'

Saturday, 23 December

22

Anderson had had a terrible night, drinking endless cups of coffee in the canteen, going through the conversation with Rogan O'Neill again and again, looking at photograph after photograph until the grit in his eyes blurred one face into another. They had taken him through every big case he'd ever worked on, considered anybody who might bear a grudge. They'd delved into his personal life only to find it squeaky clean. They'd gone through his entire career with a fine-tooth comb, digging up nothing except memories of the old DCI. And Colin could not help but think that if Alan McAlpine was here, they would be out on the streets pulling the city apart. He knew they were putting him through the motions to keep him busy, and he was grateful for something, anything to do. He had refused to talk further to Brenda, but had helped to draft the statement for her appeal, even though he knew it was getting him nowhere.

He had fallen asleep around half past six, ten minutes' shut-eye with his head down on the canteen table. But his sleep was even more tortured than his waking hours. His back was sore, his head was sore, and – worst of all – there was still no news.

Like Troy and Luca, Peter Anderson had disappeared into nowhere.

When he woke at the back of nine, Burns suggested some fresh air, some exercise to get their brain cells working. They walked back in silence, down Hyndland Road – Anderson in a borrowed coat, hunching his shoulders against the slight smirr of snow – ignoring the few very early morning commuters heading into town. As they turned into the lane, Anderson heard feet crunching in the gravel behind him.

'Colin? Colin?'

He turned. Helena was standing there, holding her hood up with a gloved hand. She looked as though she had spent most of the night crying, her eyes red raw, her lips swollen and chapped.

'Colin, how are you?'

'Not good.' He nodded at Burns, who raised a hand and went on without him. 'Worst time of my life.'

'How's Brenda?'

Anderson didn't answer. He couldn't tell Helena that he had hardly spoken to his wife, how much he blamed her. What was he supposed to say? Helena took his silence as a sign of distress.

'Oh, Colin, I am sorry. Have the police come up with nothing? Surely . . .?'

'Not much. All paedophiles are being checked out; all my old cases are being reviewed and they're bringing everybody and his dog in for interview.'

He shut his eyes, trying to hold it together. 'I can't believe it, can't admit it to myself . . .'

Helena had been a policeman's wife for too long to say the customary, calming: *Oh, I'm sure he will be all right.* 'If there's anything I can do, anything at all . . .'

'Not that I can think of.'

'Sorry, Colin, I'm going into hospital today. I should have been there at ten, I'm just on my way now . . .' her voice trailed off.

Anderson couldn't think what to say. 'Good luck,' was all he could manage.

She nodded tearfully, and turned away through the slush.

Behind him, Costello gently peeped her horn. She was sitting in her white Corolla, barely visible through the mist on the windscreen. She popped the passenger door open for him.

'Quinn has put me off the case.'

'Join the club.'

'I wanted to let you know that I have faxed Batten most of the details – of Peter, I mean. He might want to talk to you, off the record.'

'You could lose your job over that.'

'I'd like to see them try. But Quinn was OK about it. I'm going off to see Lauren now. If she knows anything, I'll find out.'

'I know you will. Thanks.' He looked out at the dull rain, and the puddles being whipped into wavelets. The forecast was for it to turn colder before they got through the day. 'The temperature's falling,' he said. 'Peter's never seen a white Christmas.'

'Well, he'll see this one.' She pointed as a few snowflakes settled on the windscreen.

It was snowing seriously now, but the air inside the Botanic Gardens was warm and cloying. Costello had made it clear: the Kibble Palace, the older part of the Botanic Gardens, at eleven. It was a fine building, and she was glad the burghers of the city had got their collective finger out at last and refurbished it. The glass of the circular Victorian dome was clean and sparkling, covered by a doily of snow where iron met glass. Costello walked in, keen to get out of the cold, immediately undoing the collar of her jacket and shaking the snow from her scarf before stuffing it in her pocket. She just hoped she would stay awake.

Littlewood had been clear: *Let Lauren run with the conversation; listen, prompt but do not lead.* Costello had had little experience of paedophiles, even less of supermodels – but when he said, *Treat her like a battered wife in denial*, she felt on more solid ground. She would be polite, interested and empathetic, no matter how much she wanted to slap the truth from Lauren's pretty but empty head.

Costello walked round the glasshouse, rehearsing the interview, breathing in the smell of damp earth, compost and warmed air. Her schoolfriend's grand-dad had had a greenhouse that smelled like that, of paraffin and sweet peas, and at the right time of year, they'd always had the smell of home-grown tomatoes on their fingertips, the taste on their tongues. How innocent those days had been: two little girls with an old man in a greenhouse at the bottom of a deserted garden. The memory brought her back to her reason for being here.

The café was a temporary-looking arrangement with pseudo wrought-iron tables and chairs on uneven slabs, and a chalk-written menu offering cappuccino spelled badly and Irn Bru spelled correctly. Two women sat with three wheelchair-bound children. Two of the kids were eating soup; the other, a boy with cerebral palsy, was being fed from a spoon during pauses in his constant writhing. Costello wasn't aware that she had been staring but the boy caught her eye, and large brown eyes stared back at her, intelligent and kind. Costello smiled, feeling awkward now about turning and walking out. She waved at him and went to stroll round the pond, where large sleepy koi carp, mottled silver and white against gold, gently undulated under the water lilies. She walked up to them slowly, not wanting them to dart away as her shadow fell.

Lauren McCrae was late; it was nearly ten past. Costello assumed it went with the job. She gazed at a large tree which stopped abruptly a few feet from the glass roof, trimmed to stay within its limitations, and stroked its trunk. 'It grows well in warm climates,' a slow Canadian drawl said from behind her.

'No chance here then,' said Costello. 'This snow will be making you feel at home.'

'Kind of.'

They walked on round the pond, the clack of McCrae's boot heels following her. Costello glanced sideways at Lauren. 'Do you mind if I say something first? This is Glasgow, Lauren, in December. Sunglasses tend to draw attention, especially indoors. I'm assuming that's not what you want.'

'I guess I just get used to being recognized everywhere I go.' Lauren pulled the Raybans from her face, but not before glancing over her shoulder.

Costello would not have recognized her. The natural sheen of Lauren's super-healthy beauty seemed to have worn off in the last twenty-four hours. Her eyes looked red and puffy, as though much-desired sleep had passed her by. She folded down her collar, shaking her hair free, and continued to walk slowly, her catwalk glide looking a little ungainly on the cobbles.

Costello considered how to approach the conversation, in the light of Littlewood's revelations; like approaching the koi, she presumed, slowly and steadily. She knew she couldn't push.

'Do you fancy a sit down and a cup of tea? I'm not sure what it will be like in here.'

She noticed, again, that nervousness about Lauren, the slight hesitation before answering. 'Yeah, sure.'

They settled on one black coffee and one black tea, in dubious-looking waxed paper cups with cardboard butterfly wings for handles. Costello warmed her hands on her cup, holding it under her chin. She was impatient, but she had to win this woman's confidence. Peter's safety might depend on it. 'I'm sorry,' she said. 'This may be pretty vile.'

'Can't be as bad as that stuff they serve at the hotel. Rogan calls it pure Madeira, I don't know why.'

Gain her confidence, thought Costello, *she's here to tell you something*. 'Glaswegian for crap,' she explained.

'Why? Madeira's a lovely island. I was there last year on a photo shoot.'

'Not the island, the cake. It's the powdery yellow cake you get at Christmas once all the good stuff with icing and marzipan and sultanas is finished. Nobody likes it, hence . . . pure Madeira.'

Lauren looked a little bemused. 'The diet of you people never fails to amaze me. Is it true you deep-fry your candy?' She stretched out long beautiful fingers tapering to perfect nails.

'Sometimes. Is that a French manicure?' she asked, in an effort to break the ice.

'What? This?' Lauren splayed her long-boned fingers on the plastic table. 'Oh, I had it done yesterday.'

Costello hid her own discoloured nails, one black from a fight with the photocopier, another bloodied and ripped to the quick. 'So, Lauren, what can I do for you?'

'Nothing really.' Lauren's forefinger circled the top of her cup.

Costello lowered her voice. 'Lauren, in my job I have seen everything and heard everything. I have had the decency to meet you. So, you should tell me what's bothering you.'

Lauren said, 'It's about me.'

'So, let's talk about you.'

Lauren looked around again, fingered her sunglasses, then thought better of it.

'Whatever it is, it was bothering you when we interviewed Rogan.'

'How did you know that?' She seemed surprised.

'I'm a policewoman, remember? I'm trained to see these things.'

Lauren raised the coffee to her lips and blew on it gently. Costello knew when to stay silent. 'I'm sorry?' She realized Lauren was speaking, but so quietly she had to lean in to hear.

'He's a good man,' Lauren was almost whispering, urgently. 'Very loyal. He's loyal to his friends, he's loyal to his business, to his fans, and he's loyal to me. You know why he brought me back to Scotland?'

To escape a criminal investigation? 'From the sunshine of LA to Glasgow?' Costello looked up through the glass overhead. 'I'd have to think a long time about that one.'

'Because a long time before he met me, he had a girlfriend who lost a baby. So, this time, he wants it all to go right, and he wants his baby born on Scottish soil. He wants to be in control.'

'How romantic.' Costello pulled a deliberate face. 'In control? That's a strange way to put it.'

'He just wants to look after me – is that so bad?'

'So, why do you keep looking over your shoulder? Does he have you followed?'

'He looks after me. He doesn't like me going out on my own.'

Costello felt her way in. 'Loyal, you say? Well, that's the Rogan I remember from years ago. Loyal to his friends. He never left the boys behind – his success was their success.' She sipped her tea; it tasted like tar. 'Dec Slater and Jinky Jones were there in my day. They were all very close.'

'They still are.'

'Still close to each other or still close to Rogan?'

'Both,' said Lauren. Again that trace of bitterness.

'Rogan seems very much in love with you.' Fishing again.

'I know. I know.' Her voice faltered.

'So, why did you leave the States?' asked Costello, bluntly.

Lauren's reply was immediate, practised. 'Like I said, Rogue wants the baby to be born here.'

'The real reason?' Costello's question punched the air. 'Why so quickly? You were out of there in a matter of days.'

'You know then. It wasn't Rogan . . .'

'So, tell me?'

Lauren sighed. 'I don't understand how it happened, but some pornographic stuff went through our computer system, and it carried our address. Our IP address, I mean. But it was somebody else using it,' she insisted. 'They could have been anywhere in the world. The computer guys said it was sophisticated and designed to cause us as much trouble as possible. The house was full of people coming and going – PR people, police, you know. I just had to get out of there. Rogan was worried about the stress having an effect on the baby.'

'I can understand that.' Costello patted the slim tanned hand.

'Oh, it was no sweat, we just jumped on a plane. The hotel's OK and we bought the castle quickly enough. We'd looked at it on the net from LA.'

As you do, thought Costello.

Lauren had her supermodel face on again. 'Well, I thought we were getting a place of our own, then I find Dec and Jinky are moving in with us.' Her voice was more bitter than before. 'I guess Rogan felt he couldn't leave them behind, not after all these years.'

Costello felt her skin creep, and she phrased the next question carefully, getting the conversation back on track. 'But surely porn's not unusual for a bunch of blokes? You should see what some of the Neanderthals back at the station look at, and that's the cops I'm talking about.'

Lauren moved slightly in her seat. 'I don't care about that. It wasn't Rogan.' She was definite about that. She sounded almost bored with the subject, as though it really didn't bother her. Yet she looked around uneasily, and Costello was alarmed to see Lauren's face turn waxy grey. 'I'm sorry, I don't feel well. I have to find the toilet.'

Luca stretched up to look through the keyhole into the room beyond. He had already tried the keyhole in the big door but he couldn't see anything apart from a small sliver of light at the side of the key.

This other door was easier. The keyhole was clear. He could see Troy lying on a narrow bed, with his bedclothes piled on top of him all higgledy-piggledy like a great pile of washing. Luca rattled at the door, but it would not open. So, he tried pulling. Nothing.

He leaned down to put his mouth against the keyhole. 'Oi,' he said quietly. 'Oi, Troy?'

Nothing.

He put his eye to the hole again, but Troy hadn't moved. He stood up, and went to the other door – the big, solid door – but he couldn't get it to budge. He didn't like this; he couldn't work out what was going on but it didn't seem right.

He didn't like it here any more, he decided. He wasn't going to stay until his mum came to get him; he was going to get out now and go and find her at the hospital. He went back to the smaller door and pushed really hard, not caring if anyone heard. The door opened a wee bit, then a bit more. Troy looked as though he had been asleep for ever. Not a normal kind of sleep. Luca watched him for a while, watched how he was breathing, in a funny way, not in and out like a normal person. It was the kind of breathing his mum did sometimes when she had to lie on the floor. There was something wrong with Troy – the shape of him, the colour of him – it didn't look normal at all.

And he hadn't eaten his dinner. The Monkey Meal lay cold and congealed in its tray at the side of the bed, and the drink was untouched, the straw still in its polythene sleeve. Troy always ate his tea, he shovelled the food in. Luca's mum said that boys who ate like that got tummy ache. Troy said he ate like that because he was always bloody starving. Luca sniffed at the chips, and opened the lid of the burger roll. It smelled of cold mustard, but it had not been touched. Troy's face was wet and waxy, and little rivulets of water were running down it. His hands looked really strange; they were big and puffy and turning black, as dark as his sleeves. And he still had not moved. He must be hungry by now so Luca knelt on the stinking floor and pulled the straw from its sleeve. He pushed it into the top of the cup and gave it a wee suck. The cola was flat but cold. He held it to Troy's mouth and whispered in his ear, 'Here's some juice.' But the cola just dribbled down the side of Troy's face as Luca squeezed the side of the cup.

Luca sat back. 'Oh, dear,' he said.

He rubbed Troy's arm, gently at first, then a bit more roughly, but he did not wake. He nudged the bed, jumping back as a movement ruffled under the bedclothes. Luca lifted up Troy's duvet and came face to face with the rat. The rodent raised itself on its hind legs, and tensed, whiskers twitching. Luca caught sight of the two yellow spickles of teeth.

All he felt as it jumped was a flick of pain on the side of his face.

Anderson was being sick again; streams of vomit flooded from his mouth, staining the water in the toilet pan a deep dark brown.

DS Littlewood opened the door. 'You OK?'

'Not really,' Anderson grunted, ripping off sheet after sheet of toilet paper and wiping his nose and mouth. 'I've seen a lot in my time, but nothing like that.'

Littlewood leaned against the wall and lit a forbidden cigarette under the extraction current of the Vent Axia, as Anderson made his way to the sink and started washing his face with cold water. 'You shouldn't have looked at those pictures. They shouldn't have been left there.'

'How can you work with people like that? How can you stand it? Jesus!'

'In Vice we got stuff like that through all the time. Until some bastard pushed it too far. It got me demoted and cost me a few grand on my salary – but, God, it felt good. It's always good to know the enemy,' Littlewood said. 'But if that's the reason these kids are being taken, it means they're still alive.'

Anderson looked up sharply. Littlewood chewed noisily on his gum, refusing to meet his stare, clearly having thought better of uttering the words *snuff movies*, which nevertheless hung deafeningly in the air. He looked at his watch, he couldn't help but count the hours, the minutes: 15 hours, 23 minutes. 'But you don't think it is, do you? And don't bullshit me.'

'Years on Vice tell me no. These children could have been taken at any time but three have gone together, which suggests an organization. We don't know of one, and I doubt our intelligence is that poor. But you can argue it either way round. The Rogan thing is a nice excuse to have a poke about, see if he's up to those tricks. But he – or whoever it is in his entourage, if it is them – has never taken more than one kid a year; two in fourteen months is as close as he gets. This is something different. There's something else we're missing.'

'So, why are you and Quinn putting so much weight behind it then?' Anderson asked. 'That's where the resources seem to be going.'

'Because we're being told to. We're being leaned on to collect intelligence about what the Rogan tour is actually up to.' Littlewood sighed. 'A report from the LAPD says they've found over four thousand images on the computer in the O'Neill household. Four thousand and not one kid in them was over the age of twelve. Somebody in that set-up likes them young. Let's hope Costello comes back with something.'

'But that won't bring us any closer to Peter, will it?' said Anderson.

'I doubt it.' Littlewood shrugged. 'I'd rather just find the kids. Work it back from there. You could pick a hundred kids off a hundred street corners, but they chose these three. There's something about these three.'

'What? What is it?'

'Who knows? Something,' Littlewood said, vaguely. 'Let's see what Costello comes up with. The way to break these guys is through the women. A pregnancy will change Lauren's priorities – we couldn't have asked for better. If that doesn't work ...' Littlewood formed his podgy hand into a fist, '... I've heard Rogan's trying to double the reward money. If I beat information out of him, do I still qualify?'

Lauren was away from the table so long, Costello thought she'd done a runner. So, she phoned the station for an update.

'The morning news broadcasts have all carried the story,' Wyngate reported. 'So, we just have to hope someone's memory gets jogged. And you've to meet Mulholland outside HMV in Sauchiehall Street as soon as you're free.' Before Costello could ask why, she had to ring off. Lauren was striding across the canteen, oblivious to people gawping and wondering where they had seen the tall blonde before. She had reapplied make-up to hide the redness around her eyes. But the dark glasses were slipped on again as she sat down. The wall was going up again. She picked up her cup, decided her coffee was cold, and put it back down.

'Lauren, does anybody know you are here?' Costello asked. Lauren shook her head, but the expression on her face had changed; she had come to some kind of decision.

'No, nobody.' Then she began, speaking like a child. 'You know how some women who live with guys will put up with anything?' The plastic table wobbled, and she put out a slender tanned hand to steady it. 'Their friends say: *I really had no idea what was going on.* Do you believe them?' She was trembling, like a smoker desperate for nicotine. 'I don't feel like sitting here any longer. Can we walk?' Lauren was already on her feet, her suede bag slung over her shoulder.

'Yes, of course.' Costello followed her, searching for casual conversation to keep Lauren talking.

'You think people will change, but they don't.'

Costello pursued her, 'Anybody in particular? Jinky Jones? Dec Slater?'

'Why do you keep going on about those two?' She kicked at a loose stone on the path with the toe of her boot. 'God, they are faithful to him, closer than brothers.'

'Lauren, how long has this been going on?' Costello asked, not sure what 'this' was.

'Since we met. He cares, I know he cares, but it

doesn't stop him. And they are there *all* the time, watching me, so I don't put a foot out of line.' Lauren paused and turned round, her eyes wide.

Costello said nothing, not quite sure of the track of the conversation. They walked on for a few minutes. Eventually Costello looked pointedly at her watch. 'I have to ask you, Lauren ...' She halted directly in front of her. 'I have to ask you: Do you think Rogan is involved, in any way, with this porn stuff?'

Lauren was instantly dismissive. 'Are you crazy? Not Rogan. He's not the type.'

Of course. They never were. Costello handed over her card. Lauren lifted her glasses, and Costello looked at the bruise on the back of her hand. She was also looking closely at Lauren's lovely face. No, she hadn't been mistaken; there really was another bruise, smaller, fainter, beside her right eye. She raised her hand as if to stroke it, and the sunglasses came down like a curtain.

'If you need me, any time – day or night – that's my number. You just call me,' said Costello, thinking that Lauren suddenly looked like the loneliest person on the planet. 'You have got to talk to somebody about this.'

'I thought I was talking to you.' Lauren shook off Costello's hand, and strode off through the jungle of exotic vegetation, her boot heels clicking into the distance. The interview was at an end.

A week ago Costello would have said Lauren

McCrae was one of the luckiest women in the world but, as her granny used to say, in rare moments of sobriety: *There's nothing like having your own front door.*

It didn't feel like a Saturday. As Christmas came closer all routine slid out of focus. It was the day after the shortest day of the year. And it wasn't that the light was fading; it had never been there to fade. The snow had eased off a little in the mid-morning, but the forecast said more was on the way and that the wind was going to get a bit rough by nightfall.

The office of McDougall, Munro and Munro was old-world, plush but understated, delicately per-fumed with the odour of old leather and good brandy. The office of Munro Property was on the top floor of the old family legal firm, and Mulholland and Costello had been halted at the first hurdle; they had to get past the reception desk before they could proceed any further. So, they were hanging around. Vik just wanted to get this over with and get out of there. And to make matters worse, Costello was in a foul mood after failing to get anything concrete out of the supermodel, and then getting frozen while he had kept her waiting outside HMV. He had come over from Partickhill Station and that meant driving past the end of Frances's street, so he had stopped. Either she hadn't been in or she hadn't answered the door. He walked over to the window of the reception area, pretending to be interested in the traffic below while furtively listening to Frances's message again.

She had left it in the early hours of the morning, a long message saying she hoped they got the wee boy back; she was upset about it, her face was sore and she was going to her bed. She'd phone again when she was up. Then a sniff, a little laugh, she'd got the hang of the mobile now. After a pause she'd said she'd like to spend Christmas with him – actually said it – and then she added *So, I'll say goodnight*, in that low husky voice of hers. She still hadn't phoned back, and there'd been no more messages. He sighed, closed the phone, switched it to silent and put it in his pocket. He didn't know why he had been detailed on this cyanide thing. He was angry at being sent to trace the credit card; that was a job for a complete plonker – any of the uniforms from downstairs could have done it, even wonderboy Smythe who was still hanging around Partickhill getting Brownie points – but DCI Quinn had sent him. She had been quite clear – Anderson's boy going missing would not make any difference; the detail for today would remain as planned. She was covering her back, and they knew it.

Across the road, the tinsel in the window of Waterstone's bookshop had half fallen down, and a column of red Squidgy McMidges shivered in the wind on either side of the doors. Mulholland looked at his watch again, then fished out his phone once more – still no more messages. He listened yet again to the one that he already had, then he texted Frances – *hope u r feeling better, luv u* – and pressed Send.

A discreet buzzer sounded. The receptionist said, 'He'll see you now, if you'd just like to go up in the lift . . .'

The lift was vintage, like an open cage. Costello shivered. 'Imagine getting your hand caught through the bars,' she said. 'And having it slowly amputated as the lift goes up . . .'

'A real bundle of laughs you are, Costello.'

On the upstairs landing, opposite the lift, was a picture of a commanding white-haired lady, like a badly painted portrait of the Queen. The eyes seemed to follow Costello and Mulholland across the carpet, as did the eyes of the dead fox that hung around her neck.

'I hope it bloody strangles her,' Costello hissed.

Douglas Munro, LLB (Hons), was casually dressed in expensive cashmere, with a slight tendency to fat round his waist, his hair sprinkled with grey at the temples.

'I'm DC Mulholland, this is DS Costello,' announced Mulholland, stepping in front of Costello, showing that he was in charge. This time she was content to let him. 'It's very good of you to see us on a Saturday, sir.'

'Just clearing my desk for the Christmas break,' he answered. 'And of course I would be pleased to help in any way I can. Do come through into my office.'

Mulholland discreetly flexed his fingers. Munro's welcome was like shaking hands with a dead haddock.

'Would you like some coffee, tea? I'm sure Stella would rustle something together for us.'

'Coffee would be fine, thank you,' said Mulholland.

'You know Stella, don't you? She's been in a terrible state since, well, since she knew she saw that wee boy.'

'We've had quite a few witnesses through our doors recently,' said Costello, evasively, adding a *no thanks* to coffee. Munro ordered coffee for himself and Mulholland, and a glass of water, over the intercom as they sat down in his long narrow office. It was mostly mahogany and burgundy leather, with sepia photographs and slightly faded oil paintings of the previous occupants on the walls. Only the architect's models of building developments around the city gave a clue to the current use of the room. Mulholland noticed another photograph of the haughty white-haired dame wearing a showy pearl choker. On anybody else it would look cheap, but she had the type of face that said 'money'. A wearily overweight spaniel sat at her feet. Both the spaniel and its owner bore a resemblance to the main portrait over the desk.

Munro smiled as he caught Mulholland looking. 'That's my mother. And that's her father – my McDougall grandfather – up there. The family have a long legal tradition.' He clasped his fingers together, leaned forward and said, 'Right, how can I help you? Something about my credit card?'

'The platinum one, MasterCard.' Mulholland reeled off the number from memory, visibly impressing Douglas Munro. 'Do you still have it in your possession?'

'Hold on a mo.' Munro eased himself from his chair, took out his wallet, had a quick look and pulled a face. 'Yes, it's in my wallet.'

'You haven't noticed it missing?'

'Can't say I have. I don't use it often but it's always in my wallet, and I don't leave it anywhere. Why?'

There was a knock on the door.

'Stella, come in. Of course, you have all met, haven't you,' he said.

Stella nodded as she laid a tray on the desk, with a silver coffee pot, two china cups and saucers, and small biscuits perfectly arranged on a doily. From the tray she lifted an envelope and handed it to Douglas. 'Excuse me,' she said to Costello, 'but do you have any news yet?'

'Nothing, but we are working on a few leads.'

Stella shot her a look that suggested they should be out looking rather than sitting in this office. 'Douglas, the police have actually just phoned, looking for the keys to three properties; the two on Rowanhill Road and the one on Crown Avenue. Shall I go down with them?'

'Just routine, sir,' Mulholland reassured him. 'The search teams will be going through the whole area.'

'Fine, fine. You never think of these things, do you?' He nodded. 'Of course, Stella. Get a taxi if you want. It's only Eve who's coming in, so I can lock up here. But can you help these officers with something else before you go? It's about my credit card.' He showed her the credit card then slit open the envelope with a fine knife.

'Miss McCorkindale, have you ever seen anything on Mr Munro's statements that you can't explain?'

Stella shrugged. 'No. But the next statement will be in any day now – you know what the post is like this time of year. I can fetch the most recent for you.'

'Please do. Does anyone else have access to your card, Mr Munro, apart from Miss McCorkindale?' asked Costello brusquely, tiring of the charade. Children were missing, the search sounded as though it was stepping up, and they might need all the ground troops they could muster.

'Nobody else. It's not a joint card.'

'Your wife?'

Stella glanced at Douglas, who was taking a glass of water from the tray, popping a capsule from its tinfoil with a well-practised thumb.

'Does anybody else have use of this credit card?'

Douglas swallowed hard. 'Only Stella. May I ask what the purchase was? There's obviously something on my card you are concerned about.'

'Just part of an ongoing enquiry,' said Mulholland.

'I was a lawyer; my discretion is assured,' said Munro. Costello noticed that Stella had silently left the room. But she hadn't seen her go.

'There was a purchase made from a firm of chemical suppliers in the USA.'

'Really?' Munro raised his eyebrow, as if that had interested him. 'And I take it you can't tell me exactly what?'

'We might have a problem with malicious product tampering, cyanide probably. The cyanide seems to have been purchased on your card.' Costello watched Munro's face; his amazement seemed genuine.

'Is that what the product recall in the papers was all about? A painkiller, isn't it?' Munro emptied the contents of his cup down his throat. 'Well, it's obviously very serious but I don't think I can help you any further.'

'You can phone the credit card company in our presence and let us hear your recent purchases.' Costello nodded at the phone. 'You can get sight of a current statement on the computer while you're at it. It would help us know whether it's fraud or something else.'

'Yes, of course.'

'Now,' smiled Costello.

Five minutes later they knew.

'That's the only one I don't recognize.' Douglas Munro's hand was trembling as he touched the screen, indicating an innocuous line of typing in a long list of items. 'You want a printout of that, I assume.'

'Thank you. We'll take it from here.' Costello got up to go, noticing a Squidgy McMidge paperweight on the table, his purple head on a spring so it would bounce. She remembered Peter having one and couldn't resist giving it a small pat for luck. She shivered, then pulled herself together. 'Squidgy did them a fair turn at the Rowanhill School do yesterday,' she beamed at Munro. 'Were you there?'

'Yes. No.' He seemed uncertain. He smiled briefly at Costello, suddenly slightly wary as he realized he was now talking to the organ grinder, not the monkey. His eyes flitted from the midge back to her face. 'I mean, yes, I heard he did us all proud, and no, I didn't make it along there myself. We're all big Squidgy fans in this office. Evelynne Calloway's a very talented young lady.' Munro tipped up the little purple face of the midge, and the head tick-tocked on the spring. 'He's so much more than a cartoon. He's an absolute gold mine.'

'Isn't he just?' said a female voice from the waiting room. It was the auburn-haired woman in the wheelchair Costello had seen briefly at the fair. The tartan rug round her legs was scattered with flecks of snow, which had not yet had time to melt.

'Hello, Miss Calloway, we were just talking about your sister,' said Douglas.

'So, you were talking about me, Mr Munro?' Eve Calloway said, knocking the snow from her rug on to the deep-pile carpet as she watched the couple walk to the lift door – well, not a couple really, she thought. The girl was dressed rather formally. So was the guy. She had seen them before; he was the cop at the fair with the hippie chick. Police. Of course. She even fancied she could see a thin film of sweat on Munro's top lip. He ignored her as he walked past, fishing a bubble pack of Headeze from his pocket. He pursed his lips when he realized it was already empty, and threw it into the nearest waste-paper basket.

Stella busied herself in the reception area, getting tagged keys from a locked cupboard, then moving one of the chairs in the waiting room so that Eve's wheelchair could fit neatly into the corner. Eve knew the secretary was wary of her; she had been since Eve was a wee girl chanting rude rhymes at her from her garden gate. Stella McCorkindale had the type of face that terrified children, with bulbous eyes behind glasses that kept sliding down her nose. When Eve was young, Stella had had a goitre, which Eve had fantasized was a small baby Stella had eaten that had got stuck in her throat.

But now Stella was a master at throwing Eve looks of distaste, the vague implication being that her employer had better things to do than sort out two dysfunctional sisters and a demanding midge.

'I'll be with you in a minute, Eve,' said Douglas.

She smirked, rippling her fingertips on the arm of her wheelchair. She could wait. She'd waited a long time to have this conversation with Douglas Reginald Munro. She'd started researching him the minute Douglas came sniffing after Lynne. The only person she could not track down was a wife; there were lots of girlfriends, and a mother, but no wife. Douglas made his money by conning stupid women out of their houses. Stupid women like Lynne – he was the 'single lady with property and no brains' specialist. Lynne had no property and no brains so she half qualified. She could have found out all about Munro if she hadn't been so besotted, but love is blind – deaf, in Lynne's case – and she would not listen. Which was why Eve was here, to give Munro one chance to redeem himself. If he left Lynne alone, she would sign. If not, she wouldn't. She didn't add that he would then be lucky to see the New Year in. She imagined the majestic stag in her sights, the cross hairs between its beautiful brown eyes, as she gently squeezed the trigger. She started to smile at her own cleverness but disguised it as a coughing fit, all the time watching the body language of the man. Was he nervous? Scared? Did he know?

Eve pretended she was adjusting her cushion, still observing Douglas as he stood in his office, quietly talking on the phone, jangling the keys in his trouser pocket. Private school, old money, his family had business ties that went back generations. She looked at the portraits round the waiting area; all that acumen and education – to come down to a bloody piranha like this.

Douglas turned, hand over the mouthpiece of the phone. 'You had better go, Stella. Take the keys and get a receipt. I'll lock up here. Do you mind, Eve? I'll be another few minutes here.'

'Be my guest,' said Eve. 'I'm not exactly going to stand up and jump the queue, am I? My legs don't work,' she explained to Stella.

She smiled a sardonic smile. 'So I see.'

'Thanks, Eve; I'll be as quick as I can,' Douglas said, closing the door with his foot.

'He's got one of his headaches again, hasn't he? I keep telling him he should wear his specs or get his eyeballs lasered or something. But men never listen, do they? Vanity thy name is man!'

Stella just smiled vaguely, and fiddled with the buttons on the phone, as if unwilling to get involved.

'Is that Douglas's mum? That portrait?' Eve carried on blithely. 'You can see the family likeness, can't you?'

'Yes. She's a lawyer too, still does a little legal work even now. Douglas does the property development. I quite enjoy it.' Stella gathered some files, tying them with a ribbon. She was getting ready to go.

Eve sat still, noticing Douglas's jacket hanging on the coat stand. 'Stella, can I ask you something?'

'I'll certainly try to help you, but it might be better if you asked Mr Munro.'

'No, it's nothing like that. I just always wonder ... actually, to be honest, I panic ... about fire exits. Since my accident, if I get into a lift, I immediately start to worry about how to get out. So, how do I get out of here – if the place goes up in flames?'

Stella looked round her, thinking. 'Well, we're supposed to use the stairs. But as you can't ...'

'... walk ...'

'... then Mr Munro would have to carry you.'

'Oh, dear. One of these days it'll happen and I'll regret all the chocolate I eat.' Eve patted her huge stomach. And she laughed the little laugh she knew made her look very pretty. 'Douglas wouldn't let me roast to death, would he? He's a nice man, in spite of being a lawyer.'

'That reminds me ...' Stella swung her coat round her shoulders. 'I was going to put this through your door.' She handed Eve an envelope addressed to Lynne Calloway. 'It's the valuation Douglas did for your house.'

Have I really just had it valued? 'Always better to know where you stand with these things,' said Eve, marvelling at her own acting ability.

Stella slung her handbag over her shoulder. 'Did your sister get her little mystery solved last night? She was expecting a visitor and thought she'd missed them. The only people I ever see are the two of you and the old lady with the grey hair — a friend of yours? She has terrible trouble with your front step.'

'Margaret?' said Eve. 'She's an old friend of Mum's. But the trouble is, she and Lynne can't stand each other. So, she always comes when Lynne is out.'

'And does she stay the night to help look after you?'

'I do need some help sometimes, and I can't always rely on Lynne,' Eve said pathetically, looking at the walls. 'Yes, sometimes I need all the help I can get.' She rubbed her leg pathetically, then tucked her blanket round her. 'Is Douglas's wife feeling better? I heard she was poorly.'

'Indeed,' said Stella curtly, not looking at her.

'You'd better go, in case the boss comes out and finds us jabbering.'

'Cheerio.'

'Bye then,' said Eve, alone at last.

23

Quinn sat behind her desk and looked out over the empty office. Everybody was somewhere else, doing something that probably was going nowhere. She sighed. She felt sick – for the first time in her career she didn't have a clue what to do next. She had put a quiet unofficial trail on anybody in Rogan's entourage who left the hotel for any reason. Littlewood would debrief Costello about Lauren. He had ideas; no evidence but at least he had ideas. The house-to-house was up and running again, properly this time, but there was nothing coming in. Alison McEwen was a waste of space, but well known. Lorraine Scott had had to be sedated when she was told about Luca. But she was a 'well kennt face' also. Or was the eyewitness mistaken? It wouldn't be the first time, and it would mean they were back to thinking about a single perp. Yet nothing had come down the wire, not a whisper, not a sniff.

Brenda's appeal had been emotional, but she was a crabbit-looking woman. The evening news report brought in a whole load of phone calls, mostly from people they had already checked. Miss Cotter and Miss McCorkindale were two names the computer threw at them all the time. But Quinn was too tired to see a connection, apart from all the legitimate connections people who live so close would have. Although part of Glasgow, Partickhill was its own little village, so the same characters popped up again and again. What might seem like coincidence was actually perfectly logical.

Through the glass, she saw the door to the Incident Room open, and Anderson came in. He looked awful; he had aged years. Burns followed him in and took two plastic cups of water from the machine. They stood looking at the wall charts, the search results, the side wall map of the USA. She knew Colin's eyes would constantly come back to the picture of a happy smiling Peter, his arms round the mouldy feathers of Pat the Penguin.

In the short term, Granny had come over and had taken Brenda home, and Graham Smeaton's mother had offered to drop Claire off at the Anderson house. Three generations of women, waiting for two generations of men to come home. But Brenda's removal had made Colin calmer and, for the moment, that was all Quinn could wish for.

Maybe Batten would come up with something. She certainly hoped so, as she had run out of ideas. She watched Anderson turn to look directly over her head and out the window behind her. He closed his eyes slowly, and then opened them again. He had been looking over the skyline of the city, thinking exactly what she had been thinking – that Peter was out there somewhere.

They walked down Gordon Street and up into the Sauchiehall Street precinct, Lewis striding out, Costello with her hands buried in her jacket pockets, deep in her own thoughts. She was trying to retain every word of her conversation with Lauren. She'd wanted Littlewood to debrief her asap, yet here she was tracing the cyanide, first with bloody Mulholland, now with bloody Lewis. Mulholland had disappeared off back to the station, no doubt to see if the gorgeous Fran had dragged herself from her bed yet. Costello had had to suffer the intimate details of Lewis and her boyfriend's early morning shagfest on her own. She halted mid-step as Lewis swerved to look at the window of Watt Brothers.

'Those are nice shoes, aren't they?' said Lewis.

'I think we should get on with our job.'

'Two minutes to try on those shoes won't do any harm.'

'Turning up on a date with the wrong shoes won't do any harm, but getting on with our job might do Peter Anderson some good. Just a thought.'

But Lewis would not be shifted. 'I have a blue D&G dress – would they go with that, do you think?'

'I don't know your blue dress and I really couldn't care less. I think we should get round to Bijou Bytes

– the internet café where they do nice chocolate croissants, remember? Where they get deliveries of cyanide?'

'Do you think they'll give us something to eat?'

'I was rather hoping for the name of the person who asked for the cyanide to be delivered there.'

'Not a chance. Too bloody clever, this guy. But we might manage to get an E-fit out of them. No wonder you're on your own, Costello. You're too focused on your job. You really are quite boring. You have all the sex appeal of a road accident. Do you know, you have the same first name as my spinster great-aunt?' she said tauntingly.

'Was she called "Sergeant" as well? If my name ever passes your lips again, you're dead meat.' Costello quickened her step, enjoying Lewis's struggle to keep up.

'You're so funny,' squealed Lewis.

Costello stopped and turned, blocking Lewis's path. She looked up into the face of the taller woman. 'I'm as funny as a Rottweiler with piles, and don't forget it,' she hissed.

Lewis took a step back, noting the sound of real menace.

Costello slowly turned round and walked on in quiet fury. It was midday but the shadow of night was still hanging over the city. It was cold, wet, and the snow had soaked through her shoes. But she had a full stomach and a home to go to. She thought of Troy, walking back through the light snow ... and

Luca and Peter. She was glad when the Christmas lights of Sauchiehall Street started to twinkle in her view, some sign of goodwill to all men.

Bijou Bytes' shopfront was constantly open to serve straight on to the street, and the queue for hot coffee was strung out, as tired folk struggled with the last of their Christmas shopping.

It was much warmer in the shop itself. Bijou Bytes made all their own bread and the sweet smell of dough and yeast hung heavily, clogging the air.

'Want me to deal with this?' asked Kate Lewis, in a way that wasn't an offer.

'Aye, go ahead,' Costello said. 'I'll stay out here and phone Littlewood. Just get this over with asap; we need to get back to the station.' She scrolled down to Littlewood's number.

'How did you get on with Lauren?' Littlewood demanded, before Costello could say a word.

'She told me nothing, John, but she hinted at a lot. She does seem scared. There's something there all right, but it wasn't the time or the place for her to tell me. I'll talk to you the minute I get back. Anything at all happening at your end?'

With a snarled 'Naah!' Littlewood put the phone down.

Costello snapped her phone shut, and leaned against the window of the shop. She needed to get her head clear and think deeply about Rogan O'Neill and the little Lauren had told her; there was a picture there that was not clear yet. Now she had to deal with this detail about the cyanide case while hoping Dr Mick Batten was having a productive working breakfast. Costello looked round her – this was a cosmopolitan city, so why should it not have its share of perverts and paedophiles?

This part of Sauchiehall Street was full of small specialist coffee shops with umbrellas over wooden tables. Somebody had said it looked like Paris after a nuclear holocaust. But in Glasgow, never a city of pretence, what you saw was what you got; the umbrellas were there to keep the rain off the smokers who preferred to die from lung cancer than pneumonia. Some Japanese tourists walked past, no doubt on their way to the Willow Tearoom to eat a toasted scone while their arses got sore sitting on a Rennie Mackintosh chair. They'd be better off in Bijou Bytes, where at least the seats looked comfortable, Costello thought.

Through the open shopfront, Costello could watch Lewis as she spoke to the manager. A hand was moving, demonstrating a height slightly smaller than herself. Lewis was being given a description, so something was moving. She turned away, noticing a row of Squidgy McMidges hanging over the bread counter. Squidgys were like shoplifters – once one had been pointed out, they were bloody everywhere.

The conversation drew to a close. Lewis nodded her thanks, folded up her notebook, and walked out of the shop, rolling her eyes heavenward.

'Was that phone call anything good?' she wanted to know. 'Any news?'

'Nothing. How did you get on?'

'Well, the number belongs to that computer in the corner, but there's no CCTV on it and the security camera is focused on the till. I have a list of everybody who's worked here over the last year, eight of them in all. Nothing's ever been delivered here from the States, except one item which was handed in at the shopfront ... *a wee box in a Jiffy bag*, the manager called it. Maybe more than a month ago, but she can't be sure. It was addressed to here and to somebody called Margaret. Turns out one of their regular customers had asked them to take in a delivery that she had ordered over the café internet ...'

'And don't tell me – said regular customer hasn't been seen since.'

'Spot on. "Margaret" apparently worked at the jewellers' over the road. She said the package was a clock, a surprise birthday present for a colleague. They wanted it to be delivered here in case she caught wind of it before the official presentation.'

'So, she collected the clock – or, to be correct, a package from the USA with a delivery address that is now a dead end. And description?'

Lewis looked at the sky, recalling. 'Older, female, grey-haired, heavy build – well, fat – small, wore a hat, thick glasses. '

'All removable.'

'Yes. The only strange thing was that she had

trouble getting up the step. She had a bad leg. Better check out the jewellers', eh?'

'It's why we're here,' muttered Costello. 'We're following in her tracks.'

The windows of Cornerstone Jewellers were covered with gold tinsel and fake snow. Costello shivered. 'Why do I feel a sort of premonition that they will have never heard of Margaret or her colleague's birthday?'

It took only two minutes in the jewellers' shop to establish that their staff had indeed never heard of 'Margaret'. They had no idea who the police were talking about and they could not recollect anyone of that description. They offered their surveillance tapes, but Lewis said no thanks. 'Margaret', whoever she may be, was clever enough never to have set foot in the place. 'Margaret' had hand-picked the staff of Bijou Bytes – helpful but not the brightest – for her purpose.

'Margaret' had played them every step of the way.

The Willow Tearoom was crowded with Christmas shoppers, but Douglas was known there so the waitress showed him and Lynne to a table at the furthest point of the mezzanine. They sat on the tall Rennie Mackintosh chairs and ordered pancakes and coffee for him, toast and Earl Grey for her. Lynne, becoming a little nervous, was wondering why Douglas had brought her to this sweet little coffee shop that sat, peculiarly, above a jewellers', and wondered what, if any, significance there was in that.

'Sorry I was late,' Douglas said pulling his coat off and placing it on the back of the chair. 'Stella was called away to give the police access to some property. God knows what they expect to find.'

'I was a little late myself,' she said, lying through her teeth. Actually, she had been kept waiting in the sleet in Sauchiehall Street for more than ten minutes, her scarf round her mouth as people coughed and sneezed as they went past. 'Why were you working the Saturday before Christmas? You work far too hard, darling.'

Douglas leaned forward and started drumming his fingers on the table. He had something on his mind. 'Look, Lynne ... I had something really nice planned for us – over Christmas.' He smiled. 'Really special. But I had a meeting this morning that means I have to be involved in an unexpected project, last-minute but very profitable.'

'Oh.' Her light-blue eyes opened flirtatiously. 'Something *really* special?'

'Very special, but not till this other thing is over. Is that OK?'

He was nervous as he asked, his fingers still drumming away on the tabletop; he could hardly look her in the eye. She was touched. 'If it has to be, it has to be. I know the stress you're under,' Lynne replied, lost for a minute in the fantasy that she was a corporate wife.

'And on top of that, I had the police in the office this morning.'

'About the keys? You said.'

'No, something else I appear to be mixed up in. Have you seen this stuff about the recall of some painkiller?' He pulled a copy of that morning's *Record* from his coat pocket, his hand shaking slightly, and passed it to Lynne. 'They're claiming that a particular batch might cause stomach problems – to prevent panic, I suppose – but it's much worse than that.'

'It's all cheap nonsense, what they sell at that shop; I would never buy anything there. What does it have to do with you?'

Douglas leaned forward. 'Keep this to yourself but from what the detective said, I think there's a product tamperer about. Cyanide.' He took a bite of his pancake. 'Imagine that, cyanide!' He backhanded a crumb from the side of his mouth and added quietly, 'Lynne, people are actually dying from this stuff!'

Lynne paused, a piece of toast halfway to her mouth, her throat suddenly dry. 'And . . .?'

'And now they've traced the cyanide and lo and behold, it was bought by me.'

'I don't understand . . .'

'Over the blasted internet. The cyanide – would you believe it, *cyanide* – was bought on my credit card.'

'How did that happen?' asked Lynne quietly.

'They're not sure about that. Somebody with access to my card. Or the number.'

'Stella?' asked Lynne, too quickly, as she thought of the many times Douglas had left his jacket lying around their living room. Around Eve.

Douglas laughed. 'Don't be daft. I asked a friend about it – an educated cop, not one of those Neanderthals that came to see me this morning. He said anybody could just have copied the strip on my card, he knows a fair bit about the mechanics of it all.'

'It's ridiculous to think you could have had anything to do with it.' Lynne went on the defensive. 'And they came to your place of work? What if you'd had an important client there? Can't you lodge an official complaint?'

'Oh, I shall expect total exoneration and an apology. But in the meantime – yes, you're right; it would be very damaging to my professional reputation if it became known. Which it could, easily; your sister was right outside my office door and her mouth is like Radio Clyde.'

'Eve? What on earth was she doing in your office?'

Douglas chewed a mouthful of pancake, giving himself time to think. He decided on an edited version of the truth. 'I think she's concerned that I'm leading you astray, me being married and all that.' He finished with a convincing lie. 'I told her it was none of her business.' In reality, he had just looked at the pathetic, obese figure in the wheelchair and hadn't listened to a word. But he *had* told her to mind her own business. Once he had the house on Horselethill, Eve would be out on the street. Even if it cost him the price of a wee ground-floor flat at the far side of Maryhill, he'd still be quids in.

But he shivered as he remembered the chill of her stare.

'Good.' Lynne took a sip of Earl Grey, only half listening, thinking about the habit Douglas had of leaving his jacket lying over a chair in their front room, where anybody – well, anybody in the house – could get to it. There weren't very many people it could be. She felt a small creep of betrayal in her stomach, and pushed her toast away, thinking about that well-fingered photocopy of Douglas walking away from court. 'So, getting back to your credit card, why would somebody do a thing like that – poison innocent people?' She spoke mechanically, thinking it through.

Douglas nodded as the bill was put in front of him. 'Because they're a mad psycho, who probably never had a job, and thinks the world owes them a living because they were hard done by.' He reached into his jacket pocket, then realized he'd put his wallet in his coat pocket. As he dug deep he pulled a face. 'What on earth . . .?' He flicked a packet on the tabletop where it landed in a saucer. The writing on the tinfoil strip was plainly visible.

Headeze.

*

Anderson was trying to contain his anger but nothing was moving forward. The boards were not getting any fuller; in fact, more and more leads were being explored and found to go nowhere.

He could think logically as far as the next move, the next person to speak to, the next thing to investigate, the next line to pursue. Then he would remember that they were looking for Peter, and his heart would crumple. Then he felt so scared he couldn't function, so he had to stay calm, stay on the fringes of the investigation, though trying to get an overview of it all. He watched Wyngate as yet another statement, originally filed as 'possible', proved to lead nowhere. Yes, the guy had been driving his cab at the time of Peter's abduction but he had seen nothing. It was dark, snowing and very busy – what did the police expect? Anderson took the red marker pen and struck the taxi driver's name off the board as Wyngate typed two lines, pressed Print, clipped the original notes to the page, signed it off and filed it. His mind kept going back to what Littlewood had said – they were missing something.

Mulholland wasn't faring much better. He was swanning around in a dwam over Frances who, no matter how many times he texted and phoned her, just wasn't answering. He was getting edgy and bad tempered with everybody except Lewis, with whom he giggled like an imbecile. They had been teamed to interview recently released paedophiles. Littlewood had voiced his own opinion – that the offender would return to the scene of his first offences – he would be there, in the shadows.

Simple.

24

At last Littlewood took Costello to one side and debriefed her about Lauren, drawing little patterns in a notebook, going from Rogan O'Neill to Dec Slater and Jinky Jones, then to Lauren. They agreed there was something there, but neither could say what. Littlewood sat back and nodded slowly. 'Something's always better than nothing,' he grunted. 'Phone Lauren tomorrow, will you? Just a friendly enquiry after her health?'

'Happy to. But I'll have to find a way to make sure that Rogan isn't around when I phone. I don't want to get her into trouble. She had a bruise on her hand, another on her face.' Costello felt her own cheek, remembered ducking blows from her own mother's fist. 'That and the way she talks about him.'

Littlewood left her to her thoughts. At the moment the only thing she could do was crack on with the cyanide lead, and leave other officers free to pursue anything that came in about the children. She couldn't understand why three of them had been detailed on it this morning when so many other matters were pressing, but Quinn would no doubt have her reasons.

She turned back her notebook and reread what she

had been doing that day. Doodles, notes, et cetera. Something was nagging at the back of her mind; something about this stuff just wasn't right. She looked up and caught Anderson staring into space, looking as lonely as any human being she had ever seen.

'How are you, Colin?'

'Desperate,' he answered.

'Any word from Mick yet? It's past two – how long does he need?'

'There's no word yet, nothing. That's why I'm here. Port, storm, any, in. Arrange them in any way you see fit.' His words caught in his throat. 'Like I said, desperate.'

Costello slipped an arm round his shoulder, but she had no words of comfort. 'Let me know the minute you hear anything, anything at all.'

He patted her hand, grateful.

'Gail,' she asked. 'Can you come over here?'

'Yes, boss,' Irvine said sarcastically. 'You got more exciting typing for me to do?'

'Can I use your brainpower?'

Irvine hesitated. 'For what it's worth.'

'Think back to your notes. You remember the date the first cyanide victim died?'

Irvine shook her head. 'That was so long ago, I'd be guessing. Remind me.'

'Duncan Thompson. The fourth,' Costello supplied without hesitation. 'I'm trying to put myself in the place of a wronged employee, perhaps unjustifiably accused. Would I take a pop at the establishment, have a go at the system? Randomly murder innocent people by way of revenge, just to show I could?'

'I think you would. I certainly wouldn't cross you,' said Irvine. 'But what are you getting at?'

'Well, it's been confirmed, it's not a bad batch. But they were all bought from the same shop, so we will deduce it's the shop the perp uses regularly. I tried to run this past Quinn but I'll run it past you instead. Why let people die if money or principle is the point? So, the point must be murder, pure and simple.'

Irvine glanced quickly over at Mulholland, still texting on his mobile, then at Lewis who was sweet-talking down her phone, and then at DCI Quinn busy in her office, doing something they were not privy to. Anderson was still sitting on the desk looking at the wallboards. 'I don't think I can handle this,' said Irvine, nervously chewing at the side of her thumb.

'Not much use to him if we don't handle it, are we? He needs to be focused on Peter, we need to leave him to get on with what's important to him. We get on with this, let the squad get on with that. You follow?'

'OK, go on,' Irvine said quietly. 'But what's in it for the poisoner – what's in it for them? Can't be the glory of it; there was no news coverage until we established the pattern.'

'For that amount of effort, I'd be killing someone

in particular,' Costello smirked as Kate Lewis walked past. 'So,' she resumed, following Irvine's glance. 'Do we go back to that old question: *Where do you hide a murder?*'

'In among a whole lot of murders,' answered Irvine slowly. 'Which would explain why there was no blackmail attempt at the time. The last thing they'd want would be anybody drawing attention to it.'

'Right, so say we wanted to kill . . .'

'Lewis.'

'We'd have to join the queue. But she's a coffee drinker. A tea drinker – me – would tamper with several lots of coffee at Waldo, and put a tampered pack beside the kettle in the Incident Room, knowing the whole squad drinks coffee except me. Lewis falls down dead, as do half the squad and several other innocent souls all over the West End – *Oh, dear. Poor Lewis, a victim of the tamperer.* Die young and stay pretty.'

'I'd be dead too. I drink more coffee than she does.'

'So, you're collateral damage. What do I care about that?'

'But the killer would have to hate the intended victim an awful lot. I mean, to kill so many other people . . .'

'Or adore her Newton Mearns lifestyle.'

Irvine's smile became thoughtful. 'So, you think maybe Sarah McGuire tampered with several packets of Headeze, kept one, put the rest back on the shelves, then gave part of a pack to her dad and carefully took some herself, knowing she would survive?'

'Best way to avoid suspicion. It wouldn't be too difficult for her to become a little old lady called Margaret. If we could just find a grey wig and sensible coat in her house ...'

'And she was prepared to let a whole lot of other people die? Just to get her hands on her dad's house?' Irvine shook her head. 'That's far too horrible, even with the amount of money that place would be worth ...'

'People have killed for a lot less, and the daughter knows how cyanide works, don't forget. She has her grandfather's books about the Third Reich in the house.'

'It may fit, but it's too far-fetched, Costello. You'd need a connection with Douglas Munro – him of the credit card – for a start. Do they know each other?'

'Tom McGuire's a builder. Douglas Munro is a property developer. Could there be a connection there? They might have worked with each other.'

'But suppose Sarah and her dad are both genuine victims – then it means somebody else is planning to murder somebody, or already has, and doesn't care who gets killed in the crossfire. And that person knows Munro well enough to get hold of his credit card.'

Costello looked out the window, thinking. 'How

many murderous friends could a property developer have? Loads, I would imagine.'

'So, there could be more deaths to come. Please can we go to Quinn with this?'

'You go. I'm going back to think about Sarah McGuire. If that bitch killed her own dad, she's not getting away with it. I'm going to chance my arm.' Costello picked up her notebook and found Tom McGuire's phone number. Their conversation was short – scarcely two minutes. John Campbell's flat had been valued by a company called Munro Property not long before his death. The initial valuation had been quite unprompted – just a prospective gambit by an avaricious property developer with an incipient paunch. But the full valuation survey had included the property upstairs and had been commissioned by Sarah herself. Tom remembered it because he had been a builder for twenty years and even he had been surprised at the quoted value of the property. Costello's heart started to race – was this her connection? No, Thomas went on, he himself did not know Munro as an individual. He regarded him as the sort of low-life who drove up property prices and gave builders a bad name. A lawyer who wanted out when the gravy train of legal aid dried up and saw a chance to make a quick buck at the property game, that was all he was.

'And how's Karen?' Costello asked.

'Terrible. I don't think she's slept at all. I'm arranging for her to have counselling; I think it's all hitting home – everything that has been going on. And how close to taking the stuff she was herself. But Sarah's showing signs of recovery now, thank God. Not much of the stuff got into her system, so we hope there'll be no permanent damage.'

'I'm glad she's doing well.' Costello finished by asking him what his own mother had died of. He seemed surprised by the question but answered, saying stomach cancer. She had been ill for a long time, and it had been a blessing in the end. Sarah had agreed the final divorce settlement a week later, so she had inherited half his mother's estate. Her dad's estate would be one hundred per cent hers. Thomas McGuire made no effort to keep the bitterness out of his voice.

Costello thanked him, rang off, and looked at the valuation figure in her notebook, whistling slowly through pursed lips. If it was accurate, that and her dad's life assurance made a tasty little package for Sarah.

She pushed her notebook across the desk to Irvine. 'Look at the value of that property.' Irvine's quiet whistle was an approximation of Costello's. 'And look who did the valuation – a firm called Munro Property. The credit card that paid for the cyanide belonged to Douglas Munro. We were at his office this morning. Smooth bastard.'

'Well, there's your connection, right enough. Are they in cahoots, Munro and Sarah McGuire? An item? Do we have any evidence?'

Costello looked across at Mulholland and Lewis, who were still chatting away about Frances and Stuart; one hadn't received a text, the other was only receiving texts. Their constant twittering was getting on Costello's nerves.

She fanned her book against her hand, listening to the ripple of paper. 'We have a connection, but it's between one investigation and the other, both ways round. Munro to the cyanide and McCorkindale to the abductions. It's not . . . Oh, for fuck's sake . . .'

Lewis's phone started to bleep annoyingly; she picked it up and laughed flirtatiously before she started stabbing her thumb over the keys in response.

Costello got up, walked over to Lewis's desk and took her mobile phone from her, threw it in her drawer then slammed the drawer shut.

'You can start work anytime you want. Come on, Irvine.'

The squad watched in silence as they walked out.

'Are you going to Quinn with this?'

'I think we can trust Quinn,' said Costello.

'You *think*? She's the DCI,' said Irvine.

'There's only one DCI I completely trusted and I'd need a spiritualist to talk to him. Fuck!' said Costello. 'But Quinn will do. She's a stroppy cow but she's not bent.'

25

Anderson flinched as Costello's phone rang. He grabbed it automatically, snapping, 'Hello?'

'That doesn't sound like Costello.'

'It isn't. DI Anderson here.'

'Colin, it's Mick Batten. Sorry to hear about Peter. Do you have time to talk?'

'I have all the time in the world, for you.' Anderson's voice cracked. *Please, God, let him have something.*

'Costello sent me some stuff . . .'

Anderson held his breath, his heart pounding. 'Was it any use?'

Costello came back in, carrying a can of Diet Coke. Anderson beckoned her and Littlewood over, and put the speaker on quiet, so only the three of them could hear.

'I've had a look at the abducted kids . . .'

They all reached for their notebooks. 'And . . .?'

'Two of them are kids who are used to being passed around, nobody's kids, to all intents and purposes . . .'

Costello remembered her own childhood, a ragged patchwork of attention and neglect. Mick was right. Luca Scott and Troy McEwen would have been happy with anybody taking them away; they wouldn't have thought twice about it, particularly if some inducement were offered. But Peter ... 'Peter wouldn't have walked off with just anybody,' she said.

'My point exactly. If he was abducted, he would have struggled, he would have screamed. And nobody saw him struggle or heard him scream.'

'Unless they just saw a kid having a tantrum. We've been through this.'

'But when the news of the abduction came out, then somebody would have clicked – you'd have a truckload of witnesses all feeling guilty that they didn't intervene. Peter walked away with whoever took him. Walked.'

'He wouldn't,' said Anderson in quiet desperation. 'Not after what I've drummed into him. He wouldn't.' Tears came to his eyes, remembering wrestling Peter to the bed, blowing raspberries on his little bare belly, Peter demanding Cheeky Chips. His little Peter.

'Peter's a well-loved, happy wee boy from a close-knit family,' Mick went on. 'How many people are there in his immediate circle?'

'A good few. I've been through the list a hundred times,' Anderson said. 'School, playground, me, Claire and Brenda, Brenda's mother. I've a sister down south. And we have a babysitter.'

'Who?'

'Girl next door.'

'And with what you do for a living that circle is

closer than it might be otherwise. Even so, what connects him with the other two boys is someone he knows, I'd say. So, who is new in his life?'

Costello scribbled a name as Mick continued, 'The other two might have a connection through the hospital. One has a mother in treatment for alcohol abuse, the other's mother has a history of being bi-polar and God knows what else, so that's one avenue to explore. Colin, has your wife ever been to that hospital – the Western?'

Anderson shook his head. 'The Southern is our hospital.'

'Claire?' asked Costello.

'No, that was the Southern.'

'Well, what about Miss Cotter? She's up at the bloody hospital with her Empire biscuits.' The hospital was not up as an active line of enquiry. Littlewood nodded and made a note to get on with it.

'But Peter – he's a different thing altogether. Who'd know him well enough to get him to walk away with them?' Mick's voice asked, his Liverpudlian accent exaggerated by being disembodied.

'But he wouldn't walk away with them.' Anderson shook his head. 'I've been over this a thousand times,' he muttered. 'Peter wouldn't walk away with anybody.'

'Colin, empty your mind, sit down with somebody, and go through everything Peter did in the last seven days, and who with. Don't you tell them, let them do the asking. Get somebody to do the same with

Brenda – both of you are missing something,' Batten said. 'Don't automatically disregard people you trust. The more you trust them, the more likely it is to be them. Look, this report says your son is intelligent, well balanced; he's described as vocal, free with his opinions . . .'

'Too right.'

'And you're a policeman. So, Peter would be more aware than most little boys of the unpleasant side of life. Which means if somebody tried to take him by reason, he would refuse. Politely, but he would refuse. He's an articulate little boy, he's bright, he'd argue back. He's been conditioned that way. So, he went with someone he trusted.'

'That's what I've been saying. I've been over this a million times. It didn't happen! My son is not a stupid wee boy, for fuck's sake. How many times do I have to tell you? Jesus!' Anderson swore, slammed his chair back and left the room, banging the door.

'Will I go after him?' asked Littlewood, rising.

Costello shook her head. 'Did you hear that?' she asked the speakerphone. 'That was Anderson's chair hitting the deck. So, let's run with this – say I know a female who has suffered recent personal loss, no family, no chance of having any kids; she knows Peter, buys him presents, knows how cops work, she might even have a uniform hanging around. And if the rumours are true, she's not a stranger to the hospital. Somebody we know Peter ran to when he was left with strangers. Good to go?'

The speakerphone was silent for a few moments. 'Who are you talking about?'

Costello and Littlewood exchanged glances.

'Who are we talking about?' repeated the speakerphone.

'Well.' Costello didn't want to say it; she was betraying Alan.

'Who are we talking about?' Batten demanded again. 'I'm supposed to be the expert here.'

Silence.

'*Who?*' demanded the speakerphone.

'Helena McAlpine.'

Silence hung round them like lead for what seemed like a long time.

'Oh, shit,' said Mick Batten eventually. 'Mrs McAlpine? Are you serious, about her being a suspect? Didn't you say she's going into hospital? She couldn't just borrow three children and then give them back. Why would she?'

'She's been through a lot; she might be that irrational.'

'Not the only one,' said Littlewood, looking at Costello.

There was another long silence as Mick Batten thought. Then he asked, 'One question – well, two. They didn't have kids, did they, she and Alan?'

'No.'

'And, Costello – does Helena McAlpine have pictures of Peter anywhere?'

'I know for a fact she does, in pride of place in the

front room,' answered Costello. 'And another thing –
all they've been looking for on the CCTV is a wee
boy with a Winnie-the-Pooh rucksack, wearing the
bottom half of a dragon outfit, but two minutes in
a toilet, a jacket with a hood, and he's not what we're
looking for any more.'

Mick Batten said nothing; he just sighed heavily.

'The other thing is that Helena sees him a lot.
They sort of hang out together. She was the one who
went to get Peter. She offered to look after his goldfish. It's as if she's trying to borrow him from his
family. Maybe she's gone one step too far. She has
everything, that woman. I mean *everything*.' Costello
paused. 'Apart from her husband, kids and a family.'

'So, she has nothing.' Batten sighed down the
speaker. 'But psychologically, the timing fits better
with that, a woman driven to irrational behaviour.'

Costello felt shivery and deathly sick. *Here, let me
take your bag, Peter; I'll put it in mine. Put your hood up,
Peter, it's cold outside – yes, we'll go and find your mother . . .*
She shoved her chair back, scraping it along the
floor. 'OK, thanks, Mick. Littlewood, we'd better go
and get hold of Colin, calm him down; I think he
might be ready to hit somebody. We'll take him
through all Peter's contacts, just as Mick suggested,
and get back to Quinn asap if any shite floats to the
top. And, Littlewood, please don't let this go any
further, but Anderson was with Helena last night,
when Peter was abducted. They were at the Theatre
Royal. Peter was taken after seven.'

Littlewood showed no sign of surprise. 'About twenty past. Colin had his phone off. We did wonder why.'

'Because he was at the concert. He only picked up our call when he got back to her house. They left at the interval. We need to find out if she was late for the curtain-up. If we ask him directly, he'll go ballistic. He's very ... protective of Helena,' said Costello.

'She's an attractive woman. I could get quite ... protective of her myself,' said Littlewood, licking his lips as if he had just tasted a good malt. 'She was with Peter at the fair. They were the best of pals, like I said.'

'OK, you ask how late she was for the concert. You get on his bad side, I'll stay on his good side.'

Costello found Colin Anderson sitting in a corner of the locker room, with his feet up on the bench, hugging a cup of tea to his chest.

'No need to ask what's going through your mind,' she said, sitting down at the other end of the same bench. They avoided each other's eyes. 'You know, Colin, you have to look at all aspects of this ... you have to talk to Littlewood, let Irvine go out and speak with Brenda ... And Batten is right about Peter.'

'Yeah, I know. I'm just sitting here thinking about how many people Peter knows, that I might not know about. How can my son know people I know nothing about? Even Claire has a boyfriend that I knew nothing about, even if he is a *borrow your pencil* boyfriend, as Helena put it.'

'And she's – how old now? – nine?' Costello carefully turned her back to Anderson, so she could watch him in the mirror on her locker door. 'So, how is Helena? How was the concert? Did she make it on time?'

'Only just. It started late but even then the lights were down as we were finding our seats. Not like her to be late; that was always Alan's job.'

'Did she say what held her up?'

That was a question too far. 'She was caught up in the traffic, like everybody else. That's why they delayed the start. Why is it any of your business?' His voice was caustic. 'What are they doing up there?'

'Well, nothing has come out of your old cases ...'

'I told them I'm not high profile enough to attract that kind of attention.'

'... So, we're tracking exactly what Rogan O'Neill has been up to in the last few days.'

'He's been house-hunting. Did you get anywhere with Lauren?'

'I don't think we'll ever be best friends,' said Costello. 'But I did find out that Dec Slater and Jinky Jones are still around, and I think they're being watched. Colin, I know it's hard, but look at the bigger picture. The kids who've gone missing across America – those cases are strung out over several years and across state lines. Compare them with three boys in one week who live so close they could all go to the same school. It's not the same thing. Any paedophile that loony would already be on the radar. It's not them. Not this time.'

'Are you saying that to comfort me?'

'I'm saying it because I believe it. Jinky and Dec were there on the tape because they're staying at the Hilton. They were only listening to the German Band.' Costello shifted slightly. 'Nothing else so far.'

Anderson shook his head. 'So, nothing I can do there then.'

'No,' Costello agreed.

'Anyone else? That woman . . .'

'Wee Miss Cotter, with her Empire biscuits and little umbrellas?'

'Or Mrs Cotter, as she actually is.'

'Where did you get that from?'

Colin looked at his watch, his face falling as he registered the relentless passage of time. 'Records Office. We looked at her earlier. Mrs Amelia Cotter. Her husband emigrated to Australia and took the children. 1954, I think it was. She didn't go, or at least we could find no record of her on the same passage.'

'You mean they deserted her? All those years ago, and she made no effort to get them back?'

'Apparently not, for whatever reason.'

'Losing your whole family like that would certainly be enough to turn a woman mental. But why our kids, why so quickly, why now? It's fifty years on.'

'The thing is, I don't see Peter being seduced by a little old lady with an Empire biscuit.'

'Why not? We nearly were,' said Costello. 'And if she said, *I know your daddy, he's that nice policeman . . .*' Her voice was cruel and mocking.

'I still don't think he would.'

'Batten agreed it might be a woman — well, it makes sense — it might be a woman who is childless, or a woman who's lost a child, who's had a life-changing event. You know how something like that can push the sanest of women over the edge. Somebody that knew Peter, somebody that Peter would trust . . .'

Colin sat up straight. 'Who are you thinking of?'

'Well . . .' Costello suddenly couldn't get the words out. 'What about Helena? She ticks all the boxes. At the fair, the way she was looking at Peter, the way she . . .'

'What? Helena McAlpine? Costello, what are you going on about?'

'She's childless, Colin; she had to face Alan's death, she's maybe facing up to her own, she . . .'

But Costello didn't get any further. Anderson leapt up so violently he knocked her shoulder, smacking her head soundly against the wall, and slammed out of the locker room. Costello slumped to the floor, letting her head fall on to her chest, waiting for her eyes to come back into focus.

Then the door of the locker room opened again and Anderson came back through it, walking backwards. He and Quinn were face to face, staring each other down, in silence. Quinn cast an eye over Costello, then looked back at Anderson before asking, 'Costello, are you all right?'

'Just bumped my head, ma'am.'

'Indeed? Well, you're going home for a rest. You look terrible. But for now, sit down, both of you.' She closed the door behind her, her trainers squeaking on the lino. 'We need to talk, and we need to talk down here. It's hell up there,' Quinn said, nodding her head upwards. 'The Press Room is crowded with journalists and a TV camera crew.'

'What's Lewis up to?' asked Costello, totally ignoring Anderson.

Quinn sat down on the bench, and shot Costello a funny look. 'Why do you ask that?'

'Just that she seems to be permanently reapplying her make-up or on the phone to bloody Stuart The-Met-Would-Fall-Apart-Without-Me. Cow.'

'Costello, you are still on duty, technically,' Quinn warned.

'I'm in the locker room.' Costello rubbed her head. 'And I'm concussed. So, *technically*, I am not responsible for anything I say. What are you doing down here?'

'I think I've got the hang of how you lot work – little huddles of gossip and information,' said Quinn, leaning back against the wall. 'So, I am joining a huddle. I want to run something past you. Much as I would love to suspend you both, I do trust you implicitly.' She looked at the door, as if daring it to open. Anderson moved away from the window and leaned casually against the door, to prevent anybody from coming in.

Quinn smiled a quick smile, as if recognizing her acceptance at last, but she looked lined and worn without her make-up; even the lipstick had gone. She was clearly troubled.

'I have no idea how – or even if – this fits together,' she said in an intense whisper. 'But I've just had a long chat with Irvine. You suspect we have a definite murder plot?' Quinn raised her eyebrows at Costello, who took that to mean she could go ahead. As she filled him in, Anderson slowly slid down the door until he was sitting on the floor.

'OK, consider this,' Quinn took over. 'We learn from O'Hare's PM report that four more deaths have been caused by cyanide, and that in there somewhere is a deliberate murder. I'm waiting for my brain to come up with an argument against it. But I can't.'

Quinn leaned forward.

'But how does any of this get me closer to my son?'

'I've no idea, Colin,' Quinn said gently. 'Sorry. And we had a no-show on Peter on the CCTV tapes near the outbuildings, where PC Smith or Smythe or whatever keeps suggesting.' Quinn reached out and touched Anderson on the arm. 'Look, you know I should put the squad on the tampering now, if that is a murder. We need to look deeper into every single one of those victims.'

'That's shite, if the stuff is off the shelf nobody is in any danger,' snapped Costello.

'This might be off the record but I am still your boss.' Quinn hesitated; Costello kept her mouth shut. 'But I agree wholeheartedly. We'll get the teams out again – the door to door again – no stone unturned. It's the Saturday afternoon before Christmas, people will be in – we need more statements, we need blanket coverage of everybody who lives or works in here. The teams should be getting access. Take a good torch and some evidence bags, go along the back lane nearest to where Peter was taken, look for anything big enough to take a car. Then do the one at the bottom end. If they took Peter off Byres Road, it would only take a minute to get up Highburgh Road and you'd be away. It mimics exactly the way we think Luca must have gone.'

Anderson stood up, opened his locker and reached in for his anorak as Quinn moved behind him, indicating to Costello that she wanted Anderson out the way.

26

Costello collected her jacket from the locker room and decided to visit the loo while she was downstairs. One of the cubicle doors was closed, and the sound of clothes coming on and off indicated that Lewis was getting changed. Her big Louis Vuitton bag was visible through the gap at the bottom of the door, and the strong smell of Lou Lou perfume was stinking the place out.

Costello trotted down the corridor, up the stairs and into the front office. She saw Anderson having a final check of the whiteboard; nothing had changed. 'Listen, I'm going home for a wee while. I've a sore head needs resting.'

'Sorry about that.' Colin looked guilty. 'Is it . . .?'

'Don't worry; I'll be back after a couple of hours' kip and a shower and a decent cup of tea. With a bit of luck, this might be a long night.'

Every time a uniform came in and walked up to the board, Colin Anderson looked over and his hopes rose. And they fell again when the uniform walked away without adding any further information. The minute the case opened, it seemed to have slammed shut immediately.

A photograph of Miss/Mrs Cotter had been circled in blue, and a photograph of Stella McCorkindale had been circled in red. Arrows, forced to bend into curved lines, were going everywhere as connections were tested and broken. Now and again, Anderson would step up, make a mark, cross it out and try again. Mrs Cotter had had the opportunity to know all three boys, and she'd been seen at the fair, but they couldn't trace any communication with Peter. Unless Mrs Cotter had spoken to Peter while he was with Helena. But Helena was in hospital, so not contactable. Mrs Cotter certainly matched the profile but the letters FTO – far too old – were scribbled next to her name. She had a bad chest but she could walk smartly enough. But was she strong enough to hold on to a struggling seven-year-old?

Stella McCorkindale may have seen Troy limping up the street, she had taken her time to come forward, she was on the verge of the credit card enquiry. She was on the verge of all sorts of things. An arrow trailed from her name, to the top of the freestanding board where the name Munro was written.

Lewis's desk phone rang and Wyngate dived across to pick it up, getting there just before Mulholland.

'Kate Lewis?' an arrogant voice snapped. No please, no thank you.

'Who's calling?' asked Wyngate.

'What business is it of yours?'

'I think you have the wrong number.' Wyngate

slammed the phone down. 'That boyfriend of hers is an arse.'

'You really are Costello's little puppy, aren't you, Wingnut?' said Mulholland.

'Whatever your problem is with your girlfriend,' said Wyngate, pulling himself up to his full five feet six, 'get it sorted. You were a much nicer human being when she was around. I'm away to see Quinn.' He nodded at Anderson. 'We won't leave until we get him back, Col.'

Anderson nodded. 'I know.'

Mulholland was seething; he was stung by Wyngate's remark about Frances. He was even starting to think that Lewis might be right and Costello wrong. After all, it was Lewis who was in the hot relationship, while Costello was just a grumpy old cow who hadn't had a man as long as he'd known her.

But Wyngate was right – Peter was priority, Fran could go on the back burner for now.

Anderson sighed, sitting down in Quinn's office, refusing yet another cup of coffee. He ignored the clock. More than twenty-four hours now. 'Is it possible that somebody just wants the reward money? Is that why they have taken Peter?' He tried to rub the tiredness from his eyes. 'But it was never made public that Rogan O'Neill was doubling the reward, was it?'

Littlewood licked his lips, answering slowly. 'You

know, I don't think it was. Wasn't there something about the wording that we didn't want released to the press just yet? In case it brought the nutters out the woodwork?'

'Then it gets us no closer to finding Peter, does it?' said Quinn.

'So, let's go at it the other way round. Who *was* privy to Rogan doubling the reward?' asked Anderson. 'Can you do me a favour? Find Lewis and ask her who she might have blabbed to – she has the biggest mouth. I don't know her and I don't trust her.'

'I do know her and I do trust her, DI Anderson,' said Quinn. 'I know she can be flighty but she's a good cop. In the same way Costello has a mouth like the Clyde Tunnel but is still a good cop.'

Anderson said nothing.

'But I'll keep Lewis out your way. Smythe will keep her in that room, looking at tapes and overseeing the door to door. The wee lad's enjoying his break with the big boys.'

'The wee lad's a good cop.'

Anderson looked through the glass to the main office; the whiteboard hadn't changed. 'I used to be one of them.'

'Last year's *Only Fools and Horses* is on! I thought you wanted to watch it,' Eve shouted from her wheeled throne in the front room.

'I'm a bit busy at the moment,' shouted Lynne

from the drawing room, turning over the page of the *Herald*, scanning column after column.

'Doing what?' came the shouted reply.

'Thinking about wringing your neck,' Lynne muttered quietly, then called out, 'Wrapping up your Christmas present, so don't come in.' She sat still, listening for the telltale squeak of the chair, but there was nothing. Eve wasn't falling asleep; she should have been, but she wasn't. She had been up most of the night playing her Rogan O'Neill CD, singing along as the old codger warbled on about saying hello to this and goodbye to that. She must have had that one on repeat as it had gone on all bloody night, and in the end Lynne had shoved her head under the pillows to shut out the racket. Once asleep, she had dreamed that Eve was getting married to Douglas and that she hadn't been invited to the reception. It turned out he had loads of Mrs Munros; tall ones, dark ones, thin ones, blonde ones … but they all had Eve's face. After that, sleep had evaded her.

Lynne yawned, closing the newspaper. She had only been able to find the product recall warnings for Headeze brand painkiller. Douglas had told her about that, but he had also mentioned deaths, that people were actually dying, poisoned by Headeze. And then, lo and behold, in his pocket – a packet of Headeze.

Eve had been there, in his office. How many times had he asked – in their house – for a glass of water and a capsule for his headache? She would know that sooner or later he would take one.

Lynne concentrated, seeing in her mind's eye where Douglas always hung up his jacket. Stella had left with some keys, he said. So, her bloody sister must have been alone in there.

She thought about the photocopied picture of Douglas, the way it had been handled over and over. Or caressed? Eve and her fat clumsy fingers, yet Lynne knew only too well the ease with which Eve opened up her painkilling capsules.

Lynne stood up quietly and crept down the hall. The last time she looked, Eve had not eaten her steak and kidney pie, so she wouldn't have eaten the sprinkling of her Zimovane on top of the gravy. She'd said she was hungry, and she never refused food. But the plate was still untouched, the pie cold, the gravy congealing, dusted with the powder of the sleeping tablet. Lynne had almost withdrawn when Eve started shouting, 'Oh, for fuck's sake, you plonker!'

Lynne wasn't sure if it was directed at her or the TV and she didn't feel like asking.

Quinn tried to steady her nerves. She had to stay calm, not let the others see her panic, not let Anderson see her panic. The boys were gone, into fresh air, and every minute that passed was screaming at her that they would not get them back. Not alive. And now the only lead they had on the cyanide had gone cold. Munro simply owned the card that had paid for the stuff, the details of the card could have been copied from anywhere. He was glad to help the police with their enquiries and would assist in any part of the investigation he could. The Headeze would go for analysis but the labs were closed for at least a week and nobody felt inclined to taste it, so Quinn had taken a chance and examined the tinfoil backing using her eyebrow tweezers. Just as Costello had described, the backing looked as though it had been pulled back on one side, then reattached. And, according to Munro, it had been placed in his jacket pocket.

And that was it.

She dropped her head into her hands and began to massage her temples, willing some inspiration. She heard a thump and a shout, the partition wall reverberated. Quinn was on her feet, hands against the glass.

She saw a hole in the wall, a scatter of photographs discarded over the floor. Burns was grabbing his coat, Littlewood was racing to the window and looking down to the street. The one person she couldn't see was Anderson. His jacket and coat were still over the back of his chair.

Burns caught her eye; she looked out into the snow. *Get after him.*

Anderson couldn't have stayed in the station another minute, sitting there and doing nothing, listening to *them* doing nothing. Watching each lead come to a dead end, every one shutting or slamming in his face.

On a lamp post, somebody had put a sticker advertising a Boxing Day sale over a poster of Luca and Troy – bastards! There was no picture of Peter.

Anderson was angry. Now he decided to get furious. Then suddenly he started to cry, tears of anger and absolute frustration pouring down his face. *Peter – where are you?*

He wrapped his arms round himself, shivering without his coat, fighting the tears. As he banged the car door, the glove compartment flew open and Peter's 'Puff the Magic Dragon' song sheet fell out, and a side piece of the Monkey Meal box, with a disembodied dragon head coming round the corner. Peter had drawn it with Helena's help. *Helena?*

He played with the cardboard in his hands, thinking, looking at the wavy lines where his son had tried to keep his pen straight. *A long, long tail*, he heard Helena say. *A long, long, long tail*, Peter's voice repeated.

Two coppers came out the back door of the station, talking loudly, almost laughing. They walked past without seeing him and continued on their way, relaxed and unhurried, disappearing into the darkness of the lane in a sudden flurry of snow caught by the rising wind.

Colin Anderson had nowhere to go. He could see Burns at the end of the lane, looking for him.

He could do without any more fucking platitudes. He gunned the engine of the old Astra, the back wheels losing it on the snow-covered camber, before slewing on to Hyndland Road. He didn't even bother stopping at the lights as he turned on to Great Western Road. And then up to Kirklee Terrace. His mood worsened as he looked at Helena's house, in intense darkness, through the falling snow. He had always thought of that house as a safe haven, with a warm fire and good coffee. Now it looked dead, cold, threatening. It was the only house in the whole terrace showing no light. Of course – Helena was in the hospital. And Alan was cold in the ground. A wheelie bin, topped by an inch and a half of snow, was still up on the pavement; that would annoy her. As he got out of the car, the wind caught the lid and lifted it slightly. Anderson opened the lid to push the contents down. There wouldn't be another collection until after the Christmas holidays, and if he left it like that the foxes would get in. He glanced at the contents of the bin. There, on the top, covered in wet coffee grounds, was Peter's tattered cartoon of Squidgy with spiky hair, the one he had drawn for Helena at the Christmas Fair, with a wonky 'H' for Helena.

He withdrew his hand as if he had been stung. He got back into the car and rammed it into gear, and the Astra jerked into speed. He took the hairpin and the lights in one, then raced up Queen Margaret Drive and on to Maryhill Road, where the car started skidding, hit the kerb with a bang and died. He bumped the pavement and got out, slamming the door with such ferocity the car rocked. He walked out into the snow and the dark, rolled up his sleeves and walked, soaked to the skin, his shoulders hunched, through the silence of the city, past front doors with Christmas wreaths, and lighted windows full of cards and Christmas trees. He turned left, up the wee hill, and found himself at the gates of the Western Necropolis. The small gravestones of those lost in the Second World War were skirted by snow but still standing to attention. He leaned against the railing that topped the wall, his face pushed hard up against the spars. He rattled the gates, and pulled at the chains in frustration. They held fast.

The moon was clear, and everything was silent, deathly quiet. Somehow getting over that gate was the most important thing in his life. If he could do this one thing, this one simple thing, Peter would be found. He would go home, and Peter would be sitting on the settee, fresh from his bath, in his Deputy Dawg pyjamas, eating toast soldiers with his eggs mashed up in a cup. It would all be OK. Anderson started to climb the wall and then the wrought-iron fence that topped it, tugging his shirt free as it got caught on the spikes at the top; he heard the material rip as he dropped down on the other side. In the cemetery itself, the path was straight to start with, then it forked off through sections of green that looked grey in the darkness. He followed it for some way before realizing why he was here, and what he wanted.

High on the hill, open to the wind, with the orange lights of Glasgow twinkling below, the cemetery was deathly silent apart from the whisper of the wind through the bare branches. He stopped at the grave, which was still unmarked, with a single bouquet of fresh flowers blowing in the wind. He knelt down and read the card: *My darling Alan, I miss you.* Anderson bit his finger, unable to stop the tears now. *And I miss you too, you sod. You should be here.* He stood up and shouted, *You should be HERE!* He staggered back on to the path, the rising wind catching him on the exposed crest of the hill, cutting through him, driving his tears across his face. He wiped his cheek on his shirtsleeve. How could anyone know what it's like to lose somebody you love more than you love yourself, someone you would gladly die for?

Anderson looked for and found another grave, off to the side, and there she was – Anna. The *someone* Alan gladly died for. He said softly, 'Of course you know, don't you, Alan? You know better than any of us what it's like.' The wind nudged him, and he lost his balance, putting a foot out on to the path to stop him overbalancing. He looked around; the branches of the trees were still thrashing in the wind, the wind still whipped his breath from him. Yet he felt that somebody had just pushed him, pushed him away from the grave.

Suddenly he realized how high up he was. He

could see right over the city, all the lights – orange sodium lights, the white lights of the motorway, red tail-lights snaking beneath them. He looked up, letting the sleet sting his face and clear his thoughts. The only noise was the wind sneaking between the gravestones, and the branches rustling. He would go back and watch that tape, again and again and again, and watch nobody but Peter, see what Peter would see. He would do what the Boss always did – he would sit and think.

And he would find his son.

27

Costello hung up. Still no Peter. No Luca. No Troy. Lewis was being babysat by somebody called Smythe. Anderson had vanished off the radar, and there was now a search party out for him as well.

Here at home, despite her headache, Costello had space to think, though the lump at the back of her head was growing now and throbbing with a pulse of its own.

Peter had been gone for twenty-four hours, and she knew – the whole team knew – that the chances of finding any of the children alive were fading. She could feel Colin's desperation.

She got up and tottered into the living room, amazed at how weary she felt now the adrenaline had gone. She thought about making a cup of tea, but instead flopped on to the settee and switched on the television for the late news. There was Brenda Anderson making an emotional appeal to get her son back – *Somebody must know something*, she kept repeating. She looked a hundred years old, a broken woman. Graphics formed and flew across the screen showing what all three boys had been wearing when last seen, times and locations flashed up, an incident number. It all looked so simple. Costello pulled her hands up into the sleeves of her jacket, letting her mind run through everything. Nothing had been missed, lists of paedophiles had been checked and rechecked, but the investigations had run into a brick wall. Except for Jinky Jones and Dec Slater, always on the fringe, never doing much but somehow always hanging around, like a bad smell. They would be kept under surveillance every time they left the hotel, but for the time being that was all that could be done.

The news switched again, to bloody Rogan O'Neill and Lauren McCrae. The image flickered on to an aerial view of a castle, the new O'Neill family home. *'Rogan's long-time road manager and engineer are already out in Thailand, preparing for the first blockbuster concert of his sell-out Pacific Rim tour,'* the newsreader announced. *'But Glasgow's very own superstar has delayed his own departure for Thailand in order to add another charity date to his Scottish tour.'*

Costello felt sick to her stomach. Jinky Jones and Dec Slater had moved one step ahead of the game already. Had Rogan got them out of the country, knowing the police were closing in? Had he shielded them in America, and then pulled the same trick over here? If Littlewood's suspicions about their US tours proved correct, the two men had probably put paid to any attempt to relocate Rogan's entire operation to a castle just forty miles up the road. Did loyalty stretch that far? Just what were the ties that bound these three, and how strong were they? However, if the American authorities were working in the same way with the Thai police, maybe Thailand was an excellent place for Jinky and Dec to be. Paedophilia still carried the death penalty there. And Costello knew enough about paedophiles to know that they don't just stop. If the Thai police caught them at it, those two bastards would swing.

And what of Lauren? Lauren of the perfect skin, of the perfect hair, the perfect teeth, Lauren who was perfect altogether? *'Rogan's supermodel girlfriend, Lauren McCrae, was today rushed to the Nuffield Hospital, having tripped and fallen in the Hilton Hotel,'* the newsreader announced, and on the screen an ambulance drove away from the hotel. A spokesman then spoke into a microphone. 'I'm happy to report that the baby is fine, and so is Lauren, but she's just being kept in for observation.'

A piece of footage from earlier in the week came on, showing Lauren proudly holding her pregnant stomach. 'I just love Scot Land,' she was cooing. 'And I really, really want my baby to be born here.' She was looking very beautiful, but seemed slightly apprehensive when the camera was focused on Rogan. As it went back to her, she beamed. Maybe that was just Costello's imagination, but she doubted it.

Shit, thought Costello, another little chink falling into place. How could she get to Lauren now?

The phone rang, and she snatched it up. 'Yes!'

'Did you see the news?' Mulholland said.

'Lauren?'

'No, Jinky and Dec.'

'How the hell did they get out?'

'Free country. And there're a lot of doors in a hotel.'

'Any sign of Anderson yet?'

'No, John Littlewood is out looking for him.'

'Let me know when you find him. Once this is all over, I owe him a sore face. I'm going for a painkiller and a kip. I'll be back in before midnight.'

'Don't take any Headeze.'

'Bugger off,' Costello said and hung up. She crawled across the floor to the television. In the Incident Room they had watched her video of Rogan's band playing in Blackfriars to an audience that hardly made double figures. They had turned the sound down, making rude comments about the mullet haircuts and the shoulder pads. Now she slipped the video into the machine and pressed Play.

And there they were – Dec Slater and Jinky Jones. Jinky was standing at the periphery of the low stage, smoking, drinking. Dec was slightly out of the picture, at the sound desk. Was it just friendship that had kept the three of them together all these years, or was it some obscene little secret, some vile pact, shared between two paedophiles and a wife beater?

Costello sat back, resting her bottom on her heels, as black and white dashes ran across the screen, then the camera spun round, wobbling slightly in an inexpert hand, as it caught Rogan in the spotlight. The sound was unprofessional. Obviously the band was playing in a pub, and you could make out lots of background noise, glasses clinking, while Rogan talked into a mic that only picked him up intermittently.

'. . . *cover version, but just this once . . .*'

The crowd clapped and cheered, and Rogan disappeared in a sea of hands. Costello knew that they were about to break into either 'Without You' or 'Rubber Bullets' – the only two cover versions the band ever did, except of course for a terrible slick version of 'Cadillac Ranch' done to relaunch Rogan on the American market.

The initial guitar riff sounded out, more Bruce Springsteen than Harry Nilsson. Costello moved back on the floor, leaning against the couch.

She had fancied Rogan in those days, in an unrealistic teenage way at first, and then it had got a bit serious as she had sat on his stool, in his spotlight, in her new jeans and the black Tukka boots that pinched her feet, and he had sung to her – *Say hello to the tambourine girl, she says hello to you.*

She watched him sing and felt the years slip away. Her brain was a mass of swirling fog, and images, thoughts and ideas were getting all mixed up. Lauren was having Rogan's baby. Lauren was uneasy, scared even. Scared of getting a fist in the face? Or worse? Costello mentally cursed the silly bitch for not being frank with her when she had the chance, while knowing deep down that she never would have been.

Rogan's guitar echoed round the pub, bum notes

and all, singing another big hit, 'The Lost Boy'. Costello had always thought it was about losing a lover, but it could equally be about the loss of a child. But did anyone actually *live* after losing a child?

What's the point of crying, with no more tears to cry?
What's the point of dying, when nothing's left to die?

Brenda had lost her child in full view of the public eye – a cruel thing, an unbelievably cruel thing. If Peter didn't come home, the poor woman would probably never sleep again. And Costello didn't see the marriage surviving either; she certainly didn't see Anderson surviving, not without his darling boy.

Somebody – who was it? Lauren? Rogan? – had said something about losing a baby. Costello's mother always used to say it was bad luck for a pregnant woman to talk about such things.

Costello leaned forward on all fours in the dark, looking at the television as though it would talk back to her.

Now Rogan was removing the guitar which hung from a strap around his neck. He was introducing 'Death of the Enchanted', a slow song with an edgy backbeat.

And she remembered something, something Lauren had said. She could remember it exactly – *He had a girlfriend who lost a baby. So, this time, he wants it all to go right.*

He had a girlfriend . . .

With Rogan back in Glasgow, and Lauren's beautiful face slapped all over every paper, the tabloids had set about tracking down Rogan's ex-girlfriends. Several had gone to town, outdoing each other to badmouth him. Public sympathy was with him, of course, and he just laughed at the stories. But what of the girlfriend who had lost the child?

What if she was here, if she was Scottish? Rogan had been in the States for a long, long time, so she would have been young. And the minute he returned to Glasgow, children had started to go missing – well, boys had gone missing. Had the lost baby perhaps been a boy? *The Lost Boy*. She lay on her back, stared at the ceiling and let her brain go into freefall.

Lynne sat back down. Her bloody sister!

She started going through the dining room systematically, humming as she went so that Eve would think she was happily engaged in present wrapping. If Eve was going to hide something, she would hide it in her desk. But Lynne had already gone through it and found nothing. She pulled open a few drawers, feeling underneath for . . . she had no idea what she was looking for. Just a clue, any clue, that her sister was guilty.

Why? The revenge would be so sweet. She pulled out a set of drawing pads, then Eve's watercolour case. She picked up Eve's pastel box and without looking at what she was doing placed it on top of the drawing pads. The box tipped over until one corner met the desk top and the contents made a slight shuffling noise. Not the noise of two hundred pastel crayons each resting in its own little groove. She lifted it up. Was it lighter than it should be?

She opened the lid. And smiled . . .

Oh, Eve. Gotcha!

The blue Astra was bumped up on the pavement on Maryhill Road, its internal light still on. Irvine approached cautiously, radio in hand, and checked that the door had not been closed properly. She circled the vehicle carefully, seeing the red light of a mobile phone flashing on a central console compartment.

'All OK?' asked Littlewood. 'Call it in, tell them we've found the car but no sign of the DI.'

'It's not been broken into; the lock's intact, and so's the door. Keys are here.' Irvine breathed out slowly, her breath billowing in the cold air. There was no need to depress the catch; the door opened easily. Irvine leaned across and lifted the phone from the console; it was flashing the word Partickhill. She reversed out of the car as the blue screen on the phone died. She held it up in gloved hands to show him. 'But where is he?'

'He must be close by. Only an idiot would be out in this weather. And he's not got his coat on.' Littlewood cursed. 'You drive this back to the station.' He turned to jog back to his own old Sierra.

'Look at the wheel – I can't drive that in this

weather,' Irvine said plaintively. 'Where are you going?' She looked round, not wanting to be alone at this time of night in the middle of Maryhill. The old Glasgow joke about it being twinned with Baghdad flashed across her mind. 'What if it doesn't start?

'It'll start. Just drive it slowly.' Littlewood looked up the hill. Behind the council estate, a few high crosses at the Necropolis were visible above the roofs. The graveyard looked still, quiet, as if comforted by the snow. 'I bet I know where that bastard is.'

Costello rolled her neck against the settee, wishing she had someone to bounce her ideas off. She could feel the two cases connecting, but she couldn't get the two ends to come together.

Rogan, his voice drowned out as the speakers buzzed angrily with feedback, was introducing 'Tambourine Girl'. The camera followed him as he walked round to his keyboard and picked up his guitar, placing it gently into an outstretched plastic hand.

An old memory surfaced – the shop-window mannequin used to hold the tambourine and a spare guitar.

Rogan took a fedora hat from the mannequin's other hand and placed it jauntily on his head.

The audience grew quiet as he sat himself at the keyboard, rippling his fingers, and the opening notes tingled from the keyboard like champagne. He leaned forward into the mike, handsome in profile.

The slow bass to 'Tambourine Girl' started and a single spotlight swung across the stage and followed as a figure moved centre stage, sliding on to the seat, nervous, shy, a small smile behind a curtain of dark hair.

Costello felt her heart stop, and she pressed Pause. A mannequin. Vik had said Fran had a mannequin. She looked at the shy smile of the girl on the chair, her beauty frozen for a moment in eternity. She had seen her often enough, with Rogan, being sung to by Rogan. She had been jealous.

Costello jumped up, forgetting the throbbing of her head until the sudden movement reminded her painfully. In the spare bedroom, she started flicking through the rack of old vinyls at the bottom of the wardrobe. She fished out Rogan's *Man Alone* album, the one with 'The Lost Boy' on it, and pulled out the inside sleeve, a collage of small black and white photos of the band before they became famous ... friends, family, fans. Costello turned it over, searching for one picture. And there it was, in the corner. In a passport-size print from a photobooth Frances stared back at her. The black hair was cut like Cher's, with a blunt fringe, but it was the same woman. The woman who had given Peter the goldfish.

She went back to the living room and pressed Play, watching the dark-haired girl playing the tambourine – young, innocent, her hand held to the side of her face ... Costello had known, when she met her, that she'd seen her before. Christ, Frances was the original tambourine girl! The whole bloody song had been written about her! Costello watched, mesmerized, as Rogan began to sing.

> She plays her tambourine, at the break of day,
> Remembers all that she's seen, places she's been,
> But the dreams fade away ...

Costello found herself singing along, the words so familiar to her.

> She plays her tambourine, when the daylight goes ...

She could remember it like yesterday, being in that seat. She'd sat nervously in the spotlight, rattling the tambourine between the lines of the song, terrified of losing the beat, but not wanting it to end. Then the lights had gone down and a hand had guided her offstage to be given a bouquet of flowers and an invitation to go back to the dressing room and wait for Rogan. And she had gone to find the room with low lights and cheap wine. She had taken the flowers and legged it. She was sixteen.

Now she sat with the wisdom of the passing years, and watched and listened to the very last lines.

> Walking away from pain and sorrow; walking to
>   somewhere new,

Walking away to her own tomorrow; walking away,
   she's through.
Oh-oh, say goodnight to the tambourine girl, she says
   goodnight to you.

Costello was waiting for the husky little whispered
Goodnight at the end of the song, which always made
the hairs on the back of her neck stand on end, but
it didn't come. She shivered, the chaos in her brain
suddenly stilled. It was a much darker song than
she had ever realized, suggesting that the tambourine
girl had taken her own life.

   But it was still a bit of a leap from Frances to Luca
and Troy. Costello drummed the phone against her
chin, knowing that there was *something*, something
she had seen, something she should have been aware
of. But she had been busy, too busy to notice. Think,
think, think, *think*. Vik's bloody gloves, folded in a
bag ... a carrier bag that Frances had brought in
and handed over. And Costello had taken it and put
it behind his desk. Frances had simply been walking
past and had handed it in. Nothing odd about that;
she lived down in Beaumont Place, a five-minute
walk around the arc of Hyndland Road ... Costello's
brain clicked round. In the middle of the Red
Triangle ...

   But Frances had also spoken to Troy's mother.
She had said hello, more than hello; she had sat down
beside her and chatted, hadn't she?

   Something Vik had said, about Fran ... About

Fran and money. Fran was on disability, for something painful – *like migraine in your face*, he'd said. Here, on the screen, the very young Frances had her hand up to her cheek in that disarming gesture. *Like migraine in your face* ... Did she have to go to the hospital with it? Costello thought of the board in the Incident Room – how the arrows connected them all – Miss Cotter, Lorraine Scott, Alison McEwen – to the hospital. And Frances?

Frances, enigmatic, shy, beautiful Frances, who was filmed going out of the market less than two minutes after Peter. Colin was right, and so was Littlewood. Peter, a clever wee boy, an obedient wee boy, would not have gone off with a man, but he might have gone off with a woman ... the woman he'd been playing with less than two hours earlier. The nice woman who had given him the fish. Kind Frances, who had put her hand on Alison McEwen's arm and had offered sympathy. At the time it had sounded like no more than empty reassurance. Costello felt sick as she remembered. Frances had said, *He'll be all right, I promise.*

Without taking her eyes from the screen, Costello reached for her mobile and speed dialled Littlewood's number.

It was Wyngate who answered. Yes, Costello snapped in answer to his question, it *was* urgent.

Anderson felt the blow on his upper arm, a dull thud into his biceps. He didn't hesitate, he didn't even think, he just swung round and caught his assailant full on the side of his jaw; he felt bone strike bone and it felt good. His body spinning, his fist came round again and caught the other guy under the chin. He felt blood splatter, heard somebody say something, didn't care ... He struck out again, but this time he wasn't quick enough. A punch landed in his midriff. Two inches further down and it would have winded him. He felt a rib crack and a stabbing pain shoot across his chest as he backhanded his opponent across the windpipe. There was a grunt, a wheeze, the noise of somebody vomiting. Then Anderson recognized the grey number two haircut, the leather jacket, and the gold bracelet on the hand that clung to his own shirt.

'For fuck's sake, Colin,' Littlewood gasped. 'Gie's a break.'

'Sorry, pal.' Anderson watched the blood forge a tortuous path from Littlewood's left nostril.

They stood on the cemetery path, gasping, hands on hips, both exhausted. The moon moved out from behind a cloud, bathing the gravestones with an eerie blue light.

A wry smile crossed Anderson's face. 'Good, though.'

'Well, a wee slap in the face wasn't gonnae stop you, pal. And it gets better,' Littlewood smiled back. 'We might have a lead. And here's your bloody phone. You're going to need it.'

28

Why didn't Troy push the rat away? It was sitting on his foot, where the skin was black and breaking, pulling at his flesh, tugging it so hard Troy's leg twitched like he was trying to kick it off. But the rat held on.

Luca took off his shoe and threw it. The rat bristled its whiskers, turned and darted away, taking its scaly tail with it as an afterthought.

Troy had not moved. He was lying still under his blanket, and the smell from his leg was getting stronger. Luca's cheek was bleeding where the rat had bitten him; a dark smear of blood came off on his fingertip when he touched it. Luca was getting more than a little cross. He wanted out of here and he wanted Troy to come with him. But Troy was lying curled up like a baby, his face to the wall, so that all Luca could see of him was his back. Luca crawled over and tapped him on the shoulder. There was no response. Luca pushed him harder, and his head moved from side to side like an old teddy bear's. The smell was worse the nearer he got, so Luca held his nose as he whispered in Troy's ear, pulling and tugging at his fleece. But he wouldn't wake up. Luca started to cry. He didn't know what to do. He'd thought his mum would have come to get him by now, but she hadn't.

He was beginning to feel very, very alone.

He lay down beside Troy, stealing the edge of the duvet, and worked his way underneath, pulling it tight around him, hiding. Troy was left with no cover, but he didn't move, he didn't seem to mind. Through the high window, he could just about see the sky, little spirals of snow dancing their way down. He began to sing. He sang the Christmas songs he had learned at school, songs about angels and stars and snow. If his mum didn't come, maybe an angel would come instead.

Anderson knocked on the door once and then again, without giving time for a response. It was three o'clock in the morning, it was minus six degrees, Glasgow lay under a duvet of snow and Anderson didn't have a coat on. Yet the sweat was running off him. He rattled the handle of the storm doors, looking up at them, judging their weight and strength, ready to kick them in if necessary.

'She's a good copper, Costello, isn't she?' The words clouded from Littlewood's mouth in the cold air. 'She won't be wrong. Even if we don't know what she's right about. But she says we need to talk to this Frances.'

'Do we think Mulholland has been feeding her information? Surely not, surely he's better than that.'

'We just want to talk to her, Colin,' said Littlewood. He wasn't going to tell Colin how far Costello's thoughts had got. They would know soon enough. He fingered the hinges to see if the strength had been rusted out of them yet. 'I'll take a crowbar to those, if need be.'

Anderson stood back, looking up at the four storeys of the tenement. Absurdly, his mind went back to his days on the desk, people phoning up in panic: *Police, please.* Yes, where are you? *At home.* Yes, where do you live? *I can't remember.* He had not understood it then but he could understand it now.

Littlewood said, taking charge, his voice determined, 'You stay here, and I'll look round the back. If she opens the door, if *anybody* opens the door, just get in there. And keep her talking.'

The sound of the traffic on Hyndland Road was muffled by the buildings. But Anderson, alone now in the dark in Beaumont Place, shrouded in uncertainty, was glad of it, finding a comforting reminder that life was still going on somewhere. He peered in through the letter box, seeing nothing in the darkness. He felt for his pencil torch, then swore. It was in the pocket of his jacket, back at the station. The letter box snapped shut as he turned to get the big torch from his car, and he swore a second time. They'd come in Littlewood's old Sierra.

He bent down to the letter box again, squinting, waiting for his eyes to adjust. A glass door, the glass heavily patterned, the wooden surround covered in white flaking paint. He could see nothing beyond the inner door at all. Just darkness. Nobody home. He flicked the brass cover of the letter box up, jamming his forehead against the frame, looking down as far as he could. He could see envelopes, and the edge of a newspaper that had fanned open as it fell. Not enough to tell if it was a build-up of mail for a day or a week. Littlewood had told him they had not spoken to Vik about this. The date-stamped image of Frances Coia walking across the screen at 7.20 p.m., her long coat swinging behind her, was imprinted on Anderson's sleep-starved brain. So too was the grainy image of Peter, just a minute ahead of her. The memory sparked a chilling flame deep within him, and his heart grew colder. They had met, Frances and Peter, at the Christmas Fair. Frances had given Peter the goldfish and they had been playing – doing a little pat-a-cake game while he talked to Mulholland. Peter would have remembered, and in the dark car park, confused and not able to see where his mother had gone, he would have been happy to see someone he knew. *Hello, Peter, do you remember me? Have you lost your mum ...?* And, trustingly, Peter would have taken Frances's hand.

That was why Littlewood had not said anything to Vik.

Anderson took a deep breath, and let the letter box snap shut, the pain in his ribs starting to dig at him. The narrow front garden, six feet below the level of the heavily curtained window, was overgrown with thistles, and he could see a milk crate, a few bricks and a car tyre. He could not see a light anywhere. He jumped down into the garden and pulled the milk crate towards the wall, stamping down the under-growth, his frustration relieved by physical activity. He set the crate against the wall, put one foot on it, then took his weight on his elbows on the mossy window ledge; there wasn't a crack in the curtain, not in the entire window. His eyes scanned the six glass panels, all with white paint flaking off the frames. Beyond the glass there was darkness and silence, and in the glass itself his own distorted reflection. He was looking into an abyss, and it was staring right back at him.

The house wasn't letting go of its secrets.

Colin Anderson stood back down into the garden, and the sudden twist of his body pulled his fractured rib. The pain was excruciating – it brought tears to his eyes – and, when he started crying, he found he could not stop. Peter could be in there, right now, and he couldn't even think what to do.

He looked up the length of the street, all brick walls, closed doors and curtained windows. A car turned into the street, and the growling of its engine was comforting. It slowed as it passed him, and he hoped it was looking for a place to park. Maybe he could ask about Frances? About what went on in number 42? He watched as the car drove on, speeding up round the arc of the road – what now? He couldn't, wouldn't, walk away from here. Costello had been so sure.

'Fuck,' he said into the night air. Then he heard the sound of footsteps, and his heartbeat quickened. Littlewood was walking up the road, head up purposefully. 'Follow me,' he said, breathing hard, and turned back into the lane between the tenements.

'Jesus.' Anderson was almost running to keep up with the big man.

'Three fences, two backyards. The one-door flats have basements.'

'A basement? We can get into the basement?' asked Anderson.

'Not legally, but Quinn isn't going to make a fuss over our justifiable entry.' He patted Anderson on the shoulder. Littlewood broke the rules as easy as cracking eggs, but Anderson was putting his career on the line and it did not come easy to him.

They climbed over a set of pre-war green palings, and padded across a concrete yard with a collection of wheelie bins in the middle. The huge creeper in the backyard veined the sandstone with snow. 'If necessary we'll kick the fucking door in, but I heard something, I'm sure of it.' Littlewood pulled the wire of the next fence down, helping Anderson across. A rat, disturbed from its nest, scurried along the wall.

'You hear that?'

'Hear what? Rats?'

'Noises. Come on, shift your arse.' This next court was paved, with small trees in containers, all pruned and trussed up for the winter.

'Did I hear what?' repeated Anderson, grasping Littlewood by the arm.

'Come on.' Another set of green palings, four feet high, and Anderson heard his shirt rip a second time as he went over. 'Here,' said Littlewood. The back of the tenement was dark and austere, dotted irregularly with small windows and desiccated window boxes, greyed with years of pollution. Littlewood walked past the door of the close. 'Down here.' He crouched down, pointing. 'This is the back of number 42, and this is the basement to the main-door flat.'

'No way in through there?'

'No chance. But, Col, look here.'

There was a long window at ground level, and beyond it the basement of the house dipping into darkness. The window was broken in one corner, the glass cracked but still hanging in its wooden frame. Anderson knelt down beside Littlewood, leaning on the foot-high ornamental railing that bordered the area below, a drop of twelve feet, its slabs littered with lager cans and rubbish. Littlewood raised his hand to his mouth, signalling that Anderson should keep quiet. They both crouched in silence but heard nothing.

Both listened intently. In the still air, something small ran across the court in among the bins. 'What was that?' Anderson said, startled.

'Fox?' Littlewood mumbled. 'Listen again.'

Both men leaned forward over the dark void, peering at the grimy frosted glass where a faint glow was just visible, as if looking harder would tell them what they were hearing, or if they were hearing anything at all. Littlewood caught Anderson's eye for a second, and neither of them breathed.

It was so faint they could hardly hear it, just a gentle stream of whispered words to no particular tune.

'That is the sound of a sick person, a child, so we have reasonable cause to go in,' declared Littlewood. He reached across the drop and worked his gloved index finger behind the piece of broken glass, stubby fingers moving delicately and carefully even though he was working at arm's length, until he could flick the broken piece outwards. It fell and shattered in the well of the area.

He leaned into the darkness, craning his neck to see through the hole.

'You see anything? Please say you see something,' said Anderson, holding back the tears.

'Too dark,' Littlewood grunted. The noise was still there, like a mermaid trying to breathe air. Littlewood reached back into the jagged gap, taking the glass between thumb and forefinger, moving it this way and that, trying to manoeuvre it out. 'I'm trying not to let any of the glass go inward; it's heavy, it could kill from this height.' He was talking to calm Anderson more than anything else. The pane of glass remained firm within the frame. Littlewood pulled his glove tight at the wrist then tugged his coat sleeve down over his hand, and shuffled forward on his knees, gaining a few more inches' reach. 'On the other hand, we'll just have to trust no one's right under the window.' He thumped the glass, once, twice, three times before it came away. Shards of glass spiralled into the darkness below and lay there, glinting like diamonds.

The formless singing stopped. The silence was absolute. Then a little plaintive voice deep within the darkness said, 'Mum?'

As they got to their feet, they heard footsteps approaching across the backyards.

'Oi! Police!'

'Police, is it?' Littlewood muttered.

Two uniformed officers were climbing the second fence. Littlewood held out his warrant card at arm's length.

'Police here too. DS Littlewood, Partickhill, and DI Anderson.' He peered at the other two officers. 'Burns, is that you?'

'Yes, sir,' came a doubtful whisper. 'Smythe's here.'

'Right, get back to the car, get a torch. Then get that front door kicked in. And get a fucking move on!'

The two figures hurried back the way they had come, a patchwork of brightness illuminating the way as lights were switched on in the flats above. When

Littlewood got back to the window, Anderson was balancing on the parapet, trying to reach the window ledge with his foot without falling to the slabs twelve feet below.

'Get round the front, Colin. They need you round the front.'

'Not leaving here. I can get in.'

'Not without breaking your fucking neck, you can't. Now get round the front.'

But Anderson knelt down again, peering through the broken glass.

More footsteps, confused chatter, a radio's static interference, all sounded across the back court. Two figures were moving quickly in the darkness, guided by the beam of a torch. It was Lewis and Wyngate. Lewis had picked up the alert at the station, and where Lewis went Wyngate had to follow.

'Give us that torch, Wingnut,' Littlewood said as the constable just managed to clamber over the final fence. He took it and handed it to Anderson, who knelt down aiming the beam through the hole in the glass.

'Any luck?' whispered Lewis. 'Is it Peter?'

'Bloody hope so,' Littlewood growled. 'And I hope you left Mulholland back at the ranch.'

'Shit,' said Lewis. 'He's round the front.' She about-turned and headed off.

'Fuckwit,' Littlewood grunted.

Anderson was very quiet; the torch had stopped moving. 'Peter?' he called.

In the beam of the torchlight a little blond boy lay on the edge of a mattress, curled up like a baby, his face to the wall.

29

It took four interminable minutes to batter the storm doors open. There was no response to the light switch as they entered the dingy hall and pushed over the mannequin that stood in their way. The tambourine it held spun and clattered to the floor, jangling tunelessly.

'Wyngate, get after Colin, just in case,' said Littlewood, as Anderson pushed past him.

Anderson ran to open the old door at the back of the hall, and nearly fell through a hole in the floor where the floorboards had rotted and given way to the joists below. It stank of damp. He shot back into the hall and tried the next one. This door was different, new, with a single key in a fresh aluminium lock. He unlocked the door and pushed it open, and almost fell headlong down the narrow stone steps beyond. He crashed into the wall as the stairwell turned sharply, then again, then down into another hall. Two more doors, both closed. He pushed one door, it did not budge. He stood back and took a well-aimed kick, ignoring the screaming pain from his ribs, and was through in a second, Wyngate right behind him.

The floor moved beneath them as the rats ran, as

one, for cover, changing direction like a shoal of black tetras. Anderson reached for the little body wrapped in its blanket, and sank to his knees, cradling the boy to his chest, repeating Peter's name over and over. He held the boy's face, disfigured and swollen, to his own, and buried his face deep in the boy's hair, holding him so tightly to his chest that Wyngate had to force them apart.

Then Anderson sat back and looked, slowly taking in the inert weight, the lack of response, the lack of breathing. 'Oh no, no, no . . .'

The hem of the boy's legging was pulled tight around the puffy flesh of his ankle. The skin was blackened and cracking, bleeding edges serrated by rodent teeth to reveal pink flesh underneath. Anderson looked up at Wyngate who was standing over him. 'He's dead, he's dead,' he said, blinded by tears. He would have stood up, except for the weight of Wyngate's hand on his shoulder.

'Yes, he's dead. But, Colin?' Wyngate said gently. 'Since when did Peter have a gold earring? It's not him.'

Littlewood was on his mobile at the top of the stairs, shouting for back-up, for an ambulance. Lewis had found another boy in the same room. It was Luca – she had seen photos of that face often enough – and he was frozen. But at least he was breathing, a slow raspy breath that stuttered on inhalation, and asking for his mum. She had removed her police jacket and wrapped it round the boy and herself, holding him close in an effort to transfer warmth from her body to his.

Irvine and Mulholland hurried past Littlewood in the dark, torches flashing, but he was paying no attention. 'Get Quinn down here,' he snapped down his phone. 'Now!' As the siren of the ambulance approached, he did a quick headcount, putting Burns on the door until they could get the tape up. 'That's Costello's Toyota pulling up; let her in, but nobody else. Give the paramedics some room. And whatever you do, don't let Mulholland in here.'

'Vik Mulholland?' asked Burns. 'He went past just a minute ago.'

Mulholland pushed the door carefully. Like the rest of the flat, the living room was in darkness. The huge velvet curtains cut off every remnant of light and shadow, and everything was pitch black except for the blue flashing lights of the cars, strobing outside. He didn't speak to anybody, and nobody spoke to him. Nobody was thinking about Frances. Yet if somebody had done this to those children – locked them in that damp freezing basement – what had they done to Frances? The room was chilly, and the only sign of life was a gentle hum from the TV or the video. He scanned the room, his eyes gradually adjusting to make out the big chair and the red settee.

All the time his heart was thumping – there was some mistake here. Where was Frances? What had happened to her?

He went back out into the hall, which was still pulsing with blue light. He looked in what passed for a kitchen; nothing there, except he imagined he could still smell their curry heating up in the oven.

In the hall, he picked up the tambourine that had been knocked from the mannequin's hand. Somebody had stood on it and dented a few of the jingles. As he looked in the bathroom, the tambourine accompanied him with its tinkling rattle. The bathroom smelled vaguely of apple shampoo, and some of Frances's clothes – the big black dressing gown, a pair of black jeans – were hung up on the back of the door. He went back into the hall, comforted, and opened the next door along, pausing as two paramedics passed with a folded stretcher. He went through the small blue door with the flaky paint, into the bedroom he knew, the bedroom he had spent a few very pleasurable nights in. He closed the door behind him, completely shutting off all the clattering and banging going on outside. The bed was tidily made – he remembered making it himself what felt like a lifetime ago, and it didn't look as if it had been slept in since. And the air was freezing; nobody had been here for some time. So, where was Frances? What danger was she in?

He made his way back into the dark hall, away from the strobing lights at the front door and the cables that were snaking their way down the old stone steps. He went to the next door, a big solid wooden one, a door he had never been through before. The single brass knob turned easily in his grasp. There was music in this room, very faint, but it was there. He could see the green light of a CD player in the corner. This room was slightly warmer, as if life had been here recently. He felt for the light switch on the damp wall, but couldn't find it. He put the tambourine under his arm and pulled out his torch.

The narrow beam of light caught the yellow brightness of a brass bedstead, and he saw the outline of a body swathed in a white silk sheet. With a shaking hand he slowly moved the beam up and there she was, her beautiful face shrouded in a cloud of dark hair. Her right hand was held up to her face, her fingers curled upwards like a child's.

Mulholland didn't move, he couldn't. 'Fran?' he said softly. 'Fran?'

She didn't respond. He reached out to touch her cheek, and her head inclined towards him. He stroked her face. She was cold. 'Oh, Frances ... Oh, Frances ... Who did this to you?'

It was then he realized he was listening to 'Tambourine Girl', to Rogan singing the final line – *she says goodnight to you*. He tensed, waiting for it ... *Goodnight* ... Then the disc clicked and the opening bars struck up again. *She plays her tambourine* ...

He heard a rattle, and something thumped at his

feet. The tambourine had fallen to the floor. As he bent to pick it up, the beam of his torch floated upwards, revealing Rogan's face in a black and white print that covered the entire wall. He reached for it, then somebody moved in behind him in the darkness, the torch was prised from his grip, and an arm crossed his body, slowly reversing him out of the room.

Costello was talking to him, repeating over and over, 'Come out now, Vik, come out. It's no place for you.' Vik didn't move. Costello tightened her grip on the damp fabric of his sleeve. 'Vik? Vik?' Nothing. He was looking at the wall, his eyes wide open, murmuring something Costello couldn't make out. Costello took hold of his chin and slowly turned his face towards hers. 'Vik, we are leaving here, now.'

She was guiding him out of the flat when Lewis passed them on the way back in, and the sombre strains of 'Tambourine Girl' grew and died as the door opened then closed.

Say goodnight to the tambourine girl ...

'God, I hate that song,' Costello said.

O'Hare considered himself an expert on cyanide deaths now. 'And in the interests of consistency,' he said, 'I'm going to be in on this at the start.'

DCI Quinn asked, 'Have you examined her body?'

'As much as I can in this light,' O'Hare said. 'The

Headeze tablets are here, the glass of water is there. The skin tone doesn't appear as red as I'd expect, but the room is very cold and this light is terrible. You can smell the cyanide on her – on her face, her skin – can't you?'

Quinn nodded. 'Yes, I can. It's horrible. Did she take her own life?'

'Strangely, I'd say it looks accidental. The fridge is stocked with food, and there are all those wrapped presents in the hall. And there's enough prescription stuff in the bathroom to kill off any number of people; so if she wanted to do it, she could have done it any time and made sure she slipped away peacefully. With cyanide, there's a lot of things you have to think about to make it as painless as possible. Why bother, when she could OD and just sleep away?' He shook his head sadly. 'Anyway Vik Mulholland is in no fit state to tell us much just yet, but from what I understand Frances never read the papers, she didn't listen to the news, she might not have heard the warnings. If I find any sign – any sign at all – that it was suicide, I'll let you know. But my first instinct is that this was an accidental poisoning.' O'Hare pulled the hair back from her face. 'Poor girl. Poor, poor girl. She looks so young.' He raised his head, suddenly, listening. 'Do I hear a baby crying somewhere?' he asked. 'Don't tell me there's a baby in here as well.'

'It's that bloody cat. Sounds just like a kid,' said Quinn.

'What do you want done with it, ma'am? The cat?' asked PC Irvine, as the cat wound its way round her ankles.

'Get on to the Cats Protection League. It's a pedigree; it'll find a home.'

PC Irvine picked the cat up and cuddled it to her face. Yoko contented herself with rubbing her chin against Irvine's body armour. Irvine looked at the figure on the bed, a pale statue, slightly bronzed in the light, her body swathed in white silk, her pillow draped with dark hair. Irvine remembered seeing Frances briefly at the fair, when she had been laughing with Peter Anderson. The cat mewed in her ear, wanting to be fed. She began to cry.

'Irvine, out!' said Quinn not unkindly. 'Go and cuddle the cat in my car. Take it back to Partickhill and lock it in my room. Find it a saucer of milk or something.'

Irvine snuffled a reply, trying to hold on to a now-struggling Yoko. As a claw narrowly missed her face, Irvine jerked her head back and stumbled off-balance, letting go of the cat as she put a hand against the wall to steady herself.

And disappeared. Her scream was loud enough to waken the whole of the West End as the cat bolted for the door, adding its own screech of indignation.

Quinn and O'Hare exchanged glances. Quinn muttered, 'Bloody Keystone Cops. Irvine, can you not look where you're going?'

'Sorry, ma'am,' Irvine sniffled, trying to disentangle

herself from the dark-red curtain. 'I got a fright. You'd better look at this.'

'Can't be worse than what we've already found,' said O'Hare, putting his arm up to open the curtain further.

They were assaulted by a stench of fungus and dampness and joss sticks as the light from Quinn's torch picked up a few mouldy cushions lying on the floor. The torch beam arced around, ghosting shadows over the pictures and photographs that adorned the walls. A mosaic of Rogan O'Neill looked back at them, a hundred, a thousand times. He was on the wall, on the floor, on the ceiling.

In the corner was a baby grand piano, with two sheets of handwritten music on the stand, complete with childish doodles and crossings out. Quinn walked over and peered at them. No one said anything for a couple of minutes. Finally Quinn straightened up. 'That,' she said, 'is very interesting. It's the music and lyrics for "Tambourine Girl", dedicated to Rogan O'Neill. *Dedicated to*, you note. Not *written by*. And the words are slightly different. *I play my tambourine* . . .' Quinn sang the line under her breath.

On the dresser, the only other piece of furniture, was a selection of framed photographs, all of Rogan and Frances, taken in the eighties from the look of the clothes. Quinn picked one up and swore under her breath.

'Jesus Christ. Look at that, Frances and Rogan –

love's young dream. Bloody nightmare, more like. Poor deluded girl.' She sighed and replaced the photograph, and played the torch over the others. 'How old does she look in these, Jack? Can't be over twenty.'

'Younger, I would say.'

'Does this explain any of it?'

Jack O'Hare was scanning the ceiling and walls with his own torch, taking in each image. 'The display of pictures is unusual, obsessional, but *this* . . .' he pointed to the old cigarette butts lined up in a row, each dated, and a location noted, '. . . is disturbing.' A selection of men's clothes, moth-eaten, was hanging from the picture rail. 'And look at this . . .' Behind the door was a collection of magazine cuttings, all half scorched. 'Look, she's burned out the girlfriend in every single one.'

Irvine leaned forward to flick through them.

'Don't do that, Gail, that's evidence. Use the end of a pen.'

'Sorry, ma'am. I'm just a bit upset by all this.'

'Yes, I know it's hard, but destroying the evidence doesn't make it any better.'

'And I think *that's* some evidence.' O'Hare pointed. 'Shine that torch over here, will you, Rebecca?' On the wall, framed in a baby's shawl that hung between two hooks, was another collection of pictures. 'Who's that?' asked O'Hare. 'They're old photographs, from the look of them.'

'Rogan as a kid. He was a natural blond,' Quinn

said. 'He and Elvis Presley were both light-haired, you know.'

O'Hare stepped closer, taking a good look. 'Well, you learn something new every day.'

'Prof?' Irvine called from the corner. Her voice was tremulous, her face eerily pale in the torchlight. 'What's this? Over here, in this glass thing?' O'Hare shone his torch towards the glass case in the corner. 'It looks like a roll of paper wrapped in a blanket,' said Irvine, her voice shaking. 'There's something taped to the glass. Hang on, can you shine that torch here? It's a poem. No, it's the lyrics for that other song, "The Lost Boy".'

O'Hare looked over her shoulder. 'It's in the same writing as the other one, and dated ...' He peered more closely. '1985.' Then his torch caught the contents of the glass case. 'Come away from that, Irvine,' he said, his voice gentle but insistent.

'What is it?' Irvine asked, her voice shaky.

'That, I'm afraid, is – or was once – a baby.'

Christmas Eve

30

'... every single bloody year since you were old enough to drink.'

'About fourteen, in my case.'

'You shouldn't boast about it, but yes, since you were about fourteen we have always had to have an Eve Christmas; we've had to put up with you slobbing about all day under your duvet and lying on the settee drinking, and eating toasted cheese and crisps and chocolate for your Christmas dinner,' Lynne shouted from the kitchen where she was digging around in the cutlery drawer. Eve had been messing things around. Again.

'Oh, who gives a shit? Christmas is for watching TV. It was only you who wanted to have bloody turkey and all that bollocks. We used to spend the other three hundred and sixty-four days of the year avoiding eating with each other and then, the one day when we're supposed to be happy and full of joy, we would sit in absolute sin and misery, making small talk, when we could be ogling Steve McQueen's arse on that motorbike.'

'What on earth are you talking about?'

'Going over the fence in *The Great Escape*. Every bloody Christmas, without fail ...'

'Eve, just come through into the kitchen and we will do it my way today. A nice Christmas lunch now, and tomorrow we will have your Christmas Day.'

Eve wheeled into the kitchen and put her hands up. 'Way-hay, hang on. You're being nice to me; it's not like you.'

'It's the season of goodwill and all that, and this might be our last Christmas together.'

'Do you really think you'll be living with Douglas next year? You arse!'

Lynne ignored her. She had spent all morning in the kitchen, keeping out of Eve's way. The rain outside pounded on the wintered detritus of her garden, and the light was already fading. She lit a few candles and placed them on the kitchen table, among the crackers, wine and party hats. Lynne had laundered and ironed the Irish linen tablecloth, embroidered at the corners with thistles and shamrock and holly and mistletoe. Their granny had made it one year during the school holidays, with Lynne sitting on her knee following every stitch.

'I've made deep-fried garlic mushrooms, your favourite.'

'Jesus, that's nice of you. What are you after?' Eve was thrilled, though. Her face lit up, and she immediately picked up a cracker and started pulling it apart.

'It's Christmas Eve and we are going to have a lovely meal . . .'

Eve pulled the snapper strip from the cracker, and

started to twist it in her fingers. 'Why are you being so nice to me? It's not like you!'

'A new start for the new year. You see, I know that you know who Douglas is ...'

Eve rolled her eyes up. 'Yes, he's Douglas. Does he ever pretend he isn't?'

'You know exactly what I'm talking about. OK so he defended the guy who then crashed into you. But you cannot punish him for someone else's bad driving and you cannot punish him for doing his job properly. And you are going to spoil the one good thing that came out of it all, the fact that I met Douglas. The only good thing to come of any of this was Douglas. I knew he was a nice man and ...'

'Oh, be quiet. You didn't know he was a nice man, you knew he was loaded; you always get those two things mixed up.'

'Look, I want you to try and forget all that, Eve, and leave Douglas and me alone. If we know, there's no point in you thinking you know something we don't. Just let's all get on with our lives, make a new start.' Lynne put a dish of deep-fried garlic mushrooms on the table, and set a ramekin of mayonnaise in front of her sister.

Eve speared a mushroom on her fork, 'I'm past caring about that. I lost interest when I found out he had more than me to be scared of,' she said with her mouth full.

But Lynne wasn't listening, she stuck her fingers in her ears and started chanting tunelessly, *La la la la ...*

Eve raised her voice, almost shouting. 'I've seen the valuation – *Oh, my dear, look how much it's worth; oh, let me buy it off you and release the capital for you.* Even if you owned it, which you don't, you'd walk away with twenty pee and he'd sell it for eighty grand more than he told you it was worth. Oh, he says, what a surprise, what a buoyant house market. He's stupid, but you're even more stupid. You think he wants you. He doesn't – he wants the house. You've never dared tell him it doesn't belong to you, have you? And if you think you can persuade me to let him buy it, you can think again. It's my house, not yours. I might leave it to you in my will – if you're lucky, that is.'

'I don't really want to hear it, Eve. It might be true. It might not be true. But the reason that Douglas and I are not together is because of his wife.'

Eve thought for a minute before replying. 'I'm not leaving you to the evil machinations of That Man. In property or in life. About men, Lynne, you don't know your arse from your elbow. Munro Properties would have you out on the street already if it wasn't for me.'

'Once he's divorced, we will live together. You'd better pull your chair in and have a nice lunch. Make the most of it.'

'Oh, you silly cow,' retorted Eve, watching Lynne arrange a few lettuce leaves and two twists of cucumber on a plate, more than a little disappointed that her sister hadn't risen to the bait, robbing her of the humiliating revelation that Eleanor was Mrs Munro, Douglas's mother, not Mrs Munro, Douglas's wife. But she could keep that one to herself a little longer. 'Only one steak?' she asked, watching the piece of meat grilling slowly, the smell of charring flesh drifting throughout the flat.

'I'm not eating too much. I have a bit of a head-ache. I'll have some salad and mushrooms, though.'

'Have one of my painkillers,' said Eve, dipping into her mayonnaise and sucking it off her fingers, making a noise like a Clyde dredger. She glanced at the clock. 'In fact, it's time for me to take the next round of mine. Where are they?'

'They're on the worktop, where you left them, as usual.'

'I'm going to have to tell the doctor I need them upped; I can't live on those. I'll need more painkilling cover once I start getting up and about. I am trying, you know.'

'Very trying,' Lynne muttered, dropping the cap-sules from her palm on to the tabletop in front of Eve.

Their eyes locked for a moment. 'Here, you have one of these.' Eve tipped a capsule back on to Lynne's still-open hand.

Colin Anderson thought he was well prepared. He would stay calm, say what he was going to say. If Helena was innocent, she would understand why he asked. If not, he needed to know.

So, how are things? he rehearsed to himself, walking down the corridor to the double doors of the ward. *Do you know where Peter is?* But how could he say that?

How could he not?

Costello might be right about Helena; but he didn't know what to think about anything any more.

There were two beds to the left, two to the right. But he couldn't see Helena. There was a fat woman to the right, an amorphous pink lump under a blue sheet, with numerous fat children crawling all over her. Beyond her was an older woman, with short spiky grey hair, who looked ill with the gauntness of cancer eating away at her; he looked away before she looked up. To the left a slim figure was lying screened from the corridor by a half-pulled curtain, arms at her side, stomach gently rising and falling, her face obscured by an oxygen mask. Even with the mask, he knew it wasn't Helena. He turned automatically to the fourth and last bed, his smile and *So, how are things?* ready, but an old grey-haired woman, her husband's hand grasping hers across the white sheet, was sitting up in bed laughing.

She wasn't here after all.

Then he caught the eye of the woman with the short spiky hair, and she smiled at him. It was only then that he recognized her. He forced the look of horror from his face, hoping it did not show how much he wanted to cut and run.

Helena held out her hand to him, and her beautiful elegant smile seemed toothy in a thinner face, her eyes darker, pain registering somewhere inside.

There were no other chairs, no visitors.

Shit.

He took a deep breath – *So, how are things?*

But she got in first. 'Hello, Colin.' She sounded a little desperate, tearful even. Her hand stretched out to him, restricted by the attached drip; he didn't know whether to reach for it, hold it, or ignore it. He put the card into it; her skin was cold and clammy, as if death had been there first. 'I heard the news,' she whispered. 'I'm so sorry – so, so sorry.'

'We've traced every movement she made, and pulled that place apart. No sign of the wee man. Back to the drawing board.' He forced a tight smile. 'How are you?'

'Better than you, from the look of it. You're absolutely worn out, I can tell.'

Anderson looked down at his trousers and his shirt, both still stained with Troy's dried blood. If only, if only . . .

'What are they going to do now?'

'I think Quinn is regrouping. There's something we're missing, and I just can't see it.' He looked at her levelly.

Her gaze did not drop. 'I don't know what to say.'

Anderson sat on the side of the bed. 'Thanks. I'm getting a little pissed off with people telling me it will be fine. You know one of the boys didn't make it?'

'It's all round the hospital. How's the other boy?'

'Wee Luca has hypothermia but he's doing well.

His mum isn't well enough to come in to see him but all the nurses are making a huge fuss of him. He's going to get more presents than anybody this year. And, you know, he still thinks of Frances as a lovely woman. She was just poorly, like his mum was poorly. *I was sitting there on her settee, watching the telly, having a great time.* It was the rat that killed Troy. He's been telling the nurses all about it.'

'So, why did she do it?'

'Who knows? Quinn and Costello are turning over every stone on that one. Batten, the psychologist, would be the man to ask.'

'Maybe because she was childless – that can play havoc with your emotions.' Helena looked out the window again. 'Maybe she wanted a child so badly, she just took one.'

Anderson looked at her profile. He couldn't help recalling Costello's words, about Helena. 'Why did you put Peter's cartoon in the bin?' he asked abruptly.

'Why did I do what?' she asked, turning to look at him.

'I found his cartoon in your bin. It was lying on the top, covered in coffee grounds and potato peelings. Why did you do that?'

Helena slowly raised her head from the pillow. 'I didn't, Colin. It must have been my cleaner.' She put her hand in his; it was skeletally thin and cold, not the same loving hand that had caressed his on her doorstep. 'Colin? I wouldn't do that. Your kids mean a lot to me. I'm their Auntie Helena. Why did you even need to ask me that?'

Colin didn't reply.

'I'm sure I left Peter's drawing on my desk, but Harriet might have moved it ...' She shrugged. 'Colin, your kids are the only young children in my life. You know I wouldn't throw away Peter's picture.'

'No,' said Colin, quietly. 'Of course not.'

Helena dropped her head back and looked at the ceiling.

The group of visitors round the opposite bed burst out laughing. Helena did not seem to hear.

'I changed my will before I came in here.'

'Really?'

'I left some money in trust for Claire and Peter, just a little something, for their good education, maybe a wee car or something. And I'm sure they'll both be around to get it. Peter has to be somewhere.'

Colin couldn't bring himself to say, *I don't quite believe you.*

Helena went on, 'I'd like you to do something for me.'

'Sorry, but I'm not doing anything but going back to the station and getting on with finding Peter.'

'You're worn out, Colin, and no use to anybody. I want you to go back to my house. The keys are in the drawer there. Have a shower, have a cup of coffee, there's stuff in the freezer if you want something to eat. And feed Peter's goldfish. The heating is still on. Lie down on the settee and think, like Alan used to. It worked for him. It might work for you.' She looked him straight in the eye. 'And you can search the premises if you're so inclined. I wouldn't blame you.' With that, she turned her back on him.

There can be few places as hopeless and depressing as the outer waiting room of a mortuary on Christmas Eve. To anybody waiting in the black plastic seats to identify the remains of their nearest and dearest, it was probably fitting that there was no acknowledgement of the festivities outside. It was oppressively warm, but a bitterly cold draught cut in each time the door opened, and a succession of wet feet shed a trail of slush in a narrow pattern from the outer doors and right through.

In the inner office, behind the glass partition, the phones seemed to be ringing constantly. Even though it was Christmas Eve, the staff wouldn't get away for a while yet. Two uniformed cops were hanging around, looking at the clock every two minutes, anxious to get back to the station Christmas party.

'Just come straight through,' said O'Hare, totally at home.

Costello followed him, and stopped, feeling ambushed, when she saw DCI Quinn sitting behind O'Hare's desk.

'I did invite you to attend the PM,' said O'Hare, indicating that she should sit down and join them.

'But I knew her. I mean, I had seen her in the flesh, so I declined.'

'How are you, Costello?' asked Quinn. 'Have you had any sleep?'

'No,' she answered quickly. Quinn was being friendly, and Costello found it unnerving. 'I'm fine, ma'am. Any news of Peter?'

'No. I'll get back to the station once we're through here.' She sighed, something she'd been doing a lot lately. 'Luca is making good progress. Miss Cotter has been up to the hospital, thinking she's sitting out-side Troy's room with his teddy bear, hoping he'll return from the dead. And nobody told her anything because she wasn't a relative. Last we heard she was walking the corridors of the hospital. She says she has nowhere else to go. I think she's a bit confused, and no wonder. Poor old dear.'

'Oh, no, that's terrible.'

Quinn sighed again. 'Anyway, Jack, what do you have for us? I'm not looking forward to writing this one up.'

O'Hare put on the X-ray box and started clipping up transparencies. Quinn handed Costello a brown envelope. 'Have a look at those.'

Costello slid out a few black and white 8×10s of Frances Jayne Coia. Dead, she looked serene and beautiful, the contrast between her pale face and dark hair exaggerated by the camera. Her hair was wet, pulled back from her face by the mortuary assistant, and Costello could picture cold, gloved hands running through Frances's long hair like a lover's.

'She looks very calm.'

'It was cyanide, no doubt of that at all, but I have not changed my opinion. It looks as though she was just another victim of the tamperer.'

'I don't think so,' Costello cut in sharply. 'She was nicking folks' kids, for heaven's sake, and we were getting close – or Vik was getting close. I think she . . .'

'But you are wrong, Costello. As I said at the time, if it was suicide she would have done it differently. Whoever is doing the tampering killed her, and in turn killed poor little Troy. This,' he pointed to Frances's picture as he looked at Costello, 'was murder. And don't contradict me. But the poisoner isn't the only one guilty of this death.'

Calming down, O'Hare looked at the X-rays again. 'These bones tell a tragic story. Look at her skull – do you see anything?'

Costello got up unsteadily and looked closely. 'Looks like a normal skull to me.'

'Look here.' He pulled a pen from his breast pocket and ran it over the screen. 'And here.' He pointed to the white arc of the cheekbone. 'And here.' The nib of the pen moved down to the jaw. 'I could go on for hours. What do you see?'

'Fine white lines?'

'Exactly. Old fractures; many old fractures, in fact, which have been left to heal on their own. They would have left a few black eyes at the time. And one of them ... that one ...' he pointed, '... damaged a nerve and left her with terrible pain, which would have led to all sorts of psychological problems.'

Costello had a sudden flash of Lauren McCrae's drawn and nervous face. 'So, you're saying she was beaten up when she was younger. Could it have happened around the time she was with Rogan?'

'I don't have the specialized knowledge to date these things exactly,' O'Hare replied. 'But they are definitely years old. Look at this elbow; the fracture has interrupted the epiphyseal line, which means she was almost fully grown when it happened.'

'Almost? Meaning she was still a child?'

O'Hare shook his head slowly. 'Some of them happened when she was a kid, some when she was adolescent. It looks as though she went from an abusive childhood to an abusive adulthood. And by that I mean a sexual, but probably not legal, relationship. Stripped of her youth, stripped of her well-being ... how long had she been in that flat?'

'Twenty years or so,' offered Quinn. 'Rogan always lied about his age, and he's still doing it. He was twenty years older than Frances. She left home at fifteen to be with him. She was only sixteen when she wrote those songs.' Quinn picked up the file. 'Frances's medical record – I'll summarize. Trigeminal neuralgia caused by a blow to the face, and psychiatric support from the age of nineteen until the date of her death. Mostly due to the consequences of living with constant pain. And ...' she looked at O'Hare.

'We found the mummified remains of a very small child, maybe a stillborn baby.' O'Hare coughed slightly. 'The woman lying on this table has given birth to a child. There is no record of her being pregnant in her notes. Absolutely nothing.'

'Rogan was the father of the baby?' asked Quinn.

'I would imagine so. But we won't get DNA from the remains.'

'He beat up a pregnant woman? Did he beat her up so she lost the baby?'

'It takes a lot to ...' O'Hare chose his words carefully. 'Babies are not fragile. They need a fair bit of trauma to be damaged. But we will never know what power O'Neill held over her, or how the baby died. Many questions will probably remain unanswered.'

'Poor Frances. But I can see it, you know. Him singing her songs round the pubs, getting some interest in his pathetic career for the first time, then she gets pregnant. He can see himself getting tied down. He beat and kicked her, she loses the baby, writes that song, he nicks the song and does a runner. Within months he'd signed a deal, didn't seem to care what it cost her.'

'If he did that to one pregnant woman, God help Lauren,' Costello said bitterly. 'What a bastard.'

'So,' Quinn resumed, thinking it through. 'When Frances was sixteen, Rogan would have been in his mid-thirties, somewhere around there, but indecently older than her. They lived in his flat with the rehearsal studio in the basement. All those mattresses must have been for soundproofing. But then she got pregnant and ... if he made her lose the baby ...' She put her hand to her mouth, unable to continue. 'Sorry,' she said, biting back tears.

'We don't *know* any of that,' cautioned O'Hare gently.

Costello ignored him. 'Does it matter? She lost the baby, and wrote the song about it. Then Rogan legged it, leaving her in the flat, and took the song with him. Charming.'

Quinn shook her head. 'But he took *all* her songs with him, his biggest hits ... which were all written ...'

'By her,' Costello said thoughtfully, then added with some venom, 'But why did she never go after him for what he owed her? I'd have sued the arse off the bastard.'

'You might, Costello,' O'Hare said. 'But this poor girl, what he did to her probably crushed the life out of her. Putting a dead foetus into a glass case and writing poetry to it is not the act of a sane woman. Sane women go to hospital.'

'He wouldn't have got away with it, not if it had been me. I'd have chased him to the ends of the earth,' she growled. 'And back.'

'I don't doubt it,' said O'Hare.

*

Colin Anderson double-parked the Astra outside Helena's house. He had stopped at McDonald's and bought a chicken burger and a latte. He had nipped into Marks and Spencer's on Byres Road and bought a change of clothes, trying three credit cards before he found one that Brenda had not maxed out with presents. And what was the use of that, he thought numbly, when Peter was not with them?

It was getting dark again already. For a minute, Anderson sat with the engine running, heater on, the radio off in case that bloody song came on again. The press were going to have a field day when the story came out. He could see it now – Rogan publicly weeping crocodile tears over Frances, and vowing to donate yet another huge sum of money to something worthy so everybody would think better of him. The bastard was probably going to come out of this even more loved by the public.

Anderson flicked the windscreen wipers off, letting a small fall of snow lie and melt, streaming down in a fine curtain of water in line with the heater. He downed the coffee in large gulps, and could feel it bringing his brain back to life.

He finished his latte and picked up the carrier bag from the passenger seat. Helena was right; even thinking about standing under the shower, cleaning his teeth, washing his face, putting on fresh clothes, was making him feel better.

He got out the car, pulling his anorak collar up round his ears. The wheelie bin had been emptied since his last visit, but it was still up on the pavement. He crumpled up the greasy smelly paper bag that had held his burger, crushed the cup, and popped them in the bin. He took hold of the handles, ready to bump it down the stairs to the basement. But he saw something trapped in the bottom of the wrought-iron fence, in among a sodden collection of leaves and litter driven there by the wind and left to rot, something that was bright green. He bent over and picked it up, letting it unfurl – five inches of bright green material, with a brown plastic hoof at the bottom.

Peter *had* been here.

'Can I have some water with them, please?'

'Of course,' said Lynne, handing over a glass, keeping the capsule in the curl of her palm. She watched Eve drink, washing the capsules down, the two pink ones, the brown one, and the white one that counteracted the constipation the pink ones caused. Lynne took the glass away when Eve had finished, and rinsed it in mild bleach, dropping her own capsule down the sink.

'Lovely.' Eve wiped her mouth with the back of her hand and burped noisily, before sticking her finger back in the mayonnaise.

Lynne put a platter of garlic bread down in front of her, using a dishcloth to protect her hands, then dolloped the whole ramekin of garlic mayonnaise on top of the brown deep-fried mushrooms. 'Thought

I'd do that for you as well; I know you were going to.'

'It's been ages since I've had these.' Eve rammed two mushrooms in her mouth sideways. 'You're being too nice. It's not like you.'

Lynne smiled back at her sister. 'Eat up before they get cold.'

Eve stuffed another huge mushroom in her mouth and bit down hard, and a dribble of grease appeared at the corner of her mouth and ran down her chin unchecked. Lynne watched, stony-faced, as Eve chewed sensuously, her tongue pulling the remnants off her teeth, missing nothing. Lynne was delicately nibbling her way round her own mushroom, her gaze fixed on Eve's face.

'Is this mayonnaise off?' Eve said, pulling a face as if she might spit the chewed mushroom out again. 'It tastes bitter.'

'Mine's fine,' Lynne said evenly, never taking her eyes from her sister.

'That's because you've not got any mayonnaise on yours. How long has the jar been open?'

'It's a new one,' Lynne said. 'It'll be the capsules, I expect. You always say they taste like a rusty can.'

Suddenly Eve's eyes opened wide, the creases on her face disappeared, and for a moment she looked vaguely surprised. She placed both hands palm down on the table, gripping the cloth, then her grip relaxed and she slumped forward, falling between the table and her wheelchair, a strange rasping sound emerging from deep within her throat.

Like a quilt slowly unfolding, Eve turned on her side, choking and trying to retch but nothing came up, and all the time the dreadful rasping sound was coming from her. She lifted one hand slowly, trembling, as if attempting to claw her face.

She looked up at Lynne, her brown cow eyes wide and frightened, but Lynne looked straight back, nibbling the batter off her mushroom with dainty teeth, and watched as saliva, then blood, started to drip from the corner of Eve's mouth and her face went pink, then red. The whites of Eve's eyes were slowly invaded by dark-red veins, like a rather pretty lily, thought Lynne, as Eve's tongue grew rigid, then softened and relaxed as the rasping ceased.

Lynne leaned over and straightened the tablecloth. She hated the way her sister made everything so untidy.

O'Hare tapped the X-ray. 'I didn't need to scan her brain; the scars are so deep, I could see them with the naked eye when I lifted it out – clear as the veins on Danish Blue cheese. And look at these – chronologically grouped, defensive, tiny fractures all the length of her ulna, as if she were holding her hands up to protect herself – all indicative of an abusive relationship,' O'Hare said. 'Frances has fractures to the maxilla, the mandible, three on the skull. She has gaps in her teeth that have not been caused by dental extraction. Multiple fractures of the ribs – impact fracture, a typical feature of domestic abuse ...'

Costello dropped her head into her hands, suddenly tired.

Quinn turned the last photograph to face her. 'Scarcely surprisingly, she seems to have suffered from clinical depression for many years.'

'Since she lost the child?' asked Costello.

'She lost the kid and then she lost Rogan. No one left to love her then.'

'*Love?*' said Costello, aghast.

'Being battered is better than being ignored, to some,' said Quinn dryly.

'So, why do *you* think Frances was taking the children?' asked Costello. 'Just because she wanted them?'

O'Hare's voice was sharp. 'I'm only saying she lost a child. And I'm suggesting that when O'Neill turned up after twenty years, bearing in mind he was both the father of the child and maybe – though I'm stretching a point – the reason for the death of the child, it dug everything up again, and destabilized her. And look at those two; they were both vulnerable children with inadequate mothers, and she looked after them, maybe in the way she wished she had been able to look after her own.'

'Or in the way she wished somebody had looked after her,' Costello said, feeling dangerously close to tears. She remembered Vik saying, *I just want to look after her, give her things, make her happy* ... and wished she'd been nicer to him.

'Very likely,' O'Hare agreed.

'But how would Frances know these children in particular were at risk?' Quinn asked. 'Do you think she saw something of herself in them?'

Costello smiled wryly. 'It was the hospital, I bet. Miss Cotter's at the tea bar with her Empire biscuits. Miss Cotter looked after Frances when she was a wee girl, as she looked after Troy. She was still close to Frances, who was in there every week. It was Miss Cotter who came and enquired after her. She's upset, to say the least. She's blaming herself, because she used to chat to Fran about Alison and Lorraine; they all used to sit there munching her homemade biscuits, gossiping the way women do while they hang around, waiting for hospital appointments.'

'Miss Cotter knew Troy well, but did she know Luca, though? Had she ever met the boy?'

'She only said she knew of him, if I remember rightly, but the important thing was that Frances would have met them too. It could have been a gradual progression in her mind, from looking out for them, to worrying about them, to thinking she was some kind of saviour to them, and then taking them. Which raises the question – why did she leave them to starve in a stinking basement?'

'That's your point of view, Costello. Frances had bought them food and bedding, and they were happy, living in their basement castle, running through that great flat during the day. Ask Luca; he was having a great time, until the end,' said O'Hare.

'So why let Troy be eaten by the rats? You don't

just lock children up and abandon them,' snapped Costello.

O'Hare looked at Costello, half-quizzically and half-enquiringly, before replying. 'The problem with Troy was a medical one; he had a throat infection, and his mother didn't see that it got treated. He was malnourished, and ill, so that innocent little scrape on his leg progressed to septicaemia and a necrotizing syndrome. His wee body was already reacting ... his tissues were dying on him. There's no way he could have fought that. Infection spreads as fast as your blood flows. He could have been fine at breakfast, dead by teatime.'

'You'd think she'd have noticed, though. You do notice when a kid's foot goes black.'

O'Hare sighed, exasperated. 'Costello, she was dead by then. I don't think she ever meant them any harm. I repeat, whoever killed Frances Coia just as surely killed Troy. And you two are still sitting here. You should be finding the tamperer. There are six dead now, that we know of. Six.'

'We need to find Peter first,' said Costello, blankly.

'Well, let's get to it.' Quinn walked towards the door and paused. 'You can't testify to any of that, can you, Jack? You'll just testify to what's in front of you — the cyanide.' O'Hare opened his mouth to protest but Quinn had turned to Costello. 'None of her history has anything to do with how she died. Legally, I mean. I'd bet good money Rogan's press office is releasing a statement this very moment, about his great tragedy, how his wee Scottish sweet-heart died, his one true love, how she wrote those songs for him. I can see it now … he'll turn the funeral into a PR triumph, donate yet more money to a good cause, and the press will love it.'

'We can't let that happen,' said Costello.

'We have no choice.'

'Watch me.'

'Costello, I'm warning you. You – we – cannot go public with this.'

'Maybe we can't. But I'm bloody sure somebody can.'

Anderson held the plastic hoof in both hands, and lifted it to his face as if it might whisper to him and tell him its secrets. It was definitely Peter's, and it was at the top of the stairs that led to Helena's basement. And she had given him the keys. Was she trying to tell him something? If so, what?

Then he realized he had a piece of evidence in his hand, the only real piece of evidence they had. He should bag it, phone it in, get a squad out; they would rip through the house in less than half an hour. He would get Helena interviewed by Little-wood, who wouldn't take any of this I'm-not-well shite. He sniffed back a few tears. He had trusted her … Of course he trusted her – what was he thinking? – but Peter *had* been here. He tried to calm his heart. He would phone Quinn, pass it to her. But not until after he had had a good look round.

He picked up his Marks and Spencer carrier bag and ran up the steps to the front door, pulling unfamiliar keys from his pocket. The storm doors were closed, and the inner glass-panelled door took a second and third smaller key. The hall was exactly how he remembered it – tall and airy, all painted in cream and beige, with some of Helena's original watercolours on the wall. He called out Peter's name, but the only answer was a click from the central heating. *The heating is still on*, she'd said. Had she left it on for a reason?

He made a quick journey through all the rooms downstairs: the living room where the goldfish was swimming happily in a large glass vase, the sitting room, the formal dining room, the huge kitchen with its Aga, the two utility rooms. He took a quick glance round each, scared of what he might find, but even more scared that he would find nothing.

In one of the utility rooms, he noticed, it was cooler, cold even. He walked into the warmth of the kitchen, then back into the cold of the utility room – a cold draught was coming from somewhere. Anderson felt the hot pipes, which came up through the floor before splitting above the worktop to go left and right. So, the boiler was below here. He moved a laundry basket away from a panelled door; there was a draught, a breeze almost, coming in through a gap at the bottom. It was locked. He went back into the kitchen, his heart pounding, and found a selection of keys hanging on a violin-shaped piece of wrought iron by the back door. He picked up the oldest one, a chunky bronze key. It slid into the lock easily, and the door opened to reveal a set of stairs going down to the basement. He stepped down, slowly. It was warmer here; he could hear the boiler and the pump. And there was the same draught. Then he saw that the basement door had been left slightly open; somebody had failed to lock it. A cold wind was coming in off the street, down the area steps and right into the basement.

He pushed the outside door closed, it scraped against the floor, jammed tight then freed itself and slammed shut. The noise of the wind ceased immediately. He leaned his head back against the door, and closed his eyes. At least nobody had noticed the unlocked door and gained access to the house. He felt the little hoof in his hand and opened his eyes. As they adjusted to the dim light that shone from the street through the narrow gap round the door, he could see something familiar, another hoof sticking out from under a little bundle of anorak huddled under the boiler.

'*Peter?*'

Lynne curled her fingers round the cup of Earl Grey and sipped slowly, relaxing. For the first time she could ever remember – from the minute Eve was born, the house had never been restful the way it was now. The house had never been hers, the way it was now.

Eve had finally stopped making that dreadful, rasping noise. It had gone on for ages – stopping then starting – as if every time life drifted away, Eve snatched it back.

The house had been quiet for ten minutes now.

It was all hers. She sipped her tea again and sighed. Total contentment. She supposed she should phone the police or somebody soon but she was too much in the moment of her deep reflection, sitting coiled into her mother's favourite armchair and looking out to the darkening garden. It looked bare, desolate, one degree above freezing; the fronds of the ferns were gathering a fine dusting of snow. It didn't look like Christmas, but it was trying.

She would plant her sweet peas again. Once the weather turned she would weed out the fish pond, restock it with koi and lilies. Douglas would help her. She wondered how long it would be before he could move in; with Eve gone the house was big enough for him to have an office upstairs. She passed her china cup under her nose, scenting the perfume of the Earl Grey, then smiled. His secretary lived across the road, after all – she could walk to work in two minutes.

It started to snow a little more heavily; the ferns became filigree ghosts, gently dancing in the dark. It was the start of something new and wonderful.

Time to get rid of the past. She stood up and went into the dining room, where Eve's drawings were still on the sideboard. She flicked through them before picking up the phone – some of them, the ones featuring Rogan O'Neill, would be worth a fortune. And then there was the chess set. She picked up the ebony king, the ivory queen – Douglas and Lynne. She rolled them in the palm of her hands and wished, before placing them back on the board, together, and tilting them so they kissed.

She smiled to herself, her stomach twisting with the pleasure of anticipation. She then glanced at her watch – time was moving on. One minute in the kitchen and the rest of the Earl Grey was down the sink, the cup washed and put away. She stepped over Eve and went to her desk. Lifting out the pastel box, she removed the upper tray and took out the plastic bag of white powder, the yellow label with the skull and crossbones now crushed and folded. She placed it and the wig in a brown paper bag and put them in the bottom of her handbag. They wouldn't be here if the police came sniffing or searching. But to them, Eve was just another victim of the tamperer, nothing more.

The tamperer had been tempered.

Hoisted with her own petard.

She took a deep breath and went to pick up the phone, then noticed Squidgy sitting on the sideboard, his rotund purple belly leaning against the handset. Lynne couldn't remember him being there before. The midge regarded her with a lifeless, black accusing eye. Lynne felt a draught snake round her feet, and she shivered.

Anderson held his son to his chest, cradling him in his arms, and breathed in the soft scent of apple blossom shampoo from Peter's hair. He buried his nose deep in his neck and kissed him again and again, the sense of relief almost unbearable.

'But why are you here, Peter? Why did you run away from Mummy?' Colin felt Peter's hands – frozen. Nose – frozen. Apart from that he was unhurt.

'I didn't run away, Daddy. I wouldn't run away,' Peter sniffled. 'I called her but she walked away.' He rubbed sleep from his eyes with the ball of his thumb.

'And why did you come here?'

'I came to see Auntie Helena. And my goldfish.'

'But you know she went to the hospital, because she's not well.'

'Claire was in the hospital but she came home, so why did Auntie Helena not come home?'

'Because . . .'

Peter wiped his nose on his damp sleeve. 'I waited for her, but she didn't come. And I got cold. So, I came in here and waited some more.'

'Why did you not come out?'

'I tried to, Daddy, but I couldn't move the door. I got a skelf, look.'

Colin took his hand. The cold, chubby little hand,

with the black thread of the skelf visible under the skin, looked red and angry. 'I think we'll have to go to hospital and get a plaster.'

'Auntie Helena went to hospital and didn't come back. I'm not going.'

'That's because she had to stay in hospital to be looked after. You and Claire have me and Mummy to look after you.'

'Auntie Helena has nobody to look after her,' said Peter, squeezing at the skelf until a bubble of blood appeared. 'And you didn't look after me, you didn't come to get me.'

Anderson had no response to that. 'Why did you come here to see Auntie Helena?'

'Because she saw me do Puff. She got up at the end and clapped – like this.' He wrestled his arms free and attempted a handclap until he remembered his thumb hurt. 'She thought I was best.'

'Peter, could you not have gone out on the street, got somebody to phone? Mummy and Daddy have been very worried about you.' Colin put his son's arms back round his neck, where they clung to his collar. The boy had had a fright.

'*Don't talk to strangers*, Daddy.' Peter wagged his finger at him. 'I just stayed here. The door banged, and it woke me up ... But I went back to sleep again. I waited for you to come and you took *ages*.'

Anderson pulled Peter under his own jacket, and cuddled him tighter. Without letting go he pulled his mobile from his pocket; the battery still showed a little life. With one thumb, he selected ten numbers and sent a text: *Stand down, Peter found safe and well.*

It was getting chilly in here now. He looked at where Peter had been lying, right under the boiler. He had been lucky. Colin pushed all thoughts of Troy from his mind. He tried to slip his arms from his son, but Peter's grip did not yield. And Colin wasn't inclined to prise off the little fingers that held on so tightly.

He opened his phone up again and phoned John Littlewood.

'Great news,' the voice at the other end said. 'Is he OK?'

'He's fine. Look, can you come and get me?'

'Course, Col. Where are you?'

'The McAlpines' place, just round the corner.' Anderson closed the phone again, and put it on the floor, and slumped his head against the wall. 'Just round the bloody corner.'

On the TV screen in the corner of Helena's room, Andy Ibrahim was returning from Pakistan to bigger cheers than those that had greeted Rogan O'Neill.

Helena smiled, looking much more like her old self. 'So, how's my young friend?' she asked. 'Is he well?'

Colin Anderson smiled, a wide relaxed happy smile. 'He's just over the road in the Children's Hospital, still being kept in to be on the safe side. He has a bit of a temperature and a penetrating wound.'

'Oh, no,' said Helena.

'He had a skelf, that's all. But with Claire having had the throat thing ... well, they're being cautious. He'll be out in time for Santa, which is all he cares about.'

'You have no idea how happy I am.' Her eyes closed in relief.

'Oh, I think I have,' he laughed.

'But why did he come to me? Why did he not tell anybody?'

Colin pulled up a seat and sat down. 'Because we weren't paying him any attention; we didn't even watch his performance. The only one who paid any attention to him was you. You'd offered to draw dragons with him. You'd taken his goldfish home. And you stood up and clapped and told him he was the best. So, he went to find you. How many times have I shown him where you live? He worked it all out for himself – when I think about it, my blood runs cold. He was so nearly following the paths Luca would have taken, a whole maze of little side roads and back alleys, adventurous places for little boys. And he found himself on Great Western Road. He went up to your house, knocked on your door and got no answer. So, he found his way down to the basement, and found the door unlocked. He just went to sleep in the warmth of the boiler, then the door got stuck.'

'Alan was always going to fix that door.' Helena smoothed an absent crease from the bedsheet. 'One of those things he was always going to do.'

'I'll fix it before you get out of here.' He stopped the movement of her hand with his. 'Peter was so lucky.'

'He's a clever wee boy, finding his way there. God, I feel guilty.'

'Not as guilty as *we* feel.'

'But he was under the house when I was in it. I thought the place was cold but I never thought to check that basement door.' Helena shook her head.

'Don't blame yourself. You weren't home when he arrived, and by the time he could hear your footsteps he would be frozen, tired, hungry and scared. Then remember, he is only five. He's only a wee boy. '

'But I should have checked, Colin. I remember feeling cold, but I thought it was me. I just went straight up to my studio, up on the third floor. It's where I go when I feel shaky. You know, I spent so much time up there when Alan –'

'Yes, I know. But the wee guy is fine.' Anderson touched her shoulder, and felt it cold and bony under his hand.

A break in the weather means that the first lot of aid is getting through, a spokesperson for Andy's Appeal was saying. *And the truckload of food and clothing donated by the people of Glasgow is on its way.*

'Thank God for that. A little cheer on the news for once.' Helena tried to pull herself up in the bed and he noticed her other arm, twice its normal size, the skin deep red, dull and furry like velvet. It looked like a big swollen, malignant sausage, overcooked and ready to burst. As she moved he could see the dressing and wadding round her chest, round her shoulder, up to her neck. He tried to stop himself from looking.

'I brought you a couple of books from the shop downstairs – Proulx's short stories and a Margaret Atwood.'

'Cheers. I'm getting fed up with bloody women's magazines. *Twenty Ways To Make Friends With Your Cellulite.*'

He settled back in his chair, ready for it now. 'So, how are things?'

She shrugged, rasping her thumb across the pages

of the book. 'We have to wait. Tests, tests and ...'

He didn't know what to say. His eyes scanned the mixture of Christmas and Get Well cards hanging from a string above the bed, appearing interested in who had sent what.

'... more bloody tests. I feel as if I don't have any blood left.' She laid her head back on the pillow. She turned to look at him, an expression in her dark-green eyes that he could not read. 'I can't get any sleep in here either. I don't drop off till half four and they wake me up at six thirty with something that's supposed to be tea. I think I see every hour of that clock.'

'So, when do you get home?' It was out before he thought, the one thing he had meant to avoid, pointing out the obvious – that there was no one to go home to. Helena turned back to the window, biting her top lip.

'They won't let me out while there's no one to look after me.' She blinked, her eyes fixed on some point of freedom outside the window. Tears were not far away.

The woman in the opposite bed looked over at her, then at him, accusingly. He wished the bell would go, then he could leave. But time seemed to be stretching.

'At least you can go home now and enjoy a rest, enjoy a really nice Christmas.'

'Maybe. But we've let a poisoner slip through our fingers. Sarah McGuire is getting better with every day that passes but that's no thanks to us. We all feel terrible about that – unfinished business, shouldn't happen in our job.'

Helena nodded, and Anderson smiled. She was a cop's wife, who understood without being told.

'But you have to look forward to a family Christmas now. It'll be extra special after all you've been through.'

'I doubt it. I can't talk to Brenda, and there's more than a few things need to be said.'

Helena squeezed his hand slightly. 'Being married to a cop worked for me. But it doesn't work for all. I have – had – my own life, my own profession, my own friends. Alan worked all the hours God sent. I went to India for six months to tour and paint and draw and he didn't bat an eyelid. It worked both ways. You and Brenda have kids, you're bound together. Alan and I just collided every now and again, but we were happy. Different kind of relationship. You nearly lost Peter; don't lose anything else.'

Her hand tightened over his again, and he gripped it back, surprising himself when the tears started to fall.

Peter was lying in a hospital bed, snug as a bug in a rug, just a contented little boy who'd been on an adventure and was now back, safe and warm. They'd run a few tests, and he was on a drip to get some fluids into him. He had his arm round his favourite dragon, his thumb bound in a yellow bandage.

He was smiling in his sleep. His dad envied him.

'We need to talk, Bren,' said Anderson.

'Don't we just!'

Colin took his wife by the elbow, over to the window of the small children's ward. He was about to start but she got in first.

'You coming home for Christmas Day? I mean, will you actually be there, at the table?' Brenda spoke softly. Anderson could hardly hear.

He looked out the window of Yorkhill Hospital For Children, over to the Western where Helena was. Brenda was looking in the same direction. Neither of them seemed capable of facing the other.

'Sure, I'll be there,' he said.

'And what about the rest of it?'

'The rest of what?'

'Last year we talked, and I agreed that I wouldn't go back to work. Before that, the agreement always was that I would.'

'Yes, I know. But you changed your mind. You wanted to stay at home.'

'No. You got the chance to work in Edinburgh, a well-paid nine-to-five desk job and weekends off. Like a normal person. Long hours, I know, but we had a family life. I couldn't go back to work because of the commute you had every day. But then,' Brenda's voice became harsh with anger, 'DCI Alan McAlpine snaps his fingers and without even asking me, you came right back here, to the Murder Squad. Without even asking me,' she repeated.

'The Crucifixion Killer was the biggest murder case in our history, and I was to ask *your* permission to go and work on it?'

'It has to do with being a husband, a father.' Brenda looked back to make sure Peter was still asleep. 'Never home for the kids' tea, not even home for Christmas Day. You didn't pick up Peter's dragon suit. You even volunteered your own flesh and blood for a dangerous reconstruction, and look what happened. You spend more time with Costello and Mulholland than you ever do with us. Wouldn't be like that if you were a bloody milkman, would it? You never even switch your phone off.'

'I have responsibility . . .'

'You have a responsibility to us.' Brenda was well into her stride and wasn't about to be stopped. 'And that is the problem. You're more married to your job than you ever will be to me. Don't deny it; I know you too well. But you have to decide what is more important. The hurtful thing is, I don't think you'll find that easy. And it should be.'

Colin smiled at her reassuringly and pulled his phone from his pocket, pressing Off. He showed her the blue display as it swirled and died.

32

Vik Mulholland sat there, his head in his hands, and waited.

And waited. He had made a mistake in telling the only member of staff he could find that he was a cop. So, he guessed he shouldn't expect the niceties and condolences reserved for the bereaved. He'd just been told to have a seat.

And that had been twenty minutes ago.

He looked at the posters opposite him for the tenth time. Bereavement counselling, Cruse, the Samaritans. In the past, they had just been numbers he had handed out to people on a card, solutions to other people's problems. Now he was grieving for somebody, in need of somebody to talk to, somebody who had known her. He couldn't think of anybody. It was warm in the corridor, yet he was chilled, shivering and wretched. He had no idea where he was going to go. Where *was* he going to go? Home, with his family, was the last place he wanted to be when he had just had his heart ripped out. It was Christmas, and he had no idea how he was going to get through it. Something inside him had died.

He heard the rattle of a deep cough from the other side of the swing doors; one door opened a little then closed, then opened fully, as though somebody was gaining strength to come through it. He considered getting up to help, but thought, 'Fuck it.' He turned away, pulling his coat round him, resenting the intrusion.

An old woman walked in backwards, her raincoat soaked through, her hat dusted with snow. In the crook of her arm was a teddy bear dressed in a Scotland strip, its toorie bunnet hanging by a thread. She came towards him, walking slowly on stick-thin legs, coughing and wheezing.

'Oh son, oh son.'

Mulholland got up, offering her the only seat, and laid a guiding hand on her elbow.

'It's awful weather out there. Why don't they have all the hospital under the same roof? Oh, my legs. Is there a buzzer or something that we press?'

'Somebody will be here in a minute.' Once she was settled, Mulholland turned his back, angry that his solitude had been interrupted.

'You see, I'm looking for my poor Frances.'

Mulholland turned his head sharply. 'I'm sorry — who?'

'My wee Frances. That's who I'm here to see.' The woman looked directly up at Vik, and he saw the tears in her faded eyes.

'I'm here to see Frances as well. It's Miss Cotter, isn't it? I'm ... well, I was a friend of Fran's.'

Miss Cotter's face trembled into a smile. 'A friend of Fran's?' She leaned forward, reaching out with cold reptile hands, a single, gnarled finger outstretched, and looked at him intently. 'You're Vik, aren't you?' she said. 'Oh, she talked about you; she always talked about you. She was so fond of you ...'

'Fond of me? Did she say that?'

'She did. You gave her some lovely flowers, she said. Nobody ever gave her flowers before. They made her very happy.'

Vik bit back his tears. 'I hope so,' was all he could say.

Miss Cotter was dabbing at her eyes with a sodden hanky, and Vik automatically took out his own, immaculately laundered, and gave it to her.

'Thank you, thank you,' she said, sniffing hard. 'Oh, I can see why she liked you – such a nice young man. She'd a sad life, you know, a hard life. There weren't many who were kind to her. I did what I could when she was a wee girl, though it wasn't much ...'

Vik was desperately wondering whether he would make it out of there before he fell apart, when he heard a light, hurried tick-tock of footsteps approaching from beyond the door, and Gail Irvine came in.

'Oh, good,' she said. 'I was looking for you.'

Gail Irvine went over to Miss Cotter, and crouched at her feet, taking the old woman's hands in hers. 'Miss Cotter,' she said. 'Miss Cotter, I've something to tell you.'

The reddened eyes struggled to focus on her, uncomprehendingly. 'What's that?'

Gail hesitated, clearing her throat slightly. 'Miss Cotter, you remember the *Daily Record* mentioned that you'd helped us with our enquiries?'

'Aye – yesterday, was it? I can't remember ...'

'They've just sent over a fax.' Irvine unfolded a sheet of paper. 'Someone in Australia saw that piece ...'

Miss Cotter looked straight into Gail's eyes, with a glimmer of sharp intelligence. But then she shook her head. 'I don't know anyone in Australia,' was all she said.

Irvine took a deep breath and ploughed on determinedly. 'This fax is from a young boy – he's fourteen, he says – who reads the Scottish papers sometimes on the internet, because his dad and granddad both came from Glasgow. He thinks he might be related to you.'

Miss Cotter's head was shaking agitatedly, Vik's handkerchief, now a crumpled rag, pressed to her face. 'No, no, no,' she was saying over and over.

Gail shot a frantic look up at Vik, as if asking him to help.

He turned his back to Miss Cotter. 'Irvine, do you think this is a good idea?' he whispered under his breath.

She nodded. 'We've checked it out. It's fine.' She reached up to take the old woman's face in her hands, trying to stop the distressed shaking. 'Miss Cotter, this boy says his dad's name is Ruari. Do you know a Ruari Cotter?'

The shaking stopped, and Miss Cotter's hands dropped to her lap. She gave a great sigh, and two tears ran down her damp cheeks. 'My son was called Ruari,' she whispered at last.

'Well, he still is,' Irvine said, sitting back on her heels. 'Now, why don't you come back to the station with me, and have a nice cup of tea? Then when you're ready, we can put a call through to Australia. You can talk to him.'

'Talk to him? What'll I say?'

'Hello? Happy Christmas? These conversations take care of themselves. Come on now.'

'Oh, I can't take it in. It's too much ...' Miss Cotter started gathering her things together. She picked up the Scotland teddy, and looked at it for a moment, as if confused. 'I wanted to give this to Troy,' she said.

'Bring it along,' Irvine told her. 'I'll take you so you can give it to him yourself. But maybe just not now.'

'Oh, you're all so kind,' Miss Cotter quavered. She stood up.

'Miss Cotter?' Vik said, and she turned round. 'Later – sometime – could I come and see you?'

'I'd like that,' she said. 'We can talk about Frances. And I can give you your handkerchief back, all nicely washed and ironed.' She walked up close to him and laid her hand on his arm. 'I'm that grateful to you,' she said. 'You made my wee Frances happy.'

And she let herself be led away by Irvine through the swing doors.

Lynne was sitting in an old plastic armchair, her coat pulled round her. The relatives' room at the Western was overheated, but her bones refused to warm up. Somebody had made her a cup of tea, and slopped it so that two Rich Tea biscuits lay one each side of the cup, slowly dissolving into mulch. She shuddered with disgust.

'Lynne, I'm so sorry.' She looked up at the sound of Douglas Munro's voice.

'Oh, hello, Douglas, how lovely to see you. Thank you for coming.' She rose, turning her cold cheek for him to kiss, then sat down again, still holding his hand, on the edge of the chair, ankles crossed like the Queen. She seemed remarkably composed.

'I can't believe what you've been through.'

'But what about you? Are you all right?'

'Yes, I'm OK, thank you. How about you?' Douglas was discomfited. Maybe it hadn't hit her yet. 'Lynne?'

'Yes, darling?'

'You do know that Eve ... that Eve ... she didn't make it?'

'Oh, yes, she was dead before she went in the ambulance,' said Lynne matter-of-factly. She smiled at him, a thin tight-lipped little smile. 'She was eating her starter – you know the way she used to stuff food down her – she must have choked and that was it.'

'It must have been awful for you.' Douglas covered his mouth with his hand, imagining.

She shrugged. Her smile was wider now. 'I'm fine. I really am.'

'Maybe, but maybe not. I should drive you home. I'll arrange to take you to the police station afterwards; you might have to speak to somebody about this. I think you're still in shock.'

'No, I'm not. I am perfectly aware of everything. In fact, I feel happier than I've felt for ages.' She laughed a little. 'It's for the best, you know.'

'Eve was your sister, Lynne. How can her death be for the best? OK, she was still in pain, but she was getting over it. Every day she was getting stronger and stronger. And such a talent.'

'She was going to ruin everything for us.' She twiddled with her ring. 'But now you can leave your wife and move in with me – you've always said how much you like our house. And it will be mine now. Eve was never going to sign that contract, never in a million years. But I'm her legal next of kin. So, now all her intellectual property is mine, and I own the rights to Squidgy McMidge. Computer graphics can do the rest. She meant to kill you, you know, Douglas. But I had my chance and I took it.' She seized his hand and gazed adoringly at him. 'I've saved your life, Douglas.'

'Lynne, you are in shock.'

'Once again, I am not in shock.'

'Why don't you have a lie-down?'

'The best bit is, we can have our Christmas together.' She kissed his cheek, her pale hair lighter under the fluorescent light, her blue eyes turning green. Strangely, she had a look of her sister. 'After what we've both been through, I think we deserve our wee bit of happiness.'

'What are you saying, Lynne?'

'Didn't you hear me? Eve was going to kill you.'

Douglas's voice was quiet. 'Oh, I don't think so, Lynne.'

'Then you're a fool,' Lynne laughed, a cruel dismissive laugh. 'Of course, you believed her. Even I believed she couldn't walk. She fooled all of us. But I have the evidence with me.' She patted her handbag. 'She got hold of your credit card, and she put a pack of Headeze in your pocket. She probably did it while she was in your office. She knew you'd take it sooner or later. When they're analysed, I'll be proved right. She played you, Douglas. I'm sure she's killed God knows how many other people too. All those people who shopped at that horrible supermarket.' Lynne sniffed fastidiously. 'So, it's for the best that she's dead, really.' Lynne folded her arms with triumph. 'I think it's all going to turn out just fine.'

He looked at her, and saw a hard flinty-eyed woman, older than her years. He didn't reply. Instead he said, 'Come on, let's go.' With a wave of his hand he gestured that she should go first. He followed her as she walked to the lift and down the back corridor to the car park. They walked past a dark-haired man sitting on a single plastic chair against a featureless, cold wall. The young man didn't look up at the sound of Lynne's voice; he sat motionless, an image of desolation, hands deep in the pocket of his coat, weary. Munro recognized the face, the immaculate cut of his coat – the policeman who'd come to enquire about his credit card. It didn't look official, but he supposed the police suffered bereavement like everybody else.

Douglas walked Lynne back to the car park, careful to keep two steps behind. Lynne didn't stop talking.

'We can be together now. I'll have it all, the house, her money, Squidgy – you said yourself that he's a gold mine. I'll have the house and you and I can get married. Life will be wonderful.'

He opened the Corsa door for her. 'Are you sure you're safe to drive, Lynne?'

'Yes, yes, I'll be fine.' She got into the driver's seat. 'As long as we can be together.' She leaned over and opened the passenger door invitingly.

But Douglas leaned his head close to her car window and took a deep breath. 'But you know that isn't really going to happen, Lynne. It was very nice while it lasted but – well, sometimes these things run their course.'

Lynne looked smug. 'Douglas, I killed her so that we could be together, so it will be fine.' She kissed him on the nose through the open window.

He drew back as though she had bitten him. He knew he had been kissed by a monster.

He stepped away from the window as his phone went. 'That'll be the wife,' he lied. 'And that will always be the problem. I'm sorry, Lynne. I'm truly sorry. But – well, recently there has been a lot of water under the bridge.'

Munro paused as he looked at the caller ID number; it was his mother, she'd be wanting to know where he was. He flipped the phone open quickly as he walked away from the car.

Many times in his career Colin Anderson had thought about taking up smoking, and now, standing outside the A&E entrance to the Western Hospital, in the rain and bitter cold sleet, with Harry Secombe belting out a Christmas carol from a radio somewhere within, he thought it might be his only hope of sanity. He could hear the revellers in the Byres Road end of the hospital getting wound up and ready to go, while outside a small group was puffing in silence along the hospital wall, huddled against the weather. The only movement was the occasional cloud of smoke, which swirled high before being swallowed by the sleet.

Colin opened his car door and slipped into the cold seat; he had no particular place to go. He couldn't even summon up the energy to be miserable. Peter was in good hands in a drug-induced sleep. Brenda was at his bedside, and her mother had taken Claire home with her. Luca had regained consciousness, and his mother had smiled for the first time in years. Troy was lying cold in the morgue, along with Frances.

Putting his hands in his pockets in an effort to keep them warm, he found a half-eaten packet of Starburst and the sticky plastic wrapping of a toffee apple, remnants of Peter's feasting at the fair. Only two days ago. In those two days he had so nearly lost his son.

And there was still more unfinished business; the tamperer was still out there, evil, malevolent, unseen and dangerous. There were rumours in the hospital that the sister of the author of the Squidgy McMidge books had succumbed, but Colin found that hard to credit. Not after all that publicity; surely not.

He saw Vik Mulholland trudging across the car park, pulling up the collar of his Crombie. The poor boy was exhausted – he had aged, and he bore the posture of the old and weary.

Anderson leaned over and opened the car door. 'Vik?' he called. 'Can I give you a run somewhere?'

Mulholland slipped into the passenger seat. He didn't look at Anderson. 'Nowhere to go, mate,' he grunted. 'Not now.'

'Ditto.' Anderson stared out through the windscreen. 'Did you see her?'

'No, I'll leave it for another day. She's not going anywhere.'

'I'm sorry, Vik. I didn't really know her, but I'm sorry.'

'Can't help thinking I should have noticed something – Christ, I was there when those kids were downstairs. But she was so nice, Col, so ... so *loving*. I still don't believe it.'

'God knows, women are complex enough at the best of times. And your Frances never had the best of times.' He shifted in the car seat and sighed heavily. 'But that's someone else's problem now. I've a family of my own to look after. I'm even keeping my phone off.'

'No, you won't. You'll turn it on again, just in case.'

'What makes you say that?'

'You're more like the old boss than you think.'

'I'll take that as a compliment.'

'It wasn't meant as one.'

And Anderson knew he did not relish going home, not with Peter still in the hospital. However, Vik needed some support. And Quinn had come good for him in the end – so had Costello. They all needed a drink. It might be like the old days – Christ knew, he owed it to them. He might even invite O'Hare. How much fun could a pathologist have at Christmas with a full morgue?

They sat for a minute in total silence, watching two nurses nip out for an illicit fag break. Both had tinsel round their necks.

'Vik? You fancy going out and getting absolutely rat-arsed?'

Vik took a deep breath. 'I've never been known to disobey a superior officer, DI Anderson.'

'Glad to hear it, DC Mulholland.'

The two nurses were joined by Santa, who immediately cadged a fag and lit up.

Anderson turned the key in the ignition, and the engine roared to life, the lights and the radio coming on with it. The closing strains of 'Tambourine Girl' filled the car.

'Sorry, mate,' said Anderson, reaching out to turn it off.

'No, leave it,' said Vik.

They sat and listened, Anderson's finger on the Off switch, Vik's hand on his wrist, until the song finished. *She says goodnight to you.*

They waited for what felt like an eternity, though it was no more than a second or two. At last, the husky little voice said *Goodnight*.

He was walking away. Douglas was actually walking away!

Lynne had called after him but he didn't even look back. She had watched him go. She had watched him talking on his mobile, chatting away to his bloody wife and ignoring her; she had watched him as he leaned on the roof of his car and stuck his finger in his ear to hear better. He then snapped the phone shut, looking worried. She thought he was reconsidering. Maybe in a few seconds he would come walking back to her. He was still standing in the angle of the door as he pulled his coat tight round him. She called out to him again but all he did was open his phone again – he was calling *her* back! Lynne frowned, then turned on the ignition, gunned the engine, closed her eyes and put her foot down – hard.

33

O'Hare was sitting with an espresso on a big comfy settee, regarding the misty reflection of a rather excellent Christmas tree in the huge front window of the Nuffield hospital. The gardens beyond were beautifully lit with fairy lights. And the coffee was excellent too. He had no real idea what he was doing here, sitting in the reception area of a plush private hospital, waiting while Costello brought moral pressure to bear on a patient upstairs, but he was glad of a moment's peace, some thinking time. He was glad too that he only had the vaguest idea what Costello and Quinn were up to, as he suspected it was highly unethical and probably illegal.

He drained his cup, thinking about the product tampering, about the kind of keen, patient and dangerous intelligence behind it. Six dead. Six. And how many more? He shut his eyes for a moment.

Costello bounced on to the settee beside him, looking dog-tired but happy. O'Hare could not help but notice that she no longer had the buff-coloured file she had held clamped to her chest on the way over. He hadn't asked what was in it but he was content it was nothing from his office, nothing to do with Frances. The original lyrics, in Frances's handwriting – that old sheet of folded, stained paper – had disappeared from the crime scene. Maybe Frances would have her revenge in the end.

'Was it a success?' he asked.

'Some kind of justice will be done.'

O'Hare placed his cup and saucer down on the table. 'So, can we now have some justice for the others? For the ones who aren't supermodels or superstars? You think the tamperer will stop. He won't, you know. Barbara Cummings's kids are without a mum this Christmas. Moira McCulloch's mum's without her daughter.'

'I know,' she agreed. 'I'm on the case.' She leaned forward tensely, peering out into the darkness. She put her hand on the window. 'Somewhere out there is the tamperer; they don't stop, you have to stop them. They are terrorists.' Then she looked back at him, as if suddenly remembering he was there. 'Look, it's gone eight. You can go home now, if you want.'

'The tamperer can wait. I'll run you somewhere if *you* want.'

She shrugged, her mind elsewhere already, her gaze back on the car park, as if she were waiting for something.

'Don't you think you should have something to eat?' O'Hare enquired.

She ignored the question. 'How long would it take to get from the M8 at Govan to here?'

'In this traffic? On Christmas Eve? Bloody ages.'

She sighed impatiently.

'What are you waiting for?'

'Justice,' she said. 'She told Rogan, you know.'

'Lauren told Rogan? About what?'

'About our meeting. He went nuts, then Jinky Jones and Dec Slater were on the next flight out. Interesting, isn't it?'

'Somebody else's problem now.'

'So it's OK as long as it's not on our doorstep?' asked Costello pointedly.

'The Americans will go after them, even in Thailand. It is really not your problem now. That was a good bit of work. My job's simpler in many ways. The dead may smell, but at least they don't trot off round the world.'

Costello's mobile rang, and she answered it quickly. *Colin*, she mouthed to O'Hare. 'Yeah, it went well. I'm hanging around for a wee while, though.' She glanced at her watch, then smiled. 'Yeah, he's here. I'll ask him.' She addressed O'Hare. 'Colin says do you want to go out for a quiet drink? He doesn't think Vik should be on his own. He's trying to get hold of Quinn. Just for a couple of hours, then we'll get back to the job in hand. I promise.'

'Maybe we could all do with a bit of company now, sad though the occasion is.' O'Hare nodded. He didn't really want to go back to his flat and his Marks and Spencer ready meal. An evening out with the squad, especially Costello, even in these terrible circumstances, was much more inviting.

'Yeah, we'll meet you there . . . oh, I don't know

... not much longer. I hardly think he'll pass up on – R ... right ..., yeah, I heard it. Sure.' She snapped the phone shut. 'Sounds like somebody just rear-ended their car.'

'Hope they're OK. I'd like a night off,' said O'Hare dryly. 'Is this who you're waiting for?' He nodded at the roar of a motorbike racing into the car park.

Costello ducked down in the settee, invisible to anybody looking in at the window or coming in through the door.

'Prof?'

'Jack.'

'Jack? Look out the window for me. That motorbike – driver and pillion?'

'Yes. Newspaper bike. Passenger's taking his helmet off.'

'Don't make it obvious you're looking, but is he blond? Spiky hair?'

'It's Dave Ripley, if that's what you want to know,' said O'Hare, faintly amused.

'Great.' Costello hid behind a copy of the *Tatler*, until after Ripley had had a quick word at Reception, shown his ID and been directed up to Lauren McCrae's room.

'Costello, am I supposed to ask what that was about?'

'That,' said Costello with a huge grin, 'was the shit getting ready to hit the fan.' O'Hare cocked a quizzical eyebrow. 'That brown folder ...'

'Yes, I was wondering.'

'... contained photocopies of the original lyrics and music to Rogan's two big hits ...'

'Which were written by Frances Coia.'

'... and a map of the USA, a list of names and dates, the dates of Rogan's US tours ... She'll work it out.'

'And then the lovely Lauren blows Rogan sky-high. Oh dear, Costello, I'm beginning to think you're as much of a devious old cynic as I am. Well done, though.'

'And Quinn, don't forget. Quinn's come good.' Costello was on a roll. 'For all that fluttery blonde airhead stuff she does, Lauren's no fool. And she's not a bad person. Right now, she's shocked and distressed. But she's angry too. Rogan's turned out to be a fake, a thief and a world-class sleazeball, and she thinks her relationship with him could damage her career. Though his fists might have done that eventually,' she finished grimly.

'So, she'll get her retaliation in first,' observed O'Hare, who was glad to see Costello so animated, with the old spirit sparking. He hadn't seen that for far too long. 'Do you really think she had no idea?'

'No, I think she did have an idea. Certainly about Jinky and Dec. That was what she was trying to tell me. But she was effectively on her own with it, and in a foreign country, and didn't know how to go about it.'

'We're pretty certain, aren't we, that Rogan had

nothing to do with the killings of all those boys in the States? Though I'd say he has one death on his conscience – he killed the soul of Frances Coia, twenty years ago.'

Costello nodded. 'But he knew about Jinky and Dec; I'd put money on it. None so blind as those who will not see. And I'd also bet they knew that he stole Frances's songs and made big money out of them. And maybe that he beat her to a jelly as well. Three nasty pieces of work that thoroughly deserve each other. It'll catch up with them, though.' Costello pulled a face. 'It *will* catch up with them.'

O'Hare took one look at her and didn't doubt it.

'Well, it looks as though justice of a kind is going to be done at last,' he said. Then he looked at his watch. 'Costello, why are we still sitting here? This foyer is extremely comfortable and I'm in danger of falling asleep.'

'Right, Prof,' said Costello, jumping to her feet. 'Let's go and celebrate.'

Both Anderson and Mulholland jumped at the noise, as violently as if something had struck the car they were sitting in.

'What the fuck was that?' said Mulholland.

Anderson cut the phone call to Costello and looked round, his hand already reaching for the door handle. In a second, both men were out of the car, running, the two nurses following in hot pursuit.

'Christ!' said Anderson. The Audi had been hit on

the side, pushed up on to the small grassy knoll in the car park. The bonnet of the Corsa was concertinaed against the driver's door, and a limp and bloodied figure was caught between the two vehicles. Anderson leapt on to the Audi's bonnet to reach the victim. He recognized Douglas Munro. Leaning up over the windscreen he steadied Munro's head, cradling his face in his hands.

'You're OK, mate, you're OK,' he lied. Munro's head lolled as he struggled to say something, and fine streams of frothy blood erupted from the corner of his mouth. Anderson wrestled to hold him still as an oxygen mask appeared. Munro got more agitated, pulling his face from the oxygen that could save his life. His eyes were rolling and darting frantically, as he tried to mouth his words.

'Hold still, hold still,' Anderson kept telling him. 'Just breathe – that's it . . . You'll be fine.'

Mulholland ran to the Corsa. A blonde woman sat at the wheel, her face masked with blood. He heard Anderson insisting the other victim took the oxygen, telling him help was on its way. Lights and sirens suddenly fractured the night, as two ambulances screeched across the car park. Yet even through the deafening racket, Vik could hear Munro, pinned against the Audi, still trying desperately to say something, only to be silenced as the oxygen mask was clamped over his face.

Instinctively, Vik tried to open the driver's door of the Corsa, but it was hopelessly buckled and jammed.

He ran round the back, and got into the passenger seat. The engine had come free from its bearings. He tried to ignore the mess that had once been the woman's legs. She was just breathing, barely conscious.

'You're OK, you're OK,' he said, reaching for her hand and feeling for a pulse. The woman gurgled slightly, and he pulled the bloodied hair from her face, knowing he had seen her before but with no cognizance of where or when. He checked her airway. She muttered something incomprehensible.

'That's right – you keep talking to me. Just keep talking.' Through the windscreen, he could see the others trying to free the man from the Audi. A nurse was lying across the car roof, trying to get a line into him.

All the noise and the shouting were out there. The Corsa was a little bubble of silence, just the two of them. His face was close to hers as he felt the weakening pulse in her neck. 'My name is Vik,' he said, realizing he was kneeling on her handbag. 'We'll have you out of here in a minute. You just keep breathing now, keep breathing.' He opened the handbag, looking for a name, an ID. He pulled out some grey hair – a wig? And out fell a tiny packet of white powder. A panda car arrived, its flashing blue light illuminating the inside of the car.

One strobe, he looked.

Second strobe, he focused on the label, catching sight of the St Andrew's flag. Third strobe, he recognized it. The yellow label, the black skull and crossbones, the lettering – NACN. Sodium cyanide.

He picked it up and dangled it in front of the woman's eyes, like a mesmerist with a watch.

Through the blood, her eyes barely registered a faint flicker of emotion. 'Help me,' she whispered. 'Please help me.'

Vik looked at her and retreated from the seat. He put the white powder on top of the handbag, made sure the wig was visible. They could work it out for themselves. His foot caught something lying on the ground, which skittered a few feet, and he got out the car and picked it up. It was a mobile phone, smashed to bits. No bloody use to anyone now. He held it up, and Anderson acknowledged with a quick nod that he'd seen it. Vik put the phone back down beside the rear wheel of the Audi.

He glanced back inside the car, a bloodied hand stretched out to him, the voice so thin, it was barely audible. 'Help me?'

He slammed the car door, and walked away.

CARO RAMSAY

ABSOLUTION

The Crucifixion Killer is stalking Glasgow, leaving victims' mutilated bodies in a Christ-like pose. DCI Alan McAlpine – a renowned and successful police officer – is drafted in to lead the hunt, supported by local officers DI Anderson and DS Costello.

But the past holds horrific memories for McAlpine. He last worked this beat some twenty years earlier, when he was assigned to guard a woman – nameless and faceless after a sadistic acid attack – at a Glasgow hospital. An obsession was born in that hospital room that has never quite left McAlpine and now it seems to be resurfacing. For a reason.

As the chase to halt the gruesome murders intensifies, so Anderson and Costello find chilling cause for concern uncomfortably close to home …

'The dialogue crackles…A most auspicious debut' *Observer*

'A cracker…many shivers in store' *The Times*

He just wanted a decent book to read ...

Not too much to ask, is it? It was in 1935 when Allen Lane, Managing Director of Bodley Head Publishers, stood on a platform at Exeter railway station looking for something good to read on his journey back to London. His choice was limited to popular magazines and poor-quality paperbacks – the same choice faced every day by the vast majority of readers, few of whom could afford hardbacks. Lane's disappointment and subsequent anger at the range of books generally available led him to found a company – and change the world.

'We believed in the existence in this country of a vast reading public for intelligent books at a low price, and staked everything on it'
Sir Allen Lane, 1902–1970, founder of Penguin Books

The quality paperback had arrived – and not just in bookshops. Lane was adamant that his Penguins should appear in chain stores and tobacconists, and should cost no more than a packet of cigarettes.

Reading habits (and cigarette prices) have changed since 1935, but Penguin still believes in publishing the best books for everybody to enjoy. We still believe that good design costs no more than bad design, and we still believe that quality books published passionately and responsibly make the world a better place.

So wherever you see the little bird – whether it's on a piece of prize-winning literary fiction or a celebrity autobiography, political tour de force or historical masterpiece, a serial-killer thriller, reference book, world classic or a piece of pure escapism – you can bet that it represents the very best that the genre has to offer.

Whatever you like to read – trust Penguin.

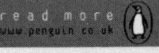